THE BATTLE FOR CHRISTABEL

Margaret Forster is the author of many successful novels, including *Lady's Maid*, *The Memory Box* and *Diary of an Ordinary Woman*, two memoirs, *Hidden Lives* and *Precious Lives*, and several acclaimed biographies, including *Good Wives*.

Margaret Forster

THE BATTLE FOR CHRISTABEL

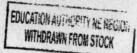

VINTAGE

Published by Vintage 2004

2 4 6 8 10 9 7 5 3 1

First published in Great Britain in 1991 by
Chatto & Windus

Vintage
Random House, 20 Vauxhall Bridge Road,
London SW1V 2SA

Random House Australia (Pty) Limited
20 Alfred Street, Milsons Point, Sydney
New South Wales 2061, Australia

Random House New Zealand Limited
18 Poland Road, Glenfield,
Auckland 10, New Zealand

Random House (Pty) Limited
Endulini, 5A Jubilee Road, Parktown 2193,
South Africa

The Random House Group Limited Reg. No. 954009
www.randomhouse.co.uk/vintage

A CIP catalogue record for this book
is available from the British Library

ISBN 0 09 945563 3

Papers used by Random House are natural, recyclable products made from wood grown in sustainable forests. The manufacturing processes conform to the environmental regulations of the country of origin

Printed and bound in Great Britain by
Bookmarque Ltd, Croydon, Surrey

For my friends and neighbours
SUE JOHN and PRUE BURNETT,
who listened

CHAPTER ONE

Today, I lost the battle for Christabel. I lost the whole war (this is a war story, make no mistake). There is nothing to salvage from it, no medals, no trophies, but my God the scars, the wounds, the shell shock . . . If I were a man, and this had been a man's war, I would have been invalided out, flown from the war zone, heavily sedated, and when the plane landed and I was put into the ambulance waiting on the tarmac, people would have wept at the pity of it and at the waste of a fine young man's life.

But nobody weeps for me. No one has given a single second's thought to my suffering. I imagine they – *they*, the hated *they* – do not think I have suffered. They certainly think I am not entitled to claim I have suffered, not as Camilla and Mrs Blake, and even Betty are acknowledged to have suffered. And, of course, Christabel. Everyone agrees Christabel has suffered. That has been the only point of unity. It is also what has made this war so bloody and savage because we all think we understand Christabel best and that this gives us the right to say what should happen to her.

Wars have long histories, don't they? I remember how tedious it was at school learning the causes of wars before we could get on to the war itself (not that this didn't turn out just as tedious too). Back and back we had to go, learning about economics and social patterns which seemed to have no relevance at all.

I

Then it would all become so neat, so tidy until you began to wonder why, if it was all so obvious, nobody had done anything about it.

Well, this war wasn't like that. It did not have complex causes. It had one cause. Rowena. Rowena was the cause, all by herself. She knew what she was starting. She knew the likely consequences – well, the possible consequences – from the very beginning, from *before* the very beginning, in fact. She knew them because I spelled them out to her and went over and over how it might all end and she was quite prepared to admit I was right. But she didn't care. She wanted what she wanted and she was going to have it. Her determination was staggering because she was not in the least determined by nature, not a strong person, such as I am (how would I have survived the war if I hadn't been strong?). Rowena was weak, vacillating, easily influenced. Easily influenced by people like me. Yet when it came to something so important, when I needed to influence her, I had no influence at all.

Thinking back, I cannot help wondering if Rowena expected me to stop her. Could she have done? If anyone were to analyse her behaviour at that time, at the time when all this began, they would surely think it odd that the only person Rowena chose to tell was me, the very person she knew would be totally opposed. Was it a test and did I fail it? But to think like that is to misunderstand Rowena. Oh, dear me – to imagine for one moment that muddled old Rowena could show such deviousness. No, there is a much simpler explanation: Rowena told me because she needed my help. She knew she could not manage without it. And she knew that I would never, never believe it was an accident, and that if I saw I had been deliberately tricked I would walk out on her. So she told me what she was going to do before she did it, knowing I would be horrified and furious, that I would rant and rave and do everything possible to dissuade her, but knowing too that once the storm of protest was over I would let her go her own way. This has been the pattern in our lives. We hide nothing from each other. We are intolerant of the other's standards – I, naturally, am much more intolerant than Rowena – but we recognise them and agree to differ.

I see I use the present tense, that I have slipped into it all too easily and that it cannot be helped. The past feels like the present at the moment and even, most alarmingly, like the future sometimes. But Rowena is dead, has been dead nearly two years, and everything about her ought to be in the past. If I were not so angry, so murderously angry, if I had not just lost the last battle, I might be more composed and able to sort my tenses out but, as it is, that doesn't seem to matter to me. Rowena is alive in my head and in my heart and in these circumstances grammatical niceties are beyond me. I still argue with her, all day, all night, and the odd thing is that whereas when she was alive she was hopeless at arguing, now that she is dead, she has developed real muscle. Often, she persuades me I am wrong and there are not many people who can do that.

I suspect that my strength has been my weakness, as it is with many women. It is still not feminine to be strong, still not an attribute admired in women unless it is concealed or unless it is glossed over with a conventional appearance and the use of what is called charm. I have no charm. I have no natural charm nor have I cultivated any of the artificial variety. I am charmless.

Rowena, of course, had charm, just through being so scatty and helpless and through smiling a great deal. It never, that I can recall, did her much good, but whenever Mrs Blake was sighing over her hopelessness she would always end up consoling herself with the words: 'But at least Rowena has a certain charm.' In her mother's eyes, in Mrs Blake's eyes, her faults would have been quite unforgivable if she had not possessed this quality. Her untidiness, her unreliability, her lack of ambition or talent, her greed, her untrustworthiness, all of this could be borne because of the charm. Or at least, borne from time to time, for Mrs Blake did not see Rowena very much before Christabel arrived. She did not see her much and was quite glad she did not, because she had little love for her second child. All her love went to Camilla who was perfect in every respect and also had The Charm.

Camilla loved Rowena. Maybe in a slightly patronising way, but if you take loving someone to mean caring about and for them then Camilla loved her little sister. There was a ten-year gap, which made things a little awkward for a long time, but once they were both adults those two were quite close, especially after the death of Henry, Camilla's husband. Of course, Rowena stayed close because she used Camilla as she used everyone. Camilla was very, very useful to her because she was rich and had a lovely home in London and never, never turned Rowena away, no matter how tiresome she was becoming. Until I took Rowena on and rented a flat with her, Camilla suffered a great deal from her darling little sister's presence. She put her up for months on end, never charging her a penny, and everyone pretended that really it was a perfect arrangement because Rowena was so useful with the child. But she wasn't. Of all the myths surrounding Rowena Blake that was the most absurd, yet it was deliberately fostered by her entire family. Oh, she *loved* children but she was not *useful* with them. She was a disaster because she was a child herself. When she died, aged thirty-six, I swear she was no more mature than she had been when I first met her, aged five. Both of us, I mean, both aged five.

We lived next door. Only for a relatively short time, five or six years, but it was long enough to cement our weird friendship. Mrs Blake procured me, if you like, for Rowena, who was already causing her constant and profound irritation. Whereas Camilla had been quiet and studious and always gainfully employed, playing her flute, Rowena as a child was hyperactive and destructive. She needed other children to play with, but when they were provided, found them hard to get on with and all social occasions would end in tears, Rowena's tears.

Mrs Blake, though an austere lady, told my mother she couldn't help holding the romantic notion that Rowena's nature had been somehow moulded by the circumstances of her birth. She had been born during a storm, on the island of Skye, where Mr Blake had taken his wife for a quiet holiday the month before she was due to give birth. Lying in bed looking out at the wind flattening everything before it, Mrs Blake had fixed

4

her gaze on a rowan-tree which, during the hours of her unexpectedly sudden labour, was lashed and whipped into a frenzy until she had felt it must be uprooted and its scarlet berries spilt like blood over the ground. But next morning, after her baby was born and all was calm she had looked out of the window again and there was the hardy little rowan-tree, bright and sparkling in the sun, looking as if it had never known what it was to be buffeted so savagely. Hence the name, hence the moral, and Mrs Blake certainly intended some moral – she is that sort of woman. The only problem was that it was lost on Rowena, who not only hated her name – it is not a very modern name – but who didn't take to being named after a tree and hearing all this stuff about it surviving storms. She would rather have been called Isobel, as I am, something traditional and plain.

Mrs Blake knew, as soon as she set eyes on me, that I would do for Rowena. I was a sturdy child, broad-shouldered, quite tall, with a square jaw and an extremely serious, *extremely* serious, expression. I make myself sound ugly but I was not. I was actually quite attractive, but I was also rather intimidating. I had this stare, probably, almost certainly, still have it – just an absolutely level look before which people tend to flinch. When I was young, really young, adults were made nervous by this stare and indeed I was told not to be 'rude'. My parents, I am glad to say, were not so stupid, though they were a little embarrassed by my famous stare. My mother suggested, gently enough, that perhaps if I smiled a little people might not be so offended, and my father thought the odd blink might help, but then almost as soon as he said this he burst out laughing at the idiocy of such an instruction. But Mrs Blake, the minute she was stared at, knew I was made to subdue Rowena.

We were put together every day. This sounds as though we were cattle and put in a pen, and indeed there are comparisons. I was the solid little calf and Rowena the lamb, skittering all over the place. But we took to each other at once for reasons neither of us have ever understood. We had nothing in common, nothing. I liked games, all games, whereas Rowena was completely uncoordinated. She couldn't catch a ball even if you dropped it carefully into her open hands, certainly couldn't hit one with any kind of bat. She couldn't run, though she looked light and thin enough to be speedy, and only just managed to doggy-paddle the width of the swimming-pool's shallow end after about a hundred lessons and was still looking for her water wings to feel safe. All Rowena had, in the way of sporting attributes, was stamina. She could keep going far longer than anyone else on walks and once, to her intense delight, won a walking marathon on School Sports Day. She wasn't clever. Reading, reading anything, even comics, was hard for her, yet she wasn't unintelligent. The Blakes had her tested, as you might expect, and she came out average. She hated reading, that was all. Curiously, she did better at writing, had no problems with that. In fact, not only did she have good, clear handwriting she also had a fairly fluent style. That was what got her by. She trailed along near the bottom of every class during the year but then at examination time she managed to pass most subjects that depended on being able to string words together.

Of course, I wasn't with her throughout her school career so my observations can't be entirely accurate. We started primary school together, in Edinburgh, but then the Blakes decided pretty quickly that Rowena needed special attention and she went to a private school. But we still saw each other regularly, even though my family moved to Cockermouth in Cumbria when I was eleven, in time for me to start secondary school there. The Blakes stayed in Edinburgh but Rowena and I spent holidays together for the next seven years, until we both left school, or rather until I did, because I was a June birthday and a whole academic year ahead of Rowena, whose birthday fell on September 25th. Then there was a gap, a long one. I didn't see much of her for the next four years, even though I went to Edinburgh University, and she was often at home. We met occasionally but lost our intimacy.

You will note a certain formality about all this biographical data. It feels a little processed, a little prepared and so it would. I seem to have written it all down many times in the last two years and I've become slick. I can reduce Rowena's life to ten lines if I have to and I have had to. Maybe that isn't too surprising, maybe we could all cover our own history in ten

6

lines, but it has always had the power to distress me. 'If you could just jot down what you knew about Rowena, her life, that kind of thing, her background, her career, it would be a help, about ten lines would do.' Ten lines? Her life, career, background? It was the odious Maureen talking. If only I'd cried. If only I'd broken down and wept. But being me the distress came out as anger. I turned turkey-cock red and roared: 'What on earth do you think you're asking?' and then Maureen went red in turn and said there was no need to be upset and it was only for the records.

The records. God, how Maureen loves the records. They are her life, her bible, her *raison d'être*. I have heard her voice high with panic when the records for something have been mislaid, shrill with anguish if they are not immediately available. And what amazes me is how unimpressive, how pitifully inadequate these revered records are. I find them embarrassing, really. When I was first allowed to see Rowena's records – though only because I had to sign my own contribution – it struck me that Maureen is virtually illiterate. Truly. It is not just that the language of officialdom is clumsy, but that she doesn't know how to put a sentence together. Her punctuation is *awful*, not a ghost of an idea about where to put a full stop, and her vocabulary impoverished. She is incapable of describing anything, flounders around using clichés culled from – well, from where? From social-work text-books? American-style psychology papers? Where did all this rubbish about being 'in touch with one's feelings' and 'making a commitment' and so forth come from? Quite simple statements are wrapped up in mumbo-jumbo, nothing is ever put down in plain, ordinary language. And yet Maureen, as a senior social worker, must have a degree, mustn't she? She must have O-level English, at any rate. You wouldn't think it from reading her reports.

Another mistake. The first time she gave me a report to read, the first one on Rowena, I couldn't get past the words 'bored of'. It said the client seemed 'bored of' her job. I looked up and said it out loud, querying it. Maureen said it was true, Rowena had seemed bored of her – and I stopped her. 'It was the grammar I was worrying about,' I said, 'not the truth of the statement. Sorry.' Well, I did say sorry, though afterwards I regretted it. And I said it nicely, and smiled. I wasn't superior about it. But Maureen, I am sure, hated me from that moment if she hadn't hated me before. She shifted her red-framed spectacles up her sharp little nose and tightened her mouth and gave me a glare worthy of my own and I knew I'd been very silly. There was no point in making an enemy of Maureen who I was only just beginning to realise had a great deal of power (though I had no idea, at that point, how much). At least I hadn't criticised her speech, which was awful too, not really much better than Betty's. Maybe this represents some sort of triumph for the social services, that its workers are no longer ghastly middle-class do-gooder types. Yes, when I think about it, it does. Of course, move up the hierarchy a bit, even just as far as Stella Freeman, Maureen's superior, what they call the Team Leader, and you're dealing with a more familiar type. Maureen is gritty, realistic, she gives the impression of being well acquainted with the way in which most of her clients live. I doubt if Stella Freeman has much idea, so on balance I prefer Maureen. I think.

I never met her when she came to see Rowena years ago. She came only twice. The first time was to inspect the living conditions and what a God-almighty clear up we had before it. We lived in a fair degree of squalor then, though we were both fond of assuring appalled visitors that, although untidy, the flat was actually clean. I doubted it. Most people probably wouldn't have thought it was clean. How often did we wash the kitchen floor, for example? Only when something particularly sticky had been spilled on it. It was a clever floor, of that kind of mottled cork which really has to be very dirty indeed before it is obvious. The bathroom floor was less fortunate. It was covered in black and white vinyl tiles but, since we had moved in five years before, it was more grey and black. Surprising, really, when you think what a good clean life a bathroom floor leads compared with the life of a kitchen floor. Before Maureen came – I bet her floors are pristine – we scrubbed the bathroom floor and I must say it was quite exciting to see it afterwards. Pleasant. I could quite see how some people can get hooked on this housework business. The pride we both felt was terrible, each screaming at the other if she so much as put a bare foot onto a white tile. And we hoovered, but that ended fairly disastrously. We hadn't realised how cleverly the dark grey haircord carpet concealed gunge, and when Rowena pushed the hoover – one of those upright jobs – over the living-room floor it seized up almost immediately and made horrible noises. We couldn't get it to work again even though we took out of its jaws a motley collection of elastic bands, bottle tops, hair clips, one-penny pieces and matchsticks. We had to do both bedrooms with a brush and pan. Luckily most of the floor space there was covered. The little box-room, up to now full of junk, we really transformed. Maureen herself admired it extravagantly, said it was ideal for a 'kiddy'. There was nothing in it, of course. It is only a slot of a room, nine foot by six, with a small window, but painted white and with a new dark blue carpet and a blue and white blind it looked very inviting.

But it didn't work, the clean-up, that is. I came home one day to find Rowena's eyes had quite disappeared with crying. Maureen had rejected her as a foster-mother. The letter, couched in Maureen's dreadful English, said Rowena wasn't suitable. At least it was typed, though that had the effect of making the errors worse. What pigs they'd been, to string her along, though of course they were quite right in their judgement. Rowena would have been a disaster as a foster-mother. Even now that I am so intimately acquainted with Betty and know the full horror of the system I have to agree with Maureen. I can't think why she went through the motions of visiting our flat at all because, however perfect she found it, she wasn't going to recommend Rowena as a foster-mother, no more than the adoption societies were going to hand over a child. I would have had more chance. I am being perfectly serious. Look at what these people go on, look at what they have to go on: background, career, references, general demeanour. See how I score compared to Rowena: university education, excellent well-paid job, impeccable and impressive references, sensible exterior. The only thing which would have been against me – and it would have proved as fatal to my chances as it did to Rowena's – would have been my single status, my lack of a stable relationship.

I think Maureen may have imagined Rowena was a lesbian. It annoys me to think this would have mattered, but I'm damn well sure it would have done, that it does. When she was questioned about these wretchedly important 'stable relationships' the only one Rowena could come up with was with me. She said Maureen said friends didn't count, that sharing a flat for three years with someone you've known virtually all your life did not count. What was important was stable relationships with the opposite sex or – and Rowena said she left it hanging in the air.

She was asked later if she had boyfriends. Unfortunately, Rowena made a frivolous reply. 'Yes,' she said, 'when I can get them.' That didn't go down at all well. The line of questioning which followed was of the 'Do you try to get them' variety and 'When you do, why don't you form . . .' yes, here it comes '. . . stable relationships?' Rowena, in her naivety, said she would like to have done but the men she was attracted to were always married or else didn't want to commit themselves. Those who were willing to do so she usually found boring. She expected Maureen to agree. How could she have thought that? Didn't she notice Maureen's wedding ring? Couldn't she tell Maureen was the sort who married the boy next door, equally dreary, equally terrified he'd never find anyone else? Everything Maureen stood for was written in her clothes, her hair, her very walk. But Rowena had no insight. She never received signals. Maureen did, though. Maureen saw it all, she recognised Rowena's hunger, her desperation and she recoiled from it. Women who are panic-stricken at the thought of never having a child should never, ever, be given them. Simple, isn't it?

I hate Maureen. All my life I have been saying I hate people and it has rarely been true. 'All this hate,' my mother used to say, and 'Save your hate for something worth hating, for heaven's sake.' Maureen is worth hating. She is worth hating for her lack of sympathy, for her lack of originality, for the absence in her of any true compassion. I hate her silly little coughs of embarrassment, her fidgety habits, her solemnity, her utterly,

utterly conventional attitudes. I asked her once, in the early days, when we were still on a reasonably friendly footing, I asked her why she had wanted to be a social worker. 'I like helping the under-privileged,' she said, without the trace of a blush. *You are under-privileged yourself, my dear, I thought, and you have nothing to give.* Yet what could I expect her to say? It is the stock-answer, surely, maybe even the right answer, as correct as a nurse wanting to make the sick better. No nurse says she is morbid, that she is fascinated by blood and sores and disease, or that it makes her feel great to be in a position of power.

Of course, what was at the bottom of Maureen's unprofessional hostility to Rowena was the fact that she was clearly *not* under-privileged. She was on supplementary benefit when she applied to be a foster-mother, but that didn't fool Maureen for a moment. For a start, there was the car, Rowena's natty little Metro, all too obviously spanking new. Mrs Blake had bought it for her when her husband had died. The girls both got a holiday and new cars out of the life insurance. Very foolishly, Rowena told Maureen about the car, thinking it would make her a better prospective foster-mother. 'I have the time,' she told me she'd said, 'and I've got transport, I could take children to the park and to school in my car, it's a very safe car, brand-new.' I wasn't there so I cannot claim to know Maureen's reaction to this, but it's easy to guess, isn't it? I bet – in fact, I know – Maureen doesn't own her own car. She can't afford to run one without a Council car loan. Many other people on her salary manage to afford it, but Maureen was saving to buy a house. Every penny she and her civil servant husband save goes towards this dream: 'My life-time dream,' as she described it once. So the shiny red car plus the supplementary benefit went down very badly indeed, though I expect Maureen struggled not to be judgemental, as all good social workers should. Then there was the holiday in Kenya. Six weeks, if you please. 'I shan't be here for the next month or so,' the stupid Rowena said to Maureen when she came to inspect our flat. 'Mummy is treating me to a holiday in Kenya.

But I don't suppose I'll be on the list before next month anyway, will I?' Not a chance, petal, not next month or any other.

And it was when she came back from Kenya that she got the cold, illiterate little letter from Maureen thanking her for her enquiry 'as to wanting to be a foster-parent' but regretting that 'owing to borough policy' she was deemed unsuitable. I ought to have suspected something when there were no tears, no hysterics. Rowena screwed the miserable letter up and tossed it aside and said it didn't matter anyway, she really didn't care now. Why didn't I jump on that 'now'? I think I was just so relieved to avoid a scene. Scenes with Rowena went on for a long, long time and drained me. She was capable of crying for forty-eight hours at a stretch, and it wasn't done in private, no head buried in a pillow with the bedroom door locked. Crying was an *occupation* with Rowena, something she laboured at diligently, striving to keep the tear-ducts flowing, exerting great powers of concentration on the bawling, hiccuping sobs and throwing herself from chair to sofa to bed and back again in shattering paroxysms of grief. To avoid all that was quite something and I was duly grateful. I wasn't quite so pleased with what came next. This was an announcement that she was going to become a baby-minder. Of handicapped children. Of mentally disturbed, handicapped children. 'Rowena,' I said. 'What do you think you're talking about? I have never in my life heard anything quite as patronising and absurd and arrogant. Who do you think you are? Mother Teresa? Maureen wouldn't let you on a child-minder's register any more than she'd put you on a fostering one.'

The laugh was on me there. What did Maureen know about it? Nothing. There is this dark underworld of child-minding which the social services know nothing about, or rather which they know about but cannot control. London is packed with mothers who have no alternative, who have to leave their babies and under-school-age small children with 'aunties'. And they pay through the nose for it. You can see the pathetic notices in any newsagent's window around our neighbourhood – 'Baby-minder wanted for sweet little girl of fifteen months; no trouble;

£4 an hour; nine to six each weekday'. Nine to six, every day, except one.

Later, when Christabel was weaned, I investigated these notices. We put one in our local newsagent's window, just like everyone else: 'Baby-minder wanted for girl of ten months, three hours weekday mornings, £5 an hour'. Five pounds, which was ridiculous, because we thought we'd get a better class of applicant. All I can say is that if what turned up was of a better class, then God help the rest. Loads of offers we had, falling over themselves these 'aunties' were. I went to see three in their homes (because the idea was that Christabel would go to *them* – it seemed better, in the circumstances, then). I went because Rowena was so hopeless but we really should have gone together so that she could share my horror and save me the trouble of convincing her.

The first woman I went to see lived in a perfectly respectable block of council flats up the hill from us, a new block, brick not concrete, not too depressing and as yet free from either litter or graffiti. This woman lived on the third floor, halfway along a row of six flats connected by a balcony. She opened the door very suspiciously, only a crack so that I could just see her face. The chain was on and she didn't hurry to take it off, appearing to think the interview could perfectly well be conducted without my entering the flat. It felt offensive when I asked if I could see where Christabel would spend her fifteen quids' worth of hours per day. Reluctantly, she let me in, mumbling something about the place being a bit of a mess and not expecting visitors. I assured her I lived in a tip myself. But there was no mess. The flat was rigidly tidy and absolutely clean. So why the horror? Hard to describe the sense of desolation I felt as I stood in the tiny living-room, plant-pots neatly lined up on the window-sill, and looked at the two prams in it. The prams were at right angles to each other with a dog, an ugly-looking mongrel, chained to the wheel of one of them. The dog appeared asleep, though its ears pricked up at my voice. One of the babies was giving snuffling noises and the baby-minder apologised for it. 'He doesn't usually make no noise,' she said, 'only he has a cold. He gets collected at dinner-time.' I stood there quite unable to understand why I'd rather give up my own job than let Christabel come here, and I could think of nothing to say. So I admired the begonia and said how well hers was doing whereas mine didn't seem to flourish. There was a momentary enthusiasm on her part and then I was out on the balcony and I could hear the chain going back on.

The second place was both worse and better. This woman was older and much more confident. No chains on the door, no dogs. She lived in a basement in an old house, the same kind of house in which we had a flat ourselves. There was a radio blaring away when she opened the door and quite a nice smell of cooking, soup I thought. The woman was smoking in the way they do in pictures of the 1930s, the fag in the corner of the mouth and never relinquished. She was sharp-eyed and cheerful and ushered me in eagerly, saying she'd nothing to hide and I must take her as I found her. I said I would. I found her dirty and dangerous. Her living-room was a death trap for small children, full of trailing wires and an unguarded electric fire and a huge television right next to the bars of a play-pen in which three children of indeterminate age were tearing at each other's hair and howling. She dealt with the howling effectively by dropping a sweet into each mouth then she lifted one of the children out, a boy, and told him he was a bloody little pest and she'd tan his hide if she had any more of it. But she kissed him and he laughed and kissed her back. So she was no bully, no cruel monster. I'm sure those children were luckier than the others. When I left, refusing a cup of tea (another mark in her favour) I knew she knew I wouldn't be back and that she was amused by my obvious disapproval. 'It isn't like home, is it, dear?' she said sarcastically. 'Not home-sweet-home when you have to farm them out. You have to take what you can get, that's the trouble, and you won't find better than this and that's the truth.'

It probably was. I didn't even go inside the third place. It was a ground-floor flat and I looked through the window before I rang the bell and there were *five*, I repeat five, small children in there, all in some way or another restrained. Three were in high-chairs, strapped in, each with a rattle; one was in a pushchair and appeared to have turned itself round in its harness so its face was hidden in the hood of the push-chair; and one was in one of those slings suspended from the door frame. There was a television on and no adult in the room. So that was that.

We gave up the idea of Christabel going to a baby-minder. But what would we have done if we had been truly poor and desperate? What option would we have had? Maureen and her official register I suppose, but then all the accredited minders would be bound to be full up. Our fancy notions of one-to-one devoted care, such as Rowena gave Christabel herself, would have looked pretty silly then. Every day she would have been obliged to go through all that agony of worry, dropping the precious baby off at a place she didn't like to be in the care of a woman whom nothing led us to trust. Unless she'd been lucky and found a genuine treasure, a woman of our own persuasion in matters of child care, a woman such as Rowena thought she was going to be when she put her notice in the shop: 'Baby-minder available, own home or baby's, handi-capped equally loved'.

It was one of the many times when I didn't know whether to laugh or scream – 'handicapped equally loved'. When she produced this gem I simply stared The Stare. How could I begin to explain what was wrong, what was *sick*, about those words? And so awkward too, the sentiment behind the words, so badly expressed. I refused to comment. I told her, bad-temperedly, to go ahead and put the notice in the window. I even made jokes, dreadful jokes, about the Lowry characters who would turn up. Wasted. Rowena had never heard of L. S. Lowry. Art was not her strong point, but then what was?

In any case, nobody turned up. Quite remarkably, Rowena was not inundated with requests to care for blind or lame or mentally deficient babies and children. Did it prove the handicapped baby is more loved than the normal? How extra-ordinary. Or maybe it simply proved people are suspicious of apparent altruism. Maybe Rowena was reckoned to be a little kinky.

There were some who thought so. Her mother for one, at least at the beginning, the beginning of her bringing home these black boyfriends. Racism, of course, racism pure and simple, or rather tainted and very complicated. Mrs Blake had no black friends. I daresay she went through years and years in Stockdale, in Edinburgh, without ever even seeing a black face. Certainly my parents, in Cockermouth, did – but there is the difference, *they* weren't racist, they didn't flinch and stiffen when eventually through me, they met black people. What used to enrage me was Rowena actually excusing her mother, saying she could hardly be blamed, that she'd had a sheltered life and the shock was great. I blame her. She told me once she thought Rowena was just doing it to annoy her, choosing black boyfriends that is. I told her nothing could be further from the truth, that Rowena was strongly attracted to black men and they to her. If there has to be a starting point somewhere in attraction, in the first instance, it was in skin colour for Rowena. Later, of course, as with everyone else, it was the man himself she liked or disliked and the blackness didn't come into it. But walking down a street with Rowena, or going into a pub, she would nudge me and comment how gorgeous some man was. He was always black. I'd tell her it made me sick to hear she wanted to get to know someone because of his looks, before she'd heard a word spoken, but she said I was the abnormal one and 'fancying' men came down to looks. Ugh. Such a hideous word. Started as a joke at first, her adoption of this 'I fancy him' jargon. But then it became real, the word 'fancy' produced a genuine leer on her face and I hated it. But then, according to Rowena, I am a prude. Good. I am glad.

Rowena was equally proud of not being one. Her sexual appetite was prodigious. Years and years we've fought for women to enjoy sex the way men do, to have the same right to glory in it as men do, but in Rowena's behaviour I saw the dangers. On the very first night of a new date she would have sex, without preamble, without thinking any was necessary. Now, if a man wanted to do that, he would still have difficulty, he would expect to go through some preliminaries, unless he was with a prostitute or perhaps with someone at a party who was drunk. Rowena dictated what was to happen far more successfully and completely than any man could have done.

Naturally, at first most of the men could not believe their luck. Rowena's availability and eagerness rightly astounded them. But in a few weeks' time, if they lasted that long, they didn't think themselves so lucky. What they had thought they had in Rowena was a classy nymphomaniac. What they discovered they had was a girl for whom sex was like an introductory handshake but who was ready to make a great many other demands on them, demands they were not necessarily able to meet. Having given the ultimate (though of course to her it was far from being the ultimate), Rowena thought she would automatically be loved and held dear. When she wasn't, she became tearful and resentful. But this didn't make her want to get rid of the man – it made her expect to be recompensed. Again and again she was left in what seemed a brutally abrupt fashion, the lover simply disappearing without trace. Then there was the agony of discovering how little she knew about the man, didn't know what his job was or even, very often, where he lived. 'How could he do it?' she would wail. 'How could *you*?' I'd say.

This is, after all, as hopeless as trying to find the cause of a regular war. It isn't just a case of saying Rowena, Rowena herself was the cause. As I ought to have known, it matters what Rowena was like, what brought her to start it all off. It is necessary, vital, to go back and back, to try to trace the pattern, if pattern there was. And yet it is pointless, now that it is all over. Why exhaust myself? Rowena is dead. I have lost Christabel. I have my own life to lead and since for the last two years I have been complaining that I have no time to lead it, I ought to get on with it and be thankful. But it cannot be done, not so easily. I know myself in a way Rowena did not know herself and I know I cannot get by without ridding myself of all this baggage I carry on her account. I do not need a psychiatrist, a therapist, a counsellor, and I definitely do not need Maureen. What I need is some sort of explanation, some rationale for everything that has happened, and I am the only person who can provide it by painstakingly sifting through the past. And yet it is so hard, because I can never know completely Rowena's past even if I knew more than anyone else.

'You've been a good friend,' Mrs Blake said. 'You stood by her, Isobel, you saw her through bad times and good.' I mumbled something about Rowena doing the same for me but Mrs Blake shook her head and smiled wearily. 'No,' she said, 'it was all take with Rowena. There was no giving. I don't know why she was like that. Camilla isn't.' Camilla, who was next to her mother and listening, said, 'We were just different, Ma, that's all.' 'Trouble,' Mrs Blake said, her brow furrowed, 'she was always trouble, all her life, and now her death is just as troublesome.' Camilla shushed her, and was clearly both embarrassed and horrified. Her mother's cold words were so inappropriate. I even heard her upbraiding her mother for not weeping. 'You haven't grieved, Ma,' she said accusingly. 'Grieved?' Mrs Blake said, surprised. 'I've grieved all Rowena's life. The grief is over, that's all, it's all finished, I haven't any left, there's nothing in me any more, I'm done.'

Weird, isn't it? Her grief was done when by rights, according to normal practice, it ought just to have begun. And yet, unlike Camilla, I saw what she meant and was not appalled. It makes me think that perhaps the circumstances of Rowena's death, and the death itself, would make a better starting point for me than all this attempt to be chronological. And perhaps, even after all this time, a whole two years, I haven't ever faced up to how terrible that death was, I have failed to do what Maureen calls my 'grief-work'. I have been too involved, too busy, too active fighting for Christabel and I have not let the tragedy itself seep through my bones. I am not, to quote Maureen again, in touch with my feelings on that score. I don't want to be.

I really do not want to be on that mountain, I do not want to see the body, I do not want to hear the screams, I do not want to carry the litter or ride in the ambulance. It was bad enough coming in where I did come in, arriving at the Intensive Care Unit in Carlisle Infirmary. I can hardly cope with remembering that, never mind with all the horrific details of what went before. And it makes me feel ashamed, though I do not know why, to think that I made no attempt to acquaint myself with those details. People kept trying to tell me but I shut them up. The newspapers had an account but I didn't read them. I was at the inquest but whatever was said passed me by. Never at any time have I allowed myself to imagine those four hours between Rowena falling and my seeing her in the ICU.

Sometimes, thoughts of her pain would begin to creep under my skin and I had to jump up and do something to block it out. It is the pain I cannot bear to think about, the hellish, searing physical agony with that rock . . . with that jagged . . . with that *thing* impaling her. *There is no point in remembering this.* It is disgusting to dwell on it. I hate people who do that, the ghouls who go over and over the horror, saying how terrible, how dreadful, but adding more and more bits of information and, while claiming to feel ill, giving every appearance of enjoyment.

I hid behind Christabel. Someone had to look after, be with her. Christabel, who was there of course, who, unlike anyone else, saw and heard, and who acted, at the age of five years old, with such heroism. Much was made, at the inquest, of Christabel's calm demeanour. I noticed, in the hours after the accident, what a curiosity this made the child. People seemed afraid of her, it was not considered normal to be so composed. A policeman confidently predicted that she would break down quite suddenly and told me to 'watch her', as though I would be doing anything else. But I had seen what the policeman had not, the small signs pointing to terror.

Christabel had not, in fact, seen that Rowena had a pointed piece of rock through her chest. She had not seen any blood and she had not heard screams – the waterfall was too loud and, later, she was neither on the mountain nor in the ambulance. The people at The Fish took her in and sensibly kept her in their own kitchen until I arrived. All Christabel saw was her mother slip and fall, fall five hundred yards down the waterfall. She turned at once and trotted down the path up which she had come. She could not get near her mother's body. The path took her in a wide arc away from the waterfall. She spoke freely of hurrying, of knowing Rowena had fallen and was hurt and needed help. Her description of what had happened and where, was precise. The two climbers she met, the people at The Fish, the mountain rescue team – they were all treated to a meticulous account without so much as a sob. But I saw, as they did not, the nail marks in the palms of her hands, the rigidity of her spine, the strange flickering of her eyes, like a nervous tick. And I saw her pallor, which they could not recognise, not realising black skins can go pale, can be drained as surely as white ones. That dull, grey-brown colour was not Christabel's usual colour. Her complexion was beautiful, a rich dark honey colour with even a trace of pink in her cheeks. In the battle of racial genes her father's triumphed over hair and eyes and nose, but his colour had been heavily diluted by Rowena's fair tones. Christabel was clearly of mixed race but her exact lineage was hard to guess. No one saw she was ashen, just that she was 'coloured'. A little coloured girl. And her white mother. 'Will you contact the father?' the policeman asked me. 'There isn't one,' I said. I let him and everyone else think Christabel's father was dead. Until I got to Maureen and then the trouble began.

CHAPTER TWO

Maybe this is how depression begins, the slow stillness of the awakening, the lethargy, the feeling of bewilderment. I wouldn't know. I have never been depressed in my life, or at least not what I would term depressed. Sad, of course, a little low in spirits from time to time, yes, but not that complete lack of faith in the prospect of any happiness or pleasure which is how I would define depression. Rowena was always wailing about how depressed she was and it made me irritable. I would tell her, constantly, not to misuse the term, I would say it was obscene for her to call herself depressed, I would remind her of all those sufferers in mental hospitals who were clinically depressed, too helpless and hopeless to see anything but darkness wherever they looked. Rowena, I knew, had far too much energy to be seriously depressed. Even the way she said it, even the fact that she said it, showed she had no idea what depression was.

But perhaps this is how it begins, with a morning like this. I wondered at first if I might be ill. I felt my forehead (perfectly cool) and stretched out my limbs (no aches or pains). I just felt, in spite of twelve hours' sleep, so weary. It was the most enormous effort to get out of bed and the moment I did so I began to weep. Now, this was ridiculous. I do not weep. With another tremendous struggle of will I made my way into the bathroom and forced myself under a stingingly cold shower.

The shock made me gasp and tremble, but I went on enduring the needle-like water until my body was quite numb. Stepping out from underneath the water, wrapping myself in a towel and going into the kitchen I felt triumphant – I had dealt with my own momentary feebleness in a way Rowena never dealt with hers. She needed other people. Me, usually. I would have had to pull the duvet off her, drag her to the shower, force her screaming under it. And it never did her the good which it did me. She would collapse, sit with her bare back to the tiled wall and crouch, head in her hands, howling for mercy. No, cold showers were no good for Rowena. What she wanted was tea and sympathy. She liked me to tiptoe in and gently draw the curtains and sit on her bed handing her Kleenex and asking her what was the matter.

The matter usually was, that she always wanted to fall in love with a man who had fallen in love with her. Oh God. I could hardly bear it. So that is what most human beings want, it is their expectation from an early age, an expectation that starts turning to fantasy as they near the age of thirty, but Rowena made a demand out of it. 'I want a lover,' she would cry. 'I want someone forever.' Nothing else mattered. She would not hear of seeking alternative satisfaction in work or other relationships or in developing absorbing interests. Her self-pity was disgusting. And then the theme song changed its tune and became: 'I want a baby – that's all I want in life. I want a baby, I want to be a mother, it's all I've ever wanted to be.' A lie. I never remember Rowena wanting to be a mother. I remember only that she wanted excitement and action all the time and that her family said she loved children. It was in their interests. What else were they to do with her? She hated school, wouldn't go into the sixth form, left at sixteen with three O-levels and no desire to do anything at all. The Blakes were in despair. They felt she needed to get away from home – they wanted her away and who can blame them – so they had to think up somewhere for her to go. What they thought up was a one-year course in nursery care in London. Rowena would stay with Camilla, who had just got married and now lived there.

So that was how dear Rowena started her career. God knows

where the Blakes found this course, but it was obvious to anyone with any common sense – me, for example – that it was feeble. Private, of course, at some impressive-sounding 'college'. Rowena was supposed to get a thorough grounding in the care of babies and young children and there was even an exam, all the college's own, at the end of the year. You got a certificate if you passed and bugger all good it did you. But that was only the first step, or only supposed to be. Rowena, the plan was, would then study for a *bona fide* qualification and become either a registered nanny or a children's nurse. She became neither, simply could not pass the exams. Her moderate intelligence and early ability to write quite well did her no good at all. The Blakes were exasperated, as they had every right to be. She wasn't stupid, so why the difficulty? She couldn't, or wouldn't, concentrate, that was the problem. She said her mind wandered. So then her parents packed her off to America where she stayed with a cousin and came back two years later with some extraordinary transatlantic qualification nobody recognised over here. She wouldn't get any kind of proper job in nursery care so she became a nanny, a nanny without any British qualification.

So what was wrong with that? Nothing. A good nanny does not necessarily have to have the right letters after her name. But Rowena was a terrible nanny, which employers quickly found out. Leaving small children with Rowena was terrifying, I imagine. But people did it, those who really just needed a seemingly high-class form of child-minder. Rowena had loads of jobs. Most of them lasted from two to six weeks, and her references became very ancient. Several times she narrowly escaped getting into real trouble, even coming near to being threatened with prosecution. That was when she lost a two-year-old in Hyde Park. What made this worse was that she didn't even know she'd lost him. She'd sat down to have a fag with the pushchair facing away from her. The hood was up and the waterproof apron on and she sat there holding the pram handle and smoking, believing the child to be asleep. Unfortunately, she dozed off herself and, when she came to, simply got up and carried on walking, congratulating herself on keeping little Jeremy asleep so long. She walked all the way home, a good forty minutes' walk, and only when she came to lift Jeremy out did she discover he had gone. The police were called by the distraught mother who then heard her nanny say she 'didn't know' in reply to almost every question. Being Rowena, she couldn't even remember which park bench she'd sat on – taken back to the park she was quite unable to retrace her steps. Oh, it ended all right – Jeremy had been found by some other nanny who had taken him to the nearest police station and it was all over in a couple of hours – but there was no reference there for Miss Rowena Blake and damned nearly a prosecution for negligence.

I paint a black picture, which is unfair. Rowena was popular, if hopeless. Small children did like her (though older ones did not). No mess ever fazed her and she was gloriously oblivious of dirty, sticky hands or wet pants or snot all over the face. She had a nice singing voice too and kept many a child happy with her endless repertoire of nursery rhymes. If she was only in charge of one child of around three she was quite a success, so long as other help was kept to deal with the more mundane and necessary facets of child care. What was disastrous was if she had more than one and if she was responsible for meals and washing clothes and so forth. Then, she couldn't cope and would gradually panic under the weight of her own newly created chaos. The mother would come home and find the house looking as if a bomb had gone off and the children wandering around naked covered in jam or honey with Rowena nowhere in sight. She'd be discovered taking a bath or watching television. Who could put up with this? Maybe the mothers, if desperate enough, but not the fathers. Oh, dear me, no. The fathers found Rowena very tiresome. Often, or so Rowena reported, they would say it was them or her, that they could not stand another minute of this anarchy. It would be bag-packing time again.

Ten years of this and then she says she wants a baby, wants to be a mother, that her *destiny*, if you please, is to be a mother. I ignored her at first, then I began making sarcastic rejoinders every time she started. 'You're so suited to motherhood,

Rowena,' I would say. 'I mean, you've proved you have all the necessary virtues. You're so patient and equable and everyone says, just everyone, you're so organised.' She would dismiss all this jeering and say that being a good mother had nothing to do with patience or organisation, that all a good mother needed was love and she, Rowena Blake, had a superabundance of love to give. Then she would say it had nothing to do with whether she would be a good or a bad mother, that it had to do with following a natural instinct. She had an overwhelming natural desire to procreate and if this was thwarted it would kill her. Nature was telling her, she said, to have a baby. I advised her to tell nature to shut up. That was when I'd finished laughing. Rowena, when earnest, something she so rarely was, had an expression of such mournfulness it always made me laugh. She had this habit of letting her mouth sag open, which pulled it down at the corners until she looked like an exaggeratedly sad clown. And she'd blink heavily while stating her case, blinked for emphasis, making an absolute caricature of herself.

At the time when she began to moan on about wanting a baby, soon after her thirtieth birthday, it so happened she had no current boyfriend. A man she'd been quite keen on, and who had been equally keen on her even after the usual cooling-off period, had just gone back to Ghana. He said he'd write. He didn't. Rowena quite enjoyed pining for him – it was a new sensation – but I don't think she was particularly hurt. It mildly perturbed her that no new man seemed on the horizon and even more that she didn't spot anyone to whom she could make ardent advances.

'The thing is,' she announced one day, with an air of revelation, 'I'm not interested in men any more. I want a baby. All my other instincts have gone. I don't want sex any more. I want a baby, I really *want* a baby.' I asked what it was going to be, a virgin birth or the old syringe. She didn't understand about the syringe. I explained, as far as possible in words of one syllable, and it was a big mistake. Rowena was thrilled to learn of the existence of artificial insemination. The idea of paying to have herself injected with the semen of an anonymous donor delighted her. She jumped up and kissed me, said I was a genius, and then it was 'Where do I go, Isobel? What do I do?' I said, pretty smartly, that I had no idea and when she pouted and asked if I would help her, I said certainly not, that I was shocked at the mere idea, that it was quite revolting to me. 'Why?' she asked, all child-like innocence. 'Why? What's wrong with it?'

Only everything. It is odd that I, the determined feminist, should be so violently opposed to women choosing to cut the father out. Oh, I have heard all the arguments, which Rowena eventually absorbed and trotted out, about nature only arranging for the man's part to be a minute and a woman's to be at the very least eighteen months. I've heard the one about society creating the family as we know it, and why shouldn't there be other types of units. I've heard the case for women going it alone, put by women far more skilled in argument than Rowena, and I still reject it. A child has a right to its father and a father to his child, and I do not confuse the issue by throwing in reservations about widows and posthumous births – it doesn't make any difference. Nor do I want to hear how this kind of single parenthood is on the increase, how it will soon be the norm and will have to be accepted as such. I won't accept it. As a feminist, I won't accept it. I won't use men as men have used women. It fills me with horror to imagine confronting a child, who asks who its father was, and saying I quite deliberately chose not to know. It is the ultimate in exploitation.

Rowena didn't care. Start any ideological argument and she'd yawn. But in her case it was superfluous to become so serious. The plain truth was she could not possibly support a child. How could she? How was she equipped in any way? Her mother bought this flat with me for Rowena so she had that kind of security, but the deal was that she must support herself and pay all bills. Her mother bought her the car, but she had to licence it and fill it with petrol herself. Then there was the cost of food and clothes and so forth and Rowena's income was erratic and small. She borrowed from Camilla, borrowed from me, borrowed from the bank and still she was in permanent financial difficulties. How, pray, could she support a child? She was a spoiled little rich girl, except that she wasn't rich, unless compared to the truly poor. The share of this flat, the car, a generous mother and sister – these did not make her rich.

I warned her. I said if this was anything but a joke, a passing whim, she had better understand one important thing: *I would not have a child in our flat.* I reminded her of the very carefully composed agreement we had, drawn up by my solicitor, at my cost, to safeguard me against Rowena's men moving in and taking over my home. Children had not been mentioned, but nevertheless they were covered by the wording. So I told Rowena she would have to move. She shrugged, said that would be no problem, she'd sell her half to me and buy something else.

How does anyone get to thirty and remain so naive? Our flat cost £30,000 in 1980. By 1985, the year I am talking about, the cost of a similar flat had doubled, *doubled*, and yet there were queues for them. Rowena's fifteen thousand would not buy her a single room, and that was if I chose to buy her out. Well, that was not a problem. In many ways, it was an opportunity I would have been eager to grab. I could afford it, just. I had had a good salary for a long time and had saved wisely. I could buy Rowena out and then sell and move to somewhere more salubrious. It was very tempting. But I refused to be tempted. I was so angry with Rowena that I took it upon myself to try to make her see sense before she went ahead and did something irrevocable. 'Think, Rowena,' I kept urging, 'think, think, think what it would be like. How trapped you'd be, how you wouldn't be able to manage, how frightened you'd get, how depressed.'

'I *am* thinking,' she'd say. 'I'm thinking how lovely it would be to have my own baby, just the two of us against the world. I'm thinking how I love babies, how sweet they are, all those gurgles and their tiny hands and . . .' Then I'd scream and tell her to stop romanticising motherhood and remind herself instead of how useless she was with babies. . . .

All the passion I spent. Not just then, but ever since, until yesterday. Maybe I'm simply drained, exhausted, battle-worn. Recuperation is what I need. This isn't depression, it is battle-fatigue. What do they do with soldiers? Send them to a convalescent home, give them complete rest, look after them. I could go home, to Cockermouth. My mother would be glad to look after me. It is what she specialises in. But the defeat is too recent for me to leave the battlefield. I need to wander around all the ruins, empty gun still smoking in my hand, all shots fired without hitting the target. People said, to my face, that I seemed to relish the battle, that I was in there with both fists flying. Was I? It didn't seem so to me. I felt I was dragged in to the fray, that I engaged reluctantly. I wonder what Maureen would say? She is coming in an hour or so, to collect the last of Christabel's stuff, the few things I was clinging on to. I am not allowed to take them to her myself. I have no access, none. When she is eighteen she can contact me if she wishes, but I must not contact her. Not even a birthday card, your honour? Oh, yes, a card will be perfectly permissible. But it will be from someone who quickly will be a stranger. Isobel? Isobel? Isobel who, Mummy?

Could this be, *could* this be not depression but jealousy? Does jealousy make you feel heavy and dull, does it make everything seem pointless? I doubt it, and yet it is true that again and again my head is filled with a certain smiling, fat face. I could hardly bear to look at her in court yesterday and yet I could not take my eyes off her unctuous expression. So confident she was, so smug and virtuous. She scored 27 out of 30, eight more than the nearest other competitor. 'This is not a competition, you know,' Maureen would say from time to time, at her most prim and severe, but of course it was. Why else have marks? She would much rather not have revealed that there were marks, but had to, when pushed. By me. When I demanded to know how their decision had been reached, her superior, Stella, and the adoption officer, Phyllis, told her to let me see the assessments and there they were, the marks: scores for what the house was like, what kind of family this was, what were the reasons for wanting a child, what was the attitude towards access for the birth family and existing friends. All marked, then added up. 27 out of 30. Go to the top of the class. And score highest of all for your husband, your ace card.

This is very childish, very Rowena. I must stop it, must return to my normal, sensible self and yet I feel outside that self. My faith in common sense, in logic, in the rule of law, has been severely shaken. What has happened is wrong. Camilla works so hard at pretending Christabel now has the best possible chance of happiness, that she has come to believe it is true, but then Camilla's guilt is far worse than my own. If I feel I have failed Christabel, think how Camilla feels. She has everything a child could want and besides she is Christabel's aunt, her blood relative.

Betty could never get over it. 'She seems a nice person,' she would say, 'kind and that, ever so gentle, but actions speak louder than words. Know what I mean?' And they did, to Betty, to Maureen, to everyone who heard about the case. I was the only one who understood Camilla's agony and agreed with her decision. But even I was shocked somewhere at the back of my mind. 'You are quite right, Camilla,' I would hear myself say, with that firmness for which I am famous, but a little internal voice would be saying: 'What has right to do with it?'

What indeed? But then what Rowena did in the first place was not right. Inevitably, the result of her action would affect Camilla and Mrs Blake, but she did not consult them until she was pregnant. She enjoyed telling them. She related how Camilla turned pale but then rallied and congratulated her whereas her mother congratulated her, stiffly, before closing her eyes and shaking her head. They questioned Rowena closely about the father. 'I suppose,' Mrs Blake evidently said, 'he is black?'

All the men Rowena tried to use to impregnate her were black. Kojo was the first. He was from Ghana too, and Rowena met him at the African Centre where she had often been with her other Ghanian friend. He was, is, a nice man. Not young, about forty, and married back home. He was rather stout and short, most unprepossessing, but he had the most beautiful smile and sweetest manner, all politeness and deference. Rowena shocked him, as she did most men, but he could not resist her and soon came to adore her, genuinely. We had already had the ceremonial ostentatious flushing down the loo of the birth-control pills – they proved almost unflushable and lay like bits of grit at the bottom of the lavatory pan for days – so I knew what was in the offing. I said nothing. When Rowena wondered aloud if Kojo was genetically fat and would have fat children, I ignored her. She was waiting for me to rise to the bait and I refused to.

In fact, I went abroad then, for nearly a month, and left them to it. When I returned, Kojo was still around but Rowena was tense and anxious. Before I was even through the front door I'd heard her worries about being infertile. In short, she had not conceived after three months of valiant endeavour. 'Rowena,' I said, tired after a long flight, 'how long have you been on the pill? Fourteen years? Well, then. If you weren't so ignorant you'd know that after such a length of time it could take months and months to conceive.'

She tried for several months. Not only with Kojo, of course, because she blamed him really. She had three other lovers after Kojo went home and only then faced up to the truth: it must be her. I must say it seemed to me the most delicious irony, if not the biggest of jokes. Is that cruel? I don't think so. It gave me the greatest satisfaction that dear old mother nature, called in to justify everything, had decided not to oblige. And besides, Rowena was no wretched, heartbroken woman whose whole life for years and years had revolved round having a child – it was still, with her, a whim, I was convinced. The longer she had to wait, the more good it would do her.

But six months after her thirtieth birthday she went to her GP and span some story about her love-affairs breaking up because she wanted a child and couldn't conceive one and about feeling she would have a nervous breakdown if she continued to fail. The GP said she could go to a clinic or she could go to a specialist, privately. Without hesitation, without even the most cursory counting of pennies, Rowena plumped for the specialist. A Mr Gordon Fyffe of Welbeck Street. 'The top man,' Rowena boasted, as people do when they pay to go to specialists – it's always the top man. I don't think she liked him much, top or not. He was very brisk. After various tests, which I was obliged to live through over every meal, he said there was nothing wrong with Rowena, but that a retroverted womb and blocked tubes were probably the cause of her apparent infertility. He said he'd have her in and blow the tubes, and then he recommened the pin-pointing of her ovulation period and concentrated intercourse on those days only.

She was in this Top Man's clinic for a day and a night and loved every minute of it. Oh, the virtue of it! You would have thought she was being noble in some great cause as she packed her bag to go in – such a line in brave smiles, such swallowings, such an air of pride. Yes, pride, she was so proud of herself. Then, once out, it was temperature-taking every morning and screams when the thermometer went up by two degrees. She ran into my bedroom brandishing it. 'This is it, Isobel,' she said, eyes shining, the thermometer held aloft like a trophy. I turned over and buried my head in the pillow, hearing, even so, Rowena already on the telephone urging Tomas, a very obliging Jamaican, to come round at once. He came and obliged, I fancy, repeatedly, but two weeks later his efforts were proved to be in vain. Rowena sobbed as she reported that her period had started. God, it was boring. I began to consider moving out. What, after all, was there in it for me, continuing to live with Rowena? You may well ask what there had ever been, but apart from convenience there had once been some fun.

There isn't much here about the fun, I realise that, but then the memory of it seems so distant. I was just so very pleased to see Rowena when I came to London after two years in Amsterdam. It was Camilla I rang, since she was a fixed point, saying I'd taken a new job and was going to be in London and did she know of any flats going, and when Camilla said Rowena was flat-hunting at this very moment, it seemed too good to be true. And Rowena found the flat. She looked so happy, pink-cheeked and eyes sparkling, and she drove me round to see it and gave me a great hug when I said it seemed perfect. Everything went so smoothly and even though that streak of caution in me made me get the legal document drawn up, protecting me from live-in 'others', I had no fears as to how it would work out. Hadn't I always got on well with Rowena? Didn't we have a long, long history, even if there had been a break in it? And the flat was big enough for us to be together but separate, should we prove incompatible after all. We each had a bedroom, a large bedroom, as well as a shared kitchen and a bathroom and living-room. Very generous. We really were very happy living together, until this pregnancy thing started.

Eventually, I got as far as telling Rowena I was thinking of moving anyway. I wanted to live in North London, not south of the river, as we did. I asked if she wanted to buy me out. She laughed bitterly and asked what with. I replied with whatever she was going to use when she became pregnant. She said when she became pregnant she'd have all the faith and energy to move mountains, nothing would be a problem. Right now, she was depressed and hadn't the energy to think about it. I could leave her in the lurch if I wanted. This enraged me of course – leave her in the lurch, indeed, as if she was my responsibility.

I started flat-hunting at once, defiantly leaving estate agents' letters around for Rowena to see. She made no comment. More and more she was at home, hardly taking any jobs, hardly contributing anything to the exchequer. It could not go on, and I was steeling myself to go and see Mrs Blake and consult her over my leaving the flat – it was, after all, her investment and not her daughter's – when it happened. Rowena became pregnant. I noticed she was a little restless, lolling about and sulking less than she had been doing, but I hadn't read anything significant into this minor change of mood. Then I came home one Friday and was amazed to find the flat immaculately tidy, a good smell of cooking coming from the kitchen, and candles lit on a beautifully laid table. No sign of Rowena. I was wary. Some new stud? Was I supposed to stay in my room tonight? I waited, and presently Rowena put her head round the door and smiled and mouthed, quite shyly, that she was pregnant.

When you see someone transformed by happiness it is hard to remember to be disapproving. I would have thought less of myself if I had tried. So I didn't. I smiled, too, and raised my glass and did not have to try very hard after all to share Rowena's delight. I didn't even ask who the father was – it could have been one of several again – and afterwards I was glad I had shown this restraint.

Three weeks later, that is to say some eight weeks after conception, maybe ten, Rowena miscarried. Very common. Nothing to it. Just an exceptionally heavy period, but oh, the drama. I heard her go to the loo in the morning and then she screamed (you will have gathered by now Rowena was a great and lusty screamer). I jumped up and there she was, standing looking down into the lavatory which was thick with blood. I got her into bed and more for form's sake than anything else rang the doctor. She was kind, said she'd pop in though there was nothing much she could do. 'Save any large clots,' she said. *What?* I couldn't believe I was hearing correctly. What were they to be saved for? How was I supposed to collect them? I recoiled with absolute disgust and did not even pass this message on to Rowena. But when the doctor came – young and harassed, though sympathetic to a remarkably convincing degree – she said that clots could be analysed and perhaps give some indication of why Rowena was miscarrying, if she went on doing so.

I thought myself that she would give up now. Surely it had gone on long enough, this farce. But not a bit of it. Becoming pregnant had spurred Rowena on – she had proved she could do it and now she was seeing the whole business as a fight. 'I won't be beaten,' she announced. 'Next time, I'll keep my son.' I looked at her in alarm. That mess of blood a son? Something with substance? How ridiculous. But she even gave 'him' a name, started to refer to 'when she was carrying Timothy'. *Timothy?* Yes, she said, Timothy because it wasn't a strong name and she felt he had been fair and artistic and not strong himself. I said it would have been a miracle if he'd been fair when his only possible fathers had all been black. She told me not to be nasty, even accused me of envying her. Again, I was like an echo – envy? *Envy?* I said, what in God's name was I supposed to envy? 'I have carried a child,' Rowena said grandly. 'I have fulfilled woman's highest function and you have not.'

Well, as a matter of fact I have, if being pregnant is what Rowena calls fulfilling, etc. etc. Twice, I've been pregnant,

33

twice, and twice I've had an abortion. Perfectly easily, painlessly and without fuss or agony, physical or emotional. What rubbish is talked about abortion these days, both about the process and the aftermath. If it is done quickly and well, it is an absolute nothing, and I saw both times that it was seen to with speed. All it was, for me, was a failure of birth control and I treated it as such. No heartache, no regret, no speculation about 'Timothys'. But I wasn't going to tell Rowena, or anyone for that matter. Both times it was an intensely private experience and I did not consult the man involved. No man has the right to dictate to me that I should bear a child neither of us wanted or deserved. I just saw to it myself and that was that. If ever I had had a child, it would have been deliberately and with the full knowing co-operation of the putative father.

Maureen asked me at one point if I 'fancied', or had ever 'fancied', having children. I said, No, I didn't see myself as cut out for mothering. I have none of the qualities I think necessary and I would miss my career tremendously. I travel, I keep odd hours, I drive myself hard and I love it. Giving it up would be like dying. She didn't believe me, of course, no one ever does. Careers are still seen as compensation for what women do not have. I can't say I cared about convincing her. Why should I? I'm not an apologist. She told me she hoped to start a family in a year or so, when a deposit had been put on a house. She didn't think it fair to have kiddies in a flat – this said with an offensively self-righteous air, condemning, as it did, virtually the entire population of London and certainly the whole of her clientele. It almost made me cheer Rowena in retrospect for not giving a damn about houses or deposits, or washing machines, for just going ahead, oblivious to all the worldly preparations the Maureens make before consenting to breed.

In the event, the conceiving of Christabel was not as sordid as it might have been. It was not really sordid at all. It was very nearly romantic. For once, Rowena was not the pursuer. She met Amos in a perfectly orthodox fashion at the house where she was currently working, looking after one little girl of three, from eight in the morning until two in the afternoon. The mother was manageress of a dress shop and the father a security guard. Amos was a security guard too, but he was about to start a university course as a mature student, the following October (this was in the summer). He used to pick up the father each day, just after Rowena started work, and so there was a good deal of all that normal exchange of pleasantries with which most people begin their friendships. Rowena was not her usual self because she was fretting after the demise of 'Timothy', and so it did not register at first that Amos was interested in her. When he asked her out she was quite amazed – it was centuries since a man had been the one to make the first move. And they did not go to bed on their first date. It was a full two weeks before their affair began – a record.

Amos was a nice man. How feeble to describe him thus, but his niceness was paramount. He was West Indian, from Barbados. Somewhere in him he had European genes, as most West Indians do, and these showed in his features rather than his skin colour. His lips were not African, nor was the size of his eyes (though he had an African nose). He was tall and heavy and carried himself very erect. Rowena's fairness and her slight build made her Desdemona to his Othello, and people turned in the street to look at them. After three months, Amos proposed. He was only a poor student, he said, or about to be one, but if Rowena would have him he would work his fingers to the bone and they would manage somehow . . .

I can bring tears to my own eyes just thinking about it. He was so sweet, so earnest, so utterly without a clue, a clue about Rowena. Because Rowena had no use for Amos except as a breeding machine. She had no intention of getting married. 'I don't want to share my son,' she said (to me, not, I trust, to Amos). She didn't even like the fact that Amos was going to be in London for the next three years or so and questioned him closely about how certain his return to Barbados was going to be (very certain, not only because his government, who were contributing to his grant, obliged him to return for at least two years, but because he could not wait to get home).

Then, dramatically, Amos was called home. His father died and his mother was ill with shock and grief, so he went home, expecting to return in a month. What happened out in Barbados

I do not know, but Amos did not return. He did not disappear, like Kojo. On the contrary, he wrote regularly and even telephoned at, I imagine, hideous expense about two weeks after he left. It seemed his mother could not manage without him and said she would die if he left her. Rowena found this pretty unbelievable, but in fact it suited her purpose very well to have Amos removed from the scene, just at the precise moment when she suspected she was again pregnant.

I remember very well the beauty of it, the magic. It was I who purchased the pregnancy testing kit at Boots, being unable to put up any longer with Rowena's minute-by-minute anxiety. I said I would rather know one way or the other and get the wretched doubt over – it was really so boring having Rowena going around as though she might expect a visit from the archangel Gabriel at any moment. So I bought the kit and sat down and absorbed the instructions carefully. It was of the type of chemical test whereby urine is left in a solution for several hours and if the woman is pregnant it turns blue, and if not it remains unchanged. Rowena provided me with the urine and I dripped the requisite number of drops into the prepared test-tube. It had to be done in the early morning, on wakening, and then left for four hours at least. Rowena, always sleepy in the morning, went back to bed after we'd set the test up. I did not.

It was September and just starting to be a little cold in the morning. I remember drawing the curtains so that I could watch the early mist lift as I sat drinking coffee while Rowena slept. Our view from the first floor is not extensive but through a gap in the buildings opposite there is a glimpse of trees, all oranges and yellows then, at the beginning of autumn. There were lights on in windows up and down the street as early risers got up for work. The lighted windows looked pretty, friendly, made our dour street sparkle momentarily.

I went into the bathroom, where the test-tube stood on top of the medicine cabinet, secure in the holder provided with the kit, and kept looking at the liquid. So still and silent and yet perhaps within it the stirrings of a life.

The newspaper arrived and I went downstairs to get it. I read it from cover to cover. The temperature in Barbados, I noticed, was 82°F. In London it was 57°F, but a fine day was forecast. It was Sunday and I planned to write to my parents and then to drive to Richmond and walk in the park. The next day I was going to Paris and wanted consciously to relax, have some exercise, get some fresh air. I knew there were all sorts of things I could be usefully doing in preparation for the next day, but for once I could not bring myself to be efficient. Again and again, at increasingly regular intervals, I went into the bathroom and stared. I wondered how Rowena could sleep. If it had been my sample, if it had been me praying for evidence that I was pregnant, I could not have slept. I would have kept the test-tube, the all-wise test-tube, in my sights for the entire four hours and more. But then I was not Rowena.

Half an hour before the time was up I took a chair into the bathroom and sat and watched, as though watching a television. There was no change. I felt already disappointed, sad, at the failure of the experiment to yield the expected evidence and I could not understand my own reaction. What vicarious thrill had I expected to get? Frowning – I could feel the heavy frown between my eyes – I ran the bath, scattering pine scented essence liberally into it, and climbed in. I closed my eyes and lay there for a long time, pondering the attraction of breeding. It was the power I decided, the power which was the cause of the excitement, just to think what one could do, what one could start. It was an irresistible force not an instinct. The water began to lose its heat and I opened my eyes and got out, wrapping myself in a white towelling robe. It was as I was tying the belt that I saw the liquid in the test-tube had surely begun to change. I froze, could hardly breathe, as I stood perfectly still, watching. There was the faintest, faintest tinge of blue, a gossamer thin circular strand of blue, forming around the rim of the tube. I shut my eyes and opened them again. I snapped the window blind up, the better to see in natural daylight. The circle was thickening, the colour deepening. My heart began to pound and I found I was smiling, saying, whispering to myself, 'How wonderful, how wonderful.' The little test-tube was like a shrine and I worshipped in front of it.

I did not know whether to waken Rowena or not, whether

to bear in front of me the test-tube, like a blazing torch, but I let her sleep on, not out of any consideration, but because I wanted to keep the secret to myself a while longer. It struck me I should just let Rowena find out for herself and so I went back to my own bedroom and dressed and started sorting out clothes for the next day. When I heard Rowena stir I went to the door and listened. She shouted my name, and I joined her in the bathroom. She flung her arms round me and kissed me and I was astonished to find myself quite overcome with emotion.

The euphoria did not last, of course. I went to Paris and came back at the end of the week feeling extremely bad-tempered. I was most of all furious with myself for having been sucked into this whole pregnancy thing – absurd. What on earth had I been thinking of to act as though Rowena's being pregnant was a cause for celebration? It was a disaster. I was *against the whole thing*. I intended, when I got home, to regain my former position and make this clear, but in the face of Rowena's happiness I could not do it. Her happiness was tangible. I could *feel* it. The minute she came into the room this bliss of hers wrapped me in its folds and I succumbed every time. Who, after all, wants to destroy happiness? Who wants to wreck and smash and tear at such a beautiful sight? Not I.

On my own, when Rowena was not in the flat, I was disapproving and angry. I formulated a whole list of questions to put to her and to which I would demand answers. Ugly questions, such as: When would she tell Amos? How was she going to manage to work? Did she realise she owed me very nearly £500, and so on. I was going to ask all these awkward questions in a loud, hectoring voice. I was going to make myself unpleasant. I never did. I rejoiced with Rowena when I was with her and groaned on my own, or with Camilla.

Camilla understood perfectly. She, too, was unable to spoil her sister's delight, though she saw the road ahead and was appalled. 'I suppose,' she said to me, 'she'll have to come here after the baby is born. I can't think of any other solution, can you, Isobel?' I wondered later if that was my cue, if she actually might have expected me to say that I was willing to care for

Rowena. If so, she mistook my attitude. About that, I was *quite* certain, so certain that I was already thinking of where I could conveniently be in eight months' time, which part of the world would be far enough away for the vital post-natal months. So I told poor Camilla that I saw no alternative except for Christabel to go to Edinburgh. I wasn't really serious when I said this. How could Mrs Blake cope with Rowena and a baby? And why should she? Why should Camilla? It had begun already, that great string of consequences in which Rowena would impose obligation upon all who were connected with her. And hadn't she always known we would rally? Wasn't it part of her calculations? 'I will manage on my own,' her proud, oft-repeated statement of intent, was hollow. I suggest she knew it.

Of course, for what seemed a long time there was the question of whether Rowena would keep this baby or miscarry again. She went straight to the doctor the day after the pregnancy test and this sensible woman told her just to carry on normally, told her that if she were going to miscarry there was little she could do to prevent it, except perhaps to abstain from sexual intercourse during the first vital weeks and even that was no guarantee of safety. But Rowena looked after herself carefully and invented all kinds of do's and dont's, some of them quite stupid. She thought hot baths very dangerous, and running, and eating spicy food. So it was tepid showers, and a pace slower than a snail and no more of her favourite curries. She was afraid to lift children and was agonising over how to get round this in her job when she had a bit of what she thought of as great, good luck. She'd moved from her last baby-minding job (it couldn't really be said that she was a nanny), the one where she met Amos, to a job with the Council at one of their adventure playgrounds, and before the authorities had time to discover how useless she was at coping with hordes of demented under-fives, they had to cut their staff and Rowena was made redundant. Since this was before Thatcherite rules were brought in, she was now entitled to supplementary benefit. Neat, eh? Just when she didn't want to work, in case she harmed this precious baby, she was given the means to loll around and do nothing.

The morals, the ethics, of this upset me very much. She could easily have found more baby-minding jobs and, besides, she needed no money for rent or the true necessities of life, which is what supplementary benefit is meant for. I could not contain myself and let fly with grand and utterly wasted speeches on how people had fought for decades to win the right to state support for those who, through no fault of their own, were unable to work and there she was, abusing the system. 'It isn't my fault I can't work,' Rowena said, sullen but defiant. 'I was made redundant, it's the Council's fault.' When I rounded on her and challenged her to say she needed that money, need as 'need', not as luxury, she said her car and her flat and the money her mother gave her had nothing to do with it, she was still entitled, and it wasn't much anyway, she complained that it *wasn't much anyway*. She was hopeless, incapable of feeling either shame or guilt.

Nor did she feel guilty or ashamed of how she treated Amos. She was extremely anxious that he should not know about the baby and wrote to him – flourished the letter, knowing I'd be disgusted – saying she was emigrating to Australia. A letter came back marked 'Please, please forward – urgent and personal' in red block capitals right across the envelope. She wouldn't open it, tore it up and burnt it in front of me, smiling as the match flared and ignited the flimsy airmail paper in a second. I knew what would happen next: he wrote to me. He begged me to tell him Rowena's new address in Australia, he said he could not believe she had intended not to give it to him and he blamed himself for putting his mother before her. He said he realised now that he must have hurt her deeply and she was giving him this chance to free himself. . . . Oh, dear. I didn't tell Rowena he had written. I wrote back saying I did not have Rowena's new address (easy to salve my conscience since there was none) and advising him to forget her since she obviously wanted to be forgotten.

He wrote to Camilla too. Camilla didn't know what he was talking about and had to be enlightened. She did not reply, but, in her tidy way, filed his letter, with the address. So did I. We both knew why, I expect, though we did not discuss it. I remember thinking it was worthy of a Shakespearean play, all these letters flying about, letters the audience knows will become terribly significant, though they aren't sure when or how. But in this case the significance was never realised because when the time came no one even thought of trying to trace Amos. He was a complication we could all do without, an irrelevance, just as Rowena had wanted him to be.

CHAPTER THREE

There are ways in which I could cheat, if I were so inclined. I have thought often of how easy it would be, with a modicum of caution, to see Christabel without anyone being aware of it. They live near Totteridge Common, a very nice area indeed, and nothing would be simpler than to walk on the common at the times I know Christabel will be there. They made such a thing of the regularity of their lives, the healthiness of their routine, and of how fortunate they were to live somewhere 'nice', where a child could be brought up with 'plenty of fresh air'. As though we'd kept Christabel down a coal hole for five years. Good God, she had all the fresh air in the world. Rowena was never inside with her. From the moment she was born Christabel was out in her pram, taken to the park every day and spending holidays in Cockermouth regularly. She climbed Mellbreak, a fell overlooking Crummock Water, when she was three years old. In that respect, there was nothing anyone could give her that she hadn't already had.

Except, of course, what she'd lacked while she had been with Betty and Norman, and that was the fault of Maureen and the Social Services Department. Not much fresh air in the High Road where Betty and Norman lived. Step out of their house and it was almost instant asphyxiation with petrol fumes. They had no garden, only the smallest of yards, and there was no path or any green area within two miles. The day Camilla and

I went to that house we could hardly bring ourselves to get out of the car. 'Houses aren't important,' I remember muttering aloud, more to reassure myself than Camilla. 'It's the people that matter.'

But, oh, how the house mattered after all, right from the moment of crossing the threshold. There was a row of shoes just inside the narrow vestibule, men's shoes, women's shoes, children's shoes, all lined up neatly in pairs. And several pairs of slippers alongside, checkered felt slippers, and children's brightly-coloured animal slippers. My eyes went automatically to Betty's feet. She was wearing pale-blue fluffy slippers. We followed them along the hall, down the stretch of fitted, flecked tweed carpet, in shades of grey and pink, into the living-room, where the carpet gave way to carpet tiles in checks of grey and darker grey with two rugs, circular, of that kind of shaggy material which looks soft but feels coarse. There was a three-piece leather suite with pink cushions arranged in a military row along the back of the sofa. It was only December 1st, but an enormous artificial Christmas tree stood in front of the window. It was covered in tinsel and decked with very large bell-shaped lights in violent green, red and yellow. A china cabinet, of 1930s vintage, stood in one corner, and the biggest television I have ever seen in my life in another. There was a gas-fire burning, and some brass ornaments on the shelf above it, each ornament exactly the same distance from the next. Clearly, all was order here.

What did we talk about on that first meeting? I cannot remember. I was obsessed with the atmosphere. I knew this woman, Mrs Elizabeth Lowe, 'but call her Betty', Maureen had said, was fully aware of being under close scrutiny and yet she was far from nervous, there was not the slightest suggestion of that. On the contrary, we were the nervous ones, we were the ones desperate to make a good impression and be liked. Betty just sat down, on the very edge of one of the leather chairs, and waited for us to say something. Her expression was not exactly hostile, but it was certainly wary and even unfriendly. I was distracted by her teeth. It was difficult to tell whether they looked so uncomfortable because they were false – yet if they were false they would not, surely, be so discoloured – or because she had an ill-aligned jaw. At any rate, her mouth dominated her rather narrow face and gave her the look of a horse. Her face was very lined, though she was only forty, and the make-up she'd liberally applied had stuck in those lines around her eyes so that, every time she smiled, cracks appeared and accentuated the parchment appearance of her skin. Not an attractive woman, then. But she had a certain dignity and a pleasant, low voice, though it was her voice, or rather her speech, which upset Camilla most. Camilla herself has a posh Scots accent, now very faint after years of living in London, and she is proud of it, she likes people to 'talk nicely'. Betty did not talk nicely. She talked working-class London, both accent and grammar, and Camilla could hardly control her wincing. Naturally, all sympathy should be with Betty, surely. Houses do not matter, accents do not matter, though I am not prepared to agree that grammar does not matter either. How can I? How can I make my living as I do and agree that grammar does not matter?

We didn't, at that first meeting, see anyone except Betty. Norman came on the scene the next time, together with Judy, Marlene, Duaine, Craig and Arthur. I was completely thrown, not having understood that Christabel would not be the only foster-child. When I expressed my amazement to Maureen she raised an eyebrow and smiled her tight, thin little smile and told me no foster-mother on their books had only one child, that wasn't how the system worked. What system? I really didn't know what she was talking about. Fostering as a job had never really struck me, though since I was so conversant with the facts of baby-minding, I cannot think why I was surprised. Betty got £40 a week for each child. With three or four placements she could make a profit which she couldn't with one. So, as well as her own son and daughter, Craig and Judy, she had three foster-children already, all much older than Christabel. Marlene and Duaine were black, aged fourteen and fifteen respectively, and Arthur, who was white, was twelve. They had all been with Betty a long time, four years in Marlene's case.

'Betty is our best foster-mother,' Maureen had assured us

before we ever met her. 'She works wonders with the children we send her. They're devoted to her, she still hears from some she had years and years ago. They all think the world of her, so you've nothing to worry about.' Even looking only at Betty, hearing her, being in her house, I did not believe it, but faced with Norman, Judy, Marlene, Duaine, Craig and Arthur, I almost had hysterics. How could Christabel come into such a household, used to the life she had led? How could she cope, not only with her grief, but with the culture shock?

Not questions to ask Maureen. Already class had reared its ugly, but insistent, head. Mrs Blake had dared to ask if her granddaughter would be placed with a 'suitable' foster-family while her adoption was arranged. Maureen had asked her, quite sharply, if she would like to define 'suitable'. 'Well,' Mrs Blake had said, fussing with the bow of her cream silk blouse, 'such as the one she belongs to.' 'Belongs?' Maureen echoed. 'But, surely, Mrs Blake, that is the point, she doesn't actually belong anywhere at the moment, does she? So she has to be placed where we can fit her in and I'm afraid our foster-mothers are all working-class – I presume that's what you wanted, is it, a middle-class home for Christabel? Well, I'm afraid the middle-classes don't take in foster-children, or not in our borough, at any rate.'

'Oh, how unfortunate,' Mrs Blake gasped, a handkerchief to her lips. It was an involuntary exclamation, out before she could stop herself, but Maureen pounced and I could not help silently cheering her on.

'Unfortunate, Mrs Blake?' she queried. 'Because Mrs Lowe is working-class? Oh, I don't think so. She's very warm and loving and sensible and I think that is more important than her class.'

'Yes, of course,' Mrs Blake said, having the grace to blush, 'it's just . . . Christabel is used to certain ways of doing things, certain habits . . . being read to, that kind of thing . . .'

'Mrs Lowe can read,' Maureen said, staring straight at her, 'and you can provide all the books you wish.'

Why did there have to be that kind of ugly confrontation? Surely it could have been otherwise? That is a silly thing to ask:

of course, it could have been otherwise by being entirely avoided. There would have been no need for social workers and foster-mothers if we had done our bit, if Mrs Blake or Camilla or I had done the right and proper and natural thing. Ah, back to my old friend nature again. The world considers it natural that if a child is orphaned it should be taken to the bosom of its remaining family. Who would hesitate? Not you, I expect. And I did not expect Mrs Blake and Camilla would either. I too heard their reasons and thought them excuses. I heard them even before Rowena was dead. She was a long time dying and what else was there to discuss as we waited? Mrs Blake discussed it too bloody quickly for anyone's liking. From the moment I met her at Carlisle station to take her to the infirmary she spoke of nothing else.

'Rowena is going to die, isn't she?' she asked me. 'The doctors haven't given much hope,' I said, slightly shocked by her apparent calm and lack of emotion. 'Then what will happen to Christabel?' she said, followed, with hardly a pause for breath, by, 'I cannot take her, Isobel, I really cannot. I'm too old, I could not manage, I really could not. What kind of a life could I give her, living as I do?' And then I realised the emotion was there but heavily masked by this concentration on arrangements, by constant thinking ahead, so that she had forgotten why the thinking was necessary. 'I've moved from our old home, you know,' she went on. I said I did know, I knew all about the very superior sheltered housing she now lived in, but that did not stop her telling me about the set-up and how impossible it would be to take in Christabel. 'And I am seventy-five, Isobel,' she finished, as we turned through the infirmary gates, 'and my heart plays up frighteningly, sometimes.'

Camilla, when she arrived from London an hour or so later, was different. I could see she was weeping as she walked slowly down the platform towards me and I felt almost afraid of her grief. I didn't know Camilla very well, even if I'd known her all my life. She was always Rowena's sophisticated older sister, very cool and remote, the brilliant one, the child prodigy who'd gone on to the Royal College of Music and become a professional flautist. I had memories of the hours and hours of practice she'd put in, when all our back gardens were filled with the sound of that flute played so beautifully. People would stop cutting their grass to listen, and she'd be held up to us all as an example of what hard work could achieve. But she was always kind to me, never lorded it over her little sister's friend. We envied her terribly – her talent, her dedication, her looks. Then when she married Henry we envied her even more because he was so good-looking and dynamic – they were the perfect couple. Right up to Henry's sudden and horrible death, they were the perfect couple producing the perfect baby exactly a year after their marriage and this made the disaster even more shocking.

Henry, aged only twenty-nine, was on that plane which blew up over Paris, when the door wasn't closed and people were literally sucked out and scattered over the French countryside. It was hideous, appalling, and I must say, Rowena, although quite young, was marvellous. She looked after the baby, Ailsa, and stayed with Camilla and helped her cope. It sounds a wicked thing to say, but Rowena was in her element. No matter how much she wept for Camilla and the dead Henry she couldn't help relishing the drama of it all. I remember suspecting this and despising her for it.

And now, poor Camilla, who had already suffered enough from this kind of random tragedy, walked down the platform towards me, crying, her face quite destroyed with grief. When I reached her, she clung to me and we stood for fully five minutes clutching each other. Then we walked to the car with Camilla saying, 'I cannot bear it, I cannot face it, Isobel. I cannot.' There was nothing I could say, no hope I could hold out. Camilla had suffered enough, she had only just seemed to be happy again, her whole life given to music and with Ailsa now off on her own, a student at Smith College in America. She'd never re-married. Like her mother, she was very self-contained, though of a gentler breed and, again as with her mother, motherhood had not brought her much joy. I'm sure she loved Ailsa, but she'd obviously found bringing her up a source of great anxiety and was clearly relieved that the girl was now independent.

'How is Christabel?' she asked, as we drove through Carlisle. I told her Christabel seemed calm at the moment and was with my parents. 'Isobel,' Camilla said, beginning to cry again, 'if Rowena dies I cannot take Christabel. Rowena always said she thought I was a rotten mother and she was right. I am. I couldn't do it again. Do you remember how she disapproved of me?'

I did. She seemed relieved when I said so. She blew her nose and fell silent, only saying as we got out of the car, 'But there is no one else, it's my duty.' I didn't reply. I took her to the ICU and we stood side by side looking at Rowena. She was naked except for a thin blanket covering her from the armpits to the knees. There were tubes coming out of her nose and throat. Her eyes appeared half open which was unnerving. I kept expecting them to open wider, for her to sit up and speak. All the right-hand side of her face and shoulder were covered in purple bruises, or what looked like bruises. There was a cut across her forehead, another in the middle of her chest, stitched so neatly that every stitch could be counted. There were other long, stitched gashes right down her arm, like red barbed-wire, nicked with black. Her beautiful hair had been half-shaved. There was a gauze patch on the shaved upper right side of her head above her ear.

There were two other patients in the unit, all similarily connected to machines. It was very eerie and yet soothing because of the silence. Not quite a total silence, because there were soft bleeping noises all around us, but a stillness, a calmness. The nurses, when they came in to take readings, did so very quietly. They'd suddenly appear without their entry having been noticed and then disappear just as mysteriously. Rowena herself made no sound.

'Can she hear?' Camilla whispered. 'Nobody knows,' I whispered back. 'Touch her, if you like.' Camilla looked appalled, but then, very hesitantly, put her hand over the edge of the cot Rowena lay in, and touched her sister's hand. 'It's warm,' she said, surprised. She squeezed it and stroked it and murmured something I could not quite catch. Afterwards, as we left the ICU to go into the small waiting-room, which adjoined it, she staggered and almost fainted. I helped her into a chair and a nurse brought some water. She was deathly white and kept saying she was sorry, sorry . . .

Mrs Blake would not go to see Rowena. 'No,' she said, 'I cannot bear it. There is no point. She is in a coma and there is no point. I would rather remember her as I last saw her, happy and lively. I really cannot bear to see her in that state, I am too old, I do not care what people think.' Nobody exerted the slightest pressure on her, but she acted as if they were about to. She sat, hour after hour, in the waiting-room, straight-backed, hands folded in the lap of her smart lavender tweed suit, eyes closed, as though meditating. Camilla clearly annoyed her. The more Camilla wept, the tighter her mother's lips closed. 'For pity's sake,' she murmured once or twice, 'for pity's sake, Camilla,' but so quietly, her daughter could not hear.

When the doctor in charge, a brain specialist, I think he was, came in late on the second day, Mrs Blake was perfectly alert and sensible, though she had had no sleep. Like most doctors, he was a very tired man, quite exhausted, it seemed to me. He tried very hard to be kind and sympathetic, to avoid euphem-isms, but not to be vague or brutal. He gave us a technical description of the state Rowena was in, but I, at least, absorbed none of it. All I took in was that the injuries to her head and chest were so massive that it was doubtful if she could recover. She was, he said, on a ventilator which was doing her breathing for her. By tomorrow, if she had not shown some flicker of life, they would have to consider taking her off the ventilator. 'Do you understand what that means?' he asked. 'Yes,' said Mrs Blake, 'she will die.' The doctor nodded. 'She will in fact have been dead in any case,' he said, 'and only kept artificially alive up to then.' He explained that a series of tests to establish life would be done, twice. They were laid down by law and must be observed scrupulously. Should there be any response, however trivial, the ventilator would not be switched off. 'Let us hope there is none,' Mrs Blake said. 'We don't want her alive, yet a vegetable. It is far better she dies.'

It was very frightening seeing this control. Probably the doctor had seen it before, seen all the reactions from gibbering terror to this kind of supreme composure, but I had not. My own distress seemed in abeyance, but then I had assured myself it was because I was in charge, because each night I had to drive back to Cockermouth and see Christabel. I could not afford to collapse. The fact that I could choose not to do so, struck me as strange, just as strange as watching Mrs Blake's reaction. What were we? Automatons? Only Camilla seemed natural. Her white face, her dizziness, her tears – they were all what one would have expected. What Rowena would have expected, would herself have given. Rowena was more than a bit of a ghoul, she liked high drama, she would have been in her element, even while screaming and bawling. Hearing her describe quite ordinary medical emergencies, I had always been struck by her zest for the details.

Take the time Christabel was suspected, wrongly, thank God, of having meningitis. You would have thought that, the emergency over, Rowena would not have wanted to dwell on it, but instead, she seemed to me to turn the whole awful incident into an entertainment. If I heard once, I heard a thousand times what each doctor had said and the way they shook their heads and how it had been touch and go – rather sickening to see her relish the drama so. But then, even before the meningitis scare, Rowena had become a hypochondriac. Each tiny ailment, not only of Christabel's, but of her own, was treated with ridiculous seriousness. For a simple cold, a running nose and cough such as half the population have from November to March, Rowena would take Christabel to the doctor. Even worse, she would often take her to hospital where, of course, she got short shrift in a busy casualty ward. If I was around, I would remonstrate, but what did I know about mothering? Maybe it is common among mothers of young children to cry fire if their children seem feverish, maybe they all rush to see their doctors. I never rush to see mine. I detest doctors and I loathe hospitals.

It was this hatred of mine, labelled by Rowena as a phobia, which made me reluctant to agree to be present at Christabel's birth. It came as a surprise to me, in any case, that Rowena was expecting me to be there. Naturally, I'd thought Camilla, if anyone, would share the experience, but Rowena laughed at the very idea and said Camilla would be the last person she would want. Her sister, she alleged, fainted at the sight of blood and had hysterics at the evidence of someone being in pain. When her own child had a wisdom-tooth out, Rowena claimed that Camilla had fainted at the mere sight of her in a hospital bed with a thin trickle of blood leaking from the corner of her mouth. She didn't want Camilla anywhere near her. I, foolishly, suggested her mother might want to come down from Edinburgh and was treated with more derision which, in that case, I deserved. Mrs Blake was too old and frail to be much use and, as Rowena said, to be present at the birth, she would need to be on hand considerably before the expected date which would mean an extended stay of some weeks. 'Besides,' Rowena said, 'you were meant to be there, Isobel.' I asked why, suspiciously, and was told that since the baby was expected on my birthday this conferred an automatic obligation. 'And there is no one else I can turn to,' Rowena finished, plaintive and, she hoped, appealing. I said she should have thought of that before, that this had been what had worried and angered me from the beginning. All these friends, whom Rowena claimed to have, simply melted away when she was in need and she was left, as she always had been, with her family. And me. I was part of the fabric of her safety-net.

My attempts to cut free had been sincerely meant, but they'd failed. The moment Rowena had passed the three-month stage and was thereafter reckoned to be going to carry her baby to term, I had begun looking at other flats. Almost immediately our own became more desirable than I had ever thought. In the five years since we'd bought it, the property market seemed to have changed radically – it was absurd of me to think I could move easily into a nicer area and still have the same space. It was obvious that even for double the investment I would get substantially less.

Then I went to Paris for three months, and when I came back I was contemplating a year's contract which would make moving flats unnecessary for the moment. Were all these complications merely excuses? Possibly, but for what, I am not sure. Certainly I wanted to be free of Rowena. I had no intention of allowing her to manipulate me. But as the time of her confinement drew near I was still living with her, with no prospect of escape. And at the same time she had become a far nicer person to live with again. Since she was at home all day, contentedly drawing her supplementary benefit, she had plenty of time to learn to be domesticated and, though it was always like a child play-acting, the results were impressive. Acutely image-conscious, she tutored herself in the art of sitting in the window, as though for the portrait *Mother Awaiting the Birth of her Child*, stitching away at tiny clothes with Brahms's *Lullaby* playing in the background, and the delicious smell of a cake baking in the oven. Neither of us ever thought we cared for cakes, but during the later months of her pregnancy, Rowena took to baking carrot-cakes. It was amusing to have this kind of home-coming and to find the flat so beautifully kept. I suppose I succumbed to the charm of it.

But never so completely that I did not have my wits about me. Rowena tried many times to get me to agree to take her baby, if she should die in childbirth, and I always, always, was steadfast and adamant in my refusal. 'Absolutely not,' I said, even when her eyes filled with tears. When she asked what would happen to him if I refused to look after him, I went through the, by now usual, routine of reminding her we'd discussed all that: her family would have to take him, who else, and her family meant Camilla. That is how I was able to back up Camilla when she asked me to agree that her sister had not wanted her to have charge of her baby. Rowena was quite violent in her protestations. 'No! No!' she said, banging her fist on the table. 'I hate the way Camilla brought up Ailsa, she was an *awful* mother. I wouldn't let her have a dog, never mind a child. Camilla was never there when Ailsa was little, never, she was always off on tour, and she didn't provide anything a mother should. Then she packed her off to boarding-school as soon as she could, and she even found the holidays a strain. *I* took Ailsa on holiday or no one would've done. No, not Camilla, never. She shouldn't have had a child and she knows it, it was a dreadful mistake. She cares more about her flute.' 'Well then,' I remember saying, 'you have a problem. You'd better think about it, and quick.'

Maybe she did, but if so she did nothing. The morning came when she woke up at dawn and announced that her waters had broken and would I ring for an ambulance if I wasn't going to take her to hospital. I took her, of course, and indeed was glad to. It was a beautiful morning, my birthday, Midsummer's Day, and there was that same irresistible feeling of excitement as there had been on the morning of the pregnancy test, only this time with rather more cause. Rowena was quiet and calm, a smile hovering round her lips and her contractions causing her no trouble at all. Her cheeks were slightly flushed and she looked prettier than I had ever seen her. Walking beside her down the hospital corridor, linking arms with her, I knew I could not possibly desert her, nor did I want to.

I felt, in the end, privileged to witness this birth and would willingly do the same again. It was all so strange and humbling, it stripped from me every vestige of sophistication I imagined I possessed, and made me see childbirth for the first time as the extraordinary process it is. I had no idea, for all the amount I have read, of how the woman's body is taken over, no idea of the strength of the force which commands it. Rowena seemed to me to be a mere instrument and, though this was frightening, it was also curiously reassuring, as though it was *meant* to be beyond her control. She was so good for the first eight hours, doing her breathing exercises dutifully and coping with the pain admirably, and as I sat by her side, chatting to her and amusing her as best I could, by reading out silly items from magazines, I had never felt closer to her, nor more fond. Why shouldn't this woman have a child if she wanted one, if she was prepared to go through all this? Wasn't her desire and determination preferable to the dutiful productions of the married woman, who merely followed convention? Who was to say Rowena's child was not more fortunate, in being so wished for, than any married woman's? And did fathers matter, when they had none of this to endure?

Where were my high-minded beliefs now? Nowhere in sight during the birth itself, that was for sure.

Oh, how everything changed during the afternoon! From being patient and compliant and somehow almost saintly, Rowena became wild and furious, and I was half-afraid of her. She thrashed about and shouted and cried, and when I became agitated myself and asked what on earth had gone wrong, I was very nearly sent out of the delivery room. The baby, it seemed, was lying across the birth canal, or something like that, and there was talk over my head of sending for someone-or-other who, it seemed, would not hesitate to do a Caesarean.

But, then whatever the problem was, it solved itself and Rowena, though still tossing and turning and groaning, began to get into a kind of rhythm. She followed instructions to push and after a while seemed to get the hang of it and opened her eyes and, like a weight-lifter approaching the weights, took great breaths and then pushed and there were cries of encouragement. I was at her side and so saw very little more than she did, but when the doctor said, 'Next push and we'll have the head – come on, now!' I half stood and saw the head emerge, saw the quick slithering body that followed, saw the twisted purple cord and then all was concealed while many hands seemed to be frantically busy, and the next thing was the sight of the baby held by its heels and rushed to a table at the end of the bed. 'It's a fine girl,' the nurse said to Rowena and, 'Aren't you clever?'

Then, Rowena cried. Hard. Seriously. She sobbed and sobbed and said she wanted a boy, not a girl. The nurse smiled, wasn't at all surprised or shocked, told her she'd feel differently in a minute and then when she brought the baby over and placed her in Rowena's arms and saw her face she said, 'There, what did I tell you? Where's your wanting a boy now?' But Rowena was disappointed and taken aback. Even the next day she kept saying she had been counting on a boy, that she couldn't take in the fact that her baby was female. I said I'd never understood this passion for a boy, anyway. She was a woman on her own, surely a girl suited her better, would make her single status easier? It seemed I'd missed the point, or rather several points. A boy was not just a matter of pride but also of more joy. Rowena did not like being female, it now transpired. She had always envied men, thought this a man's world and so wanted to bear the sex that fitted. And, then again, she could not help thinking of a girl as herself when what she wanted was to escape herself.

Nobody mentioned the baby's colour, but then, in a London teaching hospital, colour was wonderfully unnoticeable. Mrs Blake was the only one to mention it. 'If her father had known he'd have a black grandchild . . .' she murmured, and then tailed off. Even she knew she had no ground to stand on and just enough sense to hide her racist views. Or maybe not even hide them, maybe to overcome them, because there was no doubt she was charmed with Rowena's beautiful baby. 'Ailsa was such an ugly scrap,' she said, tactlessly. 'I really found it hard to take to her at all for months. But this is a lovely wee thing, and what a grand size, look at the fat on those legs.' What the baby would be called bothered her. Her own name was Mildred, which she detested, so there was no question of her expecting this grandchild to be called after her, but she thought a good Scottish name desirable or at least a 'decent' English one. I think she was afraid her daughter would come up with some totally outlandish suggestion, but, if so, she must have been relieved when Rowena said, 'How about Isobel?' This, I think, I *think*, was meant to be a compliment. Mrs Blake brightened immediately. 'Oh yes,' she said, 'what an excellent idea, after all Isobel's done for you, and she'll be the godmother, too.'

'No,' I remember saying far too sharply, 'you mustn't name her after me. She must have her own name, something special, something different.' I daresay I was ungracious but I was in a panic to avoid this 'compliment'. It was all too easy to see where it would lead, the assumptions it would give rise to. And I couldn't, wouldn't, be anyone's godmother. I don't believe in all that, it would be wrong. Rowena shrugged, she didn't care about that either, but then she said she couldn't think of any name special enough and since I was the one who had said it should be special, maybe I'd like to suggest one.

I thought about it all day and night. I thought about what this baby's life was likely to be like and about her heritage, and I decided that above all else she would need to be a fighter and that was what led me to think of the Pankhursts. Emmeline was too dated, Sylvia I did not like and so I settled on Christabel, and Rowena took to it at once. She wasn't the least interested in its derivation, waved away all references to the Pankhursts and simply said she liked the sound. Christabel it would be, and it would go very nicely with Blake. Then when she came to register the birth, she stuck her grandmother's name in the middle: Una. It wasn't until I pointed it out to her that she realised she now had a little C.U.B. – and that amused her highly. She called Christabel her cub from that day on, hardly ever using her Christian name and, in pre-school days, if the child was asked what she was called she would very often say: 'Cub Blake.' Rowena thought this funny. I thought it twee, as I did so many aspects of Christabel's upbringing. Rowena really was such a *slushy* mother, which was not too revolting when Christabel was a baby but became nauseating once she was over three. She was talked to in such a silly way. 'Mummy's going to do wee-wee,' Rowena would say. 'Does little cub want to come?' Oh, God. And Christabel very often rejected this kind of unctuous patter, turning away and wrinkling her nose and shaking her head.

She was a very sturdy and independent child, fighting to get out of her doting mother's arms from a very young age. She didn't like being kissed much, nor would she indulge in the long hugging sessions Rowena craved. She gave affection as a reward, rather as I do, and not as a right. And it was obvious she had only minimal need of demonstrative behaviour herself. Rowena was proud of this and yet alarmed by it – it was not what she had expected and looked for. She had breast-fed Christabel until the baby herself refused to suck (though since this was at a year old it was hardly remarkable). Rowena wept because she could no longer be sure of this dependable daily closeness for which there was no substitute.

I daresay I would have found all this impossibly trying, but by then I'd made the break. The moment Christabel was safely born, I acted. Mrs Blake bought me out – and I considered myself extremely generous not to demand it should be the other way round, leaving me in possession. I bought another flat about a mile away, not after all north of the river which I could not afford, but in the right direction, and was reasonably content with what I got, a large ground-floor room, very large, with a minute kitchen, bathroom, one small bedroom and another so tiny it was not worthy of the name 'room', but never mind. It was all my own and I managed very well.

Almost at once I discovered that I was much happier living entirely on my own and did not need the companionship I'd needed in my younger days. My mother worried, of course. She'd liked me living with Rowena, it made me 'sound less lonely' as she put it. It was no good protesting I was *not* lonely: she didn't believe it. 'Do I look lonely, do I seem lonely?' I would ask her when I was home. 'Do you look at me and think poor, pathetic Isobel?' She would smile at that and admit that I did indeed seem happy, lively, absorbed in my work. My father admired my independence, I think. Certainly he never chides me as my mother does. 'Still fancy free?' he says and appears amused. And my brothers, in their own way, back me up and calm my mother down.

Meanwhile, Rowena had a lodger, a paying guest. Her mother had insisted. Her purse, she said, was not bottomless and she could no longer go on helping Rowena to the extent she had done. She'd bought her the flat, which she now owned freehold, but she could not pick up the bill for rates and heating and so forth and since Rowena's supplementary benefit would hardly cover her expenses she must let out a room and pay her way. It worked out very well, so far as I could tell. The lodger was a girl who went home to Essex on Fridays and returned on Mondays. She was a student and quite happy to baby-sit from time to time. I never actually met her but deduced from the appalling state the flat was in that she was either very tolerant or extremely untidy herself. All Rowena's housewifely efforts had ceased the moment Christabel was born. Now, she was entirely devoted to the baby and didn't give tuppence for the flat. I could hardly pick my way through the debris when I went there – half-eaten apples, brown and mouldy; bits of bread, buttered side down, on the table; mugs of abandoned coffee everywhere; heaps and heaps of clothes strewn on the floor; piles of old newspapers mixed up with letters and taking up most of the sitting space. It made me feel quite ill, especially since living on my own had made me tidy. Yet, in the middle of it all, Christabel thrived and Rowena flourished.

Gradually, we fixed on a regular day, as regular as my work would allow, when Rowena would bring Christabel over for tea, and sometimes stay the night. It meant a weekly hurricane hitting my flat, but I told myself sternly that it was good for it. No sooner would she be in the front door than Rowena would have created a mess, dragging in her wake as she came the most extraordinary amount of equipment just for one baby. It was not just the nappies and baby cream and changing mat and carry-cot but the array of specially minced foods and the feeding cup and the bibs and special spoon and picture books and rattles and spare baby-gro, all spreading like a plague throughout my flat.

Rowena's entire concentration was on her child and the intensity of it scared me. How could any baby survive being made the centre of someone's world to this extent? Yet Christabel took the strain well. She was autocratic, imperious, even before she could walk and talk, and once she did both she had her mother quite helpless. At not quite two she would demand a drink in a glass, a proper glass, 'not mine cup', and Rowena would pour orange juice into a tumbler and then Christabel would totter round the room trying to drink as she went and of course spilling the sticky liquid on my pale green carpet. 'She's spilling it everywhere,' I would complain. 'Take it off her, Rowena, for God's sake, or else make her sit down.' Then we would have this ridiculous pantomime in which Rowena would say quite stupid things like: 'Come on lovey, sit down and drink it properly, it's gravity, you see, Christabel, darling. If you tip the tumbler like that the drink turns over and spills.' 'Oh just *take it off her*,' I would snap. But she wouldn't. She would beg, plead, bribe, make an absolute fool of herself, but Christabel never relinquished the glass until its contents had been sprayed over my living-room. I could see quite clearly how, by the time she was of school age, Christabel would dominate her mother completely.

So could Camilla and Mrs Blake. Mrs Blake only saw Christabel three times a year, but these visits were enough to make her declare that her granddaughter was 'a madam'. She said this quite admiringly, but nevertheless offended Rowena who, I gather, made it plain that if she were to be criticised she would not make the long trek to Edinburgh. Her mother quickly learnt to shut up, though it was as hard for her as it was for me. She was actually astonished at how Rowena had taken to motherhood, 'against all expectations', as she put it. When we were sitting in the ICU she returned again and again to this theme, and I found it quite difficult to take. 'Such a perfect mother,' she kept repeating, 'such a lovely wee mother, all those qualities in her we never thought she had, she couldn't have made a better mother, and it made her so happy at last, so fulfilled. Thank God she had that child, whatever happens. From the day she had her she'd found her vocation.' And then she'd pause and ask me to agree and I'd have to find a way of seeming to do so. But it wasn't true. Rowena was neither such a perfect mother, if there is such a thing, nor was she so blissfully content. Mrs Blake and Camilla knew nothing of the despairing phonecalls I'd had during the last year, nor of the frantic attempts to have another baby because she felt 'empty again'. There was another side entirely to this 'fulfilment'.

It was alarming when it began. The first time she phoned it was late at night, nearly midnight and I was in bed, just dropping off to sleep. I almost didn't answer. But the ringing went on and on. I began to imagine it was my mother, that some family tragedy had occurred – my younger brother was on an Arctic expedition at the time, we hadn't heard from him for months – so I answered. I thought at first it was an obscene call, so heavy was the breathing before Rowena spoke. 'What on earth is wrong?' I asked. 'Rowena? What is it? What's happened? Quick, tell me.'

There was nothing much to tell. Rowena said she was depressed, and she wept. Just like the old days. I asked what in particular, if anything, was depressing her. 'Everything,' she said, and then, 'Nothing'. She said she couldn't cope with the flat, it was a pig-sty, and the student had left, it was the end of her course anyway, and she couldn't get another lodger because the flat was too awful to let anyone see. She said she couldn't let Christabel bring her friends home because of the state the place was in. 'Then tidy it up,' I said, exasperated. 'You know you can do it when you have to.' More weeping, more despair. At last, to get her off the phone, to get to sleep myself, I said I'd come round the next day.

She met me at the door, red-eyed, wrapped in a dirty old bathrobe of mine which I'd left behind and vaguely remembered had once been white. Tears started dripping as soon as she saw me. I pushed past into my old home and felt immediately angry at the extent of the neglect it had suffered. This was serious chaos. I counted five plates on the table, all with congealed food on them. The sink in the kitchen was invisible under the weight of dirty dishes and the cooker encrusted with filth. In the middle of it all Christabel was lying on the floor watching television, apparently oblivious of her surroundings. Even though it was a lovely sunny morning the curtains were drawn. The first thing I did was to wrench them apart and open a window. Then without speaking, I set about doing the dishes. That took an hour. Rowena slumped in a chair, fists in her eyes, and Christabel carried on watching television (it was Saturday and at least they were children's programmes). I worked away all morning and by lunchtime had made tremendous progress.

'Get dressed,' I said to Rowena at one o'clock, 'we're going out.' Protesting, she was persuaded into the only pair of reasonably clean jeans I could find and a jumper Christabel produced. We went out. I drove to the park and we walked as far as the swings and when Christabel was playing in the sandpit I sat Rowena down nearby and subjected her to a cross-examination.

It seemed she didn't know what had come over her. She didn't know when she had begun to feel as she was feeling. Maybe three or four months, she couldn't be sure. She thought maybe not getting pregnant had triggered it off. She hadn't told me about trying to get pregnant again, because she knew I'd be furious. I was so stunned I couldn't even agree that I would have been, that I was. Good God, she had one child, wasn't that enough to satisfy her 'natural' maternal instincts? It was all she could do to cope with Christabel. She'd picked up some baby-minding again now that Christabel was at nursery school, but she was still on supplementary benefit and hadn't worked properly for four years. With no lodger now I knew she must be in dire financial straits. And here she was, *depressed* because she couldn't conceive. Was she mad? I finally said to her: 'Are you mad?' She closed her eyes. 'Look, Rowena,' I said, 'this has got to stop. You've got Christabel to think about, you can't be so self-indulgent.' 'It's for Christabel's sake,' she wept, 'I don't want her to be an only child, I don't want her just to have me.'

Mrs Blake knew nothing about this. She never met Leo, selected to be the father of Rowena's second child. She would probably have been pleased, since he was white and presentable, even if an American only over for a year, and divorced. She would undoubtedly have begun to hope Rowena might yet settle down with 'a nice man' and give Christabel a proper home and father. But in that respect Rowena hadn't changed, she had no wish to share Christabel with anyone. In fact, she didn't really like Leo's attachment to her child, nor the success he was with Christabel. You would have thought that lacking any male figure in her life, she would have been charmed and grateful to have such a nice man as Leo playing father or uncle to Christabel, but no. Leo had one function and that was all. I did point out to her, once I'd met this Leo, that she could not hope to treat him as she'd treated poor Amos.

'He's here, Rowena,' I said. 'He isn't going to go away, and he's going to know his rights, he's going to be around and want his child.' But she was triumphant. She'd made him sign a paper waiving all rights to any child he might sire. 'My only worry,' Rowena said, 'is his nose. Suppose the baby gets his nose? It would be awful to have a baby who looked so ugly. But his hair is nice, isn't it, and his eyes? Maybe it will have his hair and eyes, and my nose.'

Fortunately, there never was a baby. This time Mr Top Man was unable to do the trick. Rowena had her tubes blown again, but it did no good. Her depression continued, though she never got in quite such a state again. Instead, she dealt with it by trying never to be at home except to sleep. Here, there and everywhere she went, endlessly whirling Christabel from activity to activity, from friend to friend, all to stave off having to face her flat. It was my belief, though I knew I sounded like her mother when I voiced it, that it was this hectic social life which sparked off Christabel's tantrums and nightmares. The child never had any calm, never had a routine. It was out of the school and into the car, and zoom-zoom, off we go to swim, to the zoo, to see Isobel, to see Camilla, to shop, to run around somewhere, anywhere, until eight in the evening and straight to bed.

I can't remember which started first, the tantrums or the nightmares. The tantrums, I think, or maybe I think that because I was aware of them first. I witnessed them and mar-velled at how like the infant Rowena Christabel suddenly became – exactly the same frenzied heel-drumming, the piercing screams and clenched fists . . . All that was different, radically different, was the parental reaction. The Blakes had removed Rowena from wherever she was, carried her bodily to her room and locked the door on her. I well remember listening to Mrs Blake go to the locked door and ask if Rowena was ready to be a good girl now. Eventually, Rowena always was. It never actually took very long since Rowena's desire to get out was far stronger than any hurt pride. And now consider the differ-ence: when Christabel had a tantrum, Rowena lay down beside her and tried to cuddle her and got hit by her flaying fists and then she'd cry too. The sound of competition made the child redouble her efforts and oh, my God, what a sustained and ridiculous performance from them both.

It was exhausting for the onlooker and also faintly disgusting. Surely no adult should let themselves be reduced to this infantile behaviour, or is that my inexperience speaking? Why didn't Rowena simply ignore Christabel? Hardly more bearable than the tantrum itself was the long scene afterwards in which Rowena would try to unravel what had caused it. Endless ques-tions, endless analyses, and all for a small child's benefit. Inevi-tably it would all end with Rowena apologising to Christabel, apologising for not letting her have a whole packet of biscuits, or for taking a sharp knife from her or making her wear gloves because it was freezing – Rowena apologising for perfectly sensible behaviour. Then Christabel would condescend to kiss her and be hugged and cuddled, all the time fully aware she had won. How Rowena could work up the energy to carry on like this sometimes two or three times a day I do not know.

And then there were the broken nights. She told me how Christabel woke screaming at two or three in the morning, and how she could never discover what the nightmare had been about. The only way to calm the child was to take her into her bed and hold her tight. Of course, Rowena liked this, it gave her what she wanted and what Christabel would so rarely give when awake, so I suspect she did not try very hard to get her daughter back into her own bed. I don't suppose it mattered very much since no one else was sleeping in Rowena's bed (Leo was never, ever allowed there at night – all his 'work' was during the day when Christabel was at school). What mattered was the cause of the nightmares, and here I chose the obvious answer: I blamed television. Christabel was besotted by the box. She demanded that the telly be switched on as soon as she came home and, though Rowena battled valiantly to persuade her to do other things, she could not face the scenes if it was turned off. So Christabel, like half the child population, I know, watched the most unsuitable programmes and I could only presume that the stimulation was too much for her immature brain.

I suggested more exercise, if there were no chance of less television in the evenings. Maybe Christabel could be made so tired that she would not be able to keep her eyes open. But Rowena was most indignant, she said Christabel got plenty of exercise and they were out all the time (which was true). However worn out she was, she still clamoured for the television to be on as soon as they were inside and mostly fell asleep in front of it.

Oh, how tedious all this bringing up of children is, all this agonising over every damned trivial point. Except that not all mothers are like Rowena. Betty does not agonise. Everything is quite clear cut in her house: Christabel got her television fix – it was rarely off in Betty's house – but if it was bedtime, it was bedtime, and that was that. And she didn't have a single nightmare after she arrived at Betty's. 'Never has none,' Betty boasted. 'Sleeps sweet as you like, no bother.' Yet think what had happened to her by the time she got to Betty's, enough to give her nightmares to eternity. How amazed and puzzled Rowena would have been. But then she would have been amazed and puzzled at the whole train of events which her death started.

CHAPTER FOUR

This part is the hardest. Going over and over the sequence of events, as I do, over and over again, I stick on this part. The hours of Rowena's dying and her death itself are hard enough to remember and feel, feel as I did not feel them then, but what followed is much worse to bear in retrospect. I, at least, understand why. It is obvious: during those horrific three days immediately after the accident I did everything right. Examine my behaviour and you will conclude no general could have done better. But then consider my actions after Rowena died on Hallowe'en, and my blunders were disastrous. Yet I had reasons for everything. I had thought through very clearly what would be the best course of action. Nothing was done carelessly, everything was for Christabel's sake, the supreme irony. And no one contested my decisions.

There ought to have been a funeral, but at the time I admired Mrs Blake's rejection of such a ceremony. There had been no funeral for her husband either, though she had organised a memorial service some months later. Camilla, I think, would have liked some sort of simple ceremony, as she would have liked one for her father, and as she had had for poor Henry, but she said nothing when her mother emphatically turned down the suggestion that Rowena should be cremated at Carlisle Crematorium and we should not attend. 'Tell them to dispose of the body,' Mrs Blake said, 'it is only a body. I want nothing to do with it.' She made it sound as if the hospital authorities could incinerate it.

In fact, it was not so simple. The body could indeed be cremated without any ceremony but there had to be a witness apart from the undertaker. I was the natural choice, the only choice, since Mrs Blake had already been taken back to Edinburgh by Camilla. I don't even remember being asked if I would oblige – it was just assumed. And I was on hand for another few days while the post-mortem was held (there had to be a post-mortem since there was to be an inquest). I went alone to the crematorium, situated to the west of the city on a hill above the cemetery with the Cumbrian fells looming in the background, the very fells upon which Rowena had died.

It was the oddest thing, Rowena's love of climbing, hard to reconcile with the rest of her personality. And it was my fault, I had introduced her to fell-walking when she came to spend those teenage holidays with me. I think I was hoping to humiliate her, though it is not very pleasant to think that I wished to do so. I think, at thirteen, I saw myself racing up mountains and Rowena panting pathetically behind. But not a bit of it. I had forgotten her stamina. Rowena took to fell-climbing at once and together we climbed every one of the Loweswater and Crummock fells. My parents gave her Wainwright's *Western Fells* and *North Western Fells* for a birthday present and she loved ticking off each one at the front of the little books as she climbed them.

There was no ceremony. The undertaker brought the body and I watched it slowly disappear. I was asked if I wanted to say a few words and I shook my head. Silence was best. I did try to think of a poem I could recite in my head and made frantic efforts to remember Tennyson's *Crossing the Bar*, but I failed to get beyond the first line. Afterwards, I thought I ought to have taken Christabel, but the idea of exposing her to such bleakness repelled me. I'd done enough of that kind of thing, following the telephoned advice of my elder brother, who is an educational psychologist. He had urged me to take Christabel to see Rowena both before and after she died. I'd been appalled at the cruelty of this suggestion but he was adamant: small

66

children needed to see the body, needed visual evidence of what had happened, otherwise they might never believe in the death.

So I had taken Christabel into the ICU. I prepared her carefully. She asked only if her mother would be wearing pyjamas. I said no, she didn't need them, it was too warm in there. I held her hand tightly and watched her carefully as we approached the bed. She stared hard, did not even blink. Her pretty little face appeared blank of all expression. For my part, it was the nearest I had ever come to tears. The sight of Christabel standing looking at her dying mother, the small still figure in its white blouse and skirt looking so perfect and untouched, was almost too much for me in a way Rowena's damaged body had never been. I told her she could touch her mother if she wished, and did so myself, but she shook her head. A little sigh escaped her as we left the ICU, but her eyes were clear and her step firm.

Then, after Rowena was declared dead, I took her again. This time I'd seen to it that she was in those pyjamas Christabel had mentioned. They were typical Rowena, exotic pyjamas of purple and pink striped, silky material. Christabel had some the same. Lying in an ordinary bed in a side ward in these gaudy pyjamas with her eyes now closed and her head covered with a sort of muslin cap so that the injured scalp was invisible and only tendrils of blonde hair escaping on one side, Rowena looked far less terrifying. I felt relieved, thought what a good job the nurses had done. She just looked asleep, her face slightly swollen and an odd colour, it is true, but with her eyes at last sealed, that creepy feeling that she was listening had gone. But funnily enough it was then that Christabel started to tremble. Her whole frame quivered, though no tears came. I pulled her to me, went down on my knees and embraced her and her body went on shaking and shaking until my own started to do the same. I felt furious with my brother for advising this – it was monstrous, no five-year-old child should have been exposed to such an ordeal. And then Christabel said: 'Can I kiss her goodbye?' What could I say? That it was too late? That the feel of her mother's dead flesh would sicken her? I lifted her up, feeling that if she were going to do this then it was better she should be attached to someone living when the reality of it struck her.

What startled me was where she chose to kiss her mother – not on the lips (thank God), not on the cheek, not on the forehead, but on the throat. She ducked her black curly hair under the dead Rowena's chin and kissed her on her throat, near to the scar left by the tube that had been inserted in her windpipe. 'It was a butterfly kiss,' she explained. 'It tickles best there.'

Afterwards, she had a few questions, none very penetrating or upsetting, none of those I had feared. I explained what being cremated meant and was met with silence. I told her about the inquest, though I cannot think why. 'What will happen to Mummy's clothes?' Christabel asked. She was always so concerned about clothes. I said we could keep them if she liked or else give them away. She said she would like the red cardigan, the one with the knobbly buttons. It was far too long in the sleeves, but once Mummy had let her wear it and she'd rolled the sleeves up and up, and it was like a coat. I said that seemed a good idea. She smiled, swung her fat little legs contentedly. And then she said – we were driving back to my parents' at the time – 'Will I live with you, Isobel?' My hands on the steering wheel seemed to slip, and I made a great show of grasping it more firmly. 'Goodness, that's a monster,' I said, as a gigantic lorry did indeed pass us. *Coward*, I was hissing at myself, *coward, coward*. I drove a little longer and then, because the question had not been repeated, I said, 'What was that, Christabel?' She didn't reply. It was a busy stretch of the difficult road and I couldn't take my eyes off it, even for a second, to look at her. My face burned with shame – to have dodged such an enquiry so! I cleared my throat and said, 'We'll go back home on Friday, then you'll be ready for school on Monday, won't you? What's your teacher called again?' 'Miss Splint.' I laughed, said what a funny name, how could I have forgotten it. And that was how I dealt with her need to know what would happen to her. Shocking, wasn't it? I can hardly credit it myself.

We drove back on that Friday, all Christabel's and Rowena's belongings in the boot. Christabel had almost packed them herself – she had a naturally orderly mind, severely tried by her mother's disorderly one – with the help of my mother. She'd even appeared to enjoy the process, had kept up a non-stop commentary on each item as she trotted from drawer to bed where the cases were. My mother said it was obvious that, though she knew Rowena was dead, she had no idea of the finality of death. 'This is Mummy's warmest jumper,' she said, patting an Aran sweater, 'and she's going to have it dry-cleaned before the winter.' When my mother tried to throw out some socks with holes in them, Christabel would not let her. 'Mummy's going to stuff a cushion with all our old socks and tights, and make a Guy on Bonfire night,' she insisted.

Consulted over the phone my know-all brother said this was normal, it was to be expected, one half of Christabel's mind knew her mother would not return and the other refused to accept it. Gradually, the knowledge would penetrate all of her. 'And what then?' I asked. 'Well,' he said, 'then she'll be angry and finally she'll do her grief-work.' God, how I screamed at him – grief-work indeed. It was the first time I'd heard the odious jargon and I absolutely could not stand it.

But it was all part of that social worker jargon I was to come to know so well and at least my brother's phrase had prepared me. Maureen had a pamphlet she was forever consulting, written entirely in such language. One section from it I particularly remember. She read it aloud when I attacked the way she spent her time with Christabel. 'These pamphlets are written by people experienced in grief-work,' she lectured me, 'and they say (she read aloud): "It is helpful for social workers to undertake projects such as life story books. The social worker can write the child's story in simple language and illustrate it with pictures cut out from magazines. Cardboard puppets can be made, coloured and dressed to represent the people in the child's life. The puppets can be given sad/angry faces on one side and happy faces on the other. Play people can be bought, using Special Authority Form DSS 340. A flow chart can also be made . . ."' I really cannot go on.

We were not far from entering the Maureen zone that day we drove back to London. I thought the worst was over, when in fact it was only beginning. My one idea was to get Christabel back into her own home and her own routine as soon as possible, believing, as I did, that this would give her security while her future was sorted out. It had already been decided, as soon as Rowena was officially dead, that Christabel would have to be adopted. Her grandmother did not want her, her aunt did not want her, and there was no one else. I ought to rephrase that: her grandmother was too old and ill to take her and she lived in sheltered accommodation; her aunt believed her dead sister had forbidden her to take her child and knew that in any case she could not give her the family life she needed when she spent her life touring with the orchestra. Does it make any difference how it is put? Only to Mrs Blake and Camilla. To everyone whom I told, it made no difference at all.

My parents, the first people I told, were horrified, and could not credit it that Camilla, if not Mrs Blake, was not going to fold Christabel to her bosom. 'How can she?' my mother wailed. 'Her own flesh and blood – oh, how monstrous, how cruel.' I defended Camilla, I asked why her life should be ruined by starting all over again the mothering she had never liked, just at the point when she was an established flautist. 'Ruined?' my mother echoed. 'Taking in that sweet little girl would ruin her life?' Then I repeated the bit about Rowena herself not wanting Camilla to bring up her child. 'Then, who did she want?' my mother flashed at me angrily. 'Who was her choice? Who is the poor child's guardian? What arrangements did she make?'

Oh, foolish Mother. What arrangements did Rowena make? None, of course. Rowena was Rowena. Many, many times the subject had come up and always it had been dodged. I would not say Rowena did not worry about it – on the contrary, she worried about it a very great deal, even agonised upon occasions, but the trouble was she could not come to any conclusion. She would always end by saying she had 'plenty of friends' who would rally, and not all my blistering scorn would disillusion her. But on the day I hurried Christabel back to her previous life I had no thought of the disaster this lack of written provision for her would cause. From the legal point of view it was surely straightforward. Mrs Blake was Rowena's next-of-kin and I imagined all she needed to do was to choose some nice family to adopt her granddaughter, then sign a few papers.

I was supposed to set the process in motion by going to our local social services office and asking what the procedure for adoption was. Meanwhile, I would stay with Christabel for the few weeks that the necessary business took. If it seems incredible that intelligent people could be so naive, then I can only say I agree and have been embarrassed and ashamed ever since.

But what preoccupied me that November day was not any fears of legal difficulties, of which, as I say I had no inkling, so much as a deep apprehension about entering Rowena's flat. I dreaded it. Dreaded it for the pain it would cause me personally and for the effect it would have on Christabel. Surely, I reasoned, this would be the moment that she realised what 'dead' meant, when she entered her home and found it empty of her mother. It would suddenly hit her what she had lost, and I was terrified of her distress. My stomach churned as I parked the car and got out and I fussed and fidgeted with collecting the first items to take in, putting off the actual moment of opening the front door. Christabel waited patiently while I fumbled for the key (taken from Rowena's bag, an ordeal in itself, the exploring of that bag). Christabel had picked up some huge beautifully coloured chestnut leaves and was admiring the colours. It was hard to push the door open because there was a small avalanche of mail behind it. This turned out to consist of nothing more exciting than a copy of the *Yellow Pages*, countless free samples and leaflets, bills and two postcards. I made a show of stacking all this neatly, delaying opening the inner door to the stairs which led to Rowena's flat. Christabel was impatient now, appeared excited, jigged up and down and kept telling me to hurry up. I showed her the postcards and asked if she knew who they were from because I did not. She gave them a perfunctory glance and said she couldn't read real writing yet. I read them out, one from Susie and Helen and one from Leo. She showed a spark of interest in the card sent from the University of Texas, in Austin, by Leo, who had apparently returned there the month before, his year here over, but then started to hammer on the door and I could stall no longer.

She was away and up the stairs ahead of me, the moment I had opened the door, and there was nothing I could do about it. My heart thudded uncomfortably and my throat was dry. I climbed the stairs slowly, licking my lips, straining to hear any reaction from Christabel. There was an unpleasant smell of stale food and foisty air, which told its own tale of neglect and decay. The kitchen, which I came to first, was not quite as bad as I had sometimes seen it, nothing worse than a banana skin lying on the floor and a rubbish bin lid jammed open by the over-flowing contents. A tap was dripping steadily and the electric clock whirred. Slowly, I put down the box of food I'd brought and carried the case to my old bedroom next door. Rowena had clearly been using it as a dump. The floor was strewn with shoes, mostly odd ones, so far as I could see, and on the bed was a great jumble of sweaters and cardigans and jackets. But this was nothing compared to her own room and the living-room, both of which looked as if a wind-machine had been used to blow clutter into every corner. Where did Rowena get it all from? What use had she for all this stuff? It was completely beyond me. Helplessly I collapsed onto a chair covered with what looked like jig-saw pieces and stared around. To leave a flat like this, knowing you had it to come back to in a week . . . There was still no sign of Christabel and there was no sound any longer of her moving about. I felt I should go in search of her, but I dreaded finding her lying face down sobbing into her pillow, and so I convinced myself it was better to give her time to adjust (I sound like Maureen). Then the telephone rang. I sat bolt upright, not even able to see where the instrument was, and meanwhile Christabel, who had completely changed her clothes, came bounding in. She unearthed the telephone from beneath a table and lifted the receiver. 'Hullo?' she said brightly. 'Hullo, hullo, is that you, Mummy?'

Later, when she was in bed and I'd finished reading her a carefully selected and rather funny story about a little girl called Flossie who found a magic fur coat, I decided I could no longer dodge the issue. 'Christabel,' I said, trying not to sound weighty and solemn, 'you said "Hullo" to Mummy on the telephone when Grannie rang, didn't you? You thought it might be her?' She sat up in bed, her small face clenched in a fierce frown of plain resentment. 'I know Mummy is dead,' she said. 'You don't have to tell me.' There were no tears. She held herself proudly, and all thought of an embrace seemed an insult. 'Then why did you ask if it was her?' I said quietly, hating myself for pushing it. 'Well,' Christabel said, lying down again and turning away from me so that I could not judge how her expression matched her tone of voice (which was quite level and in control), 'I thought it might be her on the underground line, see?' I paused, perhaps for a fraction too long, but I could not trust my own voice. At last I said, 'You mean because you know her ashes are in the ground, is that it?' She nodded, buried herself under the duvet. 'Oh Christabel,' I murmured, 'you are such a clever little girl, you really are.' Beyond that, I made no comment. I stayed with her until she went to sleep, which she did with the same astonishing ease she had done ever since the fatal accident.

I hardly slept at all. There seemed so much to think about and it was that night I began to be haunted by Rowena. Not, you understand, haunted in the sense of seeing a ghost, but in hearing Rowena argue with me, instruct me, object to what I was doing. No sooner would my eyes close than her face would loom, a huge version of her face filling my head, and she would begin to harangue me: '*How can you let this happen?*' she would shout, '*How can you? Aren't you my friend, Isobel? Aren't you? Then why don't you act like one? How can you help my mother to pack Christabel off like a parcel? How can you do it? Have you no feelings? Have you no pity? Do you think I like being stuck here watching all this go on? Do you? What is wrong with you? I thought you were strong? I thought you were outspoken?*' I tossed and turned, put up my arms to shield my eyes, and worst of all began offering excuses and explanations, began saying it was not my fault and I had told her I would not get involved and therefore I could not be blamed for the mess she had left. Then she would jeer at me and laugh derisively, a great booming laugh which was ugly to hear, and I would wake sweating and trembling and dread going to sleep again.

In the mornings, once it was light, I felt I might drift off into a more peaceful sleep, but of course it was now life with a five-year-old which precluded any idea of such a luxury. Christabel would appear at my bedside at seven or thereabouts, already dressed and impatient. It was eerie to open my eyes and see her standing there, quite silent, looking at me. Are all children's faces so inscrutable? Is it because their skins are not lined that they can achieve this impassive expression? After she'd stared at me for some time she would say just one word – 'Up'. Not exactly a command, nor a request, but a flat statement of what should be my intent. I'd get up, shower, dress and we'd go through to the kitchen to breakfast. During all of this routine Christabel was my shadow. She did not cling, she was just there, watching. Why I did not like this I cannot say – I suppose I was worried that I was being scrutinised and found at fault or that the child was comparing me with her dead mother. It was easier at breakfast. I put the radio on, though Christabel wanted the television, and she seemed to enjoy eating her cereal and toast, and singing along with the various advertising jingles. Then we'd get her things together and set off for school.

We walked. It had never actually occurred to me to drive, since the school was only ten minutes' walk away, but Christabel was most taken aback on the first morning. She trotted straight to my car and when I said it wasn't worth driving such a short distance, especially with all the traffic there was, she told me Rowena always did. I wondered if I ought to stick to how things had always been done, if it might not perhaps be cruel and a mistake calculated to upset her, but some streak of obstinacy in me won and I suggested we tried walking just once. I saw, looking at Christabel at that moment, signs of a major tantrum about to erupt. I knew instinctively that if this had been Rowena and not me she would at once have begun screaming to be driven. I was terrified she would start, but then I saw the hesitation in her eyes, the doubt, and it was far more pathetic than any tears. She was calculating the risk, weighing up my reaction, and deciding not to challenge me, and as I sensed her do this, her helplessness overwhelmed me. I took the car key out of my pocket and said that we would drive after all but she shook her head and said, no, she could walk.

I held her hand to cross the road and was struck by the lightness of it. My own seemed huge and square and rough by comparison and I wondered if she noticed. I tried to talk to her but felt my attempts to be woefully inadequate. She replied to nothing I asked her – silly things like her favourite colour – and I began to fear her lack of response was a way of retaliating because we had walked. But then, with the school gates in sight, she came to a halt. She stood stock still, letting her hand drop out of mine. 'I want to go home,' she said.

At least I didn't do anything as crass as ask her why. I knew why, most people with a grain of sensitivity would know why. She was afraid of facing all those people at school, people who might not know about her mother. I imagined she did not know how to tell them and yet could not trust herself to keep this awful secret. I bent down to her level and said, 'Look, Christabel, Miss Splint knows about Mummy and what happened, and she won't ask you about it. And Mrs Monroe knows and Miss Kent and Mr Baines, and the dinner ladies. Everyone knows and they're so sad for you but they won't talk about it if you don't want to. Everything will just go on the same as usual.' She seemed to absorb this but then turned on her heel and repeated that she was going home and began marching in the direction from which we had come. I followed, feeling stupid. All the way back we met other children coming to school. Some of them greeted Christabel ecstatically, as though she was their bosom pal, but she stalked coldly past. The mothers gave me enquiring glances, one or two making sympathetic faces as though they, too, knew how difficult a five-year-old could be. I smiled back but began to feel something of what I supposed Christabel felt – none of these people knew and I did not want to go through the telling.

We reached home, with me in something of a panic, though trying not to show it. I made no objection when Christabel put the television on. She used the remote control to flick from channel to channel in a way I already found infuriating and which I intended to stop. We went from *Playbus* to the end of *TVam*, and then back to *Daytime on Two*. She took an apple and lay on her tummy and watched this jumble of two-minute snatches of programmes in which she did not have the least interest. I made myself some coffee, wondering what I should do. When the telephone rang, I asked Christabel to put the television sound off and answer it. She obliged readily enough, slightly to my surprise. I had the faintest glimmer of an idea who might be calling and it wasn't just because I was busy washing out the coffee jug that I wanted Christabel to answer. Naturally, I heard only her end of the conversation. 'Hello? Yes it is me . . . I don't want to . . . watching television . . . yes, she's here, she's washing up . . . I might.' There were long pauses between the words. I tried to make myself invisible, knowing Miss Splint would be wanting Christabel's whole attention. I stood behind the open kitchen door, hardly breathing. Then I heard the click of the receiver being replaced.

Five minutes later I drove Christabel to school. Everyone had already gone inside and the concrete playground was quite deserted. I had no idea which way to go, but Christabel was now in a hurry and I merely had to stick close to her. Her classroom door was open and I thought she might once more come to a halt when she heard the noise but she did not hesitate, walked confidently into the little cloakroom alongside and hung her coat on a cheerful red peg marked with her name.

Miss Splint, whom I had not yet met, though I'd spoken to her over the weekend on the telephone when Christabel was asleep, must have seen us, because she came out to meet us. I was so surprised by her appearance I worried afterwards that I must have shown it, but then she was too absorbed in Christabel to notice, never mind care. I had imagined Miss Splint, because of her name, as an old-fashioned caricature of the spinster teacher, the sort Rowena and I had had ourselves, salt of the earth, and looking rather like it. But here was this extraordinarily beautiful black girl, more like a dancer than my imagined picture of an infants' teacher. Why had Christabel not told me? Why had Rowena never mentioned how stunning the ludicrously-named Miss Splint was?

By the time Miss Splint turned to me, I was over the amazement, though still having problems readjusting. She smiled and we shook hands. I went through into the classroom with the two of them and tried to sort out what was going on. Hundreds of children seemed to be careering around shouting, but as I stood there watching, half-mesmerised, some kind of pattern did sort itself out. The group Christabel went to were tearing newspapers into shreds and dropping them into a bucket. On the table in front of them were several blown up balloons which were being enthusiastically covered with glue (or that is what it looked like). Christabel put on an apron and joined in. 'I'd go now if I were you,' Miss Splint said quietly in my ear. 'I'll watch her very carefully all day and I promise to ring you if necessary.'

So I slipped out, trusting her judgement that I should not bid Christabel a formal goodbye. The relief of being without Christabel hit me as soon as I was back in the car – oh, the luxury of not being on the alert all the time. Never, never could I have stood this strain, this sense of being responsible, which I presume all mothers have. I suppose it is called selfishness, this glorying in having only myself to consider, but if so it gives a dimension to selfishness I had never thought of. Can it really be said to be selfish not to have children? Or to like to be without hostages to fortune? I really cannot see it. It seems the other way round to me – far more selfish wilfully to create another human being and consider you are fit to do so. Which brought me back to Rowena and what I must now do.

I had an appointment with Maureen Phillips at the Social Services Area Office for eleven o'clock. I'd made it as soon as I arrived in London, feeling, once it was done, I would be less lost. On the telephone, the famous Maureen had been completely thrown. 'No! No! Oh, my goodness! Oh, no!' she kept saying as I went over what had happened and then why I was ringing her. This last bit she had hardly been able to take in. It was my first experience of how strangers would greet the news that Christabel was to be put up for adoption and I was miserably aware, as I spoke, that I blushed though there was no one to see me. Maureen was breathless with horror. 'Her own aunt?' she queried. 'She isn't going to take her?' I said No, and after another series of exclamations Maureen had seemed to get a grip on herself and remember it was not her job to censure. She'd turned brisk and set some facts before me. It would be complicated, she assured me, and a long drawn-out job.

Adoptions took a long time to arrange, a year at least, and in the interim, if no one was prepared to look after Christabel, either in her own home or in theirs, she would have to be sent to a long-term foster placement. There was a lot, Maureen said, to discuss.

The Social Services Area Office was in a high street, sandwiched between a betting shop and a branch of Sainsbury's. There was a kind of reception area on the ground floor, like a doctor's waiting-room, but with many more leaflets and posters and a much more neglected air.

A woman with two small children pulling at her skirt was arguing with another woman behind the desk. 'I'm not budging,' she was shouting, 'I'll walk out and leave these fucking kids on her doorstep if she doesn't see me, I tell you I will, and you can tell her to stick this up her arse.' She brandished a letter right in front of the receptionist's eyes, so near she almost dislodged her spectacles.

The receptionist seemed not at all put out. 'You can do what you like, Mrs Morgan,' she said calmly, shuffling some papers about, 'but no one is coming down to see you any more and you know why.'

Mrs Morgan collapsed in an instant. Instead of hitting the receptionist, which I had confidently expected, she screwed her letter up, let it drop on the desk and began to cry. 'I don't know what I'm expected to do, I don't, honest,' she wept, and began to trail towards the door followed by the children.

'Close the door on the way out,' the receptionist called after her, and then turned to me and said, 'Yes?' in the same unpleasant voice she had used to this Mrs Morgan.

I gave her my name and said I had an appointment. She sent me up to the second floor. Since I hate lifts, I went up by the stairs, stairs covered in brown linoleum with metal treads that click-clacked as feet passed over them. A frosted glass door at the top of the second flight had Maureen Phillips's name on it. I knocked and went in. It was a horrible little office, quite bare of any attempt to humanise it. The floor was the same linoleum as the stairs, though polished to a plastic sheen. There was a nasty cheap, light wood desk and several grey metal filing cabinets jammed into every available bit of wall space. Three chairs completed the furniture, two battered easy-chairs covered in maroon moquette, much split on the arms, and a swivel office chair on which Maureen sat. She got up and came round her desk to greet me. She said she was very sorry indeed to hear this awful news about Miss Blake and asked if I would like a cup of coffee. I refused the offer, perhaps too brutally, and said I'd rather get down to whatever must be done. The rest of the meeting is blurred in my memory because it is dominated by the words Maureen uttered about halfway through the hour-long session. These words were: 'Well, of course, Christabel is officially in care now, you do realise that?'

I repeated, 'In care?' and she said, 'Yes, our care, the care of the Council. You've told me there was no will and no guardian appointed which means that legally Christabel is in care. What happens to her is our responsibility and we take it very seriously.'

I think she went on speaking after that but I interrupted her. 'Just a minute,' I said. 'I'm not sure I've got this straight. Christabel has a grandmother and an aunt. Surely you're not telling me they can't decide what should happen?'

'I'm afraid I am,' Maureen said, pushing back her specs. 'But, of course, we will liaise with them closely, we want everything possible done for Christabel's welfare.'

'I think you must be mistaken,' I burst out. 'How can a grandmother and an aunt not have more power than you?'

'In the case of unmarried mothers the law has to safeguard the child,' Maureen said, in what I interpreted as a patronising tone, but may well have been merely conciliatory.

'I'll ring their family solicitor,' I said. 'I shall check this out. Her family are not fools, you know,' I said. 'You won't get away with intimidating them.'

'I haven't the slightest desire to try,' Maureen said. 'If the family want to, they could have a guardian *ad litem* appointed. Probably one would be appointed anyway, in a situation like this. That can be decided at the first Case Conference. Now, when can the family attend? I suggest we make it as soon as possible, though arranging for so many people to be present is always tricky. And meanwhile I'll come round after school today to see Christabel and make a preliminary assessment, but I'm sure we'll be able to approve you as a temporary carer. There'll be no need for a Place of Safety Order, don't worry about that.'

How could I when I had no idea what she was referring to? A kind of wonder began to dawn on me, that it was I, Isobel Clarke, sitting here in this dismal little office being dictated to by the likes of Maureen Phillips, and with the wonder came the first tinge of fear. Something had been started, which, I could even then very dimly discern, was going to turn into a nightmare over which I would have no control. My acquaintance with the power of officialdom was almost nil – never in my life had I had cause to be afraid of authority. Only once did I ever remember feeling vaguely frightened of an official and that was for a few moments in Moscow Airport, several years before. They have a routine there of making the traveller stand, alone, in front of a glass cubicle where the passport inspector sits. He stares very hard and I did not know there was a measuring pole behind me and that he was checking my height. I remember feeling trapped, with no way out backwards or forwards, and wondering what I would do if I were removed forthwith to some jail, and not allowed to contact the British Consul. Utterly foolish fears, quickly resolved, but I felt the same absurd apprehension when Maureen politely informed me that the Borough Council were now in charge of Christabel.

I rushed home and called Edinburgh straight away, speaking first to Camilla. She could not believe my news and nor could her mother, who said that she was sure Scotland didn't have such silly laws. 'But we aren't in Scotland,' I said. 'We're here, in London, it's too late. Remember? We all agreed Christabel needed to be back at school and in her own home. We agreed on that.' There was a hasty discussion, which I could not quite hear, and then Camilla said they would take legal advice and come to London the next day, both of them. I relaxed a little. I realised I had been dreading the Blakes leaving me to handle this alone. Together the three of us would surely be formidable, more than a match for Maureen and the power-drunk Council.

Their decision to have Christabel adopted did not mean that Camilla and Mrs Blake were not desperately anxious about her welfare. They did not want to get rid of her and would, if anything, be more conscientious about trying to ensure her happiness than they would have been if they had taken her – guilt was going to make them zealous.

By the time I collected Christabel from school that first day I was a changed person. I had suddenly seen her, this lovely child, shunted in my imagination from place to place – my head all day had been full of confused images of poor Christabel with a label round her neck, Christabel in a queue waiting to be chosen, Christabel on a bench in that appalling office ... And there, running towards me, was this smiling little creature, carrying her money-box pig, all ready to be painted, a child thinking only of the pleasure of bright pink paint and the fun of stippling it with black dots when it was dry. She skipped all the way home and dived straight into a cupboard and brought out a set of poster paints. There was a moment's anxiety because there was no pink but, though not famous for my artistic skills, I could at least manage to mix a suitably shocking pink with what was available and Christabel was thrilled. She painted the pig, lecturing me all the time on how it had been made and how she had pricked the balloon inside once the *papier-mâché* was hard, and how some people had pricked theirs too soon and had to start again, but she had not. She had waited until Miss Splint said it was ready ...

This, then, was the other side of the coin, the shining side of motherhood, when amusement and pride and tenderness washed over you and you wondered if there could ever be anything as sweet and touching in the world. I could have kissed Miss Splint, blessed her a hundred times for what she had given her pupil and all in the middle of that, to me, hellish hubbub.

I stayed up a long time that night. Christabel's mood had remained happy and she was asleep before eight. We had had a candle-lit tea which she loved, the table covered in a pretty cloth I'd discovered in a drawer. She beamed at me through the candle-light and ate her boiled egg and seemed very satisfied with her surroundings. She even commented on them. 'Pretty,' she said, nodding at the candles, 'like a birthday.' Then she placidly ate her toast, swinging her legs so that her feet knocked against the strut under the table. I say 'placidly' and yet what did I know? That was what terrified me, what kept me up so late that night. What I couldn't understand was the lack of questions. Christabel was only five and a half but she was intelligent and usually voluble. Rowena had answered any question the child had ever had with exhausting thoroughness and I'd expected a torrent of queries now. But none came. Christabel was not asking anything at all, apart from that one question in the car. My brother had advised me to let her go at her own pace, not to press upon her information she had not specifically requested. He told me not to go along with any fantasies but on the other hand not to sledgehammer the child with harsh reality. But the more I was with Christabel, the more I worried about what was going on in her head. Wasn't I creating a fantasy by living with her in her home? Wouldn't she begin to think that this was how life was going to be, living with Isobel, her new mother?

The thought made me sweat. It was all so seductive and that night, when finally I did go to sleep, Rowena changed tack. There she was, the same looming face, but now she was smiling and her expression was dreamy. *'Isn't she lovely, Isobel?'* she said. *'Isn't she adorable? Don't you love to see her in the bath, so fragile and yet strong? And her hair, Isobel, the feel of it, the springiness and softness? Has she given you a butterfly kiss yet, Isobel? Have you felt those gentle lips brush your skin? Isn't her smile marvellous, doesn't it transform her? It swallows her face, doesn't it? And she's smiling at you now, isn't she, Isobel? You know she loves you, don't you? Did I ever tell you how, when she was cross with me, she used to say she wanted to go and live with you? Did I tell you she thinks you're beautiful? Did I, Isobel? Oh, Isobel, how can you hand her over to a foster-mother? How can you put her up for adoption? Look at her, Isobel, how can you, how can you?'* I woke up at three in the morning with those words ringing so loudly in my ears that I was convinced Rowena was in the room. And then I cried.

Oh, not much, a few snivelling tears of self-pity, but enough to warn me that unless I pulled myself together I was going to end up a wreck.

Certainly, my looks were noted by dear Maureen. 'Bad night, had you?' she said, sympathetically, when she came round the next day with some wretched form or other that needed filling in.

'No, not really,' I said, colouring, I know.

'It's hard looking after a five-year-old if you're not used to it,' Maureen went on, 'and in these circumstances it must be dreadful.'

'Christabel's fine,' I said firmly. 'She's no trouble at all.'

'At the moment,' Maureen said. 'She can't keep it up, of course, not if she hasn't done her grief-work. It has to be done some time, that's the point, it won't stay bottled up forever.'

'How true,' I said, sarcastically, but if the sarcasm was noticed it was ignored. Wisely. Maybe Maureen was not the fool I'd taken her for.

'Now,' she said briskly, 'I've got Form 265 here for you to complete.'

I took the proffered form. It was full of questions I couldn't answer about Christabel's health. 'I don't know any of the answers,' I said, handing it back.

'Oh dear,' Maureen said. 'Will Grannie? Will Auntie?'

I stared at her. What sort of vision did she have of Mrs Blake and Camilla? Of their relationship with their dead daughter, their dead sister? Cosy? Intimate? In daily contact?

'Well,' Maureen went on, 'we shall see, and it doesn't really matter, it's the medical that matters.'

'What medical?'

'Christabel's. The Boarding Out Regulations are very strict on this – children cannot be fostered unless they've been examined within three months prior to placement. So you'll have to take her to her GP or to the clinic, and if you could do it as soon as possible that would help. Have you got her medical card? No? Then maybe you could look for it, if you have time. Are you going to work today?'

'No,' I managed to say stiffly.

'Boss is being understanding, is he?'

'I haven't got a boss,' I said, wondering why I should object to such innocent enquiries. 'I'm freelance, I work for different people all the time.'

'Oooh, how interesting. What line of work are you in then, if it isn't a rude question?'

The way she said 'rude', with a little giggle, irritated me. 'No, it isn't rude,' I said, emphasising the word insultingly. 'I'm an interpreter. I work for various organisations like the British Council, NATO, the UN. I get attached for a week or sometimes for much longer, depending what the work is.'

'So you travel, then?' Maureen said, Form 265 quite forgotten.

'Of course, though more and more work is in London.'

'And what do you speak, what languages?'

'Russian, mainly, and French, but I can manage Spanish and German too.'

'Imagine!' Maureen breathed.

'It only sounds exciting,' I said. 'It's actually very gruelling. But I love it.'

'Oh, you must. It must be ever so interesting.' Then she seemed to recollect the situation. 'Well,' she went on briskly, 'you couldn't look after a child with a job like that, could you?'

'No,' I said. 'Not unless I had a full-time nanny and even then it would be difficult.'

'Oh, it would,' Maureen agreed, nodding away. 'No question. Now, I've brought the form and you're going to arrange the medical and look for her card, OK? And I've fixed everyone for Friday for the Case Conference. Will you tell her grannie and her auntie?'

I said I would. When Maureen had gone, I applied myself to looking for Christabel's medical card knowing that I or Camilla should already have started to sort through Rowena's papers. By then I had the flat tidier than it had ever been since I vacated it, but it was a surface tidiness and I dreaded opening the overstuffed drawers of Rowena's desk. It was not the intimacy of the task which put me off – sorting out her clothes had felt much more disturbingly personal – so much as the certain knowledge that I would be confronted by chaos and yet would not be able to shovel the lot into a plastic sack and chuck it out. I dreaded the necessity of confronting the messiness of Rowena's life, the lack of order, the lack of importance of a single scrap of all this junk.

But I found, when once I had begun, that there was more structure here than I could possibly have imagined. Christabel's medical card was in a folder, clearly marked with her name, and with it was a clinic record card with each injection against the various childhood diseases filled in. Her birth certificate was there -- I noticed Amos's name was not on it, that the space was blank -- and a dentist's appointment card. There were also scraps of paper with names of music teachers and swimming instructors and so forth, the sort of information any good mother collects. Full marks to Rowena -- maybe her child did come home to a debris-strewn flat, but for anyone who did not know, the evidence of caring was all there.

I only managed to deal with three of the seven drawers that day. I threw nothing away, taking heed of my mother's warning to 'Remember you aren't a relative, Isobel.' Quite. I stacked all the old letters neatly in a shoe-box, including many from me which I was sure legally belonged to me, and had them ready to give to the Blakes. I also put an elastic band round the more important documents like the cheque book, the National Savings Certificate book, the Abbey National pass book and the bank statements. Was it insufferably nosy to look in them? Possibly. Anyway, I looked and what I found ought not to have surprised me, but did. Rowena had £8,750 in National Savings Certificates, £5,000 in the Abbey National and £2,150 in the bank. How, then, had she been able to claim Supplementary Benefit? Christabel had her own National Savings Certificate book with £20,000 in it, presumably invested for her by her grandmother at birth. It suddenly struck me how all this money would complicate things even further, because not only did Christabel possess close on £40,000 she also, presumably, inherited a flat now worth at least £80,000 (Mrs Blake had told me when she bought me out that the flat was in Rowena's name). There might even be a trust for Christabel that I did not know about, established by her grandmother for her education. Rowena had hinted at this when she began fussing over private schools for Christabel, but knowing my views on such things, she had not been encouraged to tell me more. Then, of course, there was what Mrs Blake still had. Would she leave that to Christabel, or to Camilla? Who would get this money? Would it be kept for Christabel till she came of age? I supposed so. But in that case, how would the family that adopted her feel about the child's comparative wealth, especially if they had nothing themselves?

That night, when the old rampaging Rowena began on me, I yelled back at her that she should shut up, that she'd left a bloody awful mess and everything was her fault and she had no right to harangue me, that I would never have left any child of mine at the mercy of social workers. I woke Christabel with my screaming and the shame as she stood shivering at my bedside, frightened out of her wits, was awful to bear. This had to stop. I calmed myself, calmed her and promised myself that when I saw Camilla and Mrs Blake the next day I would have to do some plain speaking to save my own sanity.

CHAPTER FIVE

It struck me yesterday that really I ought to go away somewhere, but it is precisely what I do not feel like doing. I go
away enough. Half my life seems to be spent in airports. What
I need is stability, not change, and yet I can't seem to feel stable
in my own home. I could go to my other home of course, to
my parents' house, to what my mother calls my 'real' home.
Rowena used to call it that too – 'You're so lucky,' she would
say, 'you've got a real home.' I'd retort that so had she, for
heaven's sake, but she would shake her head and deny it
emphatically. The awkward thing was that I could see what she
meant. There was nothing homely about the Blake household.
Rowena's father was in the navy, the Royal Navy, and away
for long periods of time. Once Camilla had married, this left
the adolescent Rowena and her mother alone together, and Mrs
Blake stopped 'bothering' as she called it. The giving-up of
'bothering' extended to many things: meals were not worth
bothering with, so the two of them had endless snacks and ate
them at different times; heating the sitting-room was not worth
bothering with and so the kitchen was the only warm room;
clothes weren't worth bothering with once Papa's standards did
not have to be kept up, and so both of them wore the same
things day in, day out. Mrs Blake was certainly no slattern, but
it was obvious, once her husband was away, that by nature she

was not the immaculately groomed wife she was when he was at home.

But in a way Rowena's home became even less 'real' when her father returned. Then, the routine was rigid and the 'bothering' continual. Meals were at precise times and taken formally in the dining-room, the house was spick and span, and everyone changed at least three times a day into the sort of clothes Captain Blake thought suitable for morning, afternoon and evening. It was all ghastly for Rowena, who didn't know which she hated most, the semi-neglect when her father was away or the stifling attention when he was at home. In both cases, her home was not a place she liked to take her friends, whereas our house was always a centre for half the school.

Sometimes I'd be mean about it. 'Let's go to *your* house today,' I'd say to Rowena. Her face would cloud over and she'd drag her feet but I'd insist, God knows why. I'd insist and then regret it, for what was there at Rowena's house? Certainly no cake coming out of the oven, no bright smiling mother ready to hear my complaints, no brothers to tease and mock, no warmth or activity of any sort. Only Mrs Blake looking slightly appalled that we'd come home at all and offering not so much as a biscuit or a glass of orange juice.

I see Mrs Blake differently now. She should never have had children, that was the trouble. She isn't really a cold person, but she finds all emotion difficult and children's emotional outbursts especially so. I cannot understand why the process of bearing a child does not automatically create an unbreakable bond between mother and child, but I saw in Mrs Blake, and I've seen in others, that it does not. Carrying this baby in your own body, having created it from your own being, and giving it an existence of its own and feeding it so intimately – all this, and yet you look around and see mothers and children who are strangers to each other. Very odd. But whereas when, as a small child, I lived next door to Mrs Blake I thought she was unnatural and even cruel, I saw later, when I used to return for holidays, that she was simply not made to be a mother. She was too remote from the messiness of childhood, too lacking in any sense of fun. She liked her books and her porcelain collection and going off to visit cathedrals.

She once told my mother that she had wasted her life, that what she had wanted to be was a lawyer, but her father wouldn't let her. That explained, of course, her other passion: she was a magistrate. My mother used to say it made her shiver to think of Mildred Blake trying any case she was involved in, shiver to think of the total lack of any real compassion or of any understanding of human frailty. My father would reply that she was an excellent magistrate – as a solicitor he'd seen her in action – and that no one could match her correctness. My mother would mutter: 'Exactly,' and look rebellious. She was, I think, a little jealous of Mrs Blake's expertise since she had had no career herself – she'd become a wife and mother very young, and imagined herself totally fulfilled. No one, while I was growing up, thought otherwise, but in recent times my mother has become defensive about how she has spent her life. She feels attacked by modern feminism and doesn't like the faint feeling that she may be pitied, or even despised, for her lifetime's devotion to husband and children instead of being admired.

Rowena was her biggest fan. She absolutely adored my mother and I must say my mother had a soft spot for her. 'Poor little thing,' she'd say after Rowena had gone home, reluctantly. I'd get irritated and say I couldn't see what was poor about her and my mother would try to avoid explaining what she meant. When Rowena came to stay in the holidays, after we'd moved to Cockermouth, my mother would make a great fuss of her. They'd gossip for hours, cosily installed in our lovely kitchen, about the sort of topics which didn't interest me, like the doings of the Royal Family or horoscopes. My brothers liked her, too, saying she was more like a girl than I was, by which they meant she was quite happy to be subservient to them. She'd flirt with them and flatter them and though they were perfectly aware of this – well, I was there to point it out – they liked it. Then there was her love of climbing, too, that quite unexpected stamina of hers and her zeal for tackling the higher fells. They told her she wasn't bad for a girl and she glowed with pride. Often, she'd go off just with the two of them, leaving me behind in a sulk about something or other, and she'd look so happy marching along between them, determined to keep up. 'Look after her, Andrew,' my mother would call to my older brother, 'remember she's not as strong as you, darling.' I wouldn't accept that role, ever. I would *not* be the one who needed looking after, but Rowena loved it. I think at one time she entertained romantic notions of Stephen, my other brother, though in fact it was Andrew, six years older than she was, who liked her better. He once said she'd make a good little wife for someone and I asked, why not for him? He blushed and said it was only a joke. Rowena mercifully wasn't there at the time, but she would have loved to be – she would have been enraptured to hear Andrew make that loathsome *clichéd* remark and even his insistence that it was a joke wouldn't have spoiled the effect of his blush.

At least she was truthful. 'I want to make a family like yours, Isobel,' she once told me, long after those adolescent holidays were over. It was when we met again after that longish interval and she was asking how everyone was. I'd gone through both brothers' marriages and careers and listed all their various off-spring and described how my mother doted on her grand-children, and she'd listen avidly.

'I want to be like your mother,' she said. 'Exactly like her.'

'What an ambition,' I retorted, then thought I'd better make it clear that it wasn't that I was putting my old mum down, it wasn't that I didn't appreciate and love her. 'But it isn't an ambition, Rowena,' I remember I said, piously, 'you can't call it an *ambition*.'

'I can,' Rowena said. 'I want to be what she's been and do what she's done. I don't want a job and I don't want to live on my own forever or even with you. I want a house like your mother has and a life like she has. That's what I want. That's my ambition and I don't care what you say.'

'Then you should,' I said, smartly. But I did think about what she'd said and wondered why I did *not* want my mother's life. It wasn't that I thought Rowena wrong – my mother was and is a happy person and her contentment is enviable – but that for me I knew it would never be enough.

And that's why I have not gone home to my 'real' home at this awful time. My mother could not have been more concerned, more sympathetic and I know that to travel north and be taken in by her and spoiled rotten would probably have an immediate therapeutic effect. But within a few days I would start to get restless, their blessed routine, my parents' routine, would drive me crazy and I'd turn snappy and horrible and watch them suffer as a consequence. They are so *placid*, so pleased to potter about filling their days with trivial, self-imposed tasks. I don't know how they can bear the sameness of it all without screaming. Now my father is retired, they seem to vary their days less, not more. They can sit in their conservatory forever chuntering on to each other over coffee and newspapers and in the summer it seems to me whole days are passed over one drink in the garden. It is domesticity run riot. Nothing outside of it impinges on their world and they see no reason why it should. And yet they are not smug people, not full of themselves. Their consciousness of their own good fortune does not nauseate. When I told them of Rowena's ambition they were embarrassed rather than flattered. But they understood her instinct and worried for her. 'Surely,' my mother said, 'some nice young man will snap up a pretty girl like that.' I groaned, said everything was wrong with that attitude, but I did not fill them in on Rowena's love life. Why spoil an illusion? Why wreck a mutual admiration society? Though, of course, Rowena wrecked it herself when she had Christabel.

My parents were appalled, far more shocked than Rowena's own mother. It occurred to me at the time that perhaps this was the scenario they had always feared for me. Fools. As if I'd do what Rowena did. But my mother, in particular, was so vehement in her condemnation of Rowena, up to then such a favourite of hers, that I fancied there was some message coming over loud and clear, which she wanted me to acknowledge. It threw her when I defended Rowena's decision, when I appeared to condone her action. I didn't really condone it at all, obviously, but my mother's outrage automatically made me want to play devil's advocate. I couldn't keep it up, though. Once my mother's anger had turned to distress on Rowena's account, I had to agree I shared it. It was rather pleasant to be able to share my mother's concern and we had many a long telephone conversation during Rowena's pregnancy which was a comfort to both of us. Then, when Christabel was born, my mother stopped carping. When she first saw the baby, Christabel was one. Rowena took her up to Cockermouth *en route* to Edinburgh and spent a long weekend with my parents – they were always telling her how welcome she'd be – and as you might expect they were her devoted slaves immediately. My mother said after that holiday that she couldn't think straight any more – it was all too confusing, she didn't know what she thought and she was tired trying to decide. It was sufficient that this child was adorable and her mother a changed person, happier than she had ever been in her life.

How do you judge if someone is happy? Do they only have to smile all the time and whistle under difficulties? Then no one would know I was happy. I smile only when something amuses me and I curse when in trouble. Or maybe the label 'happy' is pinned on people who fulfil that old dictum 'Happiness is activity'. What kind of activity? Doesn't seem to matter – being busy, rushing around, that is apparently happiness.

My mother used to come out with what she thought of as a damning indictment of anyone she had decided was unhappy: 'They don't seem to have many friends,' she would say, and rest her case. How on earth one's happiness can be measured by one's popularity I cannot imagine, and again I'd fail the test. My friends are few, deliberately. I reject them all the time in a way both my mother and Rowena find shocking. Friends are to me so much clutter and I like open spaces. Which is not to say I do not have *some* friends, as carefully chosen as my pictures or plates. Rowena was one, of course, and then, in three and a half decades, two others. Quite sufficient. I haven't counted my male friends since the friendship of most of them has not proved enduring once all passion was spent. Only Fergus could be called a real friend.

But Rowena had hordes of friends and was pronounced happy on account of them by my mother, to whom they were only names, lots of names. She never had the opportunity to examine these friendships and find them as wanting as I did. Some of Rowena's 'friends' closed the door in her face regularly. What was extraordinary was that she should tell me they did. 'I went to see Helen,' she would say, 'and she wouldn't let me in, said she hadn't time and I know it was a lie. She's so *mean*.' I could never resist cross-examining her – the notion of such brutal rejection had such a fascination for me. Rowena would admit that she'd *begged* this Helen to let her in, just for five minutes, because she was lonely and had no one to talk to, would even say she knew she had tears in her eyes, while she was pleading for entry and still this 'friend' said No, she couldn't be bothered with Rowena, and to come another day. Or there were the friends who were going to go on holiday with her, and come the day, had better offers and cut Rowena out. I think Rowena's fretting over her wretched friends made her more unhappy than any of the good times she had with them. Her address-book was stuffed with telephone numbers and yet I've seen her telephone a score or more and not find a single friend willing even to talk to her.

So, my mother saying that once Rowena had had Christabel she was happier than she had ever seen her, was relative. Through her child, Rowena always now had a friend, a companion, someone to cling to at all times. And it is true she thrived on it. She loved company, loved being needed, and her daughter fulfilled both functions. She had no desire to go out any more – that, at least, was one dire prophecy I had made which was not fulfilled. Rowena didn't need baby-sitters because she never wanted to leave her baby in the evening. She gave up clubbing and pubbing and could not be tempted to see a film. She wanted to be with Christabel every minute of the day. And she did blossom physically, she did glow. Pregnancy had naturally made her more substantial and after she gave birth, breast-feeding kept her more rounded than she had ever been. The extra weight suited her, made her seem less frenetic. Then her skin changed too. She wasn't as pale, had an altogether healthier appearance and her hair seemed blonder and thicker. She took to brushing it away from her face and tying it with a ribbon on the nape of her neck instead of letting it all hang in tangles round her face, and the effect was pleasing.

Her clothes changed her appearance too – she was very self-important about being a mother and no longer dragged on any old assortment of jumble-sale clothes. Now she wore either a track suit or else jeans and plain shirts and sweaters. She looked neat and trim after a lifetime of scruffiness. My mother noted and approved of all of this. Rowena's disorganisation had always upset her and the transformation convinced her that it had been a mere affectation. She never, of course, saw Rowena's flat or she would have realised all this was skin-deep.

But there were many times in those five years when I, too, marvelled at Rowena's new contentment and was obliged to concede that motherhood had worked wonders. It was the instant growth of responsibility in her that impressed me most, because the lack of it had always undermined Rowena's whole life. She took her duties as a mother extremely seriously and in doing so gave herself a sense of purpose. At the back of my mind, I always felt uneasy about Christabel's role in all this – was it right for any child to be such a fulcrum upon which its mother's very existence seemed to turn? I realised that as Christabel grew older the burden of being so central to her mother's life would prove heavier and heavier and that she would be bound at some point to want to reject it. When she did, what would happen to Rowena?

I suppose Rowena herself dimly discerned this threat, hence the agitation to have another child to latch onto, and it may have been why she made the supreme effort to have someone else look after Christabel for a few hours, three days a week, so that she could take a job at the health centre, supervising the crèche. She could have taken Christabel with her but, with an air of bravery, paid someone to look after her child in her own home (that was the time I tried to find a baby-minder for Christabel to go to). Seeing her come home to her little daughter, as I very occasionally did, was a touching sight. The hugs – which Christabel struggled against – were fierce and hungry, and the adoration on her face slightly sickening.

I don't know why I say that. I am ashamed of myself. Why

should joy nauseate? Yet I somehow despised Rowena for being so desperately vulnerable – I felt I wanted this need of hers to be less naked. And also it bored me. She was a happier person once she became a mother – well, most of the time – but she was much more boring. I realised that half the attraction of Rowena for me had always been her unpredictable nature. You could never tell what ridiculous thing she was going to do next. Even though I disapproved of most of her actions, I still got a lot of mileage out of observing them and being scornful, and I missed this. The new Rowena would never risk doing anything silly, because she was a mother and mothers were sensible. I once went so far as to say she had disappointed me, that I had thought she wouldn't give in to convention so easily, would mould motherhood to suit herself and not allow the expectations of society to daunt her. She said she wasn't daunted and didn't give a damn for society, that it was much simpler than that. She would rather, she said, spend an evening with Christabel than any other person in the world. Oh, dear me. Here we go again – that unworthy feeling of revulsion and not knowing the reason for it. Suspecting, but not really knowing.

It was hopeless, once Rowena was dead, trying to explain to those who had never known her how utterly devoted she had been to her child. 'She adored Christabel,' I told Maureen and got raised eyebrows in return. 'She worshipped Christabel,' I told Betty and was openly disbelieved.

'She's got a lot to answer for, that Rowena,' Betty said when she'd had poor Christabel only two weeks. 'I never knew her and I wouldn't speak ill of the dead, but she has a lot to answer for. That kid's five and a half and wets her knickers without a thought. It's not nerves, mind, I know about nerves, I've had bed-wetters galore and never blamed them, but Chrissie is different, she just don't care. She can do it in the toilet if she wants, but she don't always choose to want. And she's no more idea how to hold a knife and fork than a monkey. It's shocking, no manners either, shovels food in with her fingers and no thought as to others having to watch. Can't do up buttons, can't tie laces, and her a clever little thing, it's all down to the mother and no training.' The criticisms grew daily and went deeper than table- and toilet-manners. 'That child don't know how to play,' Betty informed me. 'She's like a little old woman, talk, talk, talk, it's not good for her, that mother of hers has a lot to answer for, Chrissie's old before her time, it's a damned shame.'

'Christabel,' I said defensively, 'her name's Christabel.'

'Well, she's Chrissie to me and no harm done,' Betty snapped. 'It's embarrassing for the poor little thing having a fancy name like that. She likes being Chrissie. She told me she did. Mum, she said, I like being Chrissie.'

My expression must have shown my disbelief, but Betty misunderstood the reason for it.

'She did,' she repeated, 'she said she loved being Chrissie.'

What I'd disbelieved, of course, was that Christabel could have called Betty 'Mum'. It seemed such an unlikely betrayal, I could not credit it. But it was true. I heard Christabel with my own ears call Betty 'Mum' and furthermore I heard it come out quite naturally, there was no strain about it, no suggestion that Betty extracted it under duress.

Christabel went straight over to Betty when she came into the room on my first visit and said: 'Mum, look what I made at school.'

And Betty said: 'Well, you're a clever little girl. I'll pin it up so everyone can see. Now, look who's come to see you. What do you say to her?'

Christabel turned and saw me and said: 'Good afternoon, Isobel.'

I'm afraid I burst out laughing. Who had said the child was like an old woman and who had now taught her such elderly formality? The old Christabel would have smiled, or not, as the mood took her, and maybe said Hello, maybe come over to me with her picture, but *Good afternoon*?'

'Isobel's come to see how you're getting on,' Betty said.

'Very well, thank you,' Christabel said. She didn't seem very interested in me at all, which hurt but had its own irony. I'd practised how I would deal with the little figure hurling herself at me, clinging to me, maybe sobbing, and here was this cool, composed character, who barely seemed to know me. She turned back to Betty as soon as she'd said her good afternoon and I caught Betty's look of triumph. I'd already asked how Christabel was sleeping – 'Like a top' – and eating. The eating in particular had worried me. Rowena had been obsessed, once she became a mother, with healthy eating and I was pretty sure Christabel wasn't going to get muesli and raw vegetables and pulses at Betty's table. How would she stomach the sausages and chips and fried foods I was sure Betty would provide? The answer was, very well. She 'ate like a trooper', Betty said, and added that she hoped to put some flesh on the skinny little mite before she was finished with her.

I'd hoped to take Christabel out, back to my flat, but Betty had vetoed this. 'It's not that I don't want you to,' she said, 'but it's not allowed, not without written permission and an inspection. I've been fostering a long time and believe me, I know. The Council can't be too careful, see. You might be taking her anywhere, doing anything with her, and they have to be sure. That Maureen should've told you. Didn't she tell you? Well, I'm not surprised. They're so careless sometimes, I can't hardly believe it. But I'm right, you'll see. You need written permission and that has to be applied for.'

I said it didn't matter, but I might as well have just got up and left. It was impossible to talk to Christabel in front of Betty, sitting in Betty's living-room. I was watching what I said and how I said it all the time, terrified of being patronising. And Betty knew it, she was perfectly aware of how uncomfortable I was, how ill at ease. She sat, demonstrating her power over Christabel at every turn, enjoying having the advantage. After ten minutes or so of quite excrutiatingly false chat, she sent 'Chrissie' to wash her hands before tea and change out of her 'good school clothes'. Rowena would have had a fit at such awful 'Miss Manners' stuff, but Christabel went without a murmur – and without a backward look at me.

'Well,' Betty said, smoothing down her already smooth skirt, 'when's that Gran coming again? Because I don't mind telling you I've had enough of that woman. I don't want her coming upsetting Chrissie, it's not right.'

'She is her grandmother,' I ventured.

'Funny kind of Gran, if you ask me, putting that lovely little kiddie up for adoption.'

'Well, she's old and lives in sheltered housing . . .'

'She's got money, ain't she? 'Course she has. Wouldn't matter how old I was or where I lived, but no granddaughter of mine would be abandoned.'

'Mrs Blake isn't abandoning her, she . . .'

'She's put her up for adoption, ain't she?'

'Yes, but . . .'

'But nothing. Oh, it's terrible, it makes me feel queer to think about it, her own flesh and blood, and her with all that money. And as for that aunt, that Camilla, cold? She's like an iceberg, she's not normal. She could take her niece, now couldn't she?'

'She's a musician, she tours in an orchestra . . .'

'But she's well off an' all, ain't she? That car? That address? Them clothes? She could have a nanny, could have anything if she wanted to keep Chrissie. What makes my blood boil is the two-facedness of it all, them pretending they wish they could take her but, oh, dear me, they can't and then all this rubbish about only wanting her to be happy – it's disgusting.'

Betty's face had turned bright red and a vein throbbed in her temple. There was no doubting her passion nor her concern for Christabel. And I didn't doubt either that what she said was true, that she would indeed, however old and poor, have found a way to keep her own granddaughter. All the intellectual power of the Blakes' point of view disappeared before Betty's emotional commitment, her unshakable sense of what was *right*. I didn't even consider trying to convert her to their side. Instead, I was traitorous. Up in Carlisle, in that hospital, sitting outside the ICU, I had agreed with Camilla and Mrs Blake that it would indeed be best for Christabel to be adopted since what they could offer the child was inadequate. I had defended in particular Camilla's right to reject a second term of motherhood. But now I said to Betty I thought *she* was right. I told her my own mother had said the same. I said that if any of my brothers' children were left orphans I would without hesitation have taken them into my home. I said I didn't understand the Blakes myself.

All this mollified Betty a little, but then she turned on me. Still bright red, she said, 'And I'll be honest with you, if you were that Rowena's friend and you've known Chrissie since the minute she was born, then I'm surprised at you too. You're not flesh and blood, so it isn't the same, I grant you that, but it still seems hard to me. There, I've said it, but I had to.'

It was my turn to flush. I couldn't quite think how to respond but was saved attempting to defend myself by Christabel's return. She went straight to Betty and showed her hands. Betty told her she was a good girl and could have a sweetie. Then she said she could put the television on. Christabel lay down in front of the gigantic screen and lay sucking her sweet and giving every appearance of deep contentment. When I said goodbye she murmured ''Bye', but didn't move.

Instantly, Betty snapped off the TV and said, 'On your feet, madam! The idea, the very idea, now you say goodbye properly to Isobel and thank her for coming or there'll be no more telly for you tonight.'

I started to say I really didn't mind, but Christabel had already leapt up and come to kiss me and say goodbye as instructed.

'I should think so,' Betty said, and put the TV back on. The two of us walked down the hall to the door in silence. I said I'd get that written permission from Maureen as soon as possible and give Betty a ring to discuss a date for taking Christabel out (I called her Christabel – I damned well wasn't giving in to this 'Chrissie').

It took me a while to calm down. It was hard to decide why I was quite so upset, but I was. Christabel was looking well and she clearly had the greatest respect for Betty. There had been no sign of any tears nor of any distress. She seemed settled and even happy. I could see that, as Maureen had promised, Betty was a very strong person who provided children with stability and security. Her style of mothering might be a touch military, and there might be a tinge of fear in the children's attitude to her, but while they were with her the world undoubtedly felt a safer place. But as I drove home I knew that what bugged me was the clash of standards Christabel was having to

99

face on top of everything else. In every single way Betty was not only different from Rowena she was *hostile*. She condemned everything Rowena had brought Christabel up to think good and admirable. All the child's values were challenged and she must be in such a state of confusion at every turn. Betty's house, however caring, was not the place for Christabel.

I rang Maureen as soon as I got home. I said, straight out, that I was very disturbed by Christabel's situation and that I felt she was in the wrong kind of setting. 'Betty is the best foster-mother we have available,' Maureen said, curtly. 'She's very experienced and reliable and Christabel is lucky to have her.' I dared to say I didn't think she was lucky. I said I thought there must surely be someone more in tune with Christabel's past life, able to give her the same kind of life so that she wouldn't feel so bewildered. 'Did she seem bewildered?' Maureen asked. I was obliged to agree that she did not. 'Well then,' Maureen said. 'I don't know why you're worried, and really you know it isn't up to you to worry, it's up to us and we're keeping a very close eye.'

There was nothing more I could say, except to ask for written permission to take Christabel home with me, to take her out for the day. I must admit I'd anticipated no difficulty over this simple request, so when Maureen said she would have to consult with her area group head, because, though she knew parental access rights under Sections 2 and 3 of the Child Care Act, she wasn't sure about access of mere friends. It was the 'mere' that antagonised me. I shouted louder than I intended, roared at her that I was the only person who had been intimately connected with Christabel during her entire short life, that I had watched her being born, for God's sake, and I would not take this *shit*. Maureen put the phone down on me.

I didn't ring her back. For one thing, my heart was pounding and for another I knew I would have to apologise and I wasn't yet capable. I knew Maureen would be right – she always was. She'd throw at me section this and section that, quote minutes, mention Acts and always she'd be right. The Blake lawyers had backed her up. It was absolutely true that under English law Christabel was now in care and her grandmother and aunt had no automatic right to her custody. Even if Camilla or Mrs Blake had been ready from the beginning to take her, they would have had to apply to adopt her and, although it would have been extremely unlikely for them to be turned down, they would still have had to be approved. As it was, since they did not wish to keep her, the Council assumed even greater control. It was a shock when all of us – Camilla, Mrs Blake, and I – realised this. We had all seen ourselves graciously inspecting lovely family after lovely family and finally smiling and saying that one might have her. We had certainly been quite confident that we could come and go into whatever place Christabel was put with complete freedom – we were the child's aunt, her grandmother, her friend. The idea that we would have no rights, no control, had never occurred to us.

I remember that first Case Conference vividly. The number of people who attended it astonished me. Apart from Camilla and Mrs Blake and myself there was the Blakes' solicitor, as well as the Team Leader, Maureen, Betty's social worker, whose name I never caught, a representative from the Policy Co-ordination and Liaison Section (whatever that means), a health visitor, and a representative from the Social Services Relations Unit. Ten people, all crowded into a cheerless office which would have been over-crowded with only four occupants. There was a great fuss about getting enough chairs and even more about how they should be arranged.

The Team Leader wanted 'the atmosphere to be informal', so she sat in front of the desk and we all crouched in a rough circle round her. I had plenty of time to study her and didn't like what I saw. Unlike Maureen, this Stella character was brim-full of confidence and it showed in every movement she made. She was rather stout, with very short grey hair, and she wore a dark navy suit with a white shirt, the shirt collar turned over the jacket collar giving it the air of a uniform. She looked like a traffic warden who took pleasure in slapping fines on cars one minute after the time on the meter ran out. She smiled all the time, whatever she was saying, smiled without opening her lips at all. Her eyes never rested anywhere for long but flickered here and there, avoiding all contact. She was not at all intimidated by Mrs Blake or her solicitor.

Stella – she did tell us to call her Stella – opened the Case Conference by saying she was sure we would all agree that our first concern was the happiness of Christabel. She said if we all kept this at the forefront of our minds we would find it easier to understand each other. (Mrs Blake frowned – she clearly didn't understand that remark for a start.) She then said that for the benefit of those who were not completely familiar with all the details of the situation, she would run through what had happened and then hand over to Maureen. The run-through was well done, police-report style. At the end of it, Stella expressed her sympathy for the family and managed for a moment to stop smiling her ghastly fixed smile.

Then Maureen was asked to take over. She was horribly nervous but it was more because of Stella's presence than ours, I was sure. Watching her, I decided Maureen was all right really. She was a bit stupid, a bit irritating, but she tried hard to be sympathetic. Listening to her rather shaky sing-song voice, I thought how deprived she looked herself, every bit as thread-bare as her clients. Her blouse and skirt were immaculately clean and had been freshly ironed, but you could tell they had been washed and washed almost to extinction. She was colourless, quite colourless. Brown skirt, fawn Viyella blouse, black cardigan with little pearl buttons, black boots, old but highly polished.

My mind had wandered hopelessly. When I started listening properly again Mrs Blake was busy complaining that she couldn't hear clearly and asking Maureen please to speak up. Her tone was that of a particularly fussy school-mistress. Maureen apologised, flushed, and raised her voice. She said she felt Christabel was 'not in touch with her own feelings' and that it was therefore difficult to assess her reactions. Mrs Blake said, 'I *beg* your pardon?' and Maureen repeated her statement. Mrs Blake stared at her with an expression of such contempt on her face that I found it embarrassing to witness. Then she laughed, loudly and quite falsely. It was a mistake.

Stella restrained Maureen from explaining and addressed herself to Mrs Blake. 'Do you find that amusing, Mrs Blake?' she asked, smiling glacially, tapping her pencil on the rim of the desk-top to her right.

'I find it ridiculous,' Mrs Blake said, in her posh Edinburgh drawl. 'Perfectly ridiculous.'

'And why is that?'

'It doesn't make sense. My granddaughter is a highly intelligent little girl. To say she is not in touch with her own feelings – and I think the phrase itself is gibberish – is to make her sound a complete idiot.'

'On the contrary,' Stella said, jaw tightening round her smile, 'it is a term used, quite accurately, to indicate a sensitive child having difficulty admitting how she feels and perhaps deliberately suppressing a normal reaction.'

'Oh, for heaven's sake!'

'Perhaps you don't believe in the suppression of emotion, Mrs Blake?'

'Of course I believe in it. I'm suppressing my own emotions at the moment as best I can.'

There was no doubt what those were. Stella very sensibly said, 'I think we're at cross-purposes here, so maybe we ought to let Maureen continue without interruption.'

Maureen continued. When she came to the bit about Betty being agreeable to fostering Christabel until such time as she could be adopted, Mrs Blake broke in again. 'Who is this woman?' she asked.

Patiently, Maureen went over Betty's age and experience.

'No, no,' Mrs Blake said impatiently. 'I mean what *type* of person is she? What does her husband do?'

'He's unemployed at the moment,' Maureen said.

'Unemployed? Unemployed from what?'

'He's had various jobs.'

'Various jobs? You mean he has no profession?'

'No.'

'If I might just point out,' Stella interrupted, 'it is not Mr Lowe who is on our books, it is Mrs Lowe. What Mr Lowe does or does not do is irrelevant.'

'I beg to differ,' Mrs Blake snapped. 'I was a magistrate for twenty years and I know very well the importance of the father in the home background. Half the delinquents that came before me had unemployed fathers, setting a bad example. I really do not wish my granddaughter to go into such a home. I protest most strongly.'

There was an embarrassed silence. I saw Stella narrow her eyes and the smile at last faded. She is about to put the boot in, I thought, and trembled for Mrs Blake, who seemed to have little idea of the damage she had done. She was sitting ramrod-straight, chin in the air, every inch the haughty, autocratic Captain's wife. Her contempt for Maureen, Stella and the entire Social Services Department was obvious. She was enjoying herself, enjoying putting them in their place. Even though I knew that the consequences of her arrogance would be catastrophic I could not help but admire her spirit. She wasn't going to toady to anyone, however powerful they were. She was showing them they could not mess about with her, whatever the legal position. Everything about her – her accent, her quietly expensive clothes, her real-gold jewellery, her immaculately coiffured hair – were all expected to show these social workers: here was a person who could not be pushed around or baffled with rules and regulations. Her appearance and bearing said she had position and money and she would use both to defeat officialdom.

But Camilla had more sense. 'What my mother means,' she said, hurriedly, before Stella could speak, 'is that she is very concerned that Christabel's foster-mother should be able to offer her the kind of background she is used to . . .'

'That would be difficult,' Stella said. 'We don't have single women as foster-mothers. We believe a family environment is best for a child who needs fostering.'

'Oh, I'm sure you're right,' Camilla said, 'but my mother was, I know, thinking more along the lines of, well of . . .'

'Class?' said Stella, smile returning.

'Not precisely. More . . .' But Camilla couldn't think of a substitute.

'Class,' repeated Stella firmly. 'There really isn't any other word, is there? I think we're all mature enough here to be able to label this problem as one of class, and to some extent culture, and to discuss its importance. Now, we all realise Christabel is a middle-class child, used to a certain way of life, and that her proposed foster-home is very far removed, at every level, from that way of life. We recognise, too, that Christabel is in a state of suppressed shock and that it will do her no good to be further confused. But against that we have the pressing need to give her stability as quickly as possible and that has to be our prime consideration. May I remind you that Christabel is now officially in our care and, at the end of the day, all decisions have to be our responsibility. Does this clarify the position?'

God, she was impressive – rat-tat-tat, staring straight at Mrs Blake, daring her to interrupt. Against the accent, the clothes, the other badges of class power, Stella slapped down her own statutory rights and showed she knew she had the whip-hand. The message was clear: you'd better be nice, lady, or you've had it. I'm not sure if Mrs Blake read it like that but at least she dropped her bullying tone. She switched, rather unconvincingly, and much too late to a I'm-just-a-poor-old-widow-woman-act, requesting a glass of water because she felt 'weak with all the travelling' (she'd only travelled from Camilla's place in Hampstead that morning) and asking if she could pull her chair nearer to Stella because her hearing was bad (first I'd heard of it).

There was a visible relaxing of all present. Stella resumed her smile and showed herself willing to be conciliatory. A cup of tea was brought for Mrs Blake and Stella moved closer to her instead of putting her to the trouble of having to get up to move herself. The rest of the meeting passed quickly. Stella rattled through the procedure that would have to be gone through before Christabel would even be considered ready for adoption, and arrangements were made for Mrs Blake and Camilla to visit the foster-home before Christabel was taken there. It was agreed I would go with Maureen when Christabel was transferred.

She was still living with me, of course. Living very happily with me. The way in which we had settled into a routine, without fuss, was remarkable. Every day I walked Christabel to school – she never once asked to go in the car – and every day I collected her at three-thirty. We went home, had a snack, watched television for an hour or so, then she nearly always had some sort of activity – swimming lesson, gym club, ballet class, recorder group and so on. For a five-year-old it all seemed to be a bit excessive, but she seemed to like everything and to show no signs of exhaustion. We had a sort of high tea at about six-thirty, then she had a bath and got ready for bed and sometimes I let her watch a little more television before sitting and reading to her when she was in bed. She fell asleep around eight. Everything swung along so effortlessly that during the second week I was even able to do a little work. There was a Russian trade delegation in London and I did four hours' interpreting at some very dull meetings, arriving home with plenty of time to collect Christabel.

I saw how it could all work. All it needed was organisation and efficiency and I was blessed with both. One small child was accommodated without difficulty into my life – so long, that is, as work was arranged round her and I had no social life whatsoever. I saw, actually, how I could quite easily have a social life too. It would not have been beyond me to find a reliable evening baby-sitter. The work would have been another matter. I appreciated very quickly how impossible it is to put one's career first if there is a child around. All the time I had to think carefully about any job I was offered, about whether I could or could not get back in time, and even though these were special circumstances requiring special consideration, I saw how it would always be a case of being attracted by the convenience rather than the interest of the job. All the time I was translating during those dreary trade delegation meetings I was resenting such boring work and yet I knew I had to be grateful to have work that fitted in at all. I speculated endlessly on how long I'd be able to tolerate this kind of sacrifice and thought not very long. I could feel myself becoming irritable, resenting the tedium, and waiting impatiently for the assignment to be finished.

I was also waiting for Christabel to go, but at the same time I dreaded it. It was not just that there was a surprising amount of pleasure in looking after her, but that there was also a soothing feeling of virtue. So long as I was caring for her myself, the horror of what was about to happen to her was suppressed. I felt relief in looking after Christabel, in cooking her meals and washing her clothes and generally making her as comfortable as possible. When she gave me a goodnight kiss and smiled and snuggled down into bed, I felt so happy to be making *her* happy. And, frankly, disgustingly, I enjoyed the praise and admiration. 'You are marvellous, Isobel,' Camilla said, tearful in her guilty gratitude. 'I can't tell you how much this means – it should be me – I know it should – but I'd do it so badly and I dreaded it and Christabel would have sensed it.' I graciously said it was the least I could do and I wanted to do it.

Mrs Blake was similarly appreciative but not as capable of confessing it. 'You stood by Rowena in her life, Isobel,' she said, 'and you're still doing it after her death, and I must say I've often wondered why.' She sighed and I muttered something about caring very much for Christabel. She sighed again and said, 'She tires me, as her mother did. And she's a strange little thing, don't you think? She never feels familiar to me, I'm afraid.' Then she added hastily and very firmly, 'But she *is* my flesh and blood, and I shall see that everything possible is done for her. I owe Rowena that.'

I went with them to Betty's that first time. Camilla begged me to, saying she simply could not cope with her mother on her own. 'She will be *awful*,' she groaned. 'You know how awful she can be, even though I've told her we're in no position to be critical. I dread it, Isobel, I really do.' So I went, though I dreaded it just as much. I actually drove them there, trying on the way to prepare Mrs Blake for what she would find. Even so, before ever we drew up at the house, Mrs Blake was saying, 'What a dreadful neighbourhood, not at all the place for a sensitive child.' If I hadn't been driving I'd have closed my eyes to brace myself for the next one. 'So noisy, so dangerous, and I cannot see any parks,' Mrs Blake went on. 'Where are the parks? Where will Christabel play? Dear me, what can these social workers be thinking of, I shall report them.' How could she have been a magistrate for twenty years, I wondered, and still think all children had parks on their doorsteps to play in? How could she know so little about social workers that she could imagine they could afford the luxury of choosing green and leafy locations in which to place children in care?

Then when we drew up outside Betty's – with difficulty, I may say, since there was virtually no parking space on such a busy high street – she was appalled at the sight of the house. 'It is little better than a *slum*,' she hissed. 'Mother, don't be so ridiculous,' Camilla snapped. 'It is a perfectly decent house. Look, the door is newly painted and the knocker *shines*.' Mrs Blake was silent a moment and then suddenly said, 'How awful it is to be as old as I am and be so apprehensive.' It was the first human thing she'd said and I warmed just a little towards her. 'Let it show,' I advised, before we got out of the car. 'Betty will like you better for it.'

But Betty didn't like her at all and I am obliged to report that she could not be blamed. Mrs Blake's apprehension seemed to have left her by the time we were shown into Betty's living-room, which she surveyed as though unable to believe her eyes. It was looking, it is true, pretty garish. Heavy, fancy, violently coloured paper chains were strung from corner to corner, dimming the already not very strong light and the Christmas tree, though artificial, seemed to have grown at least another foot since I last saw it. 'How jolly,' Mrs Blake said, 'but are you not a little early?'

'We please ourselves,' Betty said. 'There ain't no rules that I know of. Sit yourselves down. Would you like a coffee?'

'No, thank you,' said Mrs Blake, stupidly. There was dead silence. Betty sniffed and stared boldly at her visitors. Quite unexpectedly, Mrs Blake's eyes filled with the first tears I'd seen in them. Had she been saving them? Was this a superb piece of acting? If so, it did her no good. 'I expect you know why my little granddaughter has to come here?' she asked, her voice quavering.

'Not really,' Betty said drily.

'No? Oh, oh I thought you'd been told,' Mrs Blake said,

looking at me as though I was somehow responsible for this apparent failure of communication. 'My daughter Rowena was tragically killed a month ago, in a climbing accident.'

'Oh, I know that,' Betty said, 'and I'm ever so sorry. I thought you was meaning the little girl, why she had to come to me and that.'

'I did.' Mrs Blake said. The tears, the quavering, had gone. She recognised an adversary when she saw one. 'I am old, as you see, and not able to care for her, and my daughter here is also unfortunately unable to offer the child the sort of home she needs.' Betty said nothing, only gave the ghost of a smile. 'So we are naturally very grateful that you are able to look after Christabel for a little while.'

'More like a long while,' Betty said.

'I beg your pardon?'

'I said it'll be more than likely a long while, seeing as how tricky adoptions are, specially with the little girl being black. That'll complicate it, the Council being what it is.'

'My daughter was white,' Mrs Blake said, faintly.

'Yeh, I know,' Betty said, 'but she must've gone with a black man 'cos the little girl's black, ain't she? No two ways. So, being the Council, they'll want one of them mixed-race families for her, or a black. But not a white. And there's more of the white, that's all I was meaning. So it'll be a long job, a year I reckon. That's why they come to me. I only do the long-term ones, makes more sense, you can get them into your ways, know what I mean, get a chance to do something with them, make something of them.'

Mrs Blake was stunned. She'd had shock after shock and could hardly take it all in. She was completely silent as we all trooped upstairs to inspect the room Christabel would have. Camilla cooed over the frilly pink bedspread and the rabbits-and-ducks wallpaper, but her mother kept silent, except for gasping at the end of climbing the stairs. Actually, Camilla did quite well. She was so terrified of appearing patronising that she kept the compliments to a minimum and tried to be as self-deprecating as possible. Betty wasn't taken in but she could sense Camilla straining to please her and that mollified her somewhat. She said, as we were leaving, 'You've no need to worry about the little girl, no need at all. She'll be as safe as houses with me. I won't let her upset herself, you'll see.'

We all said we were sure we would. In the car on the way back to Camilla's, Mrs Blake said, 'I don't think I can bear that woman having Christabel. She is vulgar. Christabel will pick up her habits, she will *speak* like her. I cannot believe there is not a better place available.'

'Mother,' Camilla said wearily, 'this is pure snobbery. You can't judge Betty by her grammar nor by her taste. She is warm and kind . . .'

'Kind? She was not kind to me.'

'Nor were you kind to her. And I didn't mean just now, I meant in general. I mean that she has a tried and tested reputation for being warm and kind. It is no good criticising her before she's even met Christabel.'

'I'd rather she didn't meet her.'

'Now you're being childish, Mother. You know perfectly well we have no choice. Christabel isn't ours any more.'

'Of course she is!' Mrs Blake said angrily. 'Nothing can make her not ours, don't be absurd. We may not have absolute control over her destiny, but she is, and always will be, my granddaughter and your niece. Anyone who forgets that will regret it.'

'Oh, Mother, threats are silly.'

'I'm not making threats, I'm making a promise. I shall safeguard Christabel's future and that is a promise. No council will decide who is to adopt her. I shall take it to the highest court in the land if I do not approve of the family selected. And I am *not* putting up with this nonsense, if it is true, that my granddaughter must go to a black family.'

'Mother, calm yourself, please.'

'I am quite calm, thank you. I shall see my solicitor in the morning. If there is to be a battle, I may as well prepare myself at once.'

I kept quiet but sneaked a look at her in the driving mirror: head high, cheeks flaming, eyes glinting, mouth set firm. A grudging admiration was stealing over me and I felt some of the excitement of an approaching fight myself.

CHAPTER SIX

I can't imagine that I will see Mrs Blake in London again. She retreated, immediately after the court case, to Edinburgh and I can't see that she will come here again, even to visit Christabel, if she is allowed to. She seemed very frail when Camilla and I put her on the train and we both felt we ought to have travelled with her, but she was adamant that it was unnecessary. She'd aged such a lot in eighteen months, become quite bowed and shaky. It was pure exhaustion, she said, and once back home she would recover in time. Her eyes were red-rimmed not with weeping but with all the reading she'd done, late at night. Reading and writing, too, writing to everyone who might help, people she didn't know as well as friends dragged out of the past, anyone and everyone who might have useful advice and be on our side. Her letters were fluent, coherent, logical with not a word wasted. I hope the Council has the ones she wrote to them on file – they are models of how to set out a case. I shouldn't think they will dare to tear up these historic documents, however much they hate her.

Perhaps 'hate' is too strong a word; 'dislike' might be fairer. They – Maureen, Stella and Phyllis (who was the adoption officer we met later) all disliked Mrs Blake acutely. She was a permanent thorn in their sides, forever correcting them and pulling them up at every turn. And, of course, she was extremely fond of going to a higher authority and complaining about them. This mattered most in the case of Stella since she was responsible for the other two, whereas above her were far more important people to whom Stella herself had to answer. The head of Social Services must have made Stella's life hell, just as Mrs Blake made his. But there must have been solidarity all the same because Stella stayed where she was and Mrs Blake had polite but firm letters back from this Mr Wavell, couched in stiff, official language, terribly pompous and unreal, especially in response to the sort of letter that had been received. Mrs Blake kept a huge file of all these replies and she was always saying there wasn't a single letter in it that a child of ten could not have written. I did once point out that this was the age of the telephone and that all the people involved were very busy, but she swept this excuse aside. 'In a matter of this importance,' she said, 'getting things down on paper is what matters, and they know it.'

They probably did, which is why they were so reluctant to put anything at all on paper. The very minutes of the Case Conferences, which I saw since I was present and entitled to a copy, were flimsy things containing nothing about the arguments and differences there had been. 'It was agreed that Christabel should be visited once a fortnight by her grandmother and aunt,' the minutes said, without any mention of Mrs Blake's furious objection. She had claimed the right, at the Case Conference held immediately after Christabel moved into Betty's house, to visit her granddaughter whenever she liked. It was monstrous, she said, to keep them apart. When Stella said it was very upsetting for Christabel to be visited without warning, very disruptive, Mrs Blake asked her if she had gone quite mad. She asked which of the grandmothers Stella knew requested permission to see their granddaughters. Stella let her rant on a bit and then said that, as Mrs Blake knew, circumstances were not normal, normal conditions could not prevail. 'They are not normal,' Mrs Blake flashed back, 'because you are making them abnormal, you are conspiring with that woman to keep me apart from Christabel.' (Betty, by this time, had become 'that woman' – Mrs Blake never referred to her in any other way and it was very offensive.) Stella kept her temper. She said that as Betty was in charge of Christabel on a day to day basis, it was only right that her opinion on visitors should be respected and her opinion was that they were upsetting to Christabel. 'How can a grandmother be upsetting?' Mrs Blake shouted.

Everyone was silent. The evidence was so clear. I expected Stella to say 'by behaving as you have just behaved', but she didn't. She said instead that Mrs Blake must understand that it was dangerous emotionally for Christabel to go between two worlds: the world she had lost and the world she was now in. This was a temporary situation and, during it, great care had to be taken to maintain some kind of equilibrium. If Betty observed this balance being threatened, then it would not be wise to risk the visits which caused Christabel such confusion. She also pointed out, gently, that it was not as though Mrs Blake had been in the habit of seeing Christabel regularly. 'I live in Edinburgh,' Mrs Blake said, glaring at her. 'How *could* I see her as regularly as I wished?' 'Quite,' said Stella.

Of course, it was worse than that and I gave Stella and Maureen credit for not repeating what Betty actually had said, which I was aware of, because she'd said it to me too. 'That Gran is wicked,' Betty said, flushed with virtuous indignation, 'and Chrissie don't like her one little bit. She cries when I tell her her Gran's coming and she cries when she's gone. I'm not having her upset like that, it isn't right.' When asked in what way was Mrs Blake 'wicked', Betty came out with things like 'She tells Chrissie it's all right to cry for her mummy. I mean, I ask you, telling the kiddy to *cry*, just when we've got over that, bringing it all back. Then she give her this photograph of her mum and tells her to pin it over her bed and look at it if she's sad in the night. It's *wicked*. She's frightened to go to sleep.' It did all sound a little peculiar but, in fact, Maureen and Stella and even my brother weren't too hard on Mrs Blake over this. Maureen tried to say to Betty that it was important Christabel should do some 'grief-work', and equally important that she should keep the memory of her mother alive.

Then Betty said, 'She says she don't want to remember her anyway, she likes me better. Honest to God, she said that, you ask her.' Maureen looked a little shaken. 'I'm sure she does like you, Betty, but don't forget she knows she has to. She knows which side her bread's buttered for the moment. And wanting to forget her mother is only a way of putting off dealing with her death.' 'Oh, I'm sure,' Betty said crossly, 'I wasn't born yesterday. Anyway, I'm not having that Gran poking her nose in any time she likes, and that's final. You can take Chrissie to someone else, if I'm going to have to put up with that. And I don't like Chrissie staying overnight at her auntie's either. She hates it. What a carry-on I had making her go. Why can't I stay with you, she says, and I had to force her to go. It's not right, it isn't. She don't mind Isobel, but she don't like that Gran or her auntie.'

I thought Maureen would have hysterics over all this, but as we left together she was philosophical. 'It happens all the time,' she said, 'the foster-mother gets up-tight over the real family and the real family resent the foster-mother, even when they're dependent on her.'

'But do you think it's true?' I asked. 'I mean, do you think Christabel really said those things?'

'Probably. She feels safe at Betty's, she probably does beg to stay. But then I expect when she's with her grandmother at her aunt's she enjoys it. But she's clever, she knows Betty doesn't want to hear that.'

'Camilla says she complains that Betty shouts at her but then she begs her not to tell anyone. And I must say she said something the same to me, that she liked her new mummy, she did say that at least, but she was very "shouty" and it made her head ache.'

'Yes,' Maureen said, shrugging, 'I expect Betty does shout a bit, but then most mothers do, and she's running quite a big household. A bit of shouting won't do Christabel any harm in the long run.'

Only afterwards did that statement strike me as appalling: 'A bit of shouting won't do Christabel any harm in the long run.' She'd never been shouted at in her little life. Rowena, for all her faults, never shouted. Cried, yes, but shouted, no. And now there she was, at her most vulnerable, and she was being shouted at, living in a household where there was probably a lot of yelling going on. Like the household I'd been brought up in – everyone roaring at everyone else and thinking nothing of it. But we were born to it, it was natural, part of our rumbustious family life which Rowena so admired, and Christabel had not experienced. Maybe Betty didn't shout directly at her at all, maybe the shouting she talked about was just part of a general bawling people out and Maureen was right, it would benefit Christabel in the long run. It would do that miserable-sounding thing: 'toughen her up.' God forbid.

At any rate, visiting was firmly fixed: Mrs Blake could only see Christabel once a fortnight, but she was allowed to take her out and keep her overnight at Camilla's every second visit. This was fixed just before Christmas, but then almost immediately there was trouble. Mrs Blake said she assumed these 'outrageous restrictions' did not apply to Christmas, when Christabel would naturally want to be with her own family. Camilla's daughter Ailsa was coming specially from America for a family reunion and to be with her cousin for the first time since Rowena died.

'You cannot deny us our Christmas,' Mrs Blake said to Stella and Maureen (I'd driven her to their office because Camilla was touring Belgium). I think she thought she looked pathetic and that her plea was made with a piteous air, but if so she misjudged her performance. The words came out, as nearly all Mrs Blake's words did, sharply, challenging the listeners to disagree at their peril.

Stella disagreed instantly. 'I'm afraid Christabel must stay in her own home for Christmas, Mrs Blake, and the arrangements we made must stand, though I'm sure Betty will accommodate you as best she can and change the date of Christabel's next visit, when it's due, to suit her cousin. I think you'll find she'll have a very happy Christmas at Betty's – she goes to a great deal of trouble and there's a very nice atmosphere there.'

'The atmosphere is *awful*!' Mrs Blake burst out. 'Those dreadful decorations, that ugly tree, and all that emphasis on material things – how can you say the atmosphere is nice?'

'Children like it.'

'They may like it, but it is bad for them. What do you suppose that woman is giving my granddaughter for Christmas?

Some dreadful toy called "My little Pony"! Utterly vile, and I expect it will be paid for out of taxpayers' money. I expect she gets a grant for presents, that woman?'

'Yes,' Stella said, far too sweetly, 'she does get a grant, but in my experience she spends as much again of her own money on her foster-children.'

'Then more fool her. Christmas is not about money, it is about the spirit of giving. She would be far better off knitting the child something. I really cannot bear my granddaughter to be in that house over Christmas, absorbing all these dreadful values.'

'I don't think the values are so dreadful,' Stella said, 'just different from your own, Mrs Blake, and who is to judge which is better?'

And where did I stand in all this? You may well ask. I was never sure – an unusual frame of mind for me. The trouble was that I agreed with everything Mrs Blake said, she was right, but when I heard her saying it, I immediately felt defensive towards Betty. Norman, her husband, understood this surprisingly well (and why 'surprisingly' – dear God, there's no end to this condescension). By the time I'd met Norman two or three times, I'd decided I liked him, and that he was definitely a good influence on his wife. He was at home a lot, with being unemployed, and though at first he seemed to lurk in the background, and only speak when directly spoken to, I soon realised he was quite a formidable personality. Betty knew it, of course. She was proud of him and much given to saying, 'Norman thinks' and 'my Norman says' and he would smile and blow a little smoke out (he never had a cigarette out of his mouth) and raise his eyebrows quizzically.

He is a big man, huge, more than six foot, I would say, and burly with it. His skin, like his wife's, is very lined, although he cannot be more than forty either, and he's an awful colour, a kind of yellowy, jaundiced complexion. He has a bit of a paunch, Betty's cooking, I expect, and very big feet, almost always encased in brown and white chequered slippers which look very new. His eyes are quite twinkly – he smiles with them as well as his mouth – and he looks shrewd and amused.

He is a much better-looking man than Betty is a woman. His accent is much more pronounced than Betty's and it isn't surprising Mrs Blake says she can't understand a word he says. As well as the Cockney accent and the grammar, Norman also has a wheezy chest and coughs a lot and it is a bit of a nightmare sorting out what he's saying. I found that if I concentrated very hard on watching his lips I could decipher the sense of what he was saying, but then if I couldn't, with my training, who could? And it was worth the effort, because Norman was good at getting to the heart of the matter. I shan't attempt to reproduce all the glottal stops and so forth – it would just look like a phonetics exercise – but when talking about Christabel he was astute. 'Desperate for affection,' he pronounced, 'and she's a cunning little thing. All over me she is, and Craig too. If she weren't so little it'd be indecent, know what I mean?' I said I did. 'I reckon she ain't used to men,' Norman went on.

'No, she wasn't,' I said.

'Father scarpered?' Norman asked sympathetically (strangely, Betty had never asked at all).

'No,' I said, hesitantly. Telling the truth seemed only a way of blackening Rowena's character further. 'He went back home, to Barbados.'

'And she was left up the spout, eh?'

'Sort of,' I said, uncomfortably.

'Well, it explains a lot,' Norman said. 'Hard for the Gran to take, them being toffs and that. I'd be cut up meself if it was Judy.'

'It better hadn't be,' Betty interrupted. 'I'd tan her backside.'

'That'd do a lot of good,' Norman said. 'No good if your family hit you when you're down. That's what family means, innit, sticking together, for better for worse sort of thing.'

'Well, Chrissie's ain't doing any sticking,' Betty said.

'You watch your mouth,' Norman warned, indicating Christabel, who was watching television. 'You don't want to go putting ideas into her head, no matter what you think. It ain't right, having a go at her family.'

There spoke the voice of authority in the house and Betty appeared suitably chastened. I remember, that day, wondering more than at any other time what sort of family the Lowes really were. It was so hard to tell. I came only by appointment, when I was picking up Christabel and returning her, and I knew perfectly well that my visit was anticipated and prepared for. What I most wanted to do was to catch Betty unawares and see if this fierce tidiness was normal, to see if she was always in her pink and blue, looking so prim. She never took me into the kitchen, always into the living-room. It was like a state visit, and I hated it.

The children, if they were in, sat on the settee and stared at the television. 'Say Good Afternoon to Miss Clarke,' Betty would instruct them, and they'd mumble 'Good afternoon'. For teenagers they seemed exceptionally docile and cowed but then who could tell in such circumstances? I tried to speak to them but it was hard going, what with their guardedness and the wretched television always on. Judy, the Lowes' natural daughter, looked lively enough in the same sort of way as her mother, but appeared to regard everything I said as so extraordinary, that an answer was beyond her. She was watching *The Clothes Show* once when I returned Christabel and, since I quite often watched it myself, I felt enough of an authority to try to chat to her about it.

'Don't you hate it when they do spectacle styles and that kind of thing?' I asked Judy.

She looked at me as though I'd said something quite amazingly daring. 'Pardon?' she said, and when I repeated my question she appeared speechless.

'Do you like Selina Scott's hair short or long?' I tried, and got 'Pardon?' again, followed, eventually, by 'Dunno, really.'

How on earth did Christabel survive having Judy as her mentor? Very well, seemed to be the unlikely answer. Judy, she told me, painted her nails with the pink nail varnish she was wearing and she was going to let her borrow her Jason Donovan badge to wear at school. Judy knew all the right popular songs and all the groups and had promised to take Christabel to a Michael Jackson concert if ever there was another in London. So something went on between them.

Marlene, the foster-child daughter, seemed sullen and aggressive – Betty was always casting her deeply significant warning looks – but less alarming to me than the vacuous Judy. Christabel was a little afraid of Marlene, I think, and certainly felt no empathy because they shared the same skin colour. On the whole, the boys were infinitely preferable to the girls in that house. Craig, who was eighteen, was big and rugged like his father, with the same sort of smile and amiable air, and he would pass the time of day quite cheerfully with me. He always called me Isobel at least three times in the course of any one remark – 'Get wet, did you Isobel, on your way back, Isobel, should've had a brolly, Isobel.' He would pretend to fight with Christabel, and she shrieked and loved it, until Betty said she was behaving like a wild animal, and would Craig give over. Craig was a motor mechanic, or rather on a YTS scheme, training to be one, and the whole family were proud of him, especially his mother. Duaine and Arthur, the other two foster-children, seemed edgy in my company. Duaine, who was tall and gangly and looked older than fifteen, usually left the room as I came in. Arthur stayed, and stared. He was an unfortunate-looking boy, with a runt-of-the-litter appearance – thin face, spectacles, gingerish hair. He was quite willing to talk, though, and always replied very fully to anything I might think to ask him.

But what were they all like when I wasn't there? I couldn't credit that the same sort of silence (apart from the television) reigned. Did the place erupt the moment I left? Did Duaine and Arthur fight and Judy and Marlene argue? Did stuff get scattered around the room – jackets, comics, the ordinary detritus of family living? All Christabel said was that she had to go to bed at seven 'or else'. Everyone had carefully regulated bedtimes and Betty was very strict. She was strict about washing too. Hands and face in the morning, hands before every meal, and before bed, a bath on Sundays and Wednesdays. Clothes had to be put out neatly the night before and could not be changed at the last minute. This naturally made a deep impression on Christabel, who had spent all her short life flinging different clothes off and on. But the great compensation was that she had quite a lot of new clothes, bought for her on the grounds that she'd grown out of the ones she'd brought with her. This was all a nonsense. I'd spent a whole afternoon with Christabel sorting through her clothes and I know most of them still fitted her. But Betty didn't approve of the rather ethnic type skirts and jackets which Rowena had bought for her; lovely brightly coloured embroidered garments in which Christabel looked beautiful. Apart from those, she had only a couple of pairs of jeans and a few T-shirts and sweaters, and Betty thought this wardrobe quite inadequate. She got a clothes grant and she and Christabel went off 'up the market' – I don't know which market – one Saturday morning and came back with the most hideous things imaginable.

It hurt me to see Christabel in a bright pink nylon blouse with a bow at the neck and an electric blue viciously pleated Terylene skirt, but she was delighted. I'd always thought taste innate and if it resided in anyone I was sure it must reside in someone as pretty and naturally graceful as Christabel. But no. All in a moment I saw I must be wrong. Christabel went for the garish and was thrilled. Only over her coat – 'She's got to have a decent coat' – had there been a tussle. What she'd wanted, said Betty was a bunny-rabbit coat, whatever that is, and what she came home with was a revolting red leather one. Not real leather, of course, but a plastic version, very shiny and stiff. The awful thing was how much it changed the child. Looking at her in these new outfits I was horrified to find how she instantly looked *déclassée*. The same bright, lovely face, the same fine features and slender, elegant body, the same proud carriage – but all glossed over with these vulgar clothes and half-hidden by them. She could have been Betty's daughter, except for her skin colour.

And when Mrs Blake saw her you can imagine her reaction – she was livid and quite unable to restrain herself. 'Get that coat off,' she said to Christabel, 'off! *Off*! This instant.' But when it was off and the blouse and skirt revealed in all their tawdry glory, it was even worse. Christabel cried at her grandmother's anger and then she had to be soothed with supposedly comforting explanations. 'It isn't you I'm angry with, dearest,' Mrs Blake said, 'it is that woman. You weren't to know the difference, it isn't your fault.' But through her tears Christabel hiccuped that she had chosen her own clothes and that she liked them and wanted them, and 'Mum' said they were very nice – it really was too pitiful. Mrs Blake did feel guilty, that was one good thing. She even said, with some evidence of shame, 'I can't think what came over me, as if it mattered what the poor child wore.' Exactly. But, nevertheless, she immediately afterwards got me to purchase a pair of jeans and a jumper and a jacket which were like the ones Rowena had last bought Christabel and these were kept at Camilla's house for Christabel to change into. '. . . To keep your best clothes clean, darling.' She seemed to find this acceptable because, of course, returning to Betty clean was very important and she did not want to be scolded.

It became a game, jumping into her other clothes the minute she arrived and she quite approved. Whether she told Betty I don't know, but even if she did, I expect the real significance remained veiled. I must confess to feeling as relieved as Mrs Blake when Christabel became once more the child we knew and loved before our very eyes.

On the occasions when I myself returned her to Betty's I must say she expressed no reluctance. There was more tension evident in her face when I picked her up. What would happen was this: half an hour before I was due to collect her, Betty would telephone and say, 'I'm ever so sorry, Isobel, but Chrissie ain't well.'

'Oh dear,' I would say, my heart sinking, knowing after the first time what would now have to be gone through. 'Oh dear, what's wrong with her?'

'She can't keep out of the toilet.'

'You mean diarrhoea?'

'And sick, bringing up sick. She's in a real state, I'm ever so sorry, but, Mum, she says to me, I'll have to stay at home with you. I'm ever so sorry, Isobel, disappointing you and that.'

'Don't worry about me, for heaven's sake. Poor Christabel, poor you, having to deal with it. Did it start in the night?'

'Yeh. She come into our bed and I thought it was just nerves, 'cos she do get nervous, very, before she goes anywhere, not that she don't like you, Isobel, no offence meant, but when I say she's going out for the day, away from me, there's such a fuss.'

'What about school days – is it the same then?'

'Oh no, it's just going to other people's houses. So I'm ever so sorry, Isobel, but we'll have to cancel today.'

'That's all right, but I'll come and see her all the same.'

'Well, she isn't really up to visitors.'

'I'll just stay five minutes.'

'She should be in bed, really.'

'I'll read to her in bed if you like.'

Then I'd drop the phone pretty sharpish, pretending someone was at the door, and if it rang before I was quite ready to leave, I'd ignore it in case it was Betty telling me not to come in language I couldn't pretend I didn't understand. I'd drive to Betty's and more or less force my way in to find Christabel lying on the settee covered with a blanket and looking startled as well as very hot. Betty would be very agitated and go over and over the details of the diarrhoea and vomiting in front of Christabel. All I could do was say how awful, poor child, poor you and smile at Christabel for all I was worth. Then I'd get cunning and say something along the lines of 'Are you a little too warm, my petal? Betty's wrapped you up so cosily, hasn't she? Shall we maybe take this blanket off now? Are you feeling a little bit better? Just a bit? Hasn't Betty looked after you well – why, she's just about cured you. Do you think you're well enough to sit up now? Oh, good. Look, Betty, you've worked a miracle. She really does look better. Now, I've got this lovely funny story to read you Christabel. Listen.' And I'd read away, violently overacting, and Christabel would laugh and then I'd move on to getting her to stand up and finally turn to Betty, all innocence, and say, 'Do you know, I think maybe she's well enough to come with me after all. Do you think so, Christabel? Would you like that? You would? What do you think, Betty?'

There was nothing Betty could do but agree, through very tight lips. She would make a performance of wrapping Christabel up in the most ridiculous number of scarves and pixie hoods, and of giving me spare knickers for her which I was definitely going to need because there were bound to be accidents with the kiddie in the condition she was in and taking her so unwisely from a warm room into the raw January air . . . Christabel would get a kiss on the doorstep and then Betty would stand, arms akimbo, watching us go, obviously hoping the child would get caught short *en route* to my car. The relief of getting away made me quite faint every time. Sometimes Christabel would say, 'I think I'm going to be sick,' and I would stop the car in a side road and take all the smothering garments off her and wait a little while before going on.

Once we were at my flat there were no more problems. Within minutes Christabel would regain her normal colour and be bounding around and there was never a mention, not once, of needing to rush to the loo. Usually we spent an hour or so chatting and going through a box of so-called 'treasures', which I always managed to amass for her – bits of jewellery, little purses, anything decorative I'd seen on my travels – and she'd choose what she fancied. Then we went out for a bike ride which she adored. She couldn't have her bike at Betty's. There was nowhere for her to ride it and Betty didn't want it cluttering up the hall and scratching the paintwork with its handlebars, so I kept the bike, and if all normal methods failed it was always the final inducement to get her to come. It was a small two-wheeler with very fat wheels and stabilisers, and she was perfectly safe on it because it couldn't really go very fast or capsize. We put it in the boot of my car and drove to a park, and she was so happy trundling along ringing her bell furiously. We often had lunch out, usually spaghetti and ice-cream. Christabel apparently told Betty, indeed the whole Lowe household, about the bliss of knickerbocker glories at this Italian café we went to and she was always wanting Betty to go there. 'Do you think Mum could come one day?' she asked me, and remembering just in time who 'Mum' now was I said I didn't see why not.

The more I thought about it, the more absurd it was that I and the Blakes and Betty were all in these different compartments. It was hard enough for Christabel crossing all these real barriers every time she went from one home to another without her having to accept that none of us wanted to be altogether with her. But why not? Why couldn't Betty come to our café, or to my flat and have tea? So I asked her. I asked her if, next time I had Christabel, she would like to join us for lunch or tea and see where Christabel went when she was with me. 'I couldn't,' was the very swift answer. 'It wouldn't be right. Thank you for asking.'

'What wouldn't be right about it, Betty?' I asked.

'They wouldn't like it. And I'm busy Saturdays and Sundays, I couldn't really find the time, quite honestly, I couldn't really. I get ever such a lot done with Chrissie off my hands.' I wasn't sure what the truth was, but Betty must have told Maureen of my invitation because she brought it up when I next saw her.

'I hear you asked Betty to tea,' she said, smiling such an odd smile that I was at once on the defensive.

'Yes, what of it?'

'Well, it isn't really a good idea.'

'Why not? Is it a better one for us all to be enemies, fighting over Christabel?'

'Of course not. But you'd only confuse Christabel more, I'm afraid. She needs the demarcation lines.'

'You mean no fraternising between the enemy lines?'

'No, I don't mean that – it's you who talks about this as a battle, I'm afraid.'

'Isn't it one?'

'No.'

'Then it certainly feels like one to me, and one that's not getting very far either.'

'Things are moving at a normal pace. Actually, faster than normal. If it wasn't for Christabel being a ward of court, then they'd have moved a lot faster.' Maureen sniffed. It rankled that Mrs Blake had had Christabel made a ward of court the minute she realised she could not control her future. This meant everything to do with Christabel had to go through the Family Division and it drove the Council mad.

We'd had a very strange Case Conference soon after this move on Mrs Blake's part. She asked for it herself, sending Stella one of her magnificently cogent summaries of why one was needed. I have a copy of it, which, I remember at the time seemed to be masterly, but which strikes me now as dangerous in tone (but then I and the Blakes, were all still underestimating the Social Services Department).

'Purpose of meeting', Mrs Blake wrote: 'To clarify any misunderstanding between the various people involved in the proposed adoption of Christabel; to learn more about the procedure involved from those who will carry it out; to have explained the current thinking on suitable families; and to gain a consensus on the general direction of all concerned.' She then had a paragraph entitled: 'Particular concerns of Christabel's natural family.' These she summarised as 'Concern that the sheer weight of bureaucratic procedures may create not only delay but possibly a gridlock situation especially if the Council's Social Services Department proceeds to search for a large number of homes and then argue about the rival merits of each home (especially with regard to racial matching). The point of the wardship we took out, as we understand it, is that we, Christabel's natural family have some autonomy in this matter.' The last page of her letter held a list of all the questions she would like answered at the Case Conference.

1. What are the Council's assumptions about the necessary steps in the decision-making process to find Christabel a permanent home?
2. Whose views on this home do they seek?
3. What are the criteria by which a home will be judged?
4. Is it assumed a home must be found in London?
5. Will Christabel be consulted?
6. Will prospective adoptives meet Christabel before deciding if they wish to go ahead?
7. Will the natural family be allowed to meet them?

There was no reply, or acknowledgement, to this missive, but when Mrs Blake ranted and raved I took the Council's side. I privately imagined Stella or Maureen groaning at all this verbiage and wishing they could chuck it in the waste-paper basket, and really, they had a case. There they were, coping with quite terrible situations in which children were maltreated, or left utterly alone, and there was this middle-class old woman demanding time and attention they could not spare in a far from desperate set of circumstances. The Case Conference itself was enough, surely.

As soon as we were all seated – the usual crew – Mrs Blake said, 'Did you get my letter, may I ask?'

'We did indeed, Mrs Blake,' Stella-of-the-smile said.

'It was simply, as there was no response . . . I wondered . . .'

'*This* is the response, Mrs Blake. Now, if we're all ready I'll take Mrs Blake's questions one by one and answer them as best I can. In relation to Christabel's future placement the adoption officer in consultation with myself and Maureen . . .'

'But not with me,' Mrs Blake interrupted, already at her most haughty.

'No, not with you, Mrs Blake, not at this stage. If I could proceed?'

'Certainly, but I do think it rather remarkable, I must say, that already there seems to have been a preliminary consultative meeting deliberately excluding the child's own grandmother – quite extraordinary . . .'

'You did say I might proceed? Very well. This is a brief outline of our thinking at the moment. What we will be looking for, for Christabel, is a two-parent family, preferably middle-class. We think there should be at least a two-year difference in age between Christabel and any other child in this family and that Christabel needs to be the youngest in any family. It is now the end of January, which, with the busy matching timetable involved, together with the need for in-depth psychological reports on Christabel, makes us hesitate to anticipate being ready for the July adoption panel – we think we would be more realistic to estimate September.'

All sorts of vulgar phrases spring to mind to describe Mrs Blake's reaction to Stella's 'outline' – shit hitting the fan and all that sort of thing – but I think what I remember most clearly is the feeling of helplessness which seized me. I only half heard Mrs Blake's furious objections – to the ridiculous length of time, to the idea of psychological reports – because I felt so miserable, so wretched. All this could have been avoided if only Camilla or I had acted as we ought to have done, as we could have done. There was an expression on Stella's face of such very carefully controlled dislike, as though she was thinking we'd asked for all this, we deserved it, and to hell with us.

I was conscious of literally bowing my head. The painful memory of taking Christabel to Betty's that first time obliterated the sound of Mrs Blake's hectoring tones and I heard instead my own voice, strained and falsely bright, telling Christabel she was going to a lovely new home for a while until a permanent home was found for her where she would have a new mummy and daddy who would love her very much . . . Dear God, did I come out with all those disgustingly pat phrases? How could I have done? How could anyone who had a grain of sensitivity? And choosing my moment with such care, such *cowardice*, making sure there were only ten minutes or so to go before we set off for school and the lovely Miss Splint, who would pick up the pieces if Christabel's composure shattered.

But it did not appear to. She munched her toast and stared at me, dry-eyed. Yet again, she did not ask me any of the questions for which I'd been prepared. There was not a single 'Why?' Instead, she said, 'Will there be a telly at my new home?' I said, 'Of course.' Then she said, 'Will I be able to take my bike?' I said, 'Of course,' again (not knowing, at the time, that Betty wouldn't allow it). Then there was silence and she peeled a tangerine delicately. It was far more heartbreaking, I assure you, than wild sobs – to be so calm, so accepting, at five and a half years old, after all that had happened to her. I didn't need to come out with any of my heavily prepared explanations and justifications. And when it came to the moment of taking her to Betty's, with all her pathetic bags and toys, it was *my* stomach which seemed to be most affected, so much so that Christabel had to wait patiently for another half hour while I decided whether I was going to be sick again. I am sure that if at that moment she had flung herself into my arms and clung to me and said she was frightened and begged me to let her stay, then I would immediately have claimed her as my own with all the consequences (not, of course, that I would have been allowed to have her, but that was another fact I had yet to learn).

But there were no hysterics, no panic, and not the slightest attempt at pleading. Christabel merely waited patiently for me to get my courage up and then off we went. She even gave every appearance of anticipation, stepping out of the car quite eagerly and making her own way to the front door where I'd seen Betty already waiting for her. The handover went beautifully. 'My, you're a big girl,' Betty said admiringly. 'How old are you? Only five? Well, I never did, you look like you're seven. Are you coming in to see my Christmas tree? Eh? Do you like Christmas trees?' And Christabel took her hand and went into the ghastly living-room and stood admiring the huge, hideous tree as though it was the most lovely thing she'd ever seen. She appeared completely mesmerised by Betty, who never stopped chattering away, ignoring me completely. The television was put on immediately and Christabel was in raptures, hardly able to believe her luck. Then I left, without fuss, with the most perfunctory of goodbyes from Christabel, and went home.

I knew I ought to be glad and relieved. I felt neither. My flat seemed comfortless and dismal and unpleasantly empty. I'd taken care to make sure I was leaving for Paris the next day, not because I'd dreaded feeling suddenly lonely, but because I was cunning: should the handover not have gone well I wanted a cast-iron excuse not to be caught. I would have to go to Paris and somebody else would have to have Christabel in the event of any breakdown of what had been planned. It sounds so shabby – it was so shabby – but I had been prompted by a terrible fear that I was being trapped.

For three weeks I'd cared for Christabel and that was quite long enough to have ensnared me – one side of me, that is. Who could have known there were so many mothering skills in me? Such delight I took in the organising of Christabel's little world, the nurturing of her talents. Often in those weeks I used to find myself smiling and wishing Rowena could see the transformation I'd wrought in her child. She looked so bright and lively, those sulks and tantrums had quite gone, and there had been no nightmares. She adored the neatness of our home and drew extreme satisfaction from the regularity of our various routines. And I'd found, just as people say, that having her with me did push out the boundaries of my own life, and that those limitations it also imposed grew daily less important. I knew, in short, that I could do it. I could adopt Christabel and not only make her happy and square my conscience but enrich my own life.

Yet I let her be fostered by a stranger. As I sat listening to Mrs Blake attack Stella I could not believe I had been so cruel. And the consequence of my cruelty had very far from ended. I heard Mrs Blake ask how the Council adoption officer would set about finding a family for Christabel and felt faint when, among the methods mentioned, advertising was thought a possibility. I'd seen those advertisements – 'Adoption can give new depth of meaning to love' – that kind of headline in newspapers, followed by a winsome photograph of some child and a paragraph about how Gary, who has had a very unsettled life, needs to form a good relationship with adults he can trust and who have the emotional commitment to take him in ... But *Christabel*? Reduced to such humiliation. It was unbearable. Even as I was about to open my mouth and say so, Mrs Blake was shrieking her opposition and Stella was hurriedly intervening to say that actually, in this case, she didn't anticipate that kind of advertising would be either necessary or fruitful. They would begin the other way round, by looking through lists of prospective adoptives who had already been screened and wanted a child of Christabel's sex and age. She also said, in acid tones, that she was sure Mrs Blake would be relieved to hear that, whereas the middle-classes rarely fostered, they formed the bulk of adoptives. 'Not, of course,' she added, 'that I can guarantee Christabel's new family *will* be middle-class, because class won't be the most important factor.'

'What will be?' Mrs Blake rapped out (she really was the most alarming colour, I noticed – I'd been so absorbed in my own guilt that I'd failed to observe the alarming signs of physical distress in her).

'The character of the parents, naturally,' Stella said. 'We need exceptional people to respond to the needs of a child who has suffered as Christabel has suffered.'

'And is still suffering, quite unnecessarily,' Mrs Blake said, not at all mollified. 'Every day her stay in that woman's house is prolonged, her suffering is increased. Every time I see her, every time I am allowed a glimpse of my own granddaughter, I find further evidence of what she suffers. She can no longer speak correctly. She has forgotten how to read and write, she is saturated in what I can only call tabloid values and I shudder to think what all this is doing to a sensitive child.'

Then the poor old woman seemed to choke – it was quite dramatic and frightening. She put a hand to her throat and her eyes seemed to bulge and she seemed to strain upwards in her chair. There was pandemonium, with Stella rushing to get water and Maureen loosening Mrs Blake's jacket buttons and Camilla rummaging through her mother's handbag in search of pills. After a few minutes, order was restored. Mrs Blake's complexion went from a purple-tinged red to a greyish white and she appeared quite exhausted. Camilla took her home, helped to the car by Maureen and Phyllis, the adoption officer, and I found myself left for a moment with Stella who was clearly shaken.

'Goodness,' she said, 'I thought she'd had a stroke. That was very nasty, I must say.'

'She's not as strong as she seems,' I ventured.

'You've known her a long time, have you?' Stella said. It did not escape my attention that she had expressed no sympathy for Mrs Blake, which so annoyed me, I found I had a new desire to stick up for the old woman, so I said, 'Yes, since I was a child, actually. She's an amazing woman really. I used to think she was like one of the suffragettes, really fierce and ready to stand up for her rights.'

'I can see that,' Stella interrupted.

'. . . But she's not as hard as she appears. You'd never know, from these meetings, how terribly upset she is – it all comes out as anger.'

'Oh, I don't need to be told that,' Stella said, quite sharply. 'I can see that for myself, but it doesn't make her easy to deal with.'

'No. She isn't easy.' I saw no harm in conceding that. 'But she cares passionately about Christabel.'

'We all do, I hope.'

'But not quite in the way her grandmother does. She's old and much frailer than she looks, and I suppose she's afraid she might die before Christabel's settled. She sees it as her duty to see her settled, and I think it secretly terrifies her that she might fail . . .'

I stopped because Stella was shuffling papers about on her desk and had refixed her smile. I knew she wasn't listening. She didn't care about Mrs Blake at all, didn't even really believe she was motivated by concern for her granddaughter. She thought, pure and simple, that Mrs Blake was a snob, a pest, an irritation that she and her department could do without. When I'd stopped speaking she said, 'Sorry?' in an encouraging tone, but I didn't continue. 'It does seem wrong,' I burst out instead, 'that a grandmother can't decide what should happen to her granddaughter.'

'It depends on the grandmother,' Stella said, then added hurriedly, 'quite apart from the legal position, which safeguards the child.'

'So if Mrs Blake had been a different person you'd have let her have more say?'

'Not at all. The law decides her say, as you put it, not us. But clearly, now we're nearing the stage of looking for a permanent family for Christabel, Mrs Blake's personality will be of some importance.'

'How?'

'Well, she's a strong-minded lady and I can't imagine any parents wanting to take her on as well as Christabel. We're going to have access problems, obviously.'

'You mean she might not be allowed to see Christabel after she's adopted?'

'That will be up to the new family. Adoption means a complete new start and contact with the natural family and even with friends from the child's past isn't always wise.'

'But Christabel's past can't just be wiped out,' I said angrily. 'She can't just have her grandmother *banished*.'

'She can,' Stella said, looking me straight in the eye. 'If her new family think contact is not a good idea, if they feel her grandmother distresses her or exerts undue influence or imperils their own relationship with Christabel. Everything is for the sake of the child, not the grandmother, and so it should be, surely.'

I left the Social Services office feeling stunned. Did Mrs Blake know all this? Did Camilla? Did they realise that giving Christabel up for adoption – not that there was really any 'giving up' since legally she did not belong to them – meant they might never see her again? They had a solicitor, they must know. The chances of the new family taking Mrs Blake to their hearts were, I could see, slim. She was not an immediately attractive person and moreover she was threatening. One look at her, one earful, and anyone would sense trouble. It was not just Betty, because of all the class hostility, who found Mrs Blake intimidating – everyone did. She was abrupt, bossy, cold, and very demanding. It took years to appreciate her true worth, to recognise that a great deal of the unfortunate hectoring manner was a cover for a curious brand of shyness, the sort that is not wistful and charming, but, instead, a deeply buried lack of the very confidence that it artificially projected. Mrs Blake *expected* to be disliked and she acted up to her own expectations. And her obvious cleverness, which she could never resist flashing – she'd say things to Maureen like 'I suppose you've read the Hart Report on "Mixed Race Gender" problems?' knowing damned well Maureen had never heard of it – antagonised everyone. I could easily envisage quite disastrous meetings with prospective adoptives unless Mrs Blake totally changed her character, and how could she do that? Slowly, the real contest was looming ahead. I could see another kind of battle coming, and I remember thinking how lucky it was that Mrs Blake was rich.

CHAPTER SEVEN

It was towards the end of February, or maybe the beginning of March, that I fell foul of Maureen. God knows, she wasn't exactly a fan of mine at the best of times, but over the months since Christabel was taken into care we had at least learned how to get along. Compared to the Blakes, I suppose, I was preferable, and when Camilla went off on another tour, soon after Christmas, I suppose I was easier to deal with than Mrs Blake. She, in any case, had gone back to Edinburgh for a month to recuperate. She waived her right to one of her fortnightly access visits and hoped to trade in the time for a long weekend when Camilla returned and she herself came back to London. I was, during this period, the Blake representative, if you like.

As such, I had Christabel for a couple of overnight stays and it was during one of them that Fergus called, completely without warning. I've known Fergus Donaldson nearly as long as I knew Rowena. He was a friend of mine initially because he was a friend of hers. He arrived on my doorstep, smiling, in anticipation of what a surprise he would give me and was surprised himself when I answered the door accompanied by Christabel. He knew her, of course, though I don't suppose he had seen her more than three or four times.

During the period when Rowena was planning to become pregnant I'd been going through one of my not infrequent phases of being very involved with Fergus and I'd talked of nothing else but my fury with her. Fergus's attitude had been interesting. I'd thought he would be outraged at the idea of men, or one man, being used in the blatant way Rowena intended, but he wasn't. I asked him if *he* would like the thought of fathering a child without knowing it and then being excluded from the father role. He groaned and said I took everything far too seriously and that my feminism was too extreme. That drove me wild. I remember shouting furiously at him that it was Rowena who was being extreme, not me, and then we wrangled about it every time we met. Once Christabel was born and Rowena seemed so happy and my hostility weakened, Fergus could not resist a little told-you-so session. I lambasted him for that too, pointing out that just because Rowena was fulfilled, this in no way diminished the responsibility she'd taken on nor weakened my belief that a child is entitled to its father as well as its mother. But Fergus regarded his argument – that women with a strong maternal urge should fulfil it – as proven and nothing would make him concede there were prohibitive dangers in the carrying out.

He knew nothing of Rowena's death. Fergus is a botanist and is forever going off on expeditions to exotic-sounding locations in the Himalayas or South America, and he'd just been with a university research team to the Philippines. I remember how excited he was about this trip, not just because of the work involved but because of the other people, all of whom he regarded highly. He also judged it might be the last trip of this kind he would ever be asked to join in the current climate of research-funding and was thrilled to be able to take this last chance. So he had been out of the country since before Rowena was killed and I had had no address to which to write. Not that he was a good correspondent – from all the expeditions he'd been on I don't think I had had more than four letters and I'd been discouraged from replying to them because he'd always said there was no sure point for picking up mail. I doubt if I would have written anyway – it is horrible breaking the news of that kind of death and I preferred to do it face-to-face or not at all. I suppose, at the back of my mind, I'd realised Fergus would show up some time and would have to be told, but it had not worried me. He wasn't a close friend of Rowena's and though I knew he would be shocked, and concerned about her child, there was no point in pretending he would be likely to suffer deeply.

Funnily enough, I'd often thought of him during those difficult weeks. Firstly, I'd thought of him because he would have been useful. When he isn't away on trips he is very much available and he would have been someone objective with whom to discuss things. Then, he is so good with children and I do not say that lightly. He has a natural affinity with small children and doesn't even have to try – there is no need, on his part, for the false heartiness to be seen in so many adult men. He doesn't throw children up in the air or try to attract their attention with tricks or make a play for them with too obvious silliness. He is just his calm, benign self and they like his square, mild face and even his spectacles do not put them off. He's such a *slow* person, in everything he does, and maybe it is this which makes him unthreatening to them. It is the most appalling waste that he is not a father himself.

So Fergus stood on the doorstep and beamed and saw Christabel, and assumed Rowena was there too. It was very hard to tell him what had happened in front of the child but, on the other hand, I was afraid of doing more damage by concealing the truth. I could not send Christabel to bed and then tell him, because he said straight away, 'How's the fair lady Rowena?' And I had to say she was dead, that she'd been dead for four months. Fergus automatically picked up Christabel and sat her on his knee, producing from his pocket what looked like a handful of berries but which were actually pretty, coloured stones he'd brought for me. She played with them delightedly, setting them out in patterns on the table, and I told the sad tale as briefly as possible.

It was some time since I'd gone through it and I couldn't help noticing how I had subtly changed the telling. When it first happened and I had to tell people, people like Maureen and Miss Splint, I'd brushed aside all the details of the accident itself, but now, to Fergus, I found myself dwelling on them and could not understand why I should be doing so. I described the Red Pike path, told him how it was like a ladder of stones, and of how the variation from the path, which Rowena had taken, climbs alongside Sour Milk Gill, snaking its way up beside the beautiful cascades of the waterfall. I described the brilliant red of the soil on the east side of the Gill and the four-foot slimy rock step upon which Rowena missed her footing and crashed to her death. I even told Fergus what a beautiful day it had been, of how both lakes – Buttermere and Crummock Water – visible from the path, had been a deep, unlikely blue and the oranges and reds of the wooded fellsides had been more vivid than I had ever seen them. And when I'd finished, I found I was weeping as I had never done at the time.

'My God,' Fergus said, softly. There was a pause. I wiped my eyes and sprang up to make him some coffee. I could hear Christabel counting the stones, apparently ignoring what had been said. When I came back with the coffee Fergus said, 'So you took Christabel. I might have known you would. It's just what Rowena would have hoped. She never really approved of her sister, did she?'

'My new mum's called Betty,' Christabel suddenly said, very distinctly, 'and my dad is Norman, but you can call him Norm, he doesn't mind.'

'You can call me Ferg,' Fergus said, 'I don't mind either.'

'Betty and Norman are Christabel's foster-parents,' I said.

'Till I go to my permanent home and have my bike,' Christabel said. She struggled over 'permanent' as she did every time. It made me squirm each time she used it and I cursed Maureen for instructing me to describe her adoptive home in that way – I'd rather she had been taught straight out to say 'when I am adopted'.

'What colour is your bike?' Fergus asked.

'Red.'

'Have you got a bell?'

'Yes. And a basket on the front.'

'And a bottle with a straw in it?'

'No!' Christabel turned round to look at him.

'You need a bottle with juice in it for when you're thirsty with biking hard. I'll get you one tomorrow and fix it on.'

She went to bed in ecstasies at the thought. The last thing she asked before she fell asleep was if Fergus would stay the night so that he would be there first thing in the morning and they could go straight out and buy the bottle. I said I thought he would be. And he was. He didn't sleep with me but he stayed the night and we talked through most of it. 'She's such a lovely child,' he kept saying. 'I'd like her for myself.'

'And what would you do with her when you go off for months on end?' I challenged him.

'Oh, find someone to care for her, I suppose. Or not go away, find some other sort of work.'

'A likely story,' I said, scornfully.

'What? You don't believe that if I had a daughter like Christabel I would change my life?'

'No, I don't.'

'Well, I would. She'd be put first.'

'Rubbish.'

'There speaks a guilty conscience.'

'What have I got to be guilty about?'

'You know.'

'I do *not*. Rowena wasn't my sister.'

'But you were like a sister to her.'

'Oh, Fergus, don't be so ridiculous. You're exaggerating, romancing. We weren't in the least sisterly.'

'She depended on you, looked up to you. You know she did.'

'I was useful to her sometimes, that's all.'

'You were the only fixed point in her life, her point of reference.'

'I think you've been away too long. You're thinking of old Edinburgh days, you're getting confused.'

'No, I'm not, though I am thinking of Edinburgh too. Do you remember when you came through that time for Rowena's eighteenth? And we had to carry her to bed she was so drunk. And you told her mother you thought she'd been overworking and had collapsed with exhaustion and she actually believed it. You were always taking charge of her.'

'I was always bossy, you mean. So?'

'So she liked it. I quite liked it myself. I still do. I look forward to coming back and having you boss me, make me less of a slob. And so did Rowena.'

'Well, she's dead.'

'And Christabel is very much alive. You must have been tempted, whatever you say.'

'No, I was not,' I lied. 'I was not tempted. I love Christabel, but I don't want to be a mother.'

'You do.'

'I don't.'

'You'd make a wonderful mother.'

'I'd make a dreadful mother and anyway that is not the point, Fergus. You haven't been listening. I didn't have the choice, nobody did. Christabel is a ward of court and she's in care. I have no claim on her at all.'

'I can't believe that.'

'It's the truth. And I keep having to tell you, it doesn't make any difference, I couldn't take her on anyway. I couldn't and I wouldn't.'

The next morning, Fergus took Christabel to a bike shop and bought her a water bottle to clip on the front of her beloved bike, and then the two of them went to Richmond Park in the car, Fergus's car, and had a long bike ride. She came back glowing, her skin gleaming with all the cold air and her eyes shining. Then I took her back to Betty's and for the first time she was a little quiet. She asked if she'd see Fergus again and I said I was sure she would and that if she would like it I would ask him over the next time she came for an overnight stop. She nodded enthusiastically.

I thought no more of it. Two days later Maureen rang and asked if I could come into the office because she had 'something serious' to discuss. I couldn't go that day but I went the next, worried that there was yet another hitch in the adoption process or that the psychologist had found something disturbing in Christabel's behaviour (we had been unable to arrest the carrying out of the 'in-depth' profile the Social Services wanted).

Maureen looked grave. She didn't smile when she said, 'Good morning,' nor did she offer me coffee. She stayed behind her nasty little desk and clasped her hands in front of her; clearing her throat, repeatedly. It was like being in the headmistress's office and I resented it. Quite deliberately, I sat on the edge of her desk in a chummy, casual way to show I was not going to be treated like a child.

'What's up?' I said.

'It seems there has been a breach of the care agreement,' she said, sternly.

'What care agreement?'

'Not exactly an official agreement but the clear understanding on which you had Christabel for the night.'

'What the hell are you talking about?'

'When I inspected your premises, prior to it being cleared as a place of safety for Christabel, you told me you lived alone.'

'I do.'

'Yet it seems a man stayed with you the night you were in charge of Christabel.'

'Yes, that's true.'

'You should have informed me.'

'What, that an old friend dropped in? Don't be absurd.'

'It also seems this man took Christabel *alone* to Richmond for the morning on Saturday.'

'Also true. He bought her a water bottle for her bike. Is there anything wrong with that? Then he took her for a bike ride. She loved it.'

'That is beside the point. Christabel is in care and she is a ward of court – she is not *allowed* to go off with strange men.'

'He isn't strange. He grew up in Edinburgh with her mother. He's known Christabel since she was born.'

'Is he a relative?'

'No, he's a friend, an old family friend.'

'Unless he is a relative, and even then permission would be needed, no man should be with Christabel alone, nor any woman for that matter. She was at risk, and I don't know what I'm going to say to Stella.'

'At risk? You're being *ridiculous*. Where was the risk? For God's sake, he only took her for a ride on a Saturday morning in a public park.'

'It isn't what he did with her that matters . . .'

'I would have thought that is precisely what matters. You're implying he might have sexually abused her by the sound of all this fuss.'

'No, I am not. What I'm saying is that Christabel was allowed to be with you and no one else and that you ought to have understood this. Suppose there had been an accident, a car accident, and Christabel had been injured. Who do you think would have been blamed? The social worker, me, that's who. Who was this strange man, the court would have asked? Had he been vetted? Was he a suitable custodian? Don't you see? Can't you appreciate how careful we have to be for Christabel's sake?'

She was more upset – her face was blotchy with distress – than angry and that made me realise I had been careless, that I should indeed have anticipated this reaction. And it did have some justification. So I apologised. Maureen, clearly vastly relieved, accepted it, stiffly. I suggested she should come and meet Fergus in case Christabel met him again. She said that wouldn't be necessary. I said, surely it would. 'After all you've said, you're not now going to take him on trust, are you?'

'I don't need to,' she said, 'because Christabel can on no account go out with him again, nor stay with you if he is co-habiting with you.'

'Just a minute, he is not "co-habiting" – what a stupid word – he is neither living with me nor sleeping with me. He slept on a sofa in the sitting-room.'

'I have only your word for that and in any case the point is he was in your flat overnight, the same night as Christabel. It can't be allowed.'

'Why not? Come on, why not? I won't let it go like that, I just won't. If, as you claim, you are not suspecting Fergus of evil practices, why should his presence be taboo? What other suspicion can lie behind your objections?'

'It's a technical matter . . .'

'Then let's be technical. Which law, which rule, can you produce to show me that friends of mine, friends of Christabel herself, cannot take her for a bike ride?'

'They have to be approved, everyone who comes into contact with her has to be known to us.'

'I've just invited you to meet Fergus.'

'It's too late, the damage is done.'

'What damage? What *is* this: where does damage come into it, for Christ's sake?'

'Christabel had nightmares.'

'*What*?'

'She had nightmares for the first time, Betty says.'

'Oh, I see, "Betty says". Why didn't you begin with that? I might have guessed Betty had *said* something, and how you all jump when she does, you'd think she was in control of you, not the other way round, you're all terrified of her, you spend your entire time humouring her . . .'

'I think you'd better leave.'

'No. I refuse. I refuse to leave this miserable place until I've at least heard what dear Betty said.'

'She said Christabel woke screaming and had wet the bed and said she dreamt a man ran away with her to the underground place where dead people go, but they couldn't find her mother.'

'I see. She dreams of a man and instantly it is Fergus, whom in actual fact she adores.'

'Betty says she took hours to calm down and then it came out she'd been on her bike with a man whose name she couldn't remember except it was "furry". So Betty naturally questioned her and it came out about your friend.'

'And that proves the case, does it?'

'It proves she was disturbed by the events of the day. She hasn't had a nightmare before.'

'Then she should have done. That's what's been wrong all this time, she *should* have been letting out all her fear and distress, it's good that it's coming out, that Fergus relaxed her enough for some of it to come out.'

'That's arguable.'

'Everything is arguable, every bloody thing, and that's why it's outrageous to blame Fergus and not to meet him and clear him and let him be part of Christabel's life.'

'I'm sorry, but that's the line I have to take. I'll make a full report for Stella . . .'

'Well, I'll make one too, for Stella and Mr Wavell and whomever you damned well like.'

And I slammed out of the office, out of the building. I went home and phoned Fergus and he came round. I wished he hadn't. He spent an hour upbraiding me for my folly. He was appalled at my antagonistic approach. 'What did you expect the social worker to say?'

'If you're so smart, why didn't you point out what she'd say? It was you who suggested taking Christabel out.'

'I didn't understand the set-up properly, *you* did.'

'Thanks for your support.'

'I do support you, but not your bull-at-a-gate approach. You have very little tact, Isobel.'

'I despise tact.'

'You've always been able to afford to. Now, you can't. For the first time you're in a situation where tact can work miracles and you're too pig-headed to use it, too proud.'

'I hate Maureen and Stella and all of them.'

'They're only doing their job.'

'What a cliché.'

'What do you think they should do, then? Let Christabel, a child in their care, go off with any old unsupervised person?'

'They should trust me.'

'Why?'

'They know me, they've known me for months, they've seen how I've cared for Christabel, how I *do* care for her, they should trust my judgement – if I let a friend take her out they should know that friend is reputable.'

'That would be abdicating their responsibility. I admire them for being so careful, actually.'

'They haven't been particularly careful. It was Betty making trouble that made them care.'

'Why should this Betty make trouble?'

'Because she's competitive, she wants Christabel to love her best.'

'She only reported an unusual violent nightmare, which seems

143

good fostering to me. She might even be right. Maybe I was the cause of it, maybe Christabel is secretly afraid of someone taking her off to the land of the dead to find her mother. Maybe in her nightmare this man had my face?'

'Now you're being silly.'

'No, I'm exploring the imaginative possibilities. I think you should write a very humble letter of apology and explanation – explanation, not justification. I think you've behaved badly, worse than how you've described Mrs Blake.'

Eventually, with Fergus's help, I did indeed write, not a report, as I'd so pompously promised, but a letter of grovelling apology. Then I went with Fergus to Betty's, unannounced. It was his idea. I wasn't supposed just to turn up at Betty's, but Fergus persuaded me that in this instance it was forgivable. And he took charge. I stood aside when Betty opened the door and let him do the talking. Fergus was quite at ease. He wasn't greasy or smooth or unctuous, just quiet and polite and anxious. He told Betty who he was and said he'd come to apologise in person for upsetting Christabel without in the least meaning to. He said he could quite see, now, the danger of doing what he did and was truly sorry. Betty stared at him – never once looked at me – and then suddenly said, 'Haven't I seen you on the telly?' Fergus said she might have done, that he had been on a few programmes talking about an expedition he'd been on where he'd found one of the rarest orchids in . . .' and Betty interrupted to shout, '*Wogan*! That's it, innit? You was on *Wogan*, last week.'

We were then invited in, Betty quite flushed. Norman was lolling the morning away in front of the television, watching some schools natural history programme, so of course Fergus was well away. He didn't have to ingratiate himself, though – Betty and Norman did that. They asked him questions about flowers of quite staggering banality and he answered all of them in great detail. And they liked him, I could see at once. His style of clean shabbiness they found endearing and his soft Scottish accent – he was originally from Ayrshire – did not distance him from them the way Mrs Blake's precise Edinburgh vowels did. He drank tea, too, with sugar, and let his mug be refilled.

Christabel wasn't there, of course, since it was a school day, and nor were any of the other children. Betty eventually said she would ring Maureen and tell her she thought Fergus was a suitable person for Christabel to go out with occasionally and that it would be all right by her.

'It ain't up to me, mind,' she added, 'them social workers have their own ways, and you've put their backs up proper.' She sniffed loudly and looking at me, said, 'You want to take a few lessons, Isobel. I thought you had more sense. It don't do no good shouting at Maureen, you know.'

I blushed, but wasn't so naive as to ask how Betty knew I'd shouted at Maureen. 'I was angry,' I said.

'Oh, we all get angry,' Betty said. 'God knows, I've got enough to be angry about myself, haven't I? Haven't I, Norman?'

Norman said she had.

'What I have to put up with,' Betty went on, 'what with that Gran and them social workers all on at me and me trying to do my best. It's a good job I'm fond of Chrissie or I couldn't stand the interference, I really couldn't. And we haven't got to the worst bit yet.'

'The worst bit?' I echoed.

'When the adoption visits start. You don't know nothing, do you? When they decide who's going to have Chrissie, and she meets them, and then they have this palaver of her going to their house for the day and then for a night, and oh God, it's terrible. What a fuss they always make, clinging to me and that and not wanting to leave and I get that upset.'

'She does, she takes on something awful,' said Norman.

'I can't help it. 'Course, I'm trained not to bond with them, but however hard you try, it ain't no good. You do bond, I don't think you'd be any good if you didn't.'

'You get too fond of them,' Norman said. 'It's only natural, specially with the little ones like Chrissie.'

Betty brought this little outburst to an end by saying she would have to get off to the shops. Fergus offered to give her a lift and to my surprise she accepted (I'd offered her lifts several times and she'd refused them with the air of turning down an indecent suggestion). She sat in the front with him and explained all the way to Sainsbury's how Norman had lost his licence some years back and had resolved to 'end it all' and never drive again because he'd nearly killed someone, though it wasn't his fault. Fergus said he knew how Norman felt, because he'd actually killed a man in Greece, though it wasn't his fault either, and he'd thought he could never get into a driving seat again. Betty asked about the man who was killed, Fergus trotted out the details (none of which I'd ever heard), and Betty commented on them . . .

When finally we dropped her off, I accused him of being an old woman, the way he'd gossiped and droned on. Or was it deliberate? Was it all the Fergus-brown-nose job? He said it wasn't deliberate, he found chatting to Betty easy and she was 'fascinating'.

'Oh, for Christ's sake, Fergus – "fascinating"!'

'I really think she is. Fostering all those children, all the rejects and tragic cases, and rehabilitating so many of them by the sound of it. It takes courage.'

'It's a job.'

'Well, you phrased that a little better than saying she does it for the money, which is lucky, because she clearly doesn't.'

'I don't know how you can be so sure on one half-hour meeting.'

'I'm a good judge of character.'

That made me laugh, just because he was so very pleased with himself. But then Fergus had always been quite pleased with himself, not in any smug way, simply comfortable and happy with his life. When I first knew him I'd thought this could only mean he was complacent and dull, lacking in that ambition I thought everyone should have to be interesting, but later I revised my opinion and came to envy him his content-ment. That was when he came to London to do his post-graduate studies, soon after Rowena and I had set up house together. He was Rowena's friend, someone I'd only met during school days when I'd gone back to Edinburgh to stay with her, and of whom I'd never been too sure. I'd assumed that, since Rowena was so free with her favours, she and Fergus would have had some kind of liaison in their past, but no, they hadn't. 'He's too clever,' Rowena had said, to which I'd replied that cleverness had nothing to do with going to bed with people. 'Oh, it has,' I remember she said, 'it has a lot to do with it. Fergus is too clever ever to have got entangled with me, he knew I'd latch on to him. And I would have done. I think he's perfect.' Well, he wasn't perfect, but he was attractive in every way and did not prove too clever to get into bed with me. But then he divined, without being told, that I certainly would not latch on to him, that I would not expect more than he wanted to give. I think we were both very surprised to discover how much we came to care for each other.

Was I in love with Fergus? Was he in love with me? Rowena always said it was obvious, that it was Yes to both questions. As we drove home, to my home, I found myself wondering all over again though we were supposed to have settled this conundrum a year ago when Fergus said he thought we should marry, or if not marry set up house together, acknowledge a long-standing relationship in some way. I'd said I didn't want to, that it seemed fine to me to continue just as we had always done, off and on, for the last decade or so. He went away on his expeditions, I went off on my foreign trips, we met whenever we were both in London and lived together spasmodically. I thought that seemed fine, asked him why he wanted to change such an excellent arrangement. 'Because we're thirty-five,' he'd said. 'We're not kids anymore. I've changed, I can feel myself changing, I want stability and the certainty of a future with you. And I would like children.'

The rest of that argument had hinged on this last wish. I'd said I definitely did not want children and Fergus had said how could I know until I'd had them. That was so stupid, I'd let fly. What did he want me to do? Have a few trial children and then say, sorry, a mistake, and send them to the Battersea Dogs' Home? He'd said I was deliberately misunderstanding him and that was how it had ended.

If only Fergus had been Christabel's father. When Rowena

had been considering artificial insemination she'd come up with the suggestion herself, asking me if I thought Fergus could be persuaded to oblige. I'd been furious, disgusted. But now I wished I'd gone along with the idea. After all, Fergus wanted children. I suddenly said to him, as we drove along, 'Why don't you adopt Christabel?'

'They wouldn't let me. But I would like to.'

'Really? Or you're just saying that because you know they wouldn't even consider a single man?'

'No, I'd like to. I like children. It doesn't look as if I'm going to father any of my own, so it might make more sense to father other peoples, especially Rowena's.'

'You like the image of being a good Samaritan.'

'Isobel, sometimes you're not just sharp you're *nasty*.'

'I know.'

'Anyway, I would like to adopt Christabel.'

'How would you manage, supposing they'd let you – I know they wouldn't, you're right, but for the sake of argument, how would you cope?'

'I'd have a nanny, full time. And my mother and sisters would rally round, they'd love it. Widowers manage, divorcees manage.'

'With difficulty. It wouldn't be as good as a proper family environment.'

'Of course not. A child benefits from having both a father and a mother, it's entitled to both.'

'Then Christabel should never have been born.'

'Well, she was, and she ought to come out of all this tragedy with some gain.'

We were home by then. It was still only lunchtime. Fergus cooked an omelette – he likes cooking – and we opened a bottle of wine. It was one of those winter-is-coming-to-an-end-soon days which are so frequent in London (and often an illusion). The sun flooded into my living-room, and I suppose it was the heat as well as the brilliance of the light which induced our feeling of well-being, not to mention the wine. We gravitated automatically to bed and made love all afternoon, with a degree of passion absent for a long time. Then, to my own dismay, I cried. Hard. For fully half an hour. Fergus got up and brought me some coffee and I drank it, choking and hiccuping and saying I didn't know what was wrong with me, this was ridiculous.

'All this fierceness, Isobel,' Fergus said, 'it's obvious what's wrong with you. It's simple. You're upset, you're in a permanent state of distress because of Christabel. What's so terrible in admitting it?'

'I do admit it,' I said, lying back on the pillow, the tears still leaking, quietly now, down my face. 'It's all *wrong*. She's so sweet and pathetic and there she is, being shunted around, not knowing what's going to happen and Rowena dead.'

'She's resilient, she's a survivor. You only have to look at her to see that. Once she's settled . . .'

'But exactly, she isn't settled, and can you imagine what kind of family those social workers are going to dredge up for her?'

Fergus switched a lamp on. It was getting dark, though not dark enough to close the curtains. He went through into the shower and then came back and got dressed. I lay watching him, feeling utterly exhausted. He dressed slowly and methodically, doing his shirt buttons up with all the care of a small boy who has just mastered the art. He pulled his sweater on, tousling his thick fair hair even more, and then looked around for his spectacles. He is not massively short-sighted, but he feels happier wearing them. He is the only person I know who suits spectacles. They are those light sort, gold-rimmed, a variation on granny-glasses, and they somehow soften his rather square face. Then he brushed his hair back with his fingers – I hate men who comb their hair – and came and sat on the bed.

'You're a nice man, Fergus,' I found myself saying.

'And you're a nice woman, Isobel, whatever you may think,' he replied, half mocking. Then he said, 'And to complete the mutual niceness, Christabel is a nice child. We are all,' he said slowly, taking my hands, 'made for each other. Why don't we get married and apply to adopt Christabel? Who could refuse us?'

I said not a word. I stared at him, not removing my hands from his. I squeezed these hands and sighed and said, 'Neat. It would be neat. But I don't think I could do it, Fergus. I don't want to be a wife and I don't want to be a mother, but I think I do love you and I probably always have. I'd like to live with you. I said I wouldn't, but now I would. But it's just something really strong in me that resists marriage and motherhood. Oh, I don't know, I don't know what it is, but it's real, I can't ignore it. It's like a warning I hear all the time – don't do it, don't do it. And I'm not brave enough to take on Christabel for life, I'm frightened, it's too big a burden, I'd feel completely weighed down, I haven't that amount of self-sacrifice in me. You have, I haven't. It would be most noble to do, the right thing, but I haven't got it in me.'

I hate emotional outbursts such as that one – I cringe as I recall it. It is not *me*. Even as I was making this ghastly little speech I was thinking it couldn't be me, and yet every word, as precisely as I can remember, was true.

Fergus smiled, not a bit put out and certainly not responding with any emotion of his own. 'We'll leave it,' he said, looking for his jacket, 'for the moment, anyway.'

'I won't change my mind.'

'No, I know you won't, but circumstances could change it for you.'

'How?'

'I don't know. But circumstances do change all the time and that's why you should never say you won't change your mind. You have to change it, or what looks like change it, when what made it up in the first place changes.'

'Oh, we *are* deep this afternoon.'

'Yup. Well, I'll be off. Shall I come round this evening?'

'Of course.'

'With a bag or two?'

'With as many bags as you like.'

So that was how we came together again and I was glad about it. Whatever was wrong with me, I suddenly did not relish so much being on my own. Having Fergus around was an enormous help, stopped me feeling so edgy and tense. It was not only that his was a calming presence, but that I no longer had the feeling of total responsibility for Christabel. He was more than willing to assume a share of it and when Camilla and Mrs Blake were both back, they too welcomed his involvement. Mrs Blake had always approved of Fergus, or so she said, and was very eager to discuss strategy with him. Unlike her own daughter and myself, he seemed to be able to handle her firmly, to tell her to tone down her approach and use some diplomacy, particularly over relations with Betty. It was Fergus who suggested Mrs Blake might knit something for Betty whose fortieth birthday, Christabel had told us, was on March 20th.

'She doesn't deserve it,' Mrs Blake said at first, glaring. 'She has caused nothing but trouble.'

'Then show her you are capable of rising above it,' Fergus said. 'Show her what a kind person you are.'

'I should not like to knit the kind of vulgar garment she wears.'

'Then knit her something the same only different, choose the pink or blue she likes but a different design.'

'It isn't the colour, it isn't the design, it's the materials she goes in for – nylon and Courtelle and acrylic – horrible.'

'Well, knit her a blue cardigan in good, soft wool. Isobel will help you choose.'

Extremely grudgingly, Mrs Blake went with me to Oxford Street, and in John Lewis's we bought the wool and a pattern. She knitted furiously, frowning all the time, and when she had finished the cardigan she chose some gilt buttons 'that woman would like' for it. I'm afraid Betty's reception of this present was not all Fergus had hoped for. I took Mrs Blake over, by arrangement of course, to collect Christabel for one of her, by then, rare overnight stops with her grandmother at Camilla's. The cardigan was beautifully wrapped, first in tissue paper, then in one of those classy William Morris wrapping papers, the ones which are copies of the wallpapers, and a blue ribbon adorned the top. Mrs Blake produced it from her bag as soon as we were all formally seated in the, by now, familiar living-room – Betty perched, as ever, on the very edge of her chair – and said, 'I believe it is your birthday tomorrow, Mrs Lowe,' and handed the present over.

'Who told you?' Betty said, rather accusingly, as though

this was very private information, which should not have been divulged.

'Christabel.'

'Ooh, that Chrissie, she has a tongue on her . . . she ought never to have done no such thing, wait till she comes down, and I'll give her what for.'

Mrs Blake's lips tightened, as much over Betty's grammar as her apparent lack of appreciation. She coughed irritably.

'You got a cold?' Betty asked, the parcel still unwrapped. 'I hope our Chrissie don't catch it, she's just over one as it is, had me up all night, coughing away.'

'I have a dry throat,' Mrs Blake said, 'it is very warm in here.'

'I like the place warm, we never stint on warmth, not with Norman with his chest. Well, I must say, this is a surprise,' Betty said, fiddling with the ribbon on the parcel. 'Ever so nicely wrapped up, whatever it is, not that I want anything from anybody.'

There was silence. I could hear Christabel coming down the stairs with her bag, singing as she came. Betty opened the parcel and shook out the cardigan. It really was a lovely piece of work, exquisitely knitted. For a moment her face softened and she stroked the wool and marvelled at how light the garment was. 'It's lovely,' she said, 'it really is, you shouldn't of, you really shouldn't of.' She spread it out on her knee and smoothed it down, and probably all would have been well and some measure of cordiality established as a result, if Christabel had not at that moment come in, rushed across the room and flung her arms round her grandmother. Mrs Blake was quite startled, but also, of course, delighted and even managed to respond.

'Well,' Betty said, 'thank you, I must say. But there was no need, I've plenty of cardigans. Are you ready, Chrissie?'

'Yes, Mum,' Christabel said.

'Now, I want her back early Sunday afternoon to get ready for school, all right? She'll be tired and I'll be tired what with the party and that.'

'I'm going to Mum's party,' Christabel said to her grandmother.

'Oh, no you're not, miss,' Betty said fiercely. 'You'll be at your gran's.'

'But I want to go to your party!' Christabel wailed, and left Mrs Blake to go to Betty, who literally pushed her away, gave her a little shove back to her grandmother.

'Well, you can't, not now it's your gran's turn. It ain't my fault, so don't you start grizzling. My party's tomorrow and tomorrow you're still at your gran's and that's that. Now, stop it – stop it! I said no grizzling. Your gran don't want to take no grizzling little girl away with her. Got your bag? Got your doll? Right, off with you, I've plenty to do.'

Christabel cried all the way to Camilla's. I was so furious with Betty I could hardly keep quiet, but I knew I must. Even more, I knew I must defend Betty, try to justify her behaviour to lessen Christabel's distress. It was weary work, and Mrs Blake didn't approve but at least she kept quiet and I think realised how important it was to reinstate Christabel's foster-mother in her eyes. So we went over and over Betty's own disappointment that Christabel, whom she loved so much, wouldn't be at her party and how it was no one's fault, that arrangements were made by Maureen and sometimes they got muddled, and that Betty hadn't really been cross, only upset. 'But she *is* cross,' Christabel sobbed. 'I know she is.' I said she would have forgotten by Sunday. But the moment we were inside Camilla's house, Christabel asked if she could ring Betty. Mrs Blake wanted to say No, but I persuaded her to say Yes. Christabel rang. She said, 'Mum, are you cross with me?' I couldn't hear the reply, but it must have been satisfactory because she smiled. When the short conversation was over Christabel seemed quite restored. 'We're going to have another party when I get home,' she said, 'with jelly and ice-cream and another cake. And my Mum says when it's *my* birthday we'll have a big, big party, bigger than hers.'

I didn't see her during the rest of that weekend, and Camilla took her back, so I didn't see Betty either nor how she greeted Christabel. Camilla said everything went off fine, she thought. They'd gone to the Natural History Museum and looked at the dinosaurs and then to a matinée, some children's play at the

Arts Theatre Club. Christabel had seemed to love everything and had slept well both Friday and Saturday nights. Her grandmother had played a lot of ludo with her and taught her *Happy Families*. The only thing that had perturbed the Blakes was the frequency with which Christabel had wanted to ring Betty – every two hours, Camilla said. She'd actually got up at seven on Sunday morning and dialled herself without anyone in Camilla's house knowing – they found out only because when she asked if she could ring again at ten Camilla had done it for her and Betty had complained: 'Not again, as if it weren't enough waking me at seven of a Sunday morning and me not in bed till three after the party.' Camilla said she had sounded quite triumphant, though.

Once Christabel had been returned, Mrs Blake was very depressed. It wasn't just that she now would have to wait another month before having her granddaughter to stay (though she could have her for the day two weeks later), but that she felt Christabel was becoming too fond of Betty and would suffer accordingly when she had to move on. 'And heaven knows when that will be,' she said. 'The Council haven't done a thing, not a *thing*. Here we are, the end of March, and after five whole months they haven't even found a single family to consider. It goes on and on and nobody does anything, and the longer it takes, the more damaging it is to Christabel. Nobody answers my letters, nobody is available when I ring up, nobody tells me anything.' There were, I saw, real tears in her eyes.

'She's at least looking well,' I said, lamely. 'She's healthy and seems happy. And imagine how awful it would be if we had to take her back, screaming, to Betty.'

'If she screamed I wouldn't take her back,' Mrs Blake said. 'I would not allow it. I am beginning to think I shouldn't allow it in any case.'

'But there is no alternative. We discussed . . .'

'Yes, I know, we discussed it when Rowena died. But I did not know then what would happen. I thought Christabel would be adopted easily and quickly by some nice family with whom we could be friends. I had no idea she would have to go through all this. It is too much. I think it is time I put a stop to it.'

'How?'

'Camilla and I will care for her until a family can be found. It is what we ought to have done in the first place. I will engage a nanny and Camilla and I will supervise her.'

'Does Camilla agree?'

'She suggested it. She has been as troubled as I have been. And we shall start looking for a family ourselves, through private agencies. It is intolerable this should drag on. I intend to call the Council's bluff.'

But it was no bluff. I didn't bother wasting my breath saying so, but I knew perfectly well that the Council's Social Services Department, Maureen and Stella, would never let Christabel go to the Blakes. Moreover, I knew they *could* not let her go. Legally, the responsibility had been made theirs and in order to release themselves from it there would have to be all kinds of court orders. The Blakes had their own solicitor so they ought to know that. If they didn't, it could only be because they had not yet consulted him – he would soon disillusion them. But I knew that even if her own blood-relatives could somehow resume caring for Christabel it would not be in her best interests. Intellectually, Christabel would be stimulated, but it wasn't intellectual stimulus she was in need of. Camilla and Mrs Blake could not even begin to offer the stability and warmth Betty did. The child would be isolated in the Blake household, one small girl living in an entirely adult orientated setting. She would recover her reading and writing skills in no time, she would be the centre of very intelligent attention, but she would not be part of a family with all that that was giving her. If asked to choose I felt I would choose Betty.

I was not asked to choose, of course, and nor was anyone else. The moment Mrs Blake floated her idea, it was finished – there was no question of Christabel being removed from what was regarded as a very successful long-term fostering arrangement until such time as she was adopted. So Mrs Blake turned her energies into harassing the authorities night and day over this adoption and succeeded in driving them so crazy that within another month, by the end of April, they announced they had three suitable families ready and, if all went well, Christabel could be with one of them by the summer holidays.

And that was when war was actually declared.

CHAPTER EIGHT

Two things happened at once, after nothing seeming to happen for ages. The first was to do with holidays. Christabel told her grandmother, at the end of May, that she was going to Butlins with her Mum and Dad, and Judy and Craig. She didn't know what Butlins was or which one they were going to, but she knew she was going as soon as school broke up, and that she was going to have a very good time. Mrs Blake had a fit. She had intended taking Christabel to stay with some friends of hers in Rothesay, friends who had a little girl Christabel's age and two others a year either side, the perfect set-up. The dates clashed exactly. Since it was only May, Mrs Blake had not yet put in a formal application to take her granddaughter on holiday, but the minute Christabel came out with her news she banged one in. The Council turned it down. They said Mrs Blake's suggestion was not 'appropriate' (one of their favourite words). She was furious, rightly, I think. She consulted her solicitor and made another application, this time to the court. Christabel, being a ward of court, in fact needed permission to go anywhere outside London. The court upheld her request. She was triumphant, the Council irritated, Betty livid.

Then Phyllis, the adoption officer, came up with two families, a Mr and Mrs Lebjoy and a Dr and Mrs Ofori. The Lebjoys were Nigerian, the Oforis Nigerian and Indian (it was Dr Ofori who was Nigerian). We had another Case Conference at which

157

we had reports on both families read out to us, or the relevant parts of each, and looked at photographs. Phyllis was very pleasant about it all. Unlike Maureen, she was neither prim nor nervous, and unlike Stella, she wasn't insincerely cheerful. Of the three of them I liked her best. She was a thin, taut kind of person but had great warmth of manner and was quick to pick up innuendo and deal with it. Rather older than the other two, she seemed less antagonistic and more sympathetic to Mrs Blake. She kept saying things like 'This must be a great strain for you' and 'It must be so hard to have lost your daughter', and was altogether softer in approach. She looked alert and intelligent too, and we all related better to her. But, even so, what she brought forward, the information she gave us, was very far from satisfactory and we were bitterly disappointed.

The Lebjoys already had a son of eleven and had lost two other children at birth. Phyllis said it was long enough after the second still-birth, some four years ago, for there not to be any worry that Christabel would be thought of as a substitute. Mrs Lebjoy had since been sterilised and was in any case now forty-four. They were both teachers, Mr Lebjoy a maths teacher in a secondary school and Mrs Lebjoy a primary school teacher. They lived in Stoke Newington, owning their own house. Both belonged to large families and they went every year for a month to Nigeria to see them. In the photograph they looked very smart and clean and solemn. Mrs Blake shuddered as she looked at it. 'They do not look right for Christabel,' she said.

'They satisfy many of your own criteria as well as all of ours, Mrs Blake,' Phyllis said quietly.

'They do not look right,' Mrs Blake repeated.

'In what way?'

'They are too black.'

Stella and Maureen looked at each other and smirked, I thought. They had been waiting for such a racist reaction and were going to enjoy a full-scale self-righteous rejection of it, one I would be obliged to share because of course it was a terrible thing to have said.

But Mrs Blake would not be silent. 'My granddaughter,' she went on, 'is half white, and even the half that is black is not

Nigerian. It is West Indian. I cannot see that she has any more in common with a wholly Nigerian family than you say she would have with a wholly white family.'

'There are other considerations apart from colour,' Phyllis said. 'The Lebjoys are teachers, professional people. They would be ideal parents for Christabel, able to nurture her talents in the way you wish. And their home is very pleasant. Mrs Lebjoy is artistic and musical and Christabel would respond, I am sure, to the general atmosphere of the place.'

'What about the boy?' Mrs Blake said. 'I don't like the idea of the boy. Eleven, nearly twelve, it is too old. Christabel is not used to boys.'

'She gets on very well with the boys in her foster-home. It's surely good for her to have a sibling.'

'Not when he's so old.'

'But that is an advantage, it means there is less likely to be jealousy.'

'I don't like the idea of it.'

We passed, rather uncomfortably, on to the Oforis. Here, Mrs Blake could not say they looked too black. Dr Ofori could not have been completely Nigerian because he was much too light and his features too European, and I doubted, even before Phyllis explained, that Mrs Ofori was pure Indian. Both of them, it turned out, had white English mothers, making them 'perfect candidates'. They looked happy people too, both plump and smiling in the photograph. They had no children and were unable to have any. They were younger, in their mid-thirties, and lived in Ealing, in a flat. Dr Ofori was an academic doctor and lectured at Birkbeck College. Mrs Ofori was a dentist. Again, impeccable, middle-class credentials as well as racial ones, but this time Mrs Blake said she did not want Christabel to be an only child.

'She was an only child in any case,' Phyllis pointed out.

'Yes, but my daughter intended to adopt a companion.'

'The Oforis may well do so.'

'But we cannot be certain of that. I would like Christabel to get something out of this tragedy, to be part of a larger family from the beginning.'

'That is a little unreasonable,' Phyllis said.

'I don't think so. And I must say that to have spent seven months looking and come up with only two possibilities seems quite pathetic to me, quite pathetic.'

'It is quality, not quantity that counts,' Phyllis put in.

'Precisely. And these two families, whatever you call them, I cannot get my tongue round their names, are far from superior in my opinion. They are not what I expected. Are there no white families? No couples with at least one white person? I think that is most important. Christabel's heritage ought to be evenly balanced. I shall object to both.'

'We can of course look further,' Phyllis said calmly.

'Good. Do so.'

'But naturally it will delay matters indefinitely. If the Oforis or Lebjoys were accepted, Christabel could be in her new family and new school for the start of the new academic year in September. We could go to the July adoption panel, the last of the summer, and then when she comes back from holiday in Scotland Christabel could begin the introductory visits at the best possible time.'

'This is blackmail!' Mrs Blake burst out. She was red in the face, as she had been the other time, and we all tensed, dreading another attack. But it was Phyllis in charge this time, not Stella, and she was far better at dealing with choleric old ladies.

'No, it isn't blackmail, Mrs Blake,' she said, 'very far from it, very far. I'm so sorry if what I said appeared to you to be applying pressure – that was quite unintentional. And, of course, you are quite right, the time it takes to find the right family for your granddaughter does not really matter so long as it is the right family. Now, shall we start again?'

We started, but got nowhere. Mrs Blake remained adamant: neither the Lebjoys nor the Oforis were suitable and that was that. What I wasn't sure of was how much power she had, whether she, as Christabel's grandmother, did indeed have any right of veto. She acted as if she were certain she had, and Phyllis did not tell her she hadn't, but I thought Stella's face showed some sense of superiority – she looked as if she knew Mrs Blake was of no real consequence in this. The solicitors were not present at that meeting (their presence was apparently 'not appropriate'). But whether because Mrs Blake had this right, or because Phyllis wanted everything to be amicable, the Lebjoys and Oforis were put to one side, 'Though we may come back to them,' Phyllis added, and Stella and Maureen exchanged significant looks. The meeting was declared over, with Phyllis promising to continue looking, but Mrs Blake had an announcement to make.

'I would just like to say,' she trumpeted, at her most regal, 'that if no suitable family is found I would not let my granddaughter go to an unsuitable one.'

'Neither would we,' flashed Stella before Phyllis could speak.

'But what *you* (and Mrs Blake loaded the word with contempt), what *you* think satisfactory and what we think satisfactory may be very different. I am talking about what will happen in any difference of opinion, what I will decide if . . .'

'You will decide nothing as a matter of fact, Mrs Blake,' said Phyllis, very calmly. It was the first time she had interrupted and I had the feeling she had only done so to pre-empt Stella. 'In the event of a serious difference of opinion, the case will go to court and a judge will decide.'

'Good,' said Mrs Blake. 'I would be very glad of it. I would fight any case through the courts, whatever it cost. So long as you understand that.'

'Let us hope it will not be necessary,' Phyllis said, flushing just a little. 'It would be a failure on all our parts if it had to.'

That evening, Mrs Blake called a war council – that was literally what she called it, a war council. Fergus came too – 'So we can have a clear masculine mind present' – which made four of us. Mrs Blake appeared in excellent spirits, signs of imminent heart attack now absent, but Camilla looked even more faded and harassed than usual. I could see that she was pulled in quite a different direction from her powerful mother, that what *she* wanted to do was be conciliatory and have the whole thing over as soon as possible. She had no stomach for a fight. The idea of going to court clearly appalled her and she tried to say so only to be put down by her mother. 'After all,' Camilla said, as we sat in her very elegant sitting-room drinking sherry, 'we asked the Council to find an adoptive family, we did do that, and now they're only doing their job.'

'Badly,' said Mrs Blake. 'That is the point, Camilla. They are doing it *badly* and we must fight them.'

'I'd rather take Christabel myself,' Camilla said miserably.

'We've tried that. They won't let us.'

'We've only tried to take her until she's adopted. We haven't applied to adopt her ourselves.'

'Oh, now really, Camilla, that *is* a nonsense,' her mother said crossly. 'Quite unfeasible.'

'I should have done it in the first place,' Camilla said. 'I am to blame for all this.'

'Oh, for *heaven's* sake!' her mother snapped. 'This is so time-wasting, going back over old ground, over and over again, it serves no purpose. We had a clear objective and we still have it: to find the best possible family for Christabel and you are not in the running, Camilla, you are not a family, you are a widow like me and that is that.'

'But I could devote my life to Christabel . . .'

'Oh, don't talk such *rubbish* – devote your life indeed, it is ridiculous. It took you long enough to rebuild your life after Henry died.'

'But to save her from . . .'

'Camilla, stop it, stop it at once. You are being absurdly melodramatic, you talk as if the child was about to climb the scaffold. There is no question of sacrifices. Nobody is going to convince me that a perfectly normal, delightful little girl like Christabel cannot be found an equally normal and delightful family. It is simply through the Council's incompetence that one has not been found already. Now, do stop the histrionics and concentrate.'

Going home with Fergus afterwards I said how tired I was of it all, of these meetings and discussions, and worst of all, the feeling of being bound to the Blakes. It was taken for granted that I would be consulted at every step and would want to share in all their decisions. But I didn't want to, my involvement had got way out of hand. I was committed to Christabel, not to them, and there was a difference. I told Fergus how all the time I was with Mrs Blake I was actually being hypocritical, that I found myself agreeing with things I didn't agree with at all, just because of the sheer force of her personality. My own mother could never, ever, have that effect on me. Fergus said he could see what I meant, that he had never known me more silent or cowed. Only when Mrs Blake had wanted to draw up a list of the Council's faults under the heading 'Muddles, inefficiencies and sheer pigheadedness' to send to Mr Wavell, had I spoken out and she had relented sufficiently to leave out the alleged inefficiency and pigheadedness. But I had kept silent when she had read out her résumé of Rowena as a mother which she had written to send to Phyllis as a standard against which she could match an adoptive mother.

This was a document of almost pure fantasy and yet I had been unable to find a way of contradicting it. It was entitled: 'My daughter Rowena as a mother', and had a short introductory paragraph in which Mrs Blake stated that Rowena 'as a near perfect mother' would be impossible to emulate but that it might help if some of her 'key characteristics' as a mother were listed. Then she listed them, and Rowena gradually emerged as a saint. I heard how she had 'all the natural gifts' a mother needs and was 'supremely competent as a parent'; I heard about her 'limitless patience' and her 'entire devotion' and most of all about her 'extraordinary sensitivity to her child's needs'. Even her faults were presented as virtues, so I heard how, 'rather than enter into sexual relationships' for the sake of having the children she craved, Rowena had waited until she was able to support herself (another fantasy – she never at any point supported herself), and then 'bravely' gone ahead and had a child on her own. I heard how once she'd become pregnant she 'gave up working and went on Social Security since she believed mothers of young children should stay at home to care for them'. There was no mention anywhere of Rowena's feckless behaviour, of her depressions, of what a leech she had been on me. Even her 'mild untidiness' was made to sound endearing instead of the plague it was. At the end, Mrs Blake had asked me if I had anything to add, any 'little insight', which might complete the picture. I said, 'No,' and despised myself.

'You heard me,' I said to Fergus. 'I said "No."'

'What would you have liked to say?'

'Oh, I don't know. I'd like, I suppose, to make sure whoever mothers Christabel isn't tricked into believing Rowena was perfect. It might make any adoptive parent feel a bit better to know how bad things were becoming with Christabel. She should know of the tantrums and Rowena's helplessness in the face of them, and the not sleeping and the way Christabel challenged her mother over every damn thing and won.'

'But she did love her,' Fergus said. 'You've told me yourself, Rowena was devoted to Christabel, she really did have nothing else in her life.'

'Quite. But it wasn't a good thing. They would have had bad times coming.'

'All mothers have bad times.'

'Stop it, Fergus. I hate it when you come out with those kind of trite observations. What I mean is, Christabel and Rowena were not some sort of wonderful partnership without any kind of trouble between them. Rowena was living *through* Christabel and the strain was there. Mrs Blake writes as though they were just a normal mother and child, and they weren't. There was nothing normal about Rowena's greed for Christabel.'

'But even if all this is true, you wouldn't expect a mother to put it into words, would you? You wouldn't expect Mrs Blake to ramble on about how unhealthy, according to you, her dead daughter's maternal fixation was?'

'No, but she shouldn't go the other way and sanctify her.'

'I can't see the harm. The social workers will just ignore it anyway, they'll just chuck it in the bin. It isn't relevant. It doesn't really matter what Rowena was like now.'

True, and I knew Fergus thought I was being less than kind, and even wondered at my motives for being so determined to throw blemishes on Rowena's memory. And yet I persisted in feeling it was important the real Rowena should be remembered and not this sickly-sweet creature of her mother's description.

*

It was coming up for Christabel's sixth birthday and because of this I could not rid myself of images from that day, the day she was born. I was in London the whole of that month of June, interpreting for a group of Russian children's writers, who were over on a tour, and found my mind wandering again and again to Rowena on the day she gave birth and my own awe at the process. Phyllis had said, at one Case Conference, that Christabel would never 'bond' with any new mother until she had 'worked through' her grief for her natural mother and I found myself wondering what that grief would be for, what it was in Christabel's young mind that she missed. How was her mother alive in her memory? How did Rowena seem to her? Or did Christabel hear her mother weeping, see her in her mind's eye daily overcome by disorder, remember her so depressed she could not get up? Who did Christabel think of?

I mentioned some, only a little, of this to Phyllis, said how worried I felt at not knowing what Christabel's memories were. I said I often wanted to talk to Christabel about Rowena, especially for some perverse reason about the bad times, but that of course I'd held back, knowing it would be cruel and maybe dangerous. Phyllis said it wouldn't necessarily be either. She said it had emerged in the 'developmental assessment' of Christabel, which had to be made before she could be adopted, that she was not as attached to either her aunt or her grandmother as had been expected and that I was far more of a presence. This being so, Phyllis said, it might be a relief to her if I did talk to her about her dead mother, she might be waiting for me to give her some sort of lead. There was, Phyllis said, bound to be a good deal of anger there towards her mother and even though it might be coming out indirectly it would probably help if it could be specifically articulated.

So I tried, a few days before her sixth birthday, which was of course also my own thirty-seventh, to take Christabel back to when Rowena was alive. I had special permission that day to take her to the seaside as a pre-birthday treat (her actual birthday treat was to be a party at Betty's and then the Blakes were to have her the next day). We went to Brighton on the train. There was the usual panic call from Betty – a rash, this time, which might turn out to be German-measles-so-I-don't-want-to-take-no-chances-she's-better-off-in-bed – but I dealt with that by saying I'd take her to the doctor's first (there was no need to, the rash had cleared in the time it took me to get to Betty's). Fergus had been going to come with us and at the last minute couldn't, which I'd worried might disappoint Christabel deeply and start the day off on the wrong footing. But she took the news well and seemed as eager as ever to go on the train and I thought the fact of travelling by train as good a way into memories of Rowena as any. Once we were moving, I said, 'Do you remember the times you went on the train to Carlisle with Rowena?' She nodded. For some reason I felt very nervous and churned up at the thought of continuing and I almost left it at that, especially since she hadn't said anything, but I just managed to keep the subject going. 'It was a long way, wasn't it?' I asked. She nodded again. 'Did you get bored? Did Rowena play games all the way?'

'Noughts and crosses,' she said, 'but I broke the pencil.'

'Oh well, I expect Mummy had another.'

'I broke all the pencils, then I threw them on the floor. I did . . .' and she gestured under the table we were sitting at and smiled a funny little knowing smile.

'And what did Rowena do?'

'Nothing. She cried. Not properly, though.' She was still smiling her odd little twisted smile.

'Were you sorry?'

'No.'

There we came to a full stop for a moment. It seemed distasteful, almost prurient, to question Christabel further, to keep pressing her. And I didn't want to cast gloom over what was supposed to be a happy day. But later, when we were on Palace Pier and she was eating a hot doughnut and we were leaning on the rail watching people swimming below, she suddenly said: 'I had a doughnut, with jam in. It's bad for my teeth, but Mummy got one for the train. I ate it like this' – and she showed me how she'd taken tiny bites all the way round without penetrating the centre.

'That was nice,' I said, lamely.

'The jam went on Mummy's dress, but she didn't care.' She laughed out loud. 'I licked it off!' she shouted. 'I pretended I was a dog and I went lick, lick, and licked it off, all off the dress and Mummy's arm. She didn't mind.'

It was only several minutes later, when the doughnut was finished and we were sitting on the beach throwing stones into the sea, that the impact of this memory seemed to hit her. She stopped throwing stones and lay face down on the shingle. It was hot – a rare, perfect summer's day – and I thought she might just be tired. I'd bought her a straw hat and I put this over her head to keep the sun off her and lay down beside her myself, my eyes closed. It was very pleasant lying there. Idly, I went over what we would do for the rest of the day and calculated which train we would get back, and then I heard a small snuffling sound near my ear and realised Christabel was crying. Her head was turned away from me but I knew she was crying, her slight body shaking with sobs. I put my arm over her shoulders and raised myself high enough to peep over at her face, but she had grabbed the hat and was using it as a shield. I tried to pick her up or at least turn her over, the better to embrace her, but the sheer force of her determination to rest prone astonished me – I found I could not move her. So I lay there, as close as I could, and waited. Presently, the sobbing stopped. I knew Christabel well enough to be sure that, although only six, she would feel embarrassed because she had cried in such a way and I knew it was important to give her the chance to recover in her own way. So I waited, straining to interpret her slightest movement. When she eventually jumped up, all in a moment, and rushed down to the sea I didn't follow her. She had her bathing costume on and I saw she was longing to go in but her orange water wings were still with me. Quickly, I blew them up and joined her and put them on her arms without saying a word and we went in together.

The sea, for a Brighton sea, was relatively calm but even so there was a swell on the surface and I had to hold on tight to Christabel. She could swim in a swimming pool if she had her water wings on, but was clearly much less confident in the sea. I held her close, my body shielding hers, and together we bobbed and dipped in the gentle waves and she held her head high so she could see the next one coming. It was a wonderfully comfortable position to be in, with the sea so warm and the sun so hot. Her body was so slight that I felt I was crushing her just by holding her in my arms – I felt huge and strong and protective. And I enjoyed this feeling, enjoyed knowing I was supporting her, keeping her safe, that I could do it at no cost to myself, without effort.

We stayed in for ages and then, when the tide turned and I could feel its pull, we got out and I wrapped us both in the big towel I had brought. We didn't really need it – the sun still blazed – but there was something seductive about wrapping ourselves in its folds and lying together on the shingle, nose to nose. Christabel shivered, in spite of the heat, and held her little hands together under her chin like a squirrel. I had a sudden memory of Rowena doing that when she was tiny, of her standing on the edge of the swimming pool trembling whereas I, much fatter and heavier, scornfully walked past to the changing-rooms. It was such a natural thought to mention this to Christabel and yet I was nervous, it reminded me of that ghastly American habit of 'sharing' – 'thank you for sharing with me' a friend of mine used to say when I had told her something particularly dreadful. But I knew if I suppressed this desire to tell Christabel it would be out of cowardice, out of a Betty-type desire to keep everything happy when of course it was not. 'You look like your mother used to look when she was a little girl,' I said, tightening my grip on her shoulder. 'She used to put her hands up like that and shake.'

'Why?'

'Well, because she was cold. Only you're not really cold, are you, it's just we've been in the water a long time. When your Mummy went swimming at your age she really was cold.'

'Why?'

'The water was cold and so were the swimming baths. It was in Edinburgh, where your Grandma lives.'

'Have I been?'

'Of course. Don't you remember? The big house with the stone steps?'

'Did I jump off them?'

'I expect so. Your Mummy did and I did. We used to dare each other to jump from the top one.'

'Did you?'

'Your Mummy did but I didn't.'

'Why?'

'She was braver than I was. I was scared. So I used to pretend I didn't want to.'

'Why was she brave?'

'She just was, about things like that.'

'Was my Daddy brave?'

'I don't know. I didn't know him then.'

'Mum says he wants shot.'

She sat up, casting off the towel. Her tone had been so matter-of-fact, entirely without emotion. She didn't attempt to pursue the topic and I knew it would have been wrong to do so, but I felt furious with Betty who knew nothing at all about Amos. Why turn the child against a father she had never known and would be unlikely ever to know? It seemed so malicious. But worse was to follow. On the train back, Christabel cuddled up against me and put her thumb in her mouth. She was tired, sleepy. She looked up at me and removing the comforting thumb for a moment said, 'Will you be cross?'

'Cross?' I said. 'Why?'

'Mum gets cross if I suck my thumb. She says I'm not a baby.'

'Well, you can be a baby for an hour or so, everyone can.'

'I have to be a big girl.'

'You don't *have* to be . . .'

'I do. If I'm not a big girl nobody will want me, except my Mum.'

'Oh, that's not true. Everyone wants you.'

'No, they don't. My Mum says it ain't natural.'

'Your Mum is wrong.'

'But I don't care. I'm going to stay with her forever and ever and she says I can and my Dad says I can.'

Then she fell asleep. I sat and stared out of the train window and thought about just taking her home with me. I couldn't bear the thought of returning her to Betty and yet I knew I must. It didn't need Maureen to remind me of the consequences if I did not, and anyway I knew perfectly well Christabel would want to go. It was her party the next day and she had talked about it with great excitement. Betty had hired a conjuror and she was renting a lot of cartoon videos – it sounded hell, but Christabel was wildly excited. Mrs Blake had muttered about the cost to the taxpayer of these entertainments when she heard, but had not actually lodged one of her many complaints. She herself was planning a quiet day in the garden with her grand-daughter and then an outing to a concert where *Peter and the Wolf* was to be played. She'd played this record to Christabel many times and wanted her to have the experience of seeing it performed, convinced as she was that the child was musical (rightly, I think). Her present was going to be a piano, to be kept at Camilla's, and lessons whenever she came.

But when I went in with Christabel I hung about a bit, hoping I'd get an opportunity to register some kind of objection to the things I'd heard. Sometimes Christabel went off to find Judy and I had a chat with Betty, but today this didn't happen. Judy was out. In fact, all the children were out, and only Betty and Norman were in the living-room (even more repellent in the summer than in the winter when at least its warmth and bright lights were welcoming on raw days). Christabel flew to Betty, as she almost always did, and gave her extravagant hugs, which were returned. Betty beamed at her and I saw she really did care for Christabel. 'How's my girl?' she said. 'Have you been good?'

'Yes.'

'Did you remember what I told you? Did you say "Please" and "Thank" you to Isobel?'

Christabel looked at me uncertainly.

'There was no need,' I said.

'That's as may be,' Betty said, 'but she should of done. Now, you say "Thank you" to Isobel, say "Thank you for a lovely day".'

'Really . . .' I began, but Betty glared at me and I had to be silent while Christabel formally trotted out her thanks. There was no point in staying. I said I hoped the party would be a success and that I'd see her in two weeks, before she went on holiday with her grandmother. Betty's face darkened as I mentioned this and she sniffed and looked offended. She'd already expressed the opinion, when Mrs Blake won this privilege, that it would be 'a funny sort of holiday for a child who would be much better off with them she knew, having proper fun what a little girl likes at a holiday camp. But there's nothing I can do about it and I've told her it's no use her bawling and saying she wants to come with us.' Now, she said the less said about that the better, and she didn't want Chrissie's birthday spoiled with any reminders of that holiday hanging over her.

She saw me to the door. I asked if she'd come to my car, parked a few yards down the road, so that I could give her a present I had for Christabel which I wanted to be a surprise the next day. She walked along with me and I steeled myself to say what I wanted to say. It came out all wrong. 'Christabel says you told her her father should be shot,' I blurted out.

'Well, so he should,' Betty snapped, not seeming at all surprised I'd mentioned it. 'The lot of them should be shot when they leave a girl pregnant, put up against a wall and shot if they won't marry her, like in the old days, what was them weddings called, shotgun weddings.'

'The point is,' I said as I opened the boot, 'you don't know anything about Christabel's father . . .'

'And I don't want to. You giving me this present or what?'

'He was a lovely man,' I said, 'and it isn't true he . . .'

'Lovely?' Betty interrupted. 'Oh, very lovely his behaviour was, I must say.'

'You don't know what his behaviour was and in any case there is no need to damn him in Christabel's eyes, is there? I know you're kind and you love Christabel, but to say those kind of things, and to tell her no one will want her if she isn't a big girl . . .'

'Have you finished? 'Cos I ain't listening to no more. Here, give me that,' and she snatched the box I was holding, 'give me that and take yourself off of here. I know more about children than you'll ever know and I've had about enough of you lot, I've had more bother with Chrissie's family than I've ever had from any child's, I just don't know who you think you all are, sticking your noses in, telling me to do this and not the other, and what sort of people are you, nothing but rubbish, giving your own child away and coming out with all this double-talk about wanting her to be happy in a better home than you can give her, it *disgusts* me and that's the truth, you've no proper feeling, none of you, it makes me *sick* to hear you all going on and as for them letters what Maureen has, full of all them excuses about why Chrissie has to be adopted, I don't know how that Gran had the face to write them, I don't know who she thought she was kidding, I'd *never* give my grandchild away, never. Never mind your sheltered housing or what, I'd live in a cardboard box with her rather than do it, I would, and you, *you*, you're just as bad.'

There was no point in going after her. I managed to say, 'I'm sorry,' but the rest of my apology was lost in her tirade. I could see she was more than just furious – she was deeply insulted. She would probably never speak to me again. I had lost the slight advantage I'd had over the Blakes and now I was lumped with them.

But as I drove home I began to feel angry myself. Why was it that nobody was ever allowed to criticise Betty? Right from the beginning the Social Services Department had handled her like china and seemed far more concerned about offending her than us. Why? It could only be expediency. They had no one else who could take Christabel on and they were afraid of having to find another foster-family for this 'difficult' case. But half our complaints about Betty were true and they were surely worthy of investigation. It *was* wrong of her to tell Christabel no one would adopt her if she sucked her thumb, wrong to threaten her in any way when she was already so afraid of the future. Why didn't Maureen do something about it? Why didn't she speak to her? And then all this emphasis on Betty's experience – how relevant was her particular kind of experience to Christabel? She was used to children coming to her from broken homes, children with a long history of instability, children who no longer had any contact whatsoever with any member of their natural family. How did this make her an expert on Christabel, a child from a perfectly stable home until her mother was killed, a child with relatives who were maintaining the closest link they were allowed to? Things were going on in the Lowe household which were deeply disturbing, but which were so subtle they couldn't even be listed. It was like a kind of brainwashing and who knew what it did to a six-year-old child? Christabel was physically well cared for, she was on the surface safe and happy, but what about her fears and worries, what about how they were dealt with, or rather not dealt with? Wasn't the famous Betty at fault?

I knew my position was hopeless. I was only a friend of the family, I had no status. If I'd now lost any standing I had with Betty, and I knew I had, I must take care not to lose any more with the social workers or I would truly be useless to Christabel. It is so very, very hard for me to be humble, to ingratiate myself, but I really tried. I asked, and got, an interview with Phyllis, whom I felt might be more sympathetic and concerned even though Betty was more Maureen's responsibility. I told her, straining to hide all dangerous indignation, of what Christabel had said about the disapproved-of thumb-sucking.

'It's only her way,' Phyllis said, 'just a manner of speaking. Betty's very direct, she'll have said it without thinking.'

'I know, but shouldn't she think? I mean, in the circumstances, knowing what Christabel's been through and what's ahead, shouldn't she be more careful?'

'None of us are perfect,' Phyllis said, with a sigh. 'I expect Betty made it up to her in other ways, she'd give her a cuddle after she'd told her off to show she was joking. She's a very warm person.'

'Sometimes I fail to see it.'

'Yes, but she's not herself with you, or the Blakes. Believe me, she has as much to complain about on her side as you have on yours.'

'Really? What does she complain about?'

'Oh, snobbery, or what she thinks is snobbery. She says

Christabel comes back to her correcting her grammar and saying her grandmother tells her not to speak like Betty.'

'That's a bit different from telling her her father should be shot or that no one will adopt her if she sucks her thumb.'

'Not to Betty it isn't. It produces the same anger in her. She feels Christabel is being taught to despise her and this upsets her. And actually it *is* bad for Christabel because it does confuse her. She's living with Betty, according to Betty's ways and standards, and it isn't appropriate to make her question them at the moment.'

'I don't think I've ever corrected her grammar.'

'No, but you've told her only stupid people want to watch television all day and you know the telly is on in Betty's house all day long.'

'Did I say that?'

'Apparently. And Christabel promptly repeated it.'

'Well, I'm sorry. But it still isn't in the same category as the kind of ideas Betty's planting in her mind, is it?'

'Perhaps not, but try telling Betty that.'

'You're all so in awe of her.'

'No, we're not, but we know, which *you* don't, how lucky we are to have her. Christabel could have been in half a dozen different foster-homes by now in the normal run of things – she's fortunate only to have stayed in one.'

'The wrong one,' I said before I could stop myself.

'There's no point in going over that,' Phyllis said, frowning. 'We've been through it over and over. Betty Lowe is one of the best foster-mothers we have and that is that. Now, I've got another appointment . . .'

'But you will try to talk to Betty about what I said?'

'I'll try. And perhaps you can try to talk to Mrs Blake about all this telephoning. It's driving Betty crazy.'

'I didn't know Mrs Blake *was* phoning a lot.'

'Almost every day, Betty says. She also says Christabel doesn't want to speak to her grandmother and that she has to be persuaded.'

'I don't believe that.'

'Well, we shall see. It might all come out when we do Form D.'

'Which is?'

'We have to complete a profile of Christabel's behavioural and emotional well-being as part of the adoption procedure. Oh, there's such a lot to do, you've no idea. I haven't even done Form E yet, and that's usually the easiest, just sketching in the background, but in this case it's so complicated . . .'

The telephone was ringing most of the time she was talking and when I left her to answer it and went downstairs there was a room full of people waiting to see her. There was nothing imagined about Phyllis's work load and I felt guilty for taking up even a little of her time, especially to no purpose. I went home depressed not just by Christabel's situation but by the whole weight of life in general – everything seemed so black, so dreary, the world a place of insoluble problems. It seemed a long time since I'd felt enthusiastic about anything at all or in the least carefree.

When Mrs Blake rang I could hardly bear to talk to her. I lied and said I had a cab at the door and was leaving for Paris in an hour's time. She appeared offended, said accusingly that I hadn't mentioned anything, and I said, rather pertly, I suppose, that I hadn't realised I should. If she hadn't apologised we might have parted on bad terms, which might in turn have been quite a good thing, but when she said, 'Isobel, I'm so sorry, my dear, I forget myself sometimes, I didn't mean to be so high-handed, it is the strain of it all . . .' I said not to mention it, that I understood. 'You must get your cab,' she said, 'but when you come back from Paris might I just consult you, if you can bear it, about this holiday with Christabel? I won't keep you now, but there are complications.'

I felt so wicked having lied, so ridiculous. The thought of staying in London when I'd said I was going to be in Paris annoyed me so much I promptly rang Fergus, who'd gone back to his own flat for a couple of days to oversee a roof being mended, and said, 'Let's go away for a few days, now.' He said he couldn't. His flat had no roof still and his father was coming to see him the next day *en route* for his summer holiday in Devon.

So I went home – 'home' home, to Cockermouth. I didn't even tell them I was coming, simply rushed to Euston, got the first train and took a taxi from Carlisle station all the way. I arrived at six o'clock on the most glorious of summer evenings, and as the taxi drove out of Cockermouth and along towards Lorton, the fells loomed ahead at the end of the valley road as clearly defined as I had ever seen them. They lifted my spirits in spite of myself – just the sheer power and glory of them – and I found myself smiling to think I'd ever cursed and railed against being forced to live among them when I was young. I paid the taxi off halfway along the Whinlatter Pass, where the road turned right to dip down to my parents' house, so that I could have the pleasure of walking quietly along it and surprising them.

It was by then almost seven-thirty and, though the sun was still quite high, there was a pinkness to the horizon. Soon, Grasmoor would be dyed deep red, its forbidding western approach a sudden field of roses where no flowers grew. Once, Rowena and I had climbed it in the evening and bivouacked on top, and all the way up, on an evening such as this, we had marvelled at the illusions the light of the setting sun had given us. Rock that was slate-grey had seemed from a distance like smooth sheets of peach-coloured satin and the short, dark green grass, tufty and dry, had promised a soft carpet of purest moss. On the top, we'd set up our tent and then sat outside it, cross-legged, facing the orange sun poised to disappear over the far-off Solway Firth and we'd cried. Sat and cried, just because it was so beautiful, so perfect. To be sixteen and so sentimental . . . Then we'd made each other promise never to tell anyone we'd been so slushy. In the morning, typical Lake District trick, we woke to rain and greyness. We argued all the way down, hating the ugly dreariness of the nasty old mountain we'd found so enchanting the night before. 'Life's a bitch,' Rowena said, and I laughed so much our joint good humour was quite restored. 'Life's a bitch' – she'd been so proud of her sophistication.

This common little catchphrase became our favourite exchange forever after when something that had been good turned bad. 'Life's a bitch,' we said, and always, always, managed at least a smile.

I knew exactly what my parents would be doing. Nearly seven-thirty, so it would be finishing their pre-supper drink and about to eat. On an evening like this they'd be sitting at the back of the house, to the right of the rose-covered porch, where they had a white, wrought-iron table and a bench beside it. The view from this spot was superb, uninterrupted all the way to the sea which, on a good day, could clearly be seen. To the left, Grasmoor and Mellbreak opened like jaws to hold the lake, hidden by trees, and in the far distance Red Pike pushed into the sky above the lower peaks. Mother said she could never look at it since Rowena was killed without shuddering, but I knew she would look all the same, on an evening like this, and think how peaceful and unthreatening it seemed. Who could not? I rounded the corner of the house, and there they were, two contented people sitting mesmerised by the beauty of it all. I watched them secretly for a moment, relieved to find I did not think them old. Mother's hair was still black, Father still had all of his even though it was grey, and both of them were lean and strong-looking. Good stock, I'd come from, no doubt about it. I said it aloud as I made myself known: 'Good stock, I come from.'

I stayed three days. It was hot all the time. We took a picnic down to Crummock Water and I swam. The fells were perfectly reflected in the still waters of the lake and I swam a stately breast-stroke, trying to leave the shadows intact. Rowena and I had once raced across the lake, from near where the water gauge is to the boat-house. My father reminded me of it, said how insufferably pleased I'd been to win and how cross when he'd pointed out I was two inches taller and nearly a stone heavier, though we were both twelve, and that I swam regularly whereas Rowena didn't. 'You two were always so competitive,' he said. 'We could never see the friendship lasting. But it did, it did. You stood by each other, she was a good friend to you in trouble and you to her.' I didn't respond to that. He'd been slow to add 'and you to her'. There had been a pause after the bit about Rowena standing by me and I knew this was meant to be a subtle reminder of my 'bad' time and Rowena's staunch support. It irritated me. My parents always had exaggerated both the badness and Rowena's support.

Dear God, such a fuss there had been and all for so little, but it had been a shock to their system. All that happened, when I was eighteen, was that I was arrested with a minute quantity of cannabis on me, absolutely minute. It was my first year at university and I was doing the usual experimenting, rolling a few joints, like all students did in the late sixties. It was all so silly, so utterly unremarkable, but I'd been taking part in a demonstration – I can't even *remember* what about – and a few windows got broken in some kind of fracas and the police were called and I just got herded into a police van together with those who'd done the damage. We were all charged with obstruction and those of us with reefers in our pockets with possession of cannabis. We got a caution, that was all. The university authorities, however, informed my parents, and their reaction was one of horror, the first and only time they ever let me down. Their conformist souls were outraged at my behaviour and they were convinced I was on the primrose path to doom. Even now, we can't laugh about it, though it is so long ago and I am reckoned to have redeemed myself – as if there was any redemption needed.

Rowena had stepped into the middle of the row we'd had and been a most soothing influence. She'd said, to my fury, that she'd 'Keep an eye' on me, and my parents had gone home comforted. It became a joke, of course, this 'keeping an eye'. Such a wonderful reversal of roles, but not to my parents, whom Rowena phoned weekly for a while. Maybe that was the reason we didn't see much of each other for a good while afterwards, quite apart from her then going to America.

My parents asked me about Christabel, naturally. I had nothing good to report. The more I talked about Betty the more upset they became and, like Mrs Blake, they couldn't cope with the idea of a black family adopting Christabel. 'Such a mess, such a mess,' my mother kept saying until it sounded like a bird call. My father wished he knew more about Family Law and hoped the Blakes had a good solicitor. But as I sat with them by the lake or walked on my own on the fells, nothing seemed as terrible as it had done in London. I didn't feel so pulled down and miserable, even though nothing had changed. In a way, this was dangerous, I knew. It was all a kind of pretence: everything round me is peaceful and lovely therefore there is no horror in the world. Nor any responsibility. What did any of it have to do with me? I was only a friend.

And then, the last night, the night before I left, Rowena returned in furious form to scream at me. She came in at the window, walking with huge, fantastical strides straight off Red Pike, still in her climbing boots and with her hair sodden with water from the stream where she'd fallen, and she roared and howled at me, looming over my bed like a colossus: *'Get up! You can't hide from me here, you can't run away, you can't abandon Christabel, go back, oh how can you leave her, how can you? Go back . . .'* I woke with my heart pounding, the bedclothes gathered on top of me as though burying me. I heard my mother say, from outside the door, 'Isobel? Isobel? Are you all right, dear?' I got up and opened the door and said I'd had a nightmare about Rowena, and we went downstairs and made tea. My mother was sympathy itself, but when I confessed this was a recurring nightmare, though I hadn't had it for a while, she could not resist telling me it was my conscience, as if I did not know. 'The nightmares won't stop,' she said, unnecessarily, 'until Christabel is happily settled in a loving family that suits her.' 'Thanks, Mother,' I said, 'but I can't do anything about that.' She managed not to say 'Can't you?' but her expression was just as accusing and I resented it.

I was glad to leave that afternoon. My mother's mothering is exhausting.

CHAPTER NINE

And then along came the Carmichaels. Hardly was I back in London, and before I'd even telephoned Mrs Blake, when I had a visit from Phyllis. She'd never been to my home before and somehow it was very different meeting her in my own sitting-room instead of the dreary institutional surroundings of the Social Services office. Unlike Maureen, she was quite at ease. She admired the colours in the room – oranges, browns, yellows – and the paintings. She said she was fond of landscapes herself (this was after noticing my Sheila Fell) and that if she had the money she would like to have a Whistler. She looked around her with open curiosity – Maureen always took guilty-looking little peeps – and said what a very attractive home I had and that she was surprised, that she hadn't for some reason thought I would be so concerned about my surroundings, she'd imagined me to be more casual. I rather liked her being so bold and personal, something Maureen and Stella were most careful not to be. They always seemed so terrified of getting to know me as a person.

We sat drinking coffee and chatting about the Lake District – Phyllis had once rented a cottage in the Windermere area but it had rained solidly the whole two weeks – and I waited to hear why she had really come.

'I expect,' she said after she'd finished a second cup of coffee, 'I expect you're wondering why I've come to see you here.'

'Yes,' I said, 'of course I am.'

'Well,' she said, 'the second bit first. I wanted to see you in your own home because I think we all seem to have got off on the wrong footing, and I'm sure half the trouble is that awful room with us all squashed in, like an overcrowded classroom, and I come over as a school-mistress. It's hard to be relaxed in that situation, it tends to make meetings a case of "us" and "them".' I said that that was true. 'So I thought I'd try to break down those barriers and start again, and I thought I'd start with you because I think you've a crucial role to play.'

'How crucial?' I said, warily.

'Look,' she said, 'this is the situation: we've got another family for Christabel, one we think is as ideal as we're going to get, and I want your help in introducing them to Mrs Blake. You know her well, I don't. It was hopeless last time, showing her photographs and outlining bare details, it was a big mistake. It's how we usually work, but in this instance it isn't appropriate. I want to tell *you* about the Carmichaels and I want you to give me your advice.'

So she told me about the Carmichaels. She was clever. She began by saying the most important thing about this couple was their own happiness. They were not do-gooders and they were not frantic to have a child because they had had none of their own. In fact, they had two, both girls, aged sixteen and eighteen, but they loved children and felt they should have had more, and had a lot still to offer. Both of them were involved with children in their work, Mrs Carmichael as a speech therapist and Mr Carmichael as a swimming instructor and coach. Only then did Phyllis play her ace card: Mr Carmichael was West Indian, Mrs Carmichael English. Both daughters were therefore of the same racial mixture as Christabel. She was watching me closely as she said this, which irritated me.

'I'm not Mrs Blake,' I said, 'I'm not against her going to black parents. It's far more important what they are like and why they want her than what colour they are.'

It was the straight liberal party line, but she said, 'Good, I quite agree, but Mrs Blake won't, will she? And that's what we've got to get past. What will persuade her?'

'What they are like, I imagine,' I said.

'You mean socially?'

'Well, she'll care about that, about the middle-class bit. Where do they live?'

'Totteridge. A lovely area. They haven't got their own house, but they have one of the nicest Council flats out there I've ever seen.'

'Those won't be magic words in Mrs Blake's ears,' I said. 'Say "Council flat" and all her snobbery will pour out. It'll be almost worse than being black. Oh God, it's disgusting, I know, but she can't help it, she's just stuck in this groove, thinking "Council flat" means parasite, failure, she's hopeless.'

'They are very charming people.'

'I'm sure.'

'Do you think we can at least get Mrs Blake to meet them and visit their home? Once she does meet them and sees their flat I'm sure she'll be won over.'

'I'm not. She'll probably hurt their feelings and they'll hate her. *She* isn't a charming person, as you know. How can you inflict her on them? Have you warned them?'

'Yes, delicately.' Phyllis smiled, and raised her eyebrows. 'They're willing to risk it, but I'd like you to meet them first, without telling Mrs Blake, if you don't mind.'

I took no persuading, was actually anxious to meet these people, knowing at the back of my mind that they could remove all my own *angst* over Christabel at one stroke if they turned out to be as perfect as Phyllis implied. All the long way to Totteridge in the car I felt hopeful and excited, already fantasising a wonderful future for Christabel – I could see this beaming West Indian father playing with her, teaching her to swim and run, and I could see his rather shy, gentle wife sitting side by side with her at the piano. I heard myself telling Mrs Blake about them, giving them my whole-hearted seal of approval, and I even saw her harsh-lined old face softening when finally she met them. So I was hugely prejudiced in their favour and the disappointment was all the more bitter.

They were both extremely presentable and pleasant but they were so far from being what I expected that this hardly made any impression. My misgivings, the draining of my optimism, began as soon as we went into the flat, before I'd properly taken in either of the Carmichaels. It wasn't the right sort of place for Christabel. The block was in an attractive area – grass all round, plenty of trees, very rural indeed and the common hardly any distance – and everything was immaculately clean and painted. Clearly, only choice Council tenants ever got billeted here. But the flat, which was the top one of six, was as sterile as Betty's house. There were no pictures on the gleaming white-painted walls and only a row of about a dozen paperbacks on the bookshelves built into the alcoves either side of the gas-fire (the rest of the shelves were filled with china). The furniture was sub-Habitat, basic looking and modern, all very cheerfully covered in bright red cotton covers. The carpet was a serviceable grey. It looked like an hotel room, spotless and unlived in. I felt uncomfortable the moment I entered.

We all sat down and coffee was produced. Mrs Carmichael, Lisa, did most of the talking. She was a young-looking forty with a nice, open, friendly face, the sort that makes you think nothing could ever be hidden by this person. She was rather plump, but in a schoolgirlish, not a matronly, way. The schoolgirl-air was increased by the way she wore her hair in a ponytail with a clip above each ear to anchor stray bits. She wore trousers which, considering the size of her hips, was a mistake, and a large, baggy sweater. She chatted away, smiling all the time, and I just found myself saying over and over in my head 'Christabel will hate her, Christabel will hate her.' There was no justification for this – I just felt certain. Mr Carmichael, James, was more bearable. Physically, he was very attractive – tall, lean, with a fine, proud head.

I decided the most interesting thing about the Carmichaels was the success of their marriage. (If their daughters were sixteen and eighteen then clearly their marriage was, by any normal standard, a success.) They seemed such an unlikely pair. It was easy to see why she had been drawn to him on looks alone, but harder to see why he had been attracted to her. But then, so far as personality went, it was the other way round: she had all the vitality, the energy, but he seemed dull, hardly opening his mouth and seeming unable to express any opinion even when invited to.

Then the girls came in. One was stunning, one very plain. The younger one, Clare, had the best of both parents' looks. She was tall, slim, with her father's smile and her mother's heart-shaped face, and her skin was a honey-brown colour. The elder, Samantha, was smaller, plump like her mother, and darker-skinned. They both were talkative and, unlike so many teenagers, very willing to respond to questions. It was easier to talk to them than to the parents and I did not feel any antipathy. Probably, Christabel would love them – they were easy, relaxed, very extrovert. It was a relief to fill in the time asking them what they were doing and listening to how Clare was about to take GCSEs and hoped to do Art at A-level and how Samantha had already done them and got four A-grades, two Bs and two Cs, and was now about to take three science A-levels and wanted to be a doctor ... Well, it was certainly a different experience from trying to talk to Judy or Craig in Betty's house.

'Isobel was a close friend of Christabel's mother,' Phyllis was explaining after there had been a sudden, awkward silence. 'She grew up with her and shared a flat with her before Christabel was born.'

'It must have been a terrible shock, when your friend was killed,' Lisa Carmichael said. It was as though she was obeying stage instructions – 'expression should show sympathy/concern/pity'. I could hardly bear to reply.

'Of course,' I said, grimly, and, 'naturally.'

'Poor little girl,' Lisa said. 'Poor, *poor* little thing. And how is she? How's she coping?'

'As children do,' I said, coldly. I knew I was being unfair.

'Very well, so far as we can tell,' Phyllis said, 'but of course she needs to be settled in a permanent home before we can really find out.'

'And it will be difficult,' Lisa said, nodding sagely. 'Hard going. I work with a lot of children who are almost autistic after that kind of tragedy. They can suddenly break out, be really wild, really violent, just when they seem to be making progress. Well, we're prepared for that, aren't we James? Aren't we, girls? We *expect* trouble, we're ready for it.'

'What I was wondering,' Phyllis said, a little embarrassed, I thought, 'was whether we could arrange a meeting with Christabel's grandmother and her aunt, with her natural family. You'll appreciate they are very concerned about her future . . .'

'Oh, of course,' Lisa broke in. 'You'd expect it, wouldn't you? With them not being able to give her the kind of home they want for her. Some people might hold that against them, but we don't, do we James? Do we girls? We can quite see their point of view, they won't find us censorious, we're not those sort of people, we just want to make Christabel happy.'

'How would you do that?' I put in abruptly.

'What?'

'Make Christabel happy – how would you think you could do it? I don't think I could. What makes you think you could?'

Lisa flushed. I could see Phyllis was annoyed with me, not surprisingly. 'I only meant,' Lisa said with an impressive show of dignity, 'we would do our best to *try* to make her happy. I know we can't guarantee it – nobody could do that. But we have a lot of love to give.'

'Mum,' said Clare, warningly.

'What? What's wrong? I'm not afraid to say it – we *have* got a lot of love to give. That's the reason we want another child, we feel we can offer a child a lot of love and security and nothing is more important.'

'It's a bit different, this case,' I said, still wincing. 'A lot of other people love Christabel. How do you feel about that?'

'We feel it can only be a good thing,' Lisa said firmly. 'You can't have a surfeit of love in our opinion, can you, James? Can you, girls?'

'But you might not love the people who love Christabel. You might not like them at all and then what would you do?'

But Phyllis had had enough of my third degree. She said quickly, before Lisa could reply, 'If Lisa and James adopted Christabel then they would of course have sole control over her – it would be up to them whether links with her natural family were maintained. And in the introductory period it would not be advisable for Christabel to see her grandmother or aunt or even you, Isobel, more than once every three months. She has to be given a chance to bond properly.'

That effectively silenced me. I wondered afterwards why Phyllis had chosen that moment to come out with this, to me, startling news, why she hadn't warned me before. Or had she genuinely thought I would know? How could I have done? How could I have imagined we would be phased out of Christabel's life so quickly? But later, when I'd discussed it with Fergus, it made more sense. Christabel, disturbed at being torn from Betty's, would almost certainly give the Carmichaels, or whichever family she went into, a very rough time. Having all of us hovering in the wings would encourage her to think there was an alternative. And then, from Lisa's and James's point of view, they would be struggling hard enough with Christabel without taking Mrs Blake on board. There was no doubt that in this instance, far more than during the fostering period, the Council had a case. But who would be brave enough to put it to Mrs Blake? She didn't think she could carry on coming to London so often and staying with Camilla, to be near Christabel – in fact, during her visits she was missing Edinburgh more and more – but she certainly thought she would see her granddaughter more frequently than she had done while Christabel was at Betty's. The idea of access being reduced to only four times a year, and even then being dependent on the Carmichaels, would enrage her.

I really didn't see why I should be the one to spell this out. It was quite enough to agree to take her myself to meet the Carmichaels, where Phyllis would be waiting. All the way there I tried hard to conceal my prejudice against the couple, because that is what it was: pure prejudice based on nothing I could justify. They were an extremely nice couple. Their niceness shone out of them. And you only had to look at their daughters, to see the family together, to know that they had been brought up successfully. Christabel would be fortunate to belong to such parents. But I could not stifle my dislike of Lisa Carmichael. She was too self-satisfied, too caring, too gushing. I distrusted her, but didn't know why. I felt depressed every time I thought of

Christabel under her efficient little wing. All this had to be hidden from Mrs Blake, who was instead treated to a lyrical description of the Carmichael family. 'Really,' I found myself saying, 'Christabel might almost end up better off, losing Rowena but gaining a father and sisters as well as a new mother.' Mrs Blake took a deep breath and nodded and said it was what she had hoped, that the social workers had been quite wrong to assume she was going to object to any and every family, that on the contrary all she wanted was the best possible future for her granddaughter. 'It is my duty, Isobel,' she said, 'my bounden duty, and I shall not shirk it. If these people are the right people then I would be happy to relinquish Christabel to them, they will not find me in the least intransigent.'

Poor old girl. What? Mrs Blake a 'poor old girl'? That harridan I have described? Well, yes, at that moment I felt pity for her. She was prepared to make a huge effort and emotionally the cost was enormous. She'd brought some flowers for Lisa Carmichael, and as we parked the car, suddenly panicked about them. 'Do you think I should give her these flowers?' she asked. 'Do you think it will make me look as though I am trying to curry favour?' I said I thought it would be seen for what it was, a nice gesture, and appreciated accordingly. Mrs Blake nodded, but was still nervous. As we walked towards the flats – 'Impossible to tell these are *Council* flats,' she said approvingly – she became nervous and clutched my arm.

'Advise me, Isobel,' she said, 'how should I conduct myself? I am not at my best with new people.' It was no good reassuring her by telling her just to be herself – herself, her full-blown, powerful self, would be fatal. So I suggested she let Phyllis take the lead and said as little as possible. 'I was too critical myself,' I confessed, to make her feel better. 'Like you, I can't help it and then afterwards I regret it and I see how I must seem to new people.' She was charmed by this and gave me one of the most natural smiles I had ever seen on her stern face.

It was still there when Lisa opened the door. She was dressed differently, and to greater advantage, in a blue jersey dress, very plain, with a scarf in blues and greens knotted round her neck. Her hair was not in a pony-tail but hung loose round her face.

It was very sleek and shiny, very well brushed. And she had a little make-up on, a little pink lipstick and badly applied eyeliner. Whether all this was for Mrs Blake, or whether this was the more usual Lisa and the one I'd seen the exception, I had no way of knowing. But it made a good impression as we stood in the doorway – Mrs Blake likes women to be smart, and smart meant the kind of conventional, formal style of old-fashioned day dress Lisa had chosen to wear. So we were off to a good start, what with the older woman smiling and the younger one dressing up.

Phyllis, already seated in the sitting-room, was pleased and recognised instantly the advantage she possessed. This time we had tea. Mrs Blake took in the pretty china, the linen napkins (my God, just to eat a slice of cake) and the silver teaspoons. It was how she liked tea to be served. It was all going very well until Lisa mentioned her job. She said how fascinating it was, how gratifying to help restore, or give for the first time, clarity of speech to a child. She told us, in some detail, of a boy she was treating at the hospital where she worked and described how, even though he had one of the worst cleft palates ever operated on, he could now make himself intelligible. I could see Mrs Blake becoming restive. She was never in the least interested in stories of people she did not know. She coughed and said, 'You would miss your work if you adopted my granddaughter. Are you sure you want to give it up?'

Lisa didn't hesitate, seeing nothing at all dangerous about replying. 'Oh, I wouldn't give it up, it isn't like an ordinary job, it's more a vocation.'

Mrs Blake put her cup down. 'I don't understand,' she said, the tone of her voice thinning in that dreadful way it had when she was about to become angry.

'What don't you understand, Mrs Blake?' asked Lisa, smiling pleasantly, genuinely puzzled and quite unsuspecting.

'You appear to think you can work and look after my granddaughter adequately.'

'But of course – I looked after my own daughters and I went back to work as soon as the younger one was safely established at school. Christabel is six, there would be no problem.'

'Rowena always intended to work full-time when Christabel was settled in school,' I said hurriedly, addressing myself solely to Mrs Blake. 'I'm sure she was planning to start looking just when she was killed.'

'But a lot has happened since then,' Mrs Blake snapped. 'She has been through so much, she needs a mother who is utterly devoted to her, surely, someone who will make her their full-time concern.'

'She would be *my* full-time concern,' Lisa said. 'I'd go part-time and always be there to collect her from school. You really needn't have any worries about that. And James, my husband, works school-hours mostly, he is often around when I am not. It is all very carefully organised.'

Mrs Blake was mollified, but something had gone from her previous air of cordiality. She was back to being tense, watchful. When James Carmichael came in, a few minutes later, he got the customary frosty stare. He'd come straight from the public swimming-baths and was still in his tracksuit, the same one I'd seen him in before, a whistle round his neck.

'James is a swimming instructor,' Lisa said, unnecessarily, since we'd already been reminded of this. 'He's been taking the little ones today, haven't you James?' James nodded and smiled and sat rather awkwardly on the edge of the sofa.

'Do you find it satisfying work?' Mrs Blake asked him haughtily, plainly letting all of us see she did not.

James looked taken aback. He drank some tea, noisily enough to make Mrs Blake shudder, and said, 'Yes, thank you,' as though someone had offered him a present instead of slapped down a challenge.

Lisa, who picked up the implication, of course, flushed a little and said, 'James is a very good instructor. The children love him. He can get children to swim who won't even go in the water for anyone else.'

'Indeed,' said Mrs Blake. 'My granddaughter can in fact swim. My daughter taught her without any difficulty.'

'But she isn't a very strong swimmer yet, she still needs water wings,' I put in. 'I'm sure James would do a lot for her confidence.'

Mrs Blake shot me a hurt look, as though I'd betrayed her. With a sudden change of tack she looked straight at Lisa and asked her, 'May I enquire how long you have been married?'

I saw Phyllis close her eyes momentarily and wondered what was coming.

'We've been together nineteen years,' Lisa said.

'Quite a long time,' Mrs Blake said, grudgingly. 'I was married myself thirty years before my husband died.'

Lisa smiled politely, James drank some more tea, nobody said anything. There was an atmosphere I could not analyse. I looked at Phyllis and saw her struggling with some decision. She exchanged glances with Lisa and then said, 'In fact, Mrs Blake, Lisa and James, though married in every other way, are not officially able to marry. Lisa's first husband is a Catholic and refuses to allow a divorce and although Lisa does not practise her religion she is a Catholic too. Lisa and James are common-law husband and wife and, as you've heard, they've had an absolutely stable relationship for nearly twenty years and are known as Mr and Mrs Carmichael.'

I was amazed to find myself very nearly as taken aback as Mrs Blake. How extraordinary – it had never entered my head that this couple, this ideal couple, were not married, and yet what did it matter. I felt instant admiration for them and liked them better, surmounting as they had done that kind of convention as well as racist attitudes.

But Mrs Blake's reaction was different and swiftly articulated. 'The Council have approved an unmarried couple to adopt my granddaughter? Surely not – what can they be thinking of? The legal problems are insuperable – to whom will she belong? To him? Or to her? It is all a nonsense.'

'It is very easily settled with a properly drawn-up legal document,' Phyllis said.

'What kind of document? What are you thinking of? A document, however properly drawn up, cannot make this couple one.'

'Nothing can do that, Mrs Blake,' Phyllis said quietly.

'What if they go their separate ways? To whom would my poor granddaughter belong?'

'We've faced that with our own daughters,' Lisa said. 'It is all taken care of, not that there is the slightest chance of us parting.'

'You've parted once,' Mrs Blake flashed at her, 'from that first husband of yours. You're quite capable, it seems to me, of succumbing to temptation again in spite of your religion which, I may say, is another thing. Lapsed or not, you are a Roman Catholic and Christabel is a Scottish Presbyterian. It is quite unacceptable. I really think we had better go, Isobel.'

What Mrs Blake never seemed to suffer from was any form of embarrassment. She could come out with such straightforward disapproval and not feel in the least inhibited because of any worry about the other person's possible feelings. If she had been standing up for the underprivileged, or against discrimination, then she would have seemed admirable and brave, but since all her indignation was founded on overpoweringly conventional and outdated attitudes, she seemed instead merely unpleasant. Lisa Carmichael was not only deeply offended she was also shocked. She herself was the sort of person who enjoyed being virtuous – that was what I'd instinctively disliked in her – and she hated to be put in any position where she seemed less than noble. I saw she was preparing to defend herself, that she would not allow Mrs Blake to leave triumphant, but Phyllis had already decided to retaliate. Perhaps all along I had been mistaken and really she disliked Mrs Blake as much as Maureen and Stella did, but it seemed to me that she only made her mind up during that unpleasant little scene.

Mrs Blake was on her feet and making for the door and I was about to mutter some vague, general apology and follow, not seeing how I could leave her to battle with stairs or lift, when Phyllis said, 'Excuse me, Mrs Blake, but I think it is only fair to the Carmichaels to tell you that they have scored the highest on our points system and that we will be recommending them as Christabel's new parents to the High Court, so I think you . . .'

'Then I shall of course sue,' Mrs Blake said. She was breathing heavily but appeared to speak quite calmly and with none of that rising hysteria in her voice which we all dreaded.

'That is up to you, but . . .'

'Of course it is up to me,' she said in the same even tone, her head lifted proudly above the scraggy old neck, like a tortoise straining upwards out of its shell. 'It always has been up to me, ever since my daughter was killed. I am responsible for what happens to my grandchild and I accept that responsibility.'

'In fact, Mrs Blake, it is the Council who . . .'

'Please do not continue,' Mrs Blake said, and even raised her hand to silence Phyllis. Lisa and James were regarding her now with something like awe. 'I am well acquainted, thank you, with all the legal niceties, but they do not affect my position, in my own eyes, one iota. Now, thank you for the tea, Mrs Carmichael, Mr Carmichael. I deeply regret any distress I have caused you. I did not intend any of my objections to seem like personal attacks. I am sure you are both splendid parents. Come along, Isobel, it is time we left.'

I felt like a little dog, tamely following the old bag out of the flat. We didn't speak in the lift. Mrs Blake was humming *Onward Christian Soldiers*, and I avoided her eyes. I drove her home, neither of us speaking. I said I hadn't time to come in when she asked me. She went on sitting in the car even though the engine was still running. 'Was I rude to those people?' she asked.

'Very,' I said, determined not to let her off.

'Well, I am sorry. I shall write to them and say so.'

'I can't see that will help much.'

'Perhaps not, but I shall do it.'

'They probably won't want you to see Christabel at all now.'

'Who?'

'The Carmichaels.'

'The Carmichaels will be in no position either to grant or deny me access. They are *not* going to adopt Christabel.'

'You may not be able to stop the adoption and if you can't you'll have antagonised them forever.'

'I *will* stop it. I am in the right and right will prevail.'

'I'm not sure that you are.'

'Isobel, you cannot believe those people are the best parents for Christabel?'

'They may be. I don't know. They may be the best available. They seem very nice to me.'

'They are not married and she is a Catholic and they have two daughters of their own who are much too old.'

'And he is black.'

'That is, in fact, irrelevant.'

'Is it?'

'I cannot believe you think so ill of me, Isobel. I am not racist, I abhor racism. I really would like you to agree you did not intend that slur.'

'I'm glad,' was all I was prepared to say, knowing I sounded unconvinced and despising myself for being so half-hearted, for wanting to make Mrs Blake suffer, because I did know she was not the person I'd made her out to be.

'Nor do I object to their material circumstances,' she went on, 'though I would much rather Christabel lived in a pleasant house with a garden to play in, and I had rather her new parents were more interesting than swimming instructors or speech therapists, and so people will allege a class bias. What I want is stability for Christabel and a background in which she will flourish. Those people will not offer either.'

'There may be no alternative.'

'There is always an alternative. I will find a family myself.'

'But you haven't. You've been trying for ages and you haven't.'

'No, I have not been "trying for ages", as you put it. I have been unable to begin looking properly out of a fear that to do so might complicate the position with the Council. Once their suggestion has been vetoed I shall apply to the High Court for leave to find an alternative. The important thing is to stop the Council.'

'What does your solicitor say?'

'He says what all solicitors say: it will be expensive. We will brief a barrister, however, and proceed to challenge the Council in the High Court.'

'So Christabel will be even longer at Betty's.'

'Yes. It cannot be helped.'

I waited until she had reached the door of Camilla's house. She walked very slowly up the path, pausing to smell a yellow rose and then to pull up some weed which was offending her. She bent with difficulty to do it and put a hand on her hip as she straightened up – a sudden stab of pain, I imagined. On the doorstep she fumbled about trying to find her key and I felt mean for not being at her side to help her. Once inside, she turned and waved. I waved back, and the door closed. I knew she would go straight to a desk and start writing letters, marshalling her arguments cogently against the Carmichaels. Her whole life was now dedicated to winning this fight – she never for one moment seemed to think either of giving up or of wondering if she was wrong. How wonderful, I thought, to be so certain.

I was not so certain. I didn't think the Carmichaels were right for Christabel, though I'd taken such care to conceal this from Mrs Blake, but I couldn't imagine finding any family exactly right. Mrs Blake's contempt for the way in which the Council had conducted their search seemed to me, if not justified, then at least possibly with some foundation. They hadn't exactly come up with dozens and yet, as Mrs Blake said, Christabel was such an easy child to place, surely: attractive, no problems other than those caused by her mother's death, healthy, intelligent. I would've thought the world would be queueing up for her. But of course those wretched reports had made much of Christabel's supposed lack of contact with her own feelings and her emotional immaturity. She wasn't, the social workers maintained, the well adjusted child her grandmother claimed, and whose side was I on there? I saw her as repressed but only at the moment and only because she was clever enough to conceal what she really felt. Betty liked her to be 'happy' and 'good' and she was living with Betty, so took care to be 'happy' and 'good'. Her grandmother liked her to grieve openly for her dead mother and to remember who she really was, so when she was with her she wept and was difficult. Going backwards and forwards, meeting the two rival demands, how on earth could she allow anyone to know her real feelings? They were a luxury she couldn't afford.

It struck me, during that period, the period before the holiday, that I gave myself no place in this equation. Where did I stand? What did I demand of poor Christabel? She was bound to be a different person with me too, but I couldn't decide in what way. I liked to think it was easier for her to be with me, but Fergus said I flattered myself. He said he thought it might be harder for her to be with me than with either her grandmother or her foster-family, simply because I was such a strong link with Rowena. I was Rowena's age, I had lived with her, I would provoke memories nobody else could. This, Fergus argued, must be far more disturbing for her because with me she was expected to be the child she had once been and there could be no greater strain.

Worrying that he might be right made me dread the holiday, and I dreaded it anyway. Instead of going to Rothesay with her grandmother for the agreed fortnight, Christabel was going with Fergus and me to the Lake District. I hadn't thought Mrs ex-magistrate Blake capable of such devious conduct, but when the family she had been going to join, with Christabel, had to cancel their plans, she hadn't told the Council but had instead begged me to take Christabel and say nothing. She would come with us, to give some semblance of truth to the plot, then continue to Edinburgh, doing the same in reverse at the end of the fortnight.

I could have said No. It was, after all, an outrageous, even dangerous substitution, likely not only to distress Christabel but to cause problems later (though, in fact, it did not). I could have said No all along to Mrs Blake and I never once had done. She had clearly come to regard me as a daughter, a rather more useful daughter than Camilla had ever been, and I had done nothing to disillusion her. But I was not her daughter, I did not remotely feel in such a relation to her, and what irritated me most was not only the way she had begun to take me for granted, but the way she implied that this was a *compliment*. She seemed to think I was privileged to be of use to her and that there was nothing else I'd rather be doing – she just assumed so bloody much in a way my own mother had never done in her life. My concern was solely Christabel, not Mrs Blake, and my allegiance to the dead Rowena, not to her mother. But all the same I said Yes and landed myself with doing something not only illegal, I suppose, but something which spoiled my plans for the summer. It felt selfish to mind, but I did mind, I wanted to go away with Fergus to his parents' holiday home in Hope Cove, down in Devon, and not to the Lake District, where I would share him with Christabel. I was afraid, really, to be a threesome.

We had a very tense and uncomfortable journey north. The parting from Betty had been awful. Since the shouting-match on Christabel's birthday weekend I hadn't seen Betty – Judy had handed Christabel over and received her back each time, and I'd been relieved – and I was nervous when it came to facing her. Betty wasn't nervous, though. She was bad-tempered and trying hard to be cold and remote. Christabel was almost pushed out of the door, her case already outside it, waiting to be picked up.

'I've washed everything,' Betty said, ignoring my greeting and definitely not intending to ask me in, 'I've washed the lot and ironed it and there's enough clean knickers for the fortnight so long as she don't have no accidents. She's got her wellies, like you said, they're in that carrier bag. Well, miss, you take care and remember what I said, all right?' And she bent down to give Christabel a quick peck on the cheek. Christabel wouldn't have it. She put her arms round Betty's neck and hugged and hugged her and whispered in her ear. 'What?' Betty said. 'What? I can't help that Chrissie, so don't you start, it ain't up to me, nohow, you're to go and that's that, the judge says so, and if I don't do what he says I'll be put in prison. So get off with you and be good and send me a postcard. Good enough for a postcard, am I?' she said, glaring at me.

'Oh, we'll send lots of cards,' I said. 'And we'll ring whenever Christabel wants to talk to you.'

'That won't be no use, we're off to Margate tomorrow.'

'Will you be home before me?' Christabel asked quickly, clinging anxiously to Betty's arm.

"Course we will, the day before, we'll be all ready for you when you come back, if you want to come back to Betty?'

'I do,' Christabel said, still with this awful pleading look.

She cried in the car and when we got to Camilla's and picked up her grandmother she cried even harder. It was a hundred miles before she could be said to have calmed down and we all felt murderous towards Betty, but were careful to say nothing. Then the traffic was appalling, long queues to inch past roadworks all the way to Birmingham and even after that, when usually we zipped along. Fergus did the driving (we were in his big estate car) and Christabel sat with me in the back so that Mrs Blake could have the more comfortable front seat. I did a lot of reading of stories and a lot of simple card playing. Gradually, Christabel cheered up. It's terrible to describe the lifting of her misery like that – how lightly we say children 'cheer up', as though their sorrows are easily banished and not real, like our own. I had no desire to diminish her distress, but at the same time I dreaded its continuing, dreaded having to become truly acquainted with it, and so I was relieved when she began to smile and to respond to jokes. By the time we turned off the motorway, seven weary hours after we'd set off from London, she was playing 'I spy' with Fergus and hugely enjoying the silliness of what he claimed he spied.

Mrs Blake stayed the night with us which gave my mother a full house. It was strange to see these two older women together. Stranger still to think they had both been young mothers living next door to each other for a whole decade. My mother had made it clear, years ago, that they had never really been friends, simply good neighbours with similar-aged children. And, of course, Mrs Blake was some ten years older than my own mother which must have made a difference. I saw Mrs Blake was astonished by the tears which rolled down my mother's cheeks when she talked of Rowena. (There had been none rolling down her own that anyone had seen.) Fergus and my father took Christabel to see some day-old chicks, and we three women sat over coffee after our meal and talked. Or rather, the two older women talked and I listened.

My own mother was really more skilful than I'd ever given

her credit for, skilful at handling abrupt, stiff people like her old neighbour. Whereas I tended to meet Mrs Blake head on, Mother approached her in conversational tangents and got her to come as near to relaxing as I suspect she was capable of. I was surprised to hear Mrs Blake confess she felt she had still to absorb the fact that Rowena was dead, and that she suspected, once Christabel was settled, she might then realise it and simply collapse. She said she felt she was holding herself together through sheer will-power and if she lost her concentration for a second she would fall apart. 'The mental effort,' she said, 'is colossal. Night and day my head seethes with plans. I know I am quite obsessed. Of course, Camilla is hopeless, she simply cannot cope and I do not expect her to. Isobel here is more able to help. She is a tower of strength, the best friend Rowena could ever have had.'

It should have been a tribute which touched me – it certainly touched my mother – but it didn't. It was too much like a very clumsy pat on the back and I wanted to shrug it off. I was glad when my father drove her off to Carlisle station the next day, to put her on the train for Edinburgh. Then my mother dropped her bombshell: she and Dad were going to my younger brother's for a week or so. She had never even mentioned this and I was completely thrown by the news. 'You didn't tell me!' I almost shouted at her. She looked completely astonished and said she'd thought it would be a lovely surprise for Fergus and me to have the house to ourselves. 'We haven't got it to ourselves,' I snapped. 'We've got Christabel – remember?' She gazed at me, shocked and then pained. Of course, I then had to say, hurriedly, that I didn't mean we didn't want Christabel with us, that it was just that nothing could be called normal while she was, and there wasn't much point in being alone. Still, she was upset and didn't understand at all. I hardly understood myself, but instinctively I didn't want to be in a little nuclear family set-up. My mother being there was essential somehow to the success of the whole holiday. But she had promised to go to my brother, who was just back from his Arctic trip, and he and his wife were snatching a holiday of their own while she was there with their children, so it couldn't be changed. The two of them, my mother and father, left the following day.

And there we were, sleeping side by side, like a proper mummy and daddy, with Christabel next door, our dear little daughter. She came in and stood by our bed, just as she used to do when I was looking after her. I woke to find her slightly anxious eyes scrutinising me. She was, as ever, fully dressed. I smiled and got up. Fergus was still clinging on to sleep, the way fathers are supposed to like to do. We tiptoed from the room and ate our breakfast in front of the window looking down the valley. I thought how lucky it was that she recognised none of the fells.

'What shall we do?' Christabel said. It was six-thirty a.m. and raining heavily.

'You could read yourself a story,' I suggested, 'or listen to a record while I have a bath and get dressed.'

'Then what?' she said.

I remembered how she craved plans, exact timetables for her day. It was a stupid thing to ask but I found myself enquiring what she did at Betty's at half past six in the morning.

'I stay in bed until half past seven on school days,' she said, 'and eight o'clock on Saturdays and Sundays.'

'You don't get up?'

'No. Mum won't let me.'

'So what do you do, all that time? Read?'

'No.'

'What then?'

'Sometimes I sing.'

'What? What do you sing?'

'Songs.'

'Which songs? Sing for me now.'

But she shook her head, sadly. I left her in my mother's big, comfortable kitchen with a book propped up in front of her. She put her elbows on the table and stared at it with no interest whatsoever. I felt a tiny spark of irritation with her which disgusted me. Dear God, it was only the second day.

Things improved once Fergus was up and about. By that time

– eight o'clock – I'd thought of things for Christabel to do. Together we had carried logs in and fed the two cats and gone to the end of the lane to meet the postman. She became quite animated and that look of anxiety had vanished. The rain stopped and Fergus said we should go straight off, while it was still dry, and throw stones in the lake which he was certain would be calm and have a surface perfect for skimming stones.

We drove to the Scale Hill car park and walked along the river-bank to the lake. All the way Fergus played hide-and-seek with Christabel, each of them taking turns to run ahead and hide in the undergrowth. I didn't join in. I really don't like playing those kind of games. As I stalked along by myself, taking no part in their glee, I thought how I'd have to force myself to do what Fergus was doing if he wasn't there to do it. A child, a child of six, needs such sport. Even I, at six, had loved hide-and-seek, had begged and begged my mother to play, and she always gave in if my brothers and father were not available. I really couldn't see myself doing so.

All week this feeling persisted. I saw over and over again the roles I would have to fulfil to make Christabel happy and I knew I could never stand it. I was too selfish, because 'being selfish' is what it is called if you have children and put your own pleasure before theirs. And I wouldn't do, I knew that, I wouldn't put their pleasure after my own: if I were a mother, I would put their pleasure first. When I wanted just to sit and read and Christabel sighed with boredom at my side I always put my book down and suggested things she could do. Mostly I had to do them with her – she didn't enjoy any activity on her own except watching TV and that was something I'd vowed to give her a holiday from. I couldn't think how I could survive a decade or more, if I had a couple of children, of sticking and cutting and sloshing about with water and paint, and playing endless board-games and building pointless constructions out of bricks and straws and plastic. Outside I was all right – I liked outdoor pursuits – but on weeks like the one we unfortunately hit, when it was misty and rained incessantly, there was a limit to how many times one could let a six-year-old get soaked.

I moaned about all this to Fergus, who told me I was getting everything out of proportion.

'Like what?' I challenged him. 'What am I getting out of proportion?'

'This slavery, as you call it.'

'It *is* a form of slavery, and if she were younger it would be worse. It means subjugating all my own instincts in order to be a good mother.'

'What rubbish,' Fergus said, and actually laughed out loud. 'I've never heard such pretentious nonsense. Look, if Christabel had been your own child you would have brought her up quite differently and she would have been *your* child, *my* child, with us in her. She would have been used to occupying herself, she would have wanted to, and she would have responded to the different kind of environment we would have provided.'

'Now it's you who's prententious – and stupid,' I said. 'It doesn't matter who a child is or what its circumstances are, all small children want much the same involvement, they *have* to be watched and guided. You'd be fine, you seem to like six-year-old activities, but I don't.'

'You like them more than you'll admit.'

'That's a lie.'

'No, it isn't. I've watched you making pastry with Christabel and you loved it, you loved teaching her; the expression on your face wasn't boredom it was pleasure.'

'For five minutes.'

'So – for five minutes. Then doing that collage with her, with the rice and stuff, whatever it was you were using, you were enjoying it, I saw you.'

'Fergus, those were isolated instances. You know quite well what I mean and you even know it is true. I'm just not cut out to be a mother.'

'Well, that's OK because you aren't one and you don't ever have to be one, so let's drop it.'

We dropped it. We worked hard at making the holiday good for Christabel, and I think we succeeded – she certainly seemed wonderfully lively – but it was not a success for us. We were tense with each other once Christabel was in bed and, though good friends, genuinely, when she was around, certainly not happy lovers. In fact, we weren't lovers at all after the first couple of nights. I might as well have been in my own bed, where Christabel was. There were no passionate nights, no wicked long mornings with our heads under the sheets, no lazy post-prandial afternoons, always my favourite time. I found no problem about getting up very early because I'd usually been miserably awake half the night and longed for day to begin. It was a relief when we were out, off on trips to the seaside to amuse Christabel, though there was nothing, in that weather, very amusing about Silloth on the Solway Firth. I ticked off the days and longed to be back at work, promised myself a nice, long, foreign assignment. Russia if possible, as far away as I could get. I wasn't even sure I wanted Fergus there, in my flat, when I returned. It seemed to me that our relationship had once more changed.

And so it might have ended, that holiday. I might have returned to London absolutely convinced that I was right to be on my own forever. I would have taken Christabel back to Betty, relieved my stint as mother was over and, though as committed as ever to seeing the adoption through, feeling I had done all I could do. But instead, by the time we were ready to go and collect Mrs Blake and stay overnight with her in Edinburgh, before the long drive back, everything had changed. Fergus and I were going to marry and adopt Christabel.

CHAPTER TEN

There was nothing romantic about this decision. How can such a volte-face be romantic? But it did spring from an overpowering emotional response which I, at first, distrusted: all my life I've forced my head to rule my heart, just as Rowena did the opposite.

So it was the last day, Thursday, the day before we were due to drive to Edinburgh and pick up Mrs Blake. When I woke up, soon after dawn, Christabel was in bed with me. She lay on her left side, her little body turned in towards mine, her thumb in her mouth, her thick, long black eyelashes closed against her cheeks. Her nightdress had ridden up her legs and her bottom was bare. She was sleeping quite peacefully, a half-smile on her face and yet I saw tiny tear traces on her skin, like the paths of a snail. I lay very still. Fergus was turned away from me, one arm flung above his head. The room faced southeast and already the sun, the sun we had not seen for nearly two weeks, was flooding over the valley. Our curtains were open and I could see, lying so still in bed, a vast pale blue sky and the outline of the fells in the distance. For some reason the stillness, the two sleeping bodies either side, the promise of a perfect day – they made me want to weep. I wanted everything to stay just as it was, forever. I was trapped, unless I wished to waken the sleepers, but I did not mind. I was content to lie there and wait.

Christabel woke at six-thirty, as she usually did. Watching her waken was the most touching experience: first the eyelashes fluttered and then the legs stretched out and she seemed to tremble, to vibrate, before opening her eyes. Her look was one of astonishment – she half-lifted herself, her mouth falling open, and looked about her as though she couldn't believe her eyes and it was all a dream. She was uncertain, even nervous, as she always was in the mornings, and slipped quickly from the bed. I smiled at her and put a finger to my lips and we crept together from the room, hand in hand. The sun pouring into the house through all the front windows had transformed the place – it was now full of colour, every room we went into seemed vibrant and blessed and the big kitchen, which all those two weeks had seemed too large, too empty, was now dazzling, every pan glittering, every surface shining. We took our breakfast outside and ate it sitting on the terrace, looking down a lawn still misty-grey with heavy dew on trees gleaming with yesterday's rain. It was always the same, this shock of beauty that happened in the Lakes, this triumphant transformation from utter dreariness into perfect loveliness.

I expect, stupidly, I had tears in my eyes. I must have done because Christabel took my hand and said, 'Why are you crying?'

'I'm not.'

She put her finger up and touched a stray tear which had escaped my control and squeezed out.

'Oh, that's not crying. I was just feeling happy, I was just feeling silly.'

She frowned. obviously, nothing made sense. I tried to explain. 'I'm feeling all funny,' I said. 'Peculiar, sort of churned up because it's such a lovely day.'

'Don't you want to go back to London?'

'It isn't that. I do want to go back really, but it isn't as beautiful there. It's noisy and dirty.'

She seemed to consider this carefully. 'Mummy said we might live here one day, but I didn't want to leave school.' I'd caught the past tense, the 'Mummy' instead of 'Mum' she used for Betty. I knew the significance of it and hardly dared breathe.

'Will my permanent family live here, maybe?' she asked, stumbling as usual over the wretched 'permanent'.

'I don't think so.'

'Why not?'

'Well, they don't know about you up here, do they? It would all be strange. You said you don't want to leave Miss Splint and your school. London is your home, really.' She nodded, seemed to lose interest and at that moment Fergus appeared, all eager and energetic to make the most of this glorious last day.

This is going to sound so crass, so callous, it may well be thought unforgivable, but I swear it was not until we were well along the path that we remembered and were horrified. Yet how could we have forgotten? It doesn't make any kind of sense and I can only blame the sun and the effect it had on all of us. Tragedy of any kind seemed so far away and I suppose we wilfully suppressed all knowledge of it when we drove along to Buttermere and parked in the car park there. Certainly, Christabel seemed to have no memory of that place and never by word or look betrayed any agitation.

It was such a *friendly* day, so soft and soothing, and all we intended to do was walk along to the Low Ling Crag, a little isthmus on the western shore of Crummock where there is good swimming (though I feared it would be much too cold, after all that rain, to swim). I had a picnic packed and Christabel was carrying her own vital supplies – chocolate, raisins, apple-juice – in her own small rucksack. We sauntered along the path leading to Scale Bridge, nudging each other and giggling at the sight of the overladen climbers ahead of us and imitating their ridiculous bowed-down walks. Once we'd crossed Ruddy Beck we left the path and made our own way across the marshy land at the neck of the lake. All along our route the rowan-trees glowed with berries and looked not like trees of storm and wind but placid, fruit-bearing trees, the berries hanging in clusters so dense and thick that from a distance they looked like apples.

There is a little beach on the north side of the isthmus and at the end, where it sticks out furthest into the lake, a small hillock. Here we threw down our rucksacks and I spread out the tartan blanket, that had been in mine, on the grass. We all had swimming costumes on under our shorts and shirts. Christabel was wildly excited as we stripped off and ran down to test the lake: freezing. The sun had not even begun to warm it. She dipped her toes in and shrieked, and Fergus made to splash her, but let her splash him first and I ran away from both of them. I went into the water cautiously. It was extremely cold but I was used to it from my adolescence and had always been proud of being able to bear it. Slowly, I went in to waist level and then I took the plunge properly. I swam only a few strokes and turned to swim back at once. Fergus was carrying Christabel into the water, her legs clasped round his waist and her arms round his neck. He was bouncing her up and down and they were singing together but I was too far away to catch the words. I got out and ran to where I'd left my towel and rubbed myself vigorously before pulling on a sweater and jumping up and down to restore my circulation.

We stayed there two hours or more until other people began to arrive – not many, only one other family and another couple, but it seemed like an invasion in that remote place – and then we decided that since we could see a few white clouds building up we should do some climbing. We never intended to go anywhere near Sour Milk Gill for by that time, with Red Pike so obviously in our sights all morning, both Fergus and I were well aware of the mistake we might have made. We'd exchanged glances once or twice and had deliberately turned so that we faced down the lake, towards Loweswater, while we had our picnic. All we intended to do was go up Ruddy Beck, cross it near the top, where it is heathery, and then make our way diagonally back down to Buttermere Dubs and the bridge. We thought Christabel would enjoy going up the beck and would think she had climbed a great height because the views from the top are so spectacular and give an illusion of great distance. And she did enjoy it. The beck was full and rushed and gurgled over stones noisily so that there was no point in talking. Fergus kept stopping and showing Christabel different plants and soon she was collecting prize specimens under his expert direction. We held hands, Christabel in the middle, once we'd jumped the beck where it began to be a mere trickle, and stayed hand in hand as we set off back down. It felt companionable, easy. Christabel far from being any trouble was an asset, making me see the scene through her own fresh vision, making me notice things I'd taken for granted for years. I suddenly realised how extremely talkative she had become, how inquisitive and agreeably sharp. She wanted to know why Red Pike was called Red and Fergus pointed out to her how the soil was in fact actually red. He talked above her head, I thought, but she nodded gravely when he explained how syenite in the rock and subsoil of the fell made the colour and I was amused. It is very satisfying, I reflected, educating a bright child.

By then we were making our way down. I was leading. There was a sheep track we used to take which cut through the wooded slope and brought us out near Scale Bridge and I'd thought it would be fun for Christabel to follow it. She liked woods, enjoyed the mysterious feel to them. I'd taken that path scores of times in my youth but, of course, it was a long time since I'd used it and I can only suppose it had fallen into such disuse it had become overgrown. At any rate, the path, never very clear at the best of times, came to a halt, quite abruptly. Fergus said I was a great guide and encouraged Christabel to tease me, but none of us minded in the least. I said all we had to do was head downwards, we could come to no harm. There were no rocks, no scree. It was a little steep but quite firm underfoot and at first we made good progress, encouraged all the time by the glint of the river below.

Then Fergus saw another path which seemed to climb back up before levelling out and suggested we should take it. I tried to whisper to him that we might come out at Scale Force if we did, that I wasn't quite sure of my bearings by now. We had no map, never having thought we would need one. Fergus said we'd surely hear the waterfall before we reached it and if so could take evasive action and once more head straight down. I hesitated, but meanwhile Christabel had gone off along the new path, convinced it was her discovery.

We followed hurriedly. After only a few hundred yards I could hear the waterfall. 'Christabel! Christabel!' I shouted, and Fergus began to run to catch her, but she thought it was a race and went as fast as she could and he, in his haste, fell over a fallen tree trunk and lost his advantage. By the time he was up again I was ahead of him, still calling Christabel's name, desperately trying to reach the small flying figure in her red shorts and T-shirt, but she was so adroit, slipped so easily and skilfully in and out of the tangled undergrowth which spilled over the path, and I was clumsy and slow by comparison. She got to the waterfall first. I saw her stop just as I cleared the trees myself and there she was, looking at this torrential cataract and straight in her vision the black, wet rock where her mother had slipped and crashed to her death. It made no difference that she was looking at it from another angle – the waterfall was the same, the rock unmistakable, and by the time I got to her, by the time my arms were round her, she was screaming and screaming. I clutched her, tried to lift her, but she struggled and pounded me with her fists, her head thrown back, the sinews of her throat taut with screaming. Fergus put his stronger arms around her from behind and so the three of us stood there on the edge of the waterfall locked in an embrace in which no one knew who was holding whom.

I closed my eyes and allowed my arms to fall to my side and felt such utter relief when Fergus shouted over the roar of the water, 'I've got her, I've got her!' that I sank to my knees. I crouched on the ground, shaking, sobbing myself, feeling such anguish for Christabel that I could not bear to look at her. But then Fergus yelled out my name and I looked up and saw him with Christabel now securely locked in his arms. He nodded downwards, to indicate he was setting off and I was to follow. I stumbled behind him, not caring where my feet went, and we slipped and skidded through the trees until we reached the bank of the river below. I caught up with Fergus as he stopped. Christabel lay, limp, still hiding her face in his shirt, her body curled up tight. Every now and again she gave a small, pathetic hiccup. My own face streamed with tears and I put out my hand to touch her and, as I did so, the warmth of her skin, the feel of that curled-up body, seemed to draw me like a magnet. I longed to hold her, to protect her, to have her cleave to me as she did to Fergus. My eyes met his and I suppose it was then we silently agreed.

I sat in the back of the car with Christabel now cuddling me. The physical pleasure was extreme. I trembled with the satisfaction it gave me to have her against my body and found myself smiling with the sheer happiness of it. I felt, then, that I would kill anyone who tried to take her from me. I felt nothing in my life had been worth anything before. I felt as though emotion such as I had never known, not even at the height of sexual passion, had spilled out of me and surrounded me. I could hardly bear to lie her on the bed when we got home, hardly bear to relinquish that small body. When we saw she was deeply, truly, asleep, we left her, with the bedroom door wide open, and moved across the landing to my father's study from where we could still see her but could talk without disturbing her.

'It was my fault,' I whispered.

'Don't let's start apportioning blame, for God's sake. If it was anyone's fault it was mine, going up that stupid path.'

'You didn't actually go up it, she did.'

'Christ, this is what I meant, let's not backtrack. It's done. It couldn't have been worse.'

'What shall we do?'

'What do you suggest?'

I took a deep breath. 'I suggest,' I began slowly, 'that we, you and I, that we . . .'

'Keep Christabel,' he said, a statement not a question.

'Yes.'

'Good. I agree. But if we are to keep her, if we're to satisfy the Council . . .'

'We'll have to be respectable.'

'Right. And that means getting married.'

'A means to a worthwhile end.'

'Exactly.'

'But then what?'

'Well, we can't marry in order to become approved parents without working out what the deal would be afterwards.'

'The deal?'

'Don't pretend to be stupid, Isobel, it isn't convincing. You know what I mean. Will we stay married? Will we live together properly?'

'Of course. It wouldn't be good for Christabel if we didn't and anyway I couldn't manage on my own, I'd need her to have a father.'

'Well, that's settled then. When shall we do it?'

'Whenever you like.'

'Shouldn't we be sure, first, that we *will* get Christabel? If that's what we're marrying for? Suppose we married, then they wouldn't let us have her?'

'We'll have to risk it because they certainly won't consider either of us if we're *not* married.'

Quite apart from the words spoken it was a very strange conversation. We whispered, so as not to waken Christabel, but even so that did not explain the unusual abruptness of the exchange. We were like people speaking to each other through a prison grille, who know they have not much time and are anxious to cram significance into what they are permitted to say. It felt awkward and wrong. But afterwards we sat looking at each other, waiting for Christabel to waken, both slumped in rather uncomfortable chairs, and gradually a sweet feeling of contentment came over me.

It was right to do what we were going to do, right from every point of view. I couldn't help thinking of my parents' delight – I could see their smiles already – and of Mrs Blake's relief. She had hinted several times that if I were willing to take Christabel – but I had always interrupted her, unable to bear the longing in her voice and desperate not to have the request directly put. She would regard the union of myself and Fergus as the ideal solution. And I felt not a tinge, not a flicker of martyrdom, no lurking suspicion that this was a far, far better thing . . . In fact, before the afternoon ended and Christabel woke, I was desperate to tell everyone the good news.

We told my parents first when they rang up to speak to us before we left their house. Their ecstasy was ridiculous. My mother kept saying over and over how happy she was even when I explained the prosaic truth behind our proposed marriage. 'I don't care,' she said, 'it doesn't matter, it will be the best thing you've ever done, Isobel.' I can't say I liked that, but I let it go. She asked if we'd told Christabel and I said No. I didn't want to have to explain on the telephone, perhaps with Christabel hearing, all the circumstances behind our decision.

We were both being very careful to be as calm and quiet as possible with her, instinctively feeling that all excitement, even of the happy variety, would be bad for her. She'd woken about six o'clock and had a drink and then fallen asleep again without saying anything at all. We wondered whether we should cancel the journey the next day to Edinburgh, but decided it might be a good idea to take her right away – it would depend on how she seemed in the morning. Naturally, I rang Mrs Blake and told her, saying only that Christabel seemed a little unwell. And I told her – the door of Christabel's room firmly closed and Fergus with her – about our plan. She gave a great sigh and said, 'You have made me so happy, Isobel. Thank God for it.'

We did in fact drive to Edinburgh as planned. Christabel slept for fourteen hours and woke up with no apparent memory of what had happened the day before. She was heavy-eyed and not perhaps as energetic as usual but otherwise seemed normal (though we knew she could not be after such a trauma). When I said we were thinking of going to Edinburgh now she was quite eager and helped me pack with enthusiasm, saying she liked long drives. I laughed and said I'd remind her of that when we were stuck in a traffic jam and she was bored. But the drive was easy, even pleasant once the motorway part was over, after Carlisle, and it only took two and a half hours.

Mrs Blake gave us a convincingly hospitable welcome. She'd booked us two rooms in the place where she lived, a sort of very high-class housing co-operative set-up, which she referred to as 'sheltered housing', but which seemed more like an exclusive college. We all went to a nearby restaurant for a meal and then, once Christabel was asleep, in Mrs Blake's bedroom, we talked. It all seemed perfectly straightforward: we would marry by special licence as soon as possible and apply to adopt Christabel. We never, any of us, thought there would be the slightest problem. We thought the social workers would be delighted to be presented with such a perfect solution.

Maybe we didn't break the news to them carefully enough, but then we didn't think we had any need to take care. Maybe we assumed too much, assumed that Maureen and Stella and Phyllis knew how much we loved Christabel. Maybe social workers are always cautious, trained by the nature of their job. But, for whatever reason, our announcement was greeted with silence. Fergus and I had gone to Phyllis's office to make it. After I'd told her, and when she'd said not a word for all of two minutes, I said, 'So if you could tell us how to set the procedure in motion, I mean tell us which formalities will have to be gone through, we'd be very grateful. But we hope in the meantime it will be all right for us to keep Christabel. I'm not going to work until she's settled in school in September so you needn't worry about that.'

'Well,' Phyllis said, with a great intake of breath, 'I don't know where to start, I must say. You both seem to have taken a great deal for granted. It isn't so simple, you know. Adoption is a very, very serious business – you can't just walk in here and tell me you're getting married and keeping Christabel. It really can't be done like that, it's complicated.'

'That's why we're asking what to do,' I said. 'We know it is, we've seen enough already to know that. What do we do? How do we start?'

'You have to be approved first.'

'You mean prove we're respectable? That's easy, we can arrange character references, bank references, all that kind of thing . . .'

'That isn't what I meant. You have to be visited over a period of time in your own home by a social worker, so that your relationship and circumstances can be assessed. It takes months.'

'But Maureen's been visiting me as it is, for months, you know she has, and so have you.'

'Visiting *you*, not Mr Donaldson. She has to visit you as a couple, as a pair interested in adoption.'

'But this is a special case, you know that, we're like relatives, an aunt and uncle, a brother and sister, we're not total strangers.'

'It doesn't make any difference.'

'Then it should.'

I was beginning to get angry and Fergus put a restraining hand on my arm. He said to Phyllis that he quite understood the care that must be taken, and asked if these obligatory visits could begin next week, the day after our planned marriage. She said she supposed so. She said it so reluctantly I couldn't stop myself. I said, 'You don't seem very pleased.'

'I can't say I am.'

'Why not?'

'There are so many difficulties ahead.'

'There always were. I thought you'd think there were fewer now. Mrs Blake, for one – she's thrilled, she won't be on your back all the time, there won't need to be any court action over the Carmichaels. Aren't all those difficulties swept aside?'

'They aren't swept aside.'

'Of course they are. Mrs Blake . . .'

'It doesn't matter what Mrs Blake says or thinks. We decide to whom Christabel should go.'

'But the point is, she won't *object* to us, it will all be straight-forward.'

'It won't. We might object to you. The Adoption Panel might object to you.'

'How could you? I've known Christabel all her life and Fergus a good part of it.'

'You have not got a stable relationship.'

'Oh, don't be absurd, we've been together off and on all our adult lives.'

'Exactly – off and on.'

'But we're getting married now, precisely to prove our commitment to each other and to Christabel.'

'That in itself may not be a good thing.'

'What?'

'You're marrying out of expediency. That's suspicious.'

'What's suspicious about wanting to marry for the sake of Christabel?'

'It isn't a firm basis for marriage.'

'Oh, don't be so stupid – it couldn't be firmer, I just don't understand your argument, we're doing this to *give* her stability and the kind of home she needs. I *know* her, I love her, and I ought to have done this at the very beginning.'

'But you didn't.'

'I've just said that. Are you going to make me suffer even more guilt?'

'No, but you have to understand all this is suspiciously sudden and . . .'

'Don't keep using that word, as though we had some awful secret design, and it isn't sudden, I've been battling with this decision for months and you know I have.'

'I know you told me you didn't want to change your way of life and didn't feel you'd make a good mother.'

'That's true, but I was looking at things in the wrong way. I had them out of perspective. The only important thing is Christabel's happiness. So long as she's unhappy I could never be comfortable – oh *shit*, that isn't how I meant it to come out.'

I felt so upset, fouling up my chances as I could sense I was doing, saying pompous things, expressing myself badly, swearing, and all the time Phyllis was sitting there, as hostile as could be. I couldn't imagine how I had ever thought she was more sympathetic than Maureen and Stella when, if anything, she now appeared more implacable. Yet I couldn't walk out – I was entirely in her power. To be angry was dangerous, to be rude fatal. So I sat there, furious, trying hard to control myself, not knowing how to start again. Fergus had got up and was walking round the small office. He came and stood behind me and put his hands on my shoulders. 'What Isobel meant,' he said slowly and gently, 'was that she knows she's tried to suppress her natural instincts since Rowena was killed and she's failed. She always did want to take Christabel, but she didn't think she had enough to offer and now, seeing what is happening to the little girl, she feels she was wrong. She *has* enough to offer, more than enough. And as for our marriage, that, too, has always been likely. Christabel may have succeeded in making us go ahead, but there's nothing false or forced about our decision.'

'I didn't imply, I hope, that there was,' Phyllis said, 'but the fact remains that the normal procedures must be followed. There are no short cuts.'

'Then can you begin them? Which was all we came to ask.'

'Of course. The Adoption Panel meets on September 20th, in six weeks' time, so by then you can have made a preliminary application to be considered, but I warn you, there's very little hope. You will only have been visited perhaps twice and no assessment of any value could be made in that time. Then Christabel is a ward of court which slows everything up considerably.'

'So we'll need a solicitor?'

'In these circumstances I think so, yes. Of course, we'll be recommending the Carmichaels to the Panel, so if they approve our choice and you contest it there would have to be a High Court action.'

'But why wouldn't you recommend us?' I said, unable to remain silent any longer. 'What can you possibly hold against us?'

'I don't hold anything against you,' Phyllis said, equably enough, but I noticed she turned a little pink. 'I'm not actually in a position to judge as yet. We would need all kinds of reports . . .'

'Then let's start on them,' Fergus said quickly. 'Now, at once, please, and how can we speed things up?'

Phyllis smiled, rather pityingly. 'We have a heavy case load, Mr Donaldson,' she said, 'we can't simply set everything else aside for you, much as we would like to.'

I got up, buttoned my thin jacket, suddenly cold. 'Come on,' I said to Fergus. 'Let's go.'

'May I wish you good luck for your wedding?' Phyllis said.

'It isn't a wedding,' I said, sourly, I know, 'we're just getting married, quickly and quietly, without fuss. There will only be our parents and Mrs Blake and Christabel at the registry office.'

'Have you asked Mrs Lowe?' Phyllis said, frowning.

'Asked her? Asked her what?'

'Whether it is all right with her that Christabel attends?'

'All right with her? What are you talking about?'

'Mrs Lowe may feel that as Christabel has been unsettled for the last two weeks she should really not be disrupted again for a while, and of course, your next access visit isn't for two weeks.'

'Have you gone mad?' I said, loudly, ignoring Fergus's warning 'Isobel'. 'We're talking about a simple ceremony, a matter of an hour or so. How could Betty object to that? And in any case, she doesn't have to go back there, she's staying with us, I told you, I'm not going to work at all, I'll be her full-time companion.'

'No,' Phyllis said, 'you will not. Christabel must be returned immediately to her foster-home. The High Court is her guardian, the ultimate authority, and its permission is needed for all decisions affecting her residence. She cannot change it without express permission and it is very unlikely to be given, especially as we, as the local authority invested with her care, would not advise it.'

She said all this as though she was reading from a card, with a fixed look of resignation on her face. I kept swallowing and swallowing, in preparation to speak, but my mouth was too dry – I was literally speechless. Fergus said something conciliatory, I don't remember what, and somehow we were out of the office and down the shabby stairs and into the noisy street where it was a dull, drizzling August day. 'How can they *do* it?' I kept pointlessly asking. 'How can they, what right have they?'

'Every right,' Fergus said, driving steadily through the heavy high street traffic.

'But it's officialdom gone mad.'

'No, it isn't. Children without parents must be protected and Christabel was left without parents and without a legally appointed guardian.'

'But she has a grandmother, an aunt, why can't they automatically become her guardians? They're her relatives, her blood-relatives.'

'Isobel,' Fergus said, wearily, putting the windscreen wipers on as the rain increased, 'you're forgetting – her grandmother and her aunt voluntarily put her into care and asked for her to be adopted even before they knew the Council would have to take her into care anyway. We can't blame the Council for anything that happened. If Christabel had been taken in by a nice, cosy grannie or a lovely kind aunt immediately Rowena died then I'm sure they would have let her stay, with suitable supervision. They don't want their job made hard, they've got enough kids on their hands in far worse circumstances. They are only doing their job.'

'I hate that phrase, excuse for anything.'

'The thing to do,' said Fergus, 'is to keep calm and not antagonise them. We must fall over ourselves to placate Phyllis.'

'I hate her.'

'Don't be silly. That's pure spite, it's childish.'

'And you are so mature of course.'

'I try to be.'

'Oh, shut up.'

And this was the couple planning to marry a week later. Fergus maddened me with his stoicism, but I knew my fury was, as he said, unreasonable. All week, as we dashed about having medicals and collecting references and meeting the solicitor we'd engaged, I knew that without his reasonableness I would have been lost and quite unable to endure all this preparation. Nor would I have been able to deal with Betty as well as he did. He took Christabel back on his own – I could not face it. She was for the first time reluctant to go back, anxious about whether 'Mum' would be there and want her, and even more worried about how to explain the tear in her new skirt. She'd worn it on a walk one day, against all 'Mum's' orders, because it was her best skirt apparently, and it got snagged on barbed wire. I'd mended it quite well, I thought, for someone who finds all mending a chore, but my stitching was still evident. When she left me, all her concern was over this skirt – there were no tears or expressions of regret at leaving me. In fact, that last morning she seemed intent on evading me, ignoring me and didn't answer when I said anything to her. So it was fortunate Fergus was returning her and I didn't have to struggle to get through this resistance.

It was pathetic, as ever, watching her get her things together. Children with luggage, standing with toys in one hand and their bag in the other, look vulnerable at the best of times, but Christabel had the extra pathos of an evacuee – all she needed was a gas-mask. She'd put on, without any discussion, her 'Betty' clothes, the pleated skirt and fussy blouse and the bright pink lambswool cardigan, and she'd insisted on cleaning her patent leather shoes herself. She kept looking down at them anxiously, to see if they were shiny enough and almost at the last minute discovered she had a bicycle chain mark on one of her white socks. It had to come off and another to be found before she would go. Then she fussed over her present for Betty and for every single member of her foster-family. She'd gone on about presents almost from the beginning, saying everyone would be bringing her presents from Margate and she must have presents for them. It all made me a little irritable, but Fergus had been sympathetic and patient and had taken her off one wet day to Keswick where he was sure suitable presents could be found in the tourist shops. I thought the amount he spent absurd, but I suppose it was worth it for the sake not just of Christabel's pleasure but her prestige in the Lowe household. Betty was to receive a pair of leather gloves, Norman a tartan tie (she was supposed, after all, to have been to Scotland on holiday), Judy a scarf, Marlene a bracelet and all the boys key-rings.

Fergus said the handover had gone well, though there had been a bad moment when the door had not opened immediately (the bell was broken and he hadn't been heard till he used the knocker). Christabel had begun to whimper, so that when Betty at last appeared her first words had been, ''Ere, what they been doing to you? You look like you've had an 'oliday, I don't think.' Christabel had flung herself into Betty's arms, to her obvious gratification, and then everything had flowed from that. The presents were given and Betty loved the gloves and Norman put his tie on at once. They'd given her a doll dressed in Welsh National costume – hard to see how that had come to be thought of as a present from Margate – and some rock. Betty was clearly very pleased it had rained during Christabel's holiday, whereas in Margate they'd enjoyed a heat wave and everyone was bright red with sunburn, that proud proof of a good holiday.

At the door on the way out Fergus had told Norman about us getting married, and Norman had said he'd been caught in the end, had he, but Fergus hadn't asked if Christabel could come and watch us marry. He'd thought he'd wait, that it wouldn't be tactful at that point to talk about taking Christabel out again.

We asked the following Thursday, two days before the ceremony. Again, Fergus did the asking, and yes it was because I was too cowardly to do so. Since Betty had not yet been told that we intended to try to adopt Christabel she was apparently prepared to be generous and saw no reason why Chrissie shouldn't be there. All that slightly peeved her was that Christabel wasn't being asked to be a bridesmaid. 'She's made for it,' Fergus reported Betty as saying, 'look at her – made for it – she'd be a proper little picture in a pink dress with rosebuds in her hair and think how she'd enjoy it. Or if it isn't a church-do she could be a flower girl, carry a basket of flowers with ribbons on the 'andle, it'd look ever so sweet.' Not even the thought of how much Christabel would indeed enjoy it or how high I would soar in Betty's estimation persuaded me to relent: no bridesmaid, no flower girl. This was to be the most downbeat ceremony we could devise, as simple and straightforward and, above all, as *quick* as humanly possible.

I dreaded the day. Not the fact that I was marrying Fergus – the marrying meant nothing to me, I was quite indifferent to that part of it – but the whole fuss involved. I knew there would have to be some sort of gathering and that was what I hated the thought of, but how could we have two sets of parents coming to London specially for this ridiculous ceremony and not offer some sort of hospitality? I'd begged my parents not to come, but my mother said she had asked very little of me in my adult life and now she was asking this one favour, that she should be present to see me married. As for Fergus's parents, they just assumed he would want them and in fact he did. It was no use my taunting him – he would have had a proper wedding if I had allowed it.

As it was, it had far more of the feel of a real wedding than I had bargained for. My mother wore a new dress, new hat, the lot, and it was the first time I had seen my father in a three-piece dark suit since he had retired ten years ago. (He had a rose in his button-hole too, from his own garden.) Fergus's parents were equally smart and just as beaming. Beside this quartet Fergus and I looked distinctly shabby, though I had taken to heart my mother's almost tearful request not to look 'too defiant, dear'. I'm not quite sure what she meant by that but no fault could be found, surely, with my plain yellow silk dress even if I didn't have a hat and wore flat sandals with bare legs. Fergus wore a linen jacket and white trousers and as a joke produced a Panama hat.

But all eyes were of course on Christabel. Betty had asked what she had to wear and I'd said there was no 'had' about it – she could wear whatever she liked. I fully expected her to turn up in the fluorescent nylon blouse Betty had bought her in the market plus her pleated skirt, but not a bit of it. She wore white, white *broderie anglaise*, a simple little dress with no sleeves and a scalloped round neck and a scalloped hem ending just above her knees. Around her waist she had a pink satin sash and in her tight curly hair a ribbon the same colour. She looked enchanting and knew it. Betty had bought her a posy of small pink and white roses – such taste suddenly – and these she presented to me but I gave them straight back, because I could see she didn't really want to relinquish them. During the short ceremony – which was not nearly as meaningless in form and atmosphere as I had imagined – I could see Christabel out of the corner of my eye all the time, smiling, eyes shining, face gleaming with pleasure and excitement and after it was over we both turned to kiss her before we kissed each other. She hugged me fiercely, as fiercely as she had ever hugged Betty, and Fergus picked her up and carried her in his arms out to the car as though she were the bride.

Then we went out for lunch to a local Italian restaurant with pink tablecloths. The waiters all made a great fuss of Christabel who became more and more animated and I could see her grandmother (who had joined us for the meal together with Camilla) eyeing her and clearly wanting to tell her to calm down, but she managed to restrain herself. We stayed in the restaurant until almost four and then came the awkward bit. What I wanted to do was to go home and forget the whole thing, but there were the parents to consider. Fergus's were no problem because they were staying with his sister who lived near Cobham in Surrey and drove themselves off immediately the meal was over in order to avoid the rush-hour, but my parents were not going back to Cockermouth by train, until the following day. They were staying the night and so had to go home with us. They are always ill at ease when they stay with me and I never know if it is my fault or not – there is certainly none of this edginess when I stay with them. I think it is just that neither of them like being in other people's houses, even the homes of their own children. They are such creatures of routine, of everything being in its place, they find difficulty in reorientating themselves.

Luckily, Christabel had permission to be with us until nine o'clock so my mother and father were greatly entertained by her. They took her off for a walk and played all kinds of games with her when they came back, so that the time flew. Watching them, I thought how wonderful it would be for Christabel to have my mother as her adopted grandmother – what a gain. And it was knowing how perfect my mother was as a grannie, as opposed to Mrs Blake, which made me take her with me when I returned Christabel. I knew Betty would not be able to resist her, and that she would feel warmer towards me as a consequence, and I was right. All the things Mrs Blake did, all the ways in which she alienated Betty, my own mother had exactly right. She is such an obviously kindly, soft, gentle, *motherly* person, so benign, that no one can feel threatened or repelled or intimidated by her. She looked at Betty so shyly and asked so hesitantly if it was all right to come in, because she'd been to the park with Christabel and was afraid her shoes were not as clean as they could be, that Betty was charmed. Then when she was in the awful living-room instead of ignoring it, too embarrassed to comment on anything in it, as Mrs Blake and I had always been, my mother looked around in the most natural way possible and admired the brass candlesticks and the Wedgwood teapot on the top of the cupboard and the embroidered antimacassars which it turned out Betty's mother had made before she passed on. It was the easiest hour I had ever spent in Betty's house and I'm sure the relief was mutual.

As soon as we were in the car and on the way home, my mother started. 'But how could you mislead me so?' she asked indignantly. 'I can't think why you were so cruel.'

'How have I misled you?'

'Mrs Lowe, Betty, she isn't at all the harridan you've made her out to be all these months.'

'I never said she was a harridan, Mother.'

'Well, the equivalent, you said she was hard and difficult and very unfriendly.'

'She is. You've only met her once.'

'That's enough. She's frightened of you, Isobel, that's the trouble, you forget how alarming you can be, you make her nervous, I can see you do.'

'I can't help how I am.'

'Of course you can. You went into that poor woman's house as stiff as a poker – awful. And you sat on her sofa as though you were sitting on a bed of nails. My sympathies are all with her.'

'They wouldn't be if you knew some of the things she's said about Rowena, *and* in front of Christabel.'

'What things?'

'Oh, that Rowena had a lot to answer for, that she hadn't brought Christabel up properly. And you can't think telling the child not to cry and not to suck her thumb is a good thing, never mind telling her nobody will want her if she does, either.'

'It's only a manner of speaking. I shouldn't think Christabel takes any of it seriously. Betty seemed to me a very warm, caring person.'

This warm, caring person of my mother's imagination let it be known the following day that she didn't think Christabel ought to stay with me again because it was too unsettling. The minute I'd got home after putting my parents on the train, Maureen was on the phone telling me this and reporting that Christabel had wet the bed for the first time in months and had that nightmare again, the one in which a man was taking her to look for her dead mother. Betty described herself as having had enough, having had it up to here with all them people, having decided she couldn't keep Chrissie if she was going to be with them lot upsetting her all the time. I tried to defend myself as calmly as possible, pointing out that Betty had approved of the wedding which was clearly the cause of Christabel's over-excitement and that she had kitted her out in the new dress and so forth which had made it more of an event than I had ever suggested – in short: Betty ought to take some of the responsibility for the aftermath.

Maureen said she hadn't time to argue. She said she felt it would be better if, for the time being, Christabel stayed with Betty and they suspended the access visits. When I started to protest that Mrs Blake would be most upset and would be bound to contest this decision Maureen said the Adoption Panel were meeting next week and everything might be changed then according to what happened. It was a clear signal that we should all be good – or else.

We were good. Nobody attempted to phone or visit Christabel though we did send her several funny postcards. If Betty thought that amounted to upsetting her, then too bad – it was surely a lot less upsetting than having us appear to lose all interest in her.

Meanwhile we had amassed, in the short time available to us, as much documentation as we could to put before the Adoption Panel. Apart from the vital marriage certificate we each had a medical clearance, references from our bank managers, character references from three people each and a profile written by a psychiatrist friend of my brother's, saying why he thought we would make excellent parents. I also had a trump card I had been concealing from the social workers for some time. Once, when she had spent her one and only night apart from Christabel, Rowena had sent me a hurried note which read: 'Isobel dearest, I'm off to Jessica's wedding after all, just going down for it this afternoon and staying overnight leaving Christabel with Leo, but if I crash or anything, I know you'll call me a ghoul, will you look after her? Please? Bless you . . . will ring when I get back, why aren't you going to J's Big Day, she'll never forgive you, loveya, Rowena.' I found this note stuck in a book. I remembered the occasion. Christabel was three. I remembered Rowena ringing up later and saying she felt a fool sending me the note. I remember telling her, one of the many, many times, that she was a bigger fool not to arrange properly what *would* happen to Christabel. I remember her saying that she was going to, that very minute.

I produced this note for our solicitor to see and he thought it worth copying and submitting, though he was quick to point out it had no legal validity. I'd only found it when Fergus moved the rest of his stuff in and I struggled to make room for his books. We intended now to buy a house but until we did he had to have some space and in making it for him I found the note, peeping out of the novel I'd then been reading, I suppose. I was immensely glad I hadn't found it at the time of Rowena's death, when it would have seemed like some kind of moral imperative, and would have quite unnerved me. Now it was an asset, a clear expression of Rowena's wishes, should she be killed and, if the Adoption Panel ignored it, a High Court judge might not. In addition to all these bits of paper, quite a pile, we had Mrs Blake's very powerfully argued support in our favour, also signed by Camilla. Our solicitor had hesitated over this, fearing it might do us more harm than good, but had then decided it ought to be included. The whole package went off together and we sat and waited. Maureen – we seemed always to be dealing with Maureen again and not Phyllis now – had promised to telephone us as soon as the Adoption Panel meeting was over, even if there was no clear decision. She had reminded us constantly that there might not be, that quite often the Panel would ask for further reports or delay passing judgement for another month, especially in a contested application.

But there was no delay. Maureen rang at four o'clock. She said the Adoption Panel had unanimously decided to accept the Council's recommendation of the Carmichaels as the most suitable family for Christabel. If we wished to appeal we could, but it was unlikely to be of any use. The only alternative was to carry the case to the High Court which, she warned us, would be a very expensive and uncertain outcome as well as dragging the whole thing out for at least another six months. She said we should think carefully and submit our decision in writing. I said we'd done enough careful thinking: we would be contesting the decision, and would deliver a letter saying so at once. 'I hope you know what you're doing,' Maureen said. 'Of course we know,' I retorted, 'we're fighting for Christabel's happiness, as we always have been doing.'

Chapter Eleven

The months from September to January were an appalling mixture of tedium and fear with the fear gradually gaining the upper hand. I learned that I am frightened of the law, or rather of what the law can do. It seems to me that the law is nothing so harmless and ludicrous as an ass, but instead is vicious and stealthy like a panther, sneaking up on you out of a jungle of doubt and hypocrisy.

Everything is wrapped up in impenetrable mystery and even the solicitors and barristers, those servants of the process, very often seemed baffled themselves. What enraged me was that they seemed happy to be so, that when they confessed it was impossible to tell how something-or-other would be interpreted they would smile and shrug and look quite pleased. They never appeared to be able to give a satisfactory explanation for anything. I am not stupid but they made me feel stupid and I resented it bitterly. I also resented the cost of this legal advice, advice which was anything but. *Nobody* advised. What they did was to reply to questions, consider suggestions, veto plans. They never at any time said, 'What we think would be the best thing to do and would give you the greatest chance of success is . . .' Everything seemed to start with us. I looked down the list of their fees, all most carefully itemised to the last stamp and telephone call, and saw I was charged for every single second of their time, even for the exchange of pleasantries. I rang our solicitor one day to ask if he would let me know whether the time of our next appointment was two or two-thirty in the afternoon. He was with a client. His secretary said she would ring back. She did, and there was the cost of the call on that day's charges.

You may think this quite right and proper, but I think it is petty, considering how exorbitant legal fees are. It also irked me that appointments were so difficult to arrange – our solicitor and barrister were permanently with other clients and when they did see any of us, never stopped looking at the clock. We never felt important or worthy of their attention. There was always this subtle implication that they had far, far more serious cases to consider. All we got out of them during those dreary months were a few stiff letters to the social workers, setting out our access rights and citing the relevant wardship rules. Mrs Blake and Camilla were allowed to have Christabel twice, though not for the night, but Fergus and I were not. We were not allowed to collect or deliver her either – this was now done by Maureen. While she was at Camilla's house, we went to visit Christabel but since we were unable to take her out could do nothing more than play games with her. It was all very unsatisfactory and somehow upsetting. She had become so close to us over the summer and now we saw her slipping away, becoming less and less the child we knew.

And she was of course becoming older. Physically, she changed more in those five months than she had done in the whole of the year before. She grew in height, put on weight (Betty called it 'filling her out') and her pretty hair, which had been a thick bush had been cut very short, near to the scalp and, though nothing could spoil her lovely face, this new hair style made it curiously more serious. More new clothes were produced to keep pace with this growth-spurt and I saw that her ears had been pierced. She was very pleased about this and showed us the tiny gold sleepers with pride. Judy and Marlene had their ears pierced and she was thrilled to join the club. Mrs Blake was furious and said she intended to take it up with Maureen – it was, she argued, a mutilation and she was sure they were not allowed to authorise it. We calmed her down, pointing out Christabel's delight and saying it would be foolish to make an issue of such a thing. Instead, we bought her some earrings, ready for when the sleepers came out. They were very small gold butterflies and pre-empted Betty's choice of anything more garish.

But Christabel was older in other ways too. She was becoming less of a baby, more knowing, all the time. An element of calculation had entered into her relationships and she was not above using Betty to score off us (and vice versa, I expect). She knew, you could see she did, how it hurt her grandmother when she said, 'My Mum says I don't have to do no practising. My Mum says it's a nasty noise, anyway.' This was a reference to the recorder Camilla had bought her. Since she was unable to have a piano at her foster-home and didn't visit her aunt's often enough to learn how to play there, Camilla had given her a recorder, shown her the simple fingering and sent her back to Betty's with a book of elementary tunes to practise. She had been quite excited by her own progress which I sensed had annoyed Betty and hence the repeated remark about the nastiness of the noise. But the point was that as Christabel said this she knew perfectly well she was challenging all of us to say something derogatory about Betty. She wasn't innocent but rather fully conscious of the trouble she could make. I thought her grandmother did rather well by replying, 'Well, dear, perhaps it would be best if you left your recorder here. We don't want to annoy your foster-mother.'

In fact, Mrs Blake wanted to annoy Betty very much indeed. She worked herself up into a state of rather embarrassing hatred over Betty and would not be persuaded that it was a mistake to be so personally vindictive towards her granddaughter's foster-mother. 'I *do* hate her,' she said vehemently. 'I can't help it, and I feel justified. I have struggled to like her, to understand her, but I cannot. I think she is quite wicked. She has wilfully made this period as difficult as she can. She will not even let me speak to Christabel on the telephone . . . "Please don't ring up no more," she said last time. It's monstrous.' What was also behind this professed hatred of Mrs Blake's was the knowledge that Betty had sworn an affidavit, and signed it, in which she alleged that from her observation of Christabel over a year she judged her to be 'afraid of her grandmother'. She also expressed the opinion that 'Isobel is not motherly enough to have Chrissie, though Chrissie is fond of her.' She then, to our collective astonishment, came down heavily on the side of the Carmichaels as adoptive parents – 'it would be for the best, with Chrissie being black,' she said in this affidavit.

It was no use exploding over this. We all knew it was our biggest weakness, far more potentially disastrous than our too-recent marriage. It hadn't needed Maureen or Phyllis to explain that, since Christabel was black, and since we live in a white-dominated society, she needed to have her blackness reinforced by her own family and not feel an outcast within it. As Phyllis put it, in writing: 'As a Black child growing up in a predominantly white society she will need to be in an environment in which she can be supported and learn to deal with the racism she will inevitably encounter. This is an area of childcare practice where there has been considerable debate, but where the weight of evidence supports the proposal, that white families are not equipped to offer this support to Black children in an effective way.'

Right. That was Fergus and me out of the running, if the judge agreed. Mrs Blake bent all her energies to investigating this 'area of childcare practice' that Phyllis referred to, and in no time at all was bombarding her with references to this and that book or report which doubted the truth of the assertion she'd made. It was, Mrs Blake maintained, as a result of her research, unproven.

She also drew up a formidable document in which she argued the case for Fergus and me by matching us on the six points through which the Council had themselves selected the Carmichaels. Phyllis had been obliged to justify this selection and in doing so had listed the ways in which the Carmichaels scored, so Mrs Blake took each point and dealt with it in a masterly way.

Firstly, Phyllis had said they were looking for two parents, not a single parent. The Carmichaels had scored a maximum five on this but Mrs Blake alleged it should be only four, because of them not being married, and that Fergus and I should score five. Secondly, a middle-class, professional life-style was thought appropriate for Christabel. The Carmichaels had scored four but Mrs Blake rejected what she had seen of their life-style as middle-class and Mr Carmichael's job as a profession, so she reduced their score to two and gave Fergus and me five. Thirdly, was a requirement labelled 'able to give Christabel emotional space'. The Carmichaels scored five on this, which Mrs Blake hotly contested. She cited having two teenage children already as using up a great deal of 'emotional space' in the Carmichael family and Mrs Carmichael's job as likely to be emotionally draining, leaving her without resources to cope with Christabel's extra demands. She gave them only one mark (though, clearly, Phyllis didn't mean by 'emotional space' what Mrs Blake chose to believe). Naturally, she gave Fergus and me five, because Christabel would be without competition. Fourthly, was 'willingness to maintain contact with the natural family'. The Carmichaels scored four, which Mrs Blake refused to accept – she argued they would be hostile whereas Fergus and I were almost part of Christabel's family already. Down went the Carmichaels to one, up went Fergus and I to five again. Fifthly, was the tricky 'able to help Christabel continue to work through the loss of her mother'. Mrs Blake was scornful of the Carmichaels' ability to do more than comfort, but was prepared to give them four and also make us four on the grounds that no one could know how this 'working through the loss' could be achieved until it was begun. Lastly, was 'sharing in a mixed race family and therefore not feeling alien'. Mrs Blake was obliged to give the Carmichaels five on this but refused to assess us as nought. She asserted there were more ways than the racial ones in which to be made to feel alien, and gave us three. There are no prizes for guessing who scored most.

Meanwhile, Fergus and I were a married couple, adjusting ourselves accordingly. It wasn't too difficult. We'd always known we shared many common habits and tastes and knew we were unlikely to conflict on the domestic front. There was no soulless division of tasks – they divided up without effort. Fergus shopped and cooked, I cleaned and tidied, and dealt with bills, saw to the washing and so forth. We needed more space but that was on the agenda once we had Christabel. Indeed, Mrs Blake was lavish with promises to buy a house for us, which was unwise of her. It was not intended as a bribe but it felt like one and we were quick to reject the offer. Christabel's own money would be worry enough and we proposed to see it was even further secured for her alone.

Mrs Blake had at one point rather nastily wondered if the Carmichaels were interested in Christabel's wealth and had proposed to mention this to Phyllis, but Camilla, even before Fergus or I could, had shown an uncharacteristic toughness and had firmly slapped her mother down, saying she was to do no such thing. Instead, she had suggested that if the Carmichaels did get custody of Christabel then her mother ought also to make her offer of buying a house for them, if she really cared about her granddaughter having a more spacious environment to grow up in. Mrs Blake said there was no need even to think about that because the Carmichaels were not going to win.

Some days her own confidence inspired me and I felt, too, that the Carmichaels could surely not be preferred to us, but more often I knew she was wrong. The issue of colour would win the day and, once it had been won by the Council and Christabel taken to the Carmichaels, then we would be lucky ever to see her. Why should James and Lisa preserve any closeness with people who had opposed them? They would not have been human if they had chosen to do so. Mrs Blake and Camilla would secure some kind of bi-annual access but for me the outlook was bleak – there would be no right on my side.

It was this that Phyllis played on when she tried to get us to drop the pending High Court action. 'Don't you think,' she said carefully, 'that you might try to accept the Carmichaels? They are very anxious to meet you more than half way, they really don't like this enmity.'

'I am not their enemy,' I said irritably. 'I just think we would make better parents for Christabel, that's all.'

'All your doubts have gone, then?' Phyllis said, perfectly amicably, but I chose to think with an underlying sneer.

'I haven't any doubts about the Carmichaels,' I said, 'and

actually for a very long time now I've had no doubts about myself. I love Christabel, I know her history, I'm part of her in a way those people can never be. All I'm sorry about is waiting so long to admit all this. After Rowena's death, we should never have brought her back to London. We should have kept her in the Lake District or taken her to Edinburgh, then none of this would have happened.'

'If you'd decided to have her adopted it would have done,' Phyllis said, firmly. 'She would have had to be taken into care.'

'Some care.'

'I beg your pardon?'

'Well, it's never seemed like care. You may have done the best you could, I'm sure you have, but the best isn't much cop, is it? That's another thing we didn't realise.'

'I find that rather offensive and quite uncalled for.'

'I expect you do.'

'So you won't relent, for Christabel's sake?'

'It's for her sake we're doing all this. Do you think Mrs Blake would spend what looks like being a minimum of £20,000 on the court action if she didn't believe in what she was doing? Do you?'

'I'm not sure that the amount of *money* spent signifies anything other than Mrs Blake's determination to win.'

'But why should she want to if she didn't think she was right?'

'She may well think she is right, but that's been part of the trouble all along – she will not listen to any other opinion but her own. Our viewpoint is perfectly valid and we must act according to what we consider are Christabel's best interests.'

'So you say.'

'Am I to take it you don't believe me?'

'I find it hard. It seems to me most councils would leap at having their problem solved by the natural family coming back and saying it wanted to adopt, and . . .'

'You and your husband are *not* Christabel's "natural family". You may feel you are, but you are not. Neither of you have ever had children or worked with children or lived with them, yet you dare to set yourself up as perfect parents for a child who will need the most expert handling. It really makes me quite angry.'

I saw that it did. Phyllis sat in front of me in her office – we only ever met during those months in her office now that we were officially opposed and social visits were not on the agenda – tense with anger and as distracted as Maureen in the way she generally fussed about. It occurred to me that she might be in trouble with Mr Wavell and other superiors because, of course, this contested court action would be expensive for the Council too and, if they lost, the resulting publicity would be harmful. Presumably Phyllis was being closely questioned over the position she'd got the Council into and, whatever their policy, she would be held responsible for choosing to implement it. Perhaps there were officials in the background trying to make her back down, as she was now trying to persuade us to back down – who knew the pressures she was under? And she was, after all, as she repeatedly said, only doing her job. If I believed her to be a good woman, and I always had done, then it was impossible to credit she was deliberately seeking only to antagonise us. We had to face the fact that she genuinely thought the Carmichaels preferable.

This was tough. I felt quite sick at the thought that she might be right. What did I know, after all, about being black in a predominantly white society? But then what had Rowena known? She would have brought Christabel up without any black father present, scores of other single mothers do, maybe hundreds, maybe thousands, and it just had to be accepted. But I saw of course, that, because the Council had been asked to select parents, the situation was different. They were obliged to apply their own acknowledged standards and that, in the case of our Council, meant a clear ideological commitment to having black children fostered and adopted into black families if possible. They hadn't managed it with the fostering, which I expect they regretted, but not to have followed their own guidelines over the much more serious issue of adoption would have made them look foolish and led to uproar. I could see their point of view, unlike Mrs Blake. I even came close to doing what Phyllis wanted and backing out (though the thought of Mrs Blake's wrath, never mind anything else, made me quake), but Fergus strengthened my resolve. He, like Mrs Blake, had no doubts. He just *knew* Christabel was better off with us and could not wait to have her.

His eagerness slightly frightened me. I was glad Phyllis, who saw him only once in that period, was not aware of it. I am sure she would have labelled it unhealthy. Since we were unlikely to find a house immediately, he had started preparing the small box-room to be Christabel's bedroom. It was painted a perfectly pleasant ivory colour and had a brown cord carpet which was a good neutral background for a rug I intended to let Christabel choose, but he had other ideas. To my annoyance, he stripped the room completely – all it had in it was a spare divan and a small chest – and began constructing a wonderful sort of hanging bed which would leave the entire small floor area empty and give Christabel some feeling of space. Then he insisted on putting black and white vinyl tiles on the floor, to make it look bigger, and cork on the walls so that they became pin-boards for all the pictures Christabel would paint. The plain yellow cotton curtains were taken down and a blind, which Fergus designed himself, went up. It was a jungle scene, full of exotic flowers and plants, and was certainly colourful and dramatic when it was pulled down. The hanging bed was covered with a beautiful Mexican blanket he'd once brought back and on the floor, where the ladder for the bed rested, there was a circular rug, purple on the outer edge and fading through crimson and lavender to pale pink at the centre. He built book-shelves on the narrow walls either side of the door and spent days in bookshops stocking them.

Christabel was unaware of this, because of course we were no longer allowed to have her home. We did not even tell her about this secret room awaiting her, knowing that it would be dangerous to build up her hopes. But did she have those hopes? Who could be sure? I imagined over and over again what it would be like if Christabel's own opinion were asked: who would she choose, us or the Carmichaels? Neither, I was sure. She would choose Betty. Maureen said as much one day. She also said Betty had started to say she wouldn't mind keeping

Chrissie as a long-term foster-child as she had done Marlene. She even knew, because of Marlene, that foster-parents could become what were called, custodians, a position resting somewhere between fostering and adoption. It was designed to cover the years up to eighteen and then come to an end. Betty had been issued with the appropriate booklet when she took Marlene on and knew that the main use of the new form of legal custody was in cases like Marlene's, and now Christabel's, cases where the foster-child had been settled for more than a year in the fostering placement. To my relief, before this information had even sunk in properly, Maureen had brushed the idea aside. Betty's home was not ideal for Christabel and she would not stand a chance. Christabel was clever and it had been generally admitted by then that she was not flourishing intellectually in the Lowe household.

In fact, her reading and writing had not only not progressed but had deteriorated, though we would never have found this out if I had not suddenly thought of going to see Miss Splint, Christabel's beloved teacher. What happened was that on her pre-Christmas visit to her grandmother Christabel was unable to read the book Mrs Blake had bought her – a rather lovely edition of *The Night Before Christmas*. We all could remember how, the previous Christmas, she had been able to read words like 'night' and 'before' and had been very proud of her reading ability, telling us repeatedly she was on the highest reading book of anyone in her class. And it was one area in which Rowena had excelled from the very beginning. I could remember, when Christabel was only a baby, the cut-out pictures pasted onto boards with the words they illustrated, like 'cat', printed in big, coloured letters underneath and pinned to the wall. There had been a vogue for these 'flash-cards' at the time and I had mocked Rowena mercilessly, but she hadn't cared. Christabel was handling board books by the age of one and certainly capable at three of recognising key words in any children's book. Nor had there been anything pushy about all this – Rowena didn't force Christabel in the least – she simply left amusing books around and always, always was ready to read them.

All that had gone. With no books around, with no one reading, Christabel had come to despise the whole medium. When Camilla gave her a book for her birthday she reported Betty as saying, 'Fancy giving her a book.' Camilla had replied that she thought Christabel liked books only to be told 'Not no more, I don't. Mum says they'll hurt my eyes, and I'll end up in specs, I will.' Naturally, all our middle-class hackles rose and I'm not sure they were all class ones either – our cultural values were threatened and we felt self-righteously indignant. Maureen said that when Christabel was settled in her permanent home she would quickly regain lost ground and it was nothing to worry about.

But we did worry, and after that incident I went to see Miss Splint. I had no right to, but Maureen didn't point that out. I went to see her the first week of the new January term, two weeks before we expected to go into court, after she'd dismissed her class. I felt guilty at keeping her, knowing full well how exhausting her average day was, but if she resented my visit, she concealed her resentment well. She said she was glad someone was interested enough in Christabel's school work to come and ask about it. Betty, Mrs Lowe, had never even been in the classroom the whole year. Christabel was brought to school by Marlene, in a taxi (for which the Council paid) and collected by her. There had been a couple of phone-calls from the social worker but not one visit.

'No one,' said Miss Splint 'has asked me about Christabel in person. I've filled out a report, but that's all. And I'm very concerned about her. She's regressed alarmingly, even making every allowance for what she's going through. Her concentration has gone, she can't play with the other children, and her art work would be labelled deeply disturbed by anyone.' She showed me some of Christabel's paintings. They all seemed to be of fires, sheets of paper covered in great, slashing strokes of red and in the centre a very small figure drawn matchstick-style. Sometimes there was another, larger figure in a corner, away from the red brush strokes and in one of them there was a tree, or what I took to be a tree, growing out of the top of the flames. I couldn't really read any meaningful significance

236

into them at all, but then Miss Splint took me round the classroom and showed me the work of Christabel's classmates, and it became obvious that, for whatever reason, Christabel was wildly out of step. I thought probably it was foolish to make too much of a few erratic paintings by a six-and-a-half-year-old, but Miss Splint produced two other paintings of Christabel's from the term immediately after Rowena's death and showed them to me. She'd kept them because they were so good and she'd thought of entering them for a competition. I could see why. They were lovely things, colourful and happy and most striking of all *composed*, every detail carefully arranged and precise. It was hard to believe the same child, and an older child too, had drawn the fire pictures which were an angry mess.

A primary school classroom after hours is not exactly a place conducive to heart-to-hearts, but I came nearest to any kind of intimate discussion of Christabel's plight with a stranger than I had ever done. It struck me forcibly that Miss Splint, Eleanor Splint, had all the compassion and concern so lacking in the social workers and, though it could be argued no social worker would be able to last a day in their job if they lavished those qualities on every client, it could also be said Miss Splint was equally stressed in her profession yet she could find time and tenderness for one single child. We sat together, on those hard school chairs, talking about Christabel and though the surroundings were, with the exception of the art work and posters on the walls, not much more attractive than the social workers' offices, I felt relaxed and comfortable. I told Miss Splint – I found it hard to address or think of her by her Christian name – about the coming court case and about the Carmichaels. I watched her face closely as I said James Carmichael's colour of skin was probably going to swing the judge in his favour – it was a strong argument that Christabel, being black, should be brought up in a family which reflected her own racial heritage and which had to meet the same racism she would have to meet.

She smiled slightly and put her head on one side. 'If I were a judge,' she said, 'I wouldn't let ideological views dictate my decision. Christabel's in a multi-racial society in this very classroom, she gets plenty of experience of being black where others are white. And she has no *cultural* black heritage, she hasn't West Indian relatives in the background like so many children would have. These Carmichaels might be the right family for her, I don't know, I've never met them, but it shouldn't be because of their racial mix. That's too crude.' Then she paused and, picking up a pencil, began to sharpen it so that I couldn't see her face exactly on the level, since it was bent over the sharpener. 'Of course,' she said softly, 'Christabel doesn't think she is black and that's dangerous. It's very hard for her.'

'How do you know she doesn't think she's black?'

'She says so. We have a reading scheme with drawings of white and black and Chinese and Indian children in it. On one page there's the question: "Who am I?" and the children single out the face nearest to their own – it's a kind of exercise. Christabel always singles out the white, blonde-haired, blue-eyed girl, and when the other children point and say that the other girl, the mixed-race girl with Afro hair and brown eyes is her she gets very upset and actually says: "I'm not black."

'But she looks in mirrors, she looks round the classroom, she *must* know, she must see the evidence of her own eyes, surely?'

'Of course, but she doesn't have to admit it. And she won't admit she has a father, that she must have had one, and that he must have been black. She's only six, she hasn't thought it out and she doesn't understand the biological part, but when the other children mention fathers she is adamant she never had one and she doesn't want one. There are several children in the class whose mothers are single parents, but they don't make an issue out of denying there is a father somewhere. They simply don't consider it. They say they only have a mum, if it comes up, but they don't emphasise the lack of a father. It's taught me a lot. I'm going to be sure my baby, when I have one, knows it has a father even if he isn't living with me.'

She looked up again and gave me another of her beautiful smiles. I thought I saw a hint of mockery in it and found myself blushing stupidly. 'Are you pregnant?' I asked.

'No. But I'd like to be. It would take such a lot of courage to go ahead, though.'

'Yes, I know.'

'And I love my job. I could take maternity leave, but I'm not sure if I would want to come back.'

'How would you manage? I mean, having a baby on your own.'

'Oh, I wouldn't be on my own. My mother would care for the baby and my sisters would help. It would be difficult, I know, but I think I've seen enough in this job to be prepared for that. And in my case, the man I want to be the father would be around, even if we aren't living together.'

I was silent, and worried that she would interpret my silence as disapproval, but I couldn't think of what to say. I felt tired, wearily thinking I had been here before, and none of the old passion I'd felt on the subject of single parenthood was there any more – I didn't know what I thought.

I longed to ask her about her lover, and why she wasn't intending to marry him, whether it was through choice or because he was married already, but I didn't want to pry. It was none of my business. So I let her go home and trailed off myself, feeling slightly stunned. How Rowena would have enjoyed Miss Splint's plans, endorsing as they did her own standpoint. In no time at all, I could see, Rowena's action was going to be the norm. I wondered, though, as I always had done, what Christabel, and Miss Splint's baby, if she ever had one, would think when they reached adolescence.

It started me thinking of someone I hadn't thought of for a long time: Amos, Christabel's natural father. I found myself wondering what would happen if he were contacted and told and brought to England. Would he take Christabel home with him? Would he have the right to, if his parentage was proven? Would it be bad or good for her if Amos claimed her? I knew nothing about him, didn't know if he was married by now or even if he had stayed in Barbados. Would it be fair to drag him into this? But maybe, if he was found and brought into this mess, he would agree to Fergus and me adopting Christabel, maybe he could help us. I had visions of Christabel being whisked off to spend her life playing in the sun, slushy, silly visions in which she had flowers in her hair and ran in and out of the blue waters of the Caribbean . . . Fergus put me right. He said he couldn't think of anything more catastrophic for Christabel at this stage than the sudden appearance of a father she had never known, and who might conceivably manage to take her away to a country and culture so totally different. And he said it was too much of a burden to put on to Amos who had always been used by Rowena. This led to a huge argument in which I did not so much defend Rowena as attack Amos, attacked all men, for allowing themselves to be used.

Those first two weeks in January were full of arguments, as the dreaded day for going to court approached. I don't think there was anyone with whom I did not argue. I even argued with poor, harmless Camilla simply because she allowed Maureen to push her around. Christabel was supposed to go to Camilla's on the Saturday before the case, but at the last minute Maureen said it was not convenient and changed it to the Sunday which was not at all convenient for Camilla but she was afraid to say so. I simply could not bear Camilla being intimidated by Maureen and tried to argue her into insisting the Saturday date was kept. She wouldn't. She meekly let Maureen bring Christabel on Sunday and cancelled her own arrangements. Luckily, her mother had not yet come down from Edinburgh, where she had been since Christmas, gathering her strength, or doubtless she would have been as scornful of Camilla as I was.

I also argued with Mrs Blake herself, the moment I met her off the train, but then that was no new thing. She'd been in touch with a body of people called the Family Rights Group and was full of plans to sue the Council for not allowing her the rights she had discovered she was entitled to as a grandmother. I argued that it was too late to sue anyone and that, since Christabel was a ward of court, access had been governed by different rules. Neither of us really had the faintest idea of what we were talking about.

We all met at Camilla's house the morning we were to appear in court. By then all the arguing had petered out. We were a very silent group of people. Fergus looked odd in a suit and white shirt and tie. Mrs Blake was dressed to kill, complete with fox fur scarf – horrible thing, though I remembered Rowena and I used to adore dressing up in it when we were little. She would not be called by the judge – in fact, it had been explained that it was unlikely anyone would be called in the normal meaning of the word since this was a hearing and not a trial – but she wanted to impress, as she always did. I saw she was clinging on to her stick very tightly, but her colour was pale rather than that angry red which indicated her blood pressure was soaring. Camilla was all in black, which her mother complained about, saying it was tactless to be dressed as if for a funeral, and Camilla defended herself by pointing out she wore black most of the time and that she looked her best in it (which she did). Her mother also dared to wonder aloud if *my* clothes were 'suitable'. I was wearing trousers, but perfectly respectable trousers, pale grey and immaculately cut, and a purple shirt under a loose jacket. I said I thought I looked suitable for anything and, rather huffed, she let it go.

Lisa Carmichael looked how I think Mrs Blake thought I should look, in another of her trim, old-fashioned dresses worn with a gilt necklace and black court shoes and carrying a black handbag. She looked very clean and fresh and wholesome. James wore a dark suit, like Fergus, and looked very solemn. We could not all avoid saying 'Good morning' to each other since we had to stand about, in clusters, in a sort of ante-room before we went into the court. We stood at one end, with our solicitor and barrister (whom we'd only met once before for a brief five minutes), and Phyllis and Maureen were with the Carmichaels and the Council's solicitor and barrister at the other. Everyone spoke in whispers and looked frequently at their wrist-watches. I'd wondered if Betty or Christabel would be there, but apparently the judge had spoken to both of them already, separately.

After about half an hour of this waiting, a man came up to our barrister and said something to him and he turned and led us through the double-doors at the far side of the room. I noticed we preceded the Council's party. The courtroom was not what I had expected, but then perhaps I had seen too many courtroom dramas. It was a modern-looking room, more like a lecture hall in a new university than a venerable place of antiquity. We all seemed quite near to each other and there was no atmosphere of solemnity though I was reminded for a brief moment of a crematorium. The judge did wear a wig, though, and was adorned in robes which was almost a relief – it had all begun to feel shabby and unimportant. We all stood up when he came in, as though in church, and waited until he indicated we should sit. He settled himself before a kind of solid-looking lectern – or perhaps it was a desk – which was on a low dais. He put his spectacles on and sat reading whatever was in front of him. I wondered why he couldn't have read it before, but presumably he was doing a quick recap. For some reason, this idea made me smile and it was just at that moment the judge looked up and seemed to fix me with a disapproving stare. I was very irritated to discover I actually felt afraid.

I listened very intently to everything that was said, but I find I can remember very little of it. I remember more clearly people's facial expressions and the general atmosphere than anything that was said during those forty-five minutes. I decided within two minutes of listening to him that our barrister was quite useless and wondered how on earth we had been landed with him. He was bored, he was dull, he brought neither conviction nor cunning to his recital of our claim and I longed to push him aside and speak for myself. The Council's barrister on the other hand, a young woman, who had looked very nervous outside the courtroom, was excellent. It was a pleasure both to see and hear her, by which I do not mean she was either beautiful or particularly eloquent, but because of her absolute concentration and commitment. It was touching to see how she was pouring herself into her description of the Carmichaels, how she built up detail after detail of their background until they sounded irresistible. Naturally, she made much of the colour issue and had several well-chosen quotes taken from recent research projects which made the ones our barrister had used sound completely outdated. Phyllis and Maureen exchanged gratified looks and Lisa Carmichael lowered her eyes modestly. I noticed her neck was flushed and wondered absent-mindedly if the gilt necklace was a mite too tight – she had a thick neck.

The judge put several question to each of the barristers but beyond asking us to identify ourselves – we had to raise our hands when our names were read out, as though we were schoolchildren – he did not speak either to us or to the Carmichaels. He did a lot of hard staring but that was all. Then he put the tips of his fingers together and half closed his eyes and proceeded to summarise what he thought were the salient points of the case. My heart leapt when he appeared to come crashing down on councils who got carried away by their ideological passion and forgot children are human and again when he was most severe over the lack of co-operation with a child's natural relatives especially grandparents. I thought perhaps I had been too gloomy and that, after all, we were still in with a chance. He even, once he stopped generalising, commended Fergus and me for not hesitating to marry as a preparation for hoping to adopt Christabel and said that unlike our social worker he saw nothing in the least suspicious about this. This was followed by a rather lengthy expression over his concern at the way modern society was going and how difficult this made it for the law. The law, he said, could only follow where society led and did not, contrary to popular opinion, dictate changes in mores. I got a little lost in all this, as I think everyone did, but it sounded curiously soothing and my hopes rose even higher – so falsely high that it was a shock when the judge suddenly said that he thought Christabel would be better off with Lisa and James Carmichael.

Mrs Blake actually shouted out, 'Nonsense!' at which the judge said that if there was any more comment he would ask for the person, who had so rudely interrupted, to be removed. I don't know what he said after that. I might as well have been removed myself. It seemed cruel to have to go on sitting there for another five minutes.

The Carmichaels went out first, beaming of course. I wanted to stalk right past them but Fergus took my elbow and steered me firmly towards where they were standing, enthusiastically shaking the young barrister's hand. Lisa Carmichael put on her sympathetic look and her eyes filled with pity. 'Congratulations,' Fergus said. 'Christabel is a wonderful girl.'

'I know, I know she is,' Lisa said, eager to show her appreciation. 'I can't wait to meet her.'

'You haven't even met her?' Fergus said, though I'd told him this was Council policy.

'No, not yet, we weren't allowed to because of this court action, in case we couldn't have her after all. We haven't set eyes on her, we've just seen photographs, but we feel we know and love her all the same, don't we James?'

I thought I might be sick, but managed a tight little smile and, though I could not bring myself to congratulate them, I wished the Carmichaels good luck and hoped Christabel would be happy. Did I make this sound like a threat? Perhaps. Anyway, Lisa flushed and said, 'I hope you and your husband will come and see that she is. We bear no ill feeling.' Surprisingly, James Carmichael, without waiting for the inevitable 'do we James?', said 'No, we do not, we'd be glad to keep in touch, we don't want to rob our new daughter of her past and the people who've been so good to her. That makes no kind of sense.'

Why am I so horrible about those people? It was such a sincere little speech and it brought tears to my eyes which I turned away to hide, not being sure what those tears were for. I was in time to see Mrs Blake hit Maureen. It wasn't a violent blow, merely a thump on the shoulder, but it was so unexpected that Maureen staggered and had to be steadied by Phyllis. Fergus and I rushed over, but Camilla had already apologised and had rounded on her mother. 'Mother! That was unpardonable, how *could* you!'

'Quite easily,' Mrs Blake shouted, 'quite easily. I've wanted to do that for a long time. All this, *this* . . .' and she gestured over towards the Carmichaels, waving her stick wildly. '. . . this is your fault! I gave my granddaughter into your care and you took her away from me and you were *pleased* to do so. You gave her to that awful Betty woman, you made her life hell for a whole year, and now you have prevented her from going to her mother's oldest, dearest friend! It is all your doing, you took a dislike to me, you wished to *spite* me and now you have won the law round to your side. Well, you have won. I hope you are satisfied. But do not think I shall give up, because I shall not, nor will I be prevented from seeing my granddaughter whenever I wish. I am an old woman, an old *sick* woman, and soon I shall die and you will be very relieved, very glad to be rid of trouble, but until I die I will not, I *will* not, be separated from my granddaughter whatever the law says.'

It was all very pathetic. In a stronger, younger woman such an outburst might have been terrifying and ugly, but coming as it did from an elderly, extremely frail and very distressed woman it was embarrassing and only pitiful. The moment she'd finished this diatribe, Mrs Blake began to walk out, her head held high and, though Lisa Carmichael tried to approach her, she seemed blind to everyone and everything and stumbled out into the corridor where Camilla hurried to guide her to the outside door.

'How awful,' Lisa said, 'the poor old thing, how terrible, I mean, as if we want to shut her out, as if we want to rob Christabel of her grannie, it's dreadful to think she sees us like that, I can't think why she does. What have we done?'

'She's just upset,' I muttered.

'It's me she blames,' Maureen said, a little bitterly. 'I've only done my job. Hit the social worker, that's the solution.'

'Now, Maureen,' Phyllis said, warningly, 'you must be professional. You have to make allowances, you mustn't take it personally.'

'I know,' Maureen said, 'but it feels personal.'

'Well, goodbye,' I said, wanting to get away. 'I don't suppose we shall meet again.'

'Oh, we'll have to,' Maureen said swiftly. 'During the handover period we really need your co-operation.'

'We certainly do,' Lisa put in, 'you're our link.'

Was it flattery, ghastly unctuous flattery to make me feel better? But then I am very quick to suspect flattery, especially flattery mixed with expediency. They did need 'a link' as Lisa put it and Mrs Blake certainly wouldn't serve as one. I'd already had explained to me in some detail the laborious procedure which would be followed once it was clear who was to adopt Christabel. It was all to be very gradual, with first of all visits for the day, then an overnight stop, then a weekend and if all that seemed to go smoothly, over a period of say three months, the final move would be made. Meanwhile, the Carmichaels would want to learn as much about Christabel as possible and would have to liaise with Betty. There was also the psychological value of my giving the seal of approval to the whole thing and providing some continuity – I knew all this and had never for one moment thought of turning on either the social workers or the Carmichaels as Mrs Blake had done. Nor, of course, would Fergus and I attempt to appeal and thereby prolong all this uncertainty for Christabel.

I knew I would do my dutiful best and said so. Mrs Blake wanted to have a new council of war immediately but Fergus and I declined to attend. We wrote to her, feeling it was better to put down on paper our point of view, so she could have no more illusions about our co-operation. And, of course, we helped Camilla encourage her to go back to Edinburgh at once. Then we have all tried, this past month, to get back to normal. Only, there no longer was any state of mind called normal. For fifteen months, time had been Christabel time, every waking moment full of her. Now, although she is still at the forefront of all our minds, Christabel time has to come to an end. To help it do so, Fergus went last week on another expedition, to Botswana. It isn't a particularly exciting expedition, but he felt that his going might restore that normality we are looking for. It was worth a try. He will only be gone, this time, six weeks. But before he went he left me with this thought: we ought to have a child.

CHAPTER TWELVE

The last vestiges of Christabel's presence were removed, the last indications that she would be coming to live with us erased. Maureen came and took the bicycle. It will be too small now, but she has such an attachment to that particular model that it was important it should go with her. Where will the Carmichaels put it, in their sixth floor flat? Perhaps they have a garage somewhere, perhaps it will stay in the boot of their car. I cleaned it before I handed it over. That took me back to Stockdale, and Rowena and me out in the front garden with our bikes up-turned while we plastered the painted parts with my mother's furniture polish (Min-Cream I think it was called). Then we used a Brillo pad, dipped in warm soapy water, on the metal handlebars even though my father had told us repeatedly that this would scratch them. Virtuously, I would carry it further and clean the spokes and the rims of the wheels where the dirt clogged thickest, but Rowena would be bored by then.

Maureen, when she came on her final visit, was nicer than she had ever been. The bike had been stuck in Christabel's wonderful new room and I think the sight of it appalled her. 'Good heavens,' she said, quite flabbergasted, 'what a beautiful room, what a lot of trouble you went to.' Perhaps she thought it out of character, but it seemed to shock her. I refused to reply. I wasn't going to come out with any Lisa Carmichael statements like: 'Nothing is too much trouble for Christabel.'

I just stood there, silent. 'What a lot of books,' Maureen went on nervously. 'Christabel will enjoy them when she comes over.' Again, I said nothing. We both knew that any 'coming over' was unlikely. Christabel had been with the Carmichaels a month by then and there had been no suggestion she might 'come over'. I had asked if she might and been told that 'in the circumstances' it would be better if she had 'a period of stability'. When this period will end is not clear and I have a suspicion it will not be, in our case, for a very long time, long enough to make quite sure that Christabel has been Carmichaelised just as she had been Bettyed.

The transition between Betty and Lisa had been disastrous. I was ashamed to feel just a small grain of satisfaction that Betty had been so difficult, that she had done nothing at all to help Lisa. While, on the one hand, Betty boasted of her much vaunted experience where handing children over was concerned, on the other, she resisted the whole process. She made everything hard, filled Christabel with guilt because she was going. Then, when the child clung to her and cried, desperate to demonstrate her loyalty, Betty pushed her away and told her not to 'take on' or *she'd* get upset. How any social worker could watch all this and still allege that Betty was one of their best foster-parents I did not know.

Lisa was indignant about all this but helpless to combat it. (It was she who described these little scenes to me and I believed every word.) 'I've tried to be nice,' she complained. 'I've said over and over how lucky Christabel has been to have such a good foster-mother and how I hope we'll all see a lot of each other in the future, but it's no good, she seems to hate me, and it tears Christabel apart.' This, at least, the social workers saw and moved with some speed. The transition was accelerated and, instead of taking the predicted three months, was completed in six weeks flat. Betty actually approved. 'If they're going to take my Chrissie away,' she said, 'then I'd rather they did it quick. She don't want to go and it breaks my heart to see it happen.'

Once Christabel was living with the Carmichaels, all the problems began. It was – it is – uncharitable of me to suspect ugly motives for permission to have Christabel here being refused when I know perfectly well she is in such obvious turmoil. The rages and tantrums she had shown when Rowena was alive returned the moment she left Betty and it was I who comforted Lisa and James by recounting old incidents. I told them how Christabel had thought nothing of lying down in the middle of a road-crossing and screaming, or of sweeping crockery off a table in the middle of some attack on her mother, and I told them how desperate Rowena had become about it. Now, Christabel was older and the violence worse, but no one was in any doubt that it had to be endured and lived through rather than repressed. It needed no psychiatrist to point out that this was normal behaviour in a child who, for so long, had been struggling to suppress grief and terror. And I must say that, although I still could not say I liked Lisa, my antipathy towards her (never based on anything concrete) disappeared. I have come to respect her. She remains calm, whatever the provocation, and takes nothing personally as a lesser woman might. Unlike Betty, she does not see herself in competition with anyone nor is she straining for praise. From the start, she was dogged and determined, but not hard or demanding. She still is, and will need to be for many more months.

But in spite of the comfort of knowing that Lisa can cope and may well be good for Christabel, as Phyllis always said, the feeling of loss is terrible. Even worse is the resentment, resentment against the social workers and most of all against the judge. I object to having Christabel's fate decided by the law and I am not even convinced the law was as impartial and balanced as it is supposed to be. I do not consider that Fergus and I were judged properly. I think the colour of James Carmichael's skin settled everything and I do not think it right that it should have done. But nobody will ever be able to tell if the legal decision was the best one. Suppose Christabel grows up to hate and reject her adoptive family: that will prove nothing. She might well have rejected and hated Fergus and me and she would also certainly have had no easy ride with Rowena, her natural mother. Suppose she grows up seeming more the Carmichaels' daughter than their own two, more devoted and in tune with their principles and attitudes than their own natural children: that will prove nothing either, except perhaps the power of environment. Nobody will ever be able to say for certain that it was better for Christabel to go to the Carmichaels than to come to us. And it is that knowledge which hurts most, the knowledge that we will never know, that we will never be given the chance to find out what kind of mother I, or what kind of father Fergus, would have made. Perhaps I would have fulfilled myself in ways I do not even know.

That is what I dream about now – not the past, not nightmares about Rowena, but the future which has been taken away from me. I see myself, older, with Christabel, older, and we are doing mundane things like shopping together (which, since I hate shopping, since I have never in my life shopped with anyone, is very strange). We are arm in arm, laughing, mother and daughter, and we are choosing clothes for Christabel who has grown into a beautiful adolescent with long legs and a wild bush of hair. We choose reds and brilliant purples, exotic clothes bedecked with sequins and tiny mirrors, and Christabel pirouettes and turns to me for approval, and I give it. Or we are walking by a lake and she is talking earnestly, intimately, to me and I am listening carefully. Always, we are close, we are friends.

My daydreams are ridiculous of course. I have eyes, I have ears, I have been a daughter if not a mother. My own family life has been happy and fortunate, I love and like my mother who loves and likes me, but nevertheless I have more often made her sad than glad. So I know my dreams are absurd and show me things about myself of which I am ashamed. Did I really want Christabel only to fulfil some dreadful sentimental urge? I hope not. What I thought I wanted her for was to love. Simply to nurture and care for her. I never thought I would wish to do that for anyone.

I do not want to do this for Fergus. Oh, I am not sorry we married, saying that does not mean I don't feel attracted to, and like, and want to live, with Fergus. On the contrary, I am longing for him to return from Botswana. I am looking forward to selling this flat, complete with the Christabel Room, and buying a house together, a place which can be a real home.

Probably we will settle in Edinburgh, not just because we both like the idea of returning to our roots, but because Fergus has been offered a job there, in the university science department. I see no reason why Edinburgh cannot provide me with as many, if not more, opportunities for my work as London does. And I can still, if I wish, go abroad for months at a time. There are lovely houses in the Georgian New Town and we fancy a house on the crest of one of those hills from which the sea can be seen on one side and the castle on the other. We will, I am sure, be very happy there. Fergus is a good partner for me, we complement each other almost perfectly, and there is, besides, a degree of passion for each other which we both like to keep hidden from other people. But I do not feel I am giving myself to him utterly. That is one of the beauties of our relationship: he does not threaten me by absorbing or dominating me. I am still myself, still separate. But in motherhood, as I understand it, as I always insisted on understanding it, there *is* no separate. For me, to become a mother is to give oneself, completely, forever.

If this sounds alarming and extreme then it is because I am alarming and extreme myself. I hate what I call half-measure motherhood, the having of a child as an accessory, as a perk, as a status symbol, a proof that you are a woman. I despise those who declare that they became a mother 'without thinking, really, it just happened'. I cannot bear it when motherhood means the having of the child and then the handing-over of it to a whole chain of substitute mothers – nannies, au pair girls, child-minders. When a mother is forced into this through necessity I can understand it, but there are those who, even before the birth, *intend* to abscond, and still take pride in their bogus motherhood.

At least Rowena was not one of those, at least she had every intention of giving herself, utterly. But I never wanted to. I was afraid. In my fear I discovered strong arguments to make me feel safer, I said to myself that to give birth, to become a mother, was a form of suicide, a suicide of the self. And I did not want to commit suicide. I loved myself and I loved my life too much. But for Christabel I would have done it, finally. That 'natural' feeling I had waited for arrived at last and I was consumed for a while by the most powerful urge towards motherhood.

I suppose it is a kind of punishment, a judgement upon me, the sort of cruel trick fate plays so neatly. I can't become a mother and that is that. Fergus's suggestion is impossible to act upon, to fulfil. Because we married in order to secure Christabel, I did not feel the necessity to tell him any more than he absolutely needed to know. Which was that I would never have a child myself.

'Fergus,' I said to him, 'if we don't get Christabel, you know that I will not have a child myself, don't you? I mean it. You do believe I mean it?' He said he believed it, that with Christabel his desire to be a father would be satisfied, that unlike women who want to be mothers, who need to go through pregnancy and giving birth, before that need was fulfilled, men could manage without the biological part. He said he wanted to father, not to breed. So that was all right. Except, of course, it was not, because I didn't tell him what he did not need to know, I didn't tell him the whole truth and I hope I can get away with never telling him. If that implies guilt and even fear then there is reason for it.

I do feel guilty. I know I ought to have made a point of revealing this secret, but when a secret has been really secret, when a whole decade has passed and not a soul has been told, it becomes almost impossible to part with it. It stays in my mind as though in a tightly closed box and the prising open of the lid would be difficult and painful. If Fergus had pushed me, I would have told him. In many ways I wish he had – it would have been such a good time to tell him. I ought to have carried on, after he'd accepted that I would never have a child of our own, I ought to have said, 'The truth is, Fergus, I couldn't have a child anyway. I was sterilised ten years ago. I had an abortion, the second, and I decided it was stupid to risk this happening again when I knew I never wanted to have children. So I had myself sterilised and I've never regretted it. It was a relief. I seemed to become pregnant so easily, in spite of taking every precaution, I seemed extra fertile, and even the Pill wasn't a hundred per cent for me. I couldn't stand the thought of going on with pumping my body full of hormones when I didn't ever want a child.'

All this I should have said, a regular little speech. Fergus would have been surprised, but it would have made no difference, I am sure. Now, it somehow does make a difference. He will wonder why I concealed this startling piece of information.

I wonder myself. It isn't sufficient to say, as I have just done, that the secret had been kept so long and so securely, it was too hard to reveal. It was something else, some faint apprehension that I might be regarded differently. There is no sense in such a feeling, it does not bear logical examination. I have no doubts about Fergus, I know him very, very well indeed and he is incapable of turning against me because I cannot have children. He is incapable of it. But, I think, he might have been – might be – more concerned about the meaning of such an act than I could endure and would – will – want to know all the circumstances surrounding it. I don't want to have to go back ten years and go over that second abortion and the unhappy end to my affair with Nick. I didn't regret the abortion, it was easy, nor did I find any difficulty in getting over it, but I did regret losing Nick whom I had certainly loved. He would have liked me to have our child and could not understand why I would not, and this had a great deal to do with how his feelings changed. When he left me – though he would say I threw him out – I found it distressing to think I could have been so mistaken in him. This was the man I had lived with and loved for three years, the man whose child I might have borne and there he was, a changed person all because of an abortion.

Well, I do not want to go over any of this with Fergus. The fact that I am barren has nothing to do with me as a person, and if it does, if a man thinks I am altered in his eyes because of it, that I am not fit to be loved, then I am well rid of him. But I ought to have told Fergus and I do not like to remember that I chose not to tell him. It was a little shabby of me. And I know that if I am obliged to tell him when he returns, as I suppose I may be, he will simply shrug and say there is no point in discussing it then. If he probes, as I fear, it will be equally easy to say I don't want to talk about it. He may be silent for a while, perhaps even upset, but it will pass.

What I dread is that he may suggest adoption. He may point out that there are other Christabels and that we could seek and find and adopt such a child. But I don't want that. I wanted Christabel, I still want her, but this mothering urge does not stand on its own. I am not like Lisa Carmichael, I do not feel I have 'something still to give'. I am not like Betty, I do not simply want to cosset a child and be the centre of their world. What I want is Christabel, who drew from me this powerful desire to give myself to her, utterly. I don't believe there is any other child who could do it.

Yet I am nothing to her. Betty was someone, Miss Splint was someone, but I am nothing, so far as I can tell. The last time I saw Christabel was to take her, with Maureen, from the Lowe house to the Carmichaels' flat on her first day visit.

'I've got her ready,' Betty said, in her usual fiercely resentful way, 'and I've told her the judge says she has to go or I get put in prison.' Christabel began to cry.

'Not prison, Betty,' Maureen reprimanded her.

'How do you know?' Betty said rudely. 'You don't know nothing. It *could* be prison, it could be if you go against the law, that's what the law's for, innit?'

'It wouldn't be prison,' Maureen said firmly. 'You'd just be reminded it had to be done.'

'That's what I'm saying,' Betty shouted. 'That's what I told Chrissie, it ain't no use whining, she has to go, and the sooner the better, with her grizzling about it night after night, going on and on about wanting to stay with me and me telling her there ain't no way that can happen and her saying what about Marlene and me saying Marlene's a different kettle of fish, I'm not good enough for *you*, I don't talk proper enough or read them books your grandma sends, so you can stop that. But she told that judge, didn't she? You was there Maureen, you should know. She says she told him she wanted to stay with me.'

'Yes, she did,' Maureen said, coldly. 'She loves you very much Betty, which is why you've got to help her to let go.'

'I can't,' Betty said and suddenly started to cry. 'God knows,

I've tried, but I've had her that long and she's my Chrissie and to see her taken off to strangers . . .'

'You were a stranger,' Maureen reminded her. 'Now come on, Betty, give Chrissie a kiss and wish her a nice day or she'll feel bad, won't you Christabel?'

One look at the child was enough to see she was feeling bad already. She sat with me in the back seat of Maureen's car rigid and stony-faced. She would reply to nothing and when I took her hand she snatched it away. Maureen saw us through the driving mirror, but said nothing. Christabel turned her face away and looked out of the window. I imagined that inside she was exploding with rage, but all we could see was the tightly controlled exterior.

'Christabel,' I said, 'please talk to me, *please*. I just can't bear this.'

The silence continued. She moved even further into the corner of the seat as though she felt contaminated by me.

'Well, will you nod or shake your head if I do the talking? Please.' Neither a nod nor a shake was given. 'What I want you to know,' I began, and then stopped. What I wanted her to know was that I wanted her but was not allowed to have her and how could I tell her that? It would set her even more against the Carmichaels. 'What I want you to know,' I started again, 'is that I love you very much and I always will. Do you believe me? Do you know I do? Do you know Fergus does? Please, Christabel, nod if you *know* I love you, even if everything is a puzzle.' Not a fraction of movement from her head. Maureen coughed pointedly. 'Okay,' I said, 'then you think I hate you, you think I couldn't care less about you, you think all the good times we have had were rubbish, don't you?' There was the merest, faintest shake of her head and I let out a great sigh of relief.

'You don't want to leave Betty, do you?'

Definite shake of head.

'You're afraid to leave her, aren't you?'

Definite nod.

'You're scared you won't like the Carmichaels and they won't like you?'

Definite nod.

'And then Betty won't take you back and you'll have nowhere to go? is that what you're frightened of?'

Big nod, face turned just slightly away from the window.

'Well, it won't be like that. The Carmichaels already like you. They liked you as soon as they saw you at Betty's. They're so excited about your coming to live with them, really they are. And Miss Splint likes them.'

'How do you know?' Christabel said, aggressively, but swinging right round to look at me.

'She told me. Lisa went to see her, to look at your books and pictures, and Miss Splint told me on the telephone that she thought she was a lovely lady and you'd like her. You can ask her, she'll tell you.' Silence fell again, but the head was not turned away.

'Betty says there'll be no more videos 'cos they ain't got no video.'

'That's true,' I said. 'I don't think they do have a video, but they have a cat and two kittens and you can have your bike, and the videos were getting boring, you said.'

'I don't like cats.'

'Don't you? You used to.'

'Betty says they're nasty things, they smell. Betty says you don't have to ask no one if they've got a cat 'cos if they have, their house pongs.'

'The Carmichaels' house doesn't, and the kittens are sweet.'

'What colour?'

'One's tabby, the other's black.'

'What are they called?'

'They haven't got names yet. Lisa thought you could give them names.'

Christabel's lip curled in scorn. I could see her registering how cheap this trick was. 'I don't like cats,' she repeated. 'I don't like kittens either.' There was a short pause before she added, 'Not much, anyway.'

We were nearly there. Once we arrived, I was supposed to leave within a few minutes, whatever the scene. This was really my last opportunity to talk to Christabel, and with Maureen in front and the tension in the car, it was far from perfect. I knew what I should be doing was giving her what Phyllis had called 'a positive image' of the future, but I felt more concerned with the past and my own part in it. My head was full of regrets, of justifications, of excuses and I could not burden a six-year-old with any of that. So I said, as we approached the flats where the Carmichaels lived, 'One day, Christabel, I'll tell you all about this last year or so and maybe it will make more sense when you're older. But don't think about it now, darling, just think of all the good things ahead.' She did not reply and I was not surprised.

We got out of the car. She stood beside it while Maureen got her bags out of the boot. In one hand she had an umbrella, one of those small ones specially made for children, bright blue with white spots. Fergus had given it to her one day when it was raining and she had been devoted to it ever since. In the other hand she had a small case, the last thing Rowena had ever bought her. It held very little – a pair of pyjamas, a hairbrush, a sweater and that was it, full – but was rather attractive with its brilliantly striped handle and straps. She stood holding these things, looking up at the flats where the Carmichaels live. Her face was quite expressionless and remained so all the way up in the lift. We were quite close together since it was a very small lift (there were two for the block and the other was much bigger). Christabel's face was about level with my waist. She kept her eyes fixed on the buckle of my belt as though hypnotised by the shiny metal. I could think of nothing to say.

The younger Carmichael daughter, Clare, opened the door and immediately dropped down to Christabel's level to greet her. Maureen and I stood awkwardly in the corridor, waiting. Clare was clever. She didn't expect answers to her bright questions and knew how to withstand the cold stare of a rebellious six-year-old. She smiled a lot and hugged Christabel. I saw Christabel stiffen and struggle but Clare let her go just in time to avoid a real protest. Then Lisa appeared and ushered us all in. There was a delicious smell – a chocolate cake baking, we were told.

'Do you like chocolate cake, Christabel?' Lisa asked.

'No,' Christabel said, 'I only like bought cakes like what my mum buys.'

Lisa looked momentarily thrown but recovered her relentlessly cheerful persona quickly. 'Oh, well then, never mind,' she said, 'there are plenty of others to eat it when it's out of the oven and you might change your mind later.'

'I won't,' Christabel said. She was standing only just inside the door, still with umbrella and case in her hands, whereas the rest of us had moved further in. Again and again Clare and Lisa urged her to 'come right in' but she stuck obstinately to the threshold. Short of dragging her in, there was nothing that could be done until she chose to move. We all sat down. I looked at my watch. I was supposed to go, but in order to go I would have to get past Christabel, who blocked the door.

I saw Clare bring in two kittens and put them down on the floor. We all admired them, Maureen extravagantly. It was obvious they were meant to tempt Christabel on to the hearthrug but she perfectly understood that and ignored the kittens. But they were of course full of energy and dashed wildly in all directions and inevitably Christabel was at the end of one of their erratic little journeys. They both arrived at her feet and began trying to lick her shoes. When she lifted one foot they both clung on desperately and she could not help smiling. She held her precious umbrella out and one of the kittens jumped for it and missed and fell and gave a high-pitched cry. Christabel dropped her case and her umbrella and picked it up and cradled the kitten in her arms. I thought it was time I left.

I haven't seen her since, though I have spoken to her on the telephone – very unsatisfactorily. There never seems any way for me to ask decently the things I really want to know, nor any way for her to answer.

'How are you?' I ask.

'All right,' Christabel says, her voice sounding very thin and wavering.

'Are you sleeping well?' I ask, stupidly, and she says, 'Nearly.'

'Nearly?'

'Sometimes I wake up.'

'Why? Do you have bad dreams again?'

'I don't know.'

'How are the kittens?'

'All right.'

'Have you given them names yet?'

'Yes. One's called Betty and the other is Norman.'

'Funny names for kittens.'

'They're named after my mum and dad.'

'I see.' Pause. 'Are you having good bike rides?'

'No.'

'Why not?'

'My bike is too small. My feet touch the ground.'

'I think your grandmother is going to buy you a new, bigger one for your birthday.'

'I don't want one.'

'Why not?'

'I don't like bikes any more.'

'What about swimming? Is James helping you to swim better?'

'No.'

'Why not?'

'I don't like swimming, I don't want to go in the water.'

'That's a pity. Swimming is fun when you can do it properly. Maybe in the summer you'll feel like it.'

'I won't.'

That was how our stilted exchanges progressed until I came to dread them. Christabel sounded so flat and bleak, though Lisa would later assure me she was settling in very well, 'considering'.

The worst part of the move had been moving schools, naturally. Christabel cried for Miss Splint. When the rages and tantrums started, Lisa told me about them quite openly and was determined to see them as a good sign, but that was when she asked me not to telephone for a while. She also banned Mrs Blake, who took it ill. Mrs Blake was back in Edinburgh of course and had had to reconcile herself to giving up all thought of appealing against the judge's decision. She told me she had already spent over £20,000 and that, if she engaged in a further legal battle, she would sadly deplete Christabel's inheritance, so she had withdrawn. She'd written to the Carmichaels saying all her anger had been directed at the social workers, not them, and that she hoped she might be allowed to see her granddaughter occasionally in the few years that were left to her. The Carmichaels had been cautious: certainly they wanted Christabel to know her grandmother, but they were anxious to get her truly settled first and would prefer six months to do it in. They proposed that Mrs Blake should telephone Christabel every two weeks and visit her in the school summer holidays. But then, when Christabel became so difficult towards the end of March, they asked for the phone-calls to cease temporarily, and I had Mrs Blake on to me at once.

'It is outrageous,' she stormed, 'to prevent me speaking to Christabel. It is cruel, quite cruel, and for no reason.'

'Well, it is for a reason,' I said, 'she is very disturbed at the moment and I suppose we are reminders of her past.'

'She cannot discard her past.'

'No, but so long as she clings on to it, the present hasn't much chance. I think the Carmichaels just want to establish themselves more securely.'

'It is a very strange way to do it, in my opinion, but, I suppose, nothing can be done.'

'No.'

'If only you and Fergus had her, Isobel, how different things would be, all this unpleasantness avoided.'

I doubted it, but did not say so. Perhaps there would even have been more unpleasantness, perhaps Fergus and I would have been equally keen to keep Mrs Blake off the telephone, perhaps the rages would have been worse with us and, unlike Lisa, I would have been unable to cope with them. It was so temptingly easy to blame the judge's verdict for everything, when, if blame had to be apportioned, it lay with fate, which is a kinder way of saying that the fault had been Rowena's. Mrs Blake had long since stopped admitting that. We all had. Rowena's responsibility for all this mess was now almost forgotten. We could not speak ill of the dead, nor was there any point in doing so. We had become so antagonistic towards the social workers and then towards the legal profession that Rowena's negligence seemed nothing and yet from it all else stemmed. We made Maureen and Phyllis suffer for Rowena's sins, and yet never once did they point this out, never once did they turn on us and say they had not wanted this burden we thrust upon them. If only . . .

But I cannot allow myself to go on like this. I have become maudlin and wallow in self-pity. I have lost Christabel. I doubt if I shall ever get her back. Will she, at eighteen, seek me out and choose, as soon as she is able, to desert the Carmichaels and come to me? Why on earth should she? I will be nothing to her – a few hazy memories, a person who sends birthday and Christmas cards, and presents, a vague figure on the periphery of her new life. And I do not deserve her, never did, though if mothers had to deserve children, there would be precious few who'd make the grade. I must learn to stifle this rush of maternal feeling, and no doubt I will. It can be conquered, with determination, and I am very determined. I shall learn clever tricks to deal with it, I shall focus my mind on my own selfishness (so-called) and how I would hate to give it up. I shall concentrate on stories of teenage horrors and be glad never to have to endure them. When the longing is at its greatest I shall work hardest and exhaust myself into relief. And when Fergus returns we will move back to Edinburgh and that in itself will cut ties and help to heal my wounds. None of the injuries I have sustained are, after all, fatal.

POSTSCRIPT

What a magnificent day for a birthday – that slightly misty start which, in England, especially in the Lake District, heralds good weather far more surely than a clear blue sky from early morning. This light, veil-like mist looped and swathed its way from fell to fell without obscuring the land and over the lakes it hung suspended, nicely judging its resting place just above the surface so that it looked like smoke blown by some giant mouth with great evenness. I stood at the edge of Crummock Water on my birthday morning, on Midsummer's Day, and looked down the lake to where the tip of Red Pike rose above the gentle mist, dark blue against the as yet paler blue of the grey-tinged sky. There was no sound, not a bird, not a fish, not a single car moving along the far-off lakeside road.

Slowly, I walked along the path to the boat-house, each twig that snapped underfoot echoing in the silence. My heart thudded, but not with fear. When I came to the boat-house, where there is only ever a single rowing-boat, I crouched on the little stony beach and watched the mist finally disperse from above the water and the brazen sun break through to transform what had been soft and unsure, into a hard, dazzling surface. It was only eight o'clock, but the heat was powerful.

I took off my shorts and sweater – I'd run all the way down from my parents' house, all three miles, two hours ago – and went slowly into the lake, slowly for pleasure and not to brace myself against any cold. It was not cold. The water was silky, clear, and released from its depths the heat of the last two hot months. I swam out, my eyes on Mellbreak where I could see sheep stuck like gravel to the sides of the fell. When I was a long way out I stopped and floated on my back and closed my eyes. I felt exhilarated, elated, and for no other reason than that I was well and strong and happy. Such a rush of energy and well-being I felt, such a sense of reclaiming my true self.

I arrived here a month ago, pale and drawn and so apathetic my mother wondered, with eager concern, whether I was pregnant. No, Mother. I was tired, worn out with all the emotion of those months after Rowena's death, drained by my thwarted desire for Christabel, exhausted by guilt and shame and finally regret. Fergus had decided to stay in Botswana another month and somehow I could not cope with the weight of my misery any longer. So I packed up, came home, and after a while my bewildered mother left me alone. She fed me, cared for me, followed me with anxious eyes, but she left me alone, there were no third degrees. I pitied her. I knew she had given herself to me, utterly, and that my unhappiness was hers. She will never free herself. All her life, her children will have this power to paralyse her with anguish for them. There is no such thing as our growing up and severing the bond, because it is not ours to sever, it is no umbilical cord that can be cut.

But I have no such bond. I swam, I floated and there was nothing to anchor me. I care for my parents, I care for Fergus, I even care for my brothers, but they have no real hold on me. Only a child could have had that effect on me, perhaps my own, perhaps Christabel, but without a child my happiness is not dependent upon another. I need suffer for no one but myself and that is an almighty blessing. Vigorously, disturbing the calm waters I had taken such care to slip through, I swam noisily back to the boat-house, arms and legs pounding furiously. Getting out, I saw I had left behind me a great wake of waves. I watched it settle before I left. Nobody could tell there had ever been a swimmer.

'Happy Birthday, darling,' my mother said, when I reached

home. 'What a beautiful morning, just like the day you were born, the happiest day of my life.'

'Now, why was that, Mother dear?' I asked gravely, knowing of course how she would like to tell me.

'Because you were a girl and I already had two lovely boys.'

'So if I'd been another boy it wouldn't have been the happiest day of your life?'

'Now, Isobel, you know what I mean.'

'I know what you mean. I'm very glad to have given you the happiest of days.'

We kissed. She gave me a bag, a dark brown, soft leather shoulder bag of the type she knew I admired. Very thoughtful. We kissed again. My father came down and we all sat outside breakfasting in the sunshine. Then the telephone rang and my mother rushed to answer. She called out excitedly that it was Fergus. He wished me a happy birthday and gave me the date of his return. My mother studied my face as I returned to the outside breakfast table.

'Everything all right?'

'Fine. Fergus will be back next week.'

'Oh, wonderful. That's wonderful. You must have missed him so much.'

'I've missed him,' I agreed. I wouldn't spoil her illusions by exaggerating how much. My mother wants me to miss Fergus passionately, to have been made ill by his absence, as she was made ill by my father's and I cannot oblige.

'It's been a good year, in the end,' she ventured. My father looked at her warningly. 'Getting married,' she went on hurriedly. 'I mean, such a happy event since your last birthday.' Then she paused. I could see she could not resist it. 'Who knows what next year will bring?' she added.

'Who indeed?' I said solemnly. I was not going to be so cruel as to put an end to all her hopes unless it involved an outright lie in the maintaining of them.

'Thirty-eight,' my father said thoughtfully. 'A good age.'

'Why?' I asked.

'Oh, half way, that kind of thing. Half way but not yet in your prime,' and he laughed.

264

'Thirty-eight is quite old for a woman,' my mother said, frowning. 'I wouldn't say it was young.'

'I didn't,' my father said, a touch irritated, as he always was when my mother misunderstood him, usually deliberately. 'I said Isobel was not yet in her prime at thirty-eight.'

'I'm sure I was, I'm sure I was past my prime. I had three children, of course.'

'Of course,' I said, 'and children accelerate one's prime.'

'Do they?' my mother said, looking anxious, as though she had stumbled on some secret she didn't quite like.

'Well, that was what I thought you meant.'

'I just meant I feel my prime was earlier.'

'You're still *in* your prime, love,' my father said, and laughed. Having started all this, he was withdrawing, but my mother wouldn't let him.

'Don't be silly,' she said, frowning. 'I'm nearly seventy and in my dotage.'

'I've never seen anyone less in their dotage,' I said. 'If I'm as active and healthy as you are at seventy, I'll be thrilled.'

'Then I hope you'll be as lucky as I've been,' my mother said, and added, with unmistakable emphasis 'in *every* way.'

I won't be, not in the way she means, but it is of no importance. I spent my birthday peacefully in the garden, basking in the sun, and nothing could rob me of my newly recovered contentment. I thought of Christabel, of course. I rang her – phone-calls were in order once more and even a visit was to be allowed before we left London for Edinburgh – and wished her a happy seventh birthday. She sounded cheerful and talked quite animatedly, quite naturally, about her presents and the swimming party 'Daddy' had organised for her. So James had become 'Daddy' as quickly as Norman had become 'Dad' (though I noticed Lisa remained 'Lisa' in her conversation). Christabel was all right. Rowena could rest in peace at last.

It was only as I thought this that I realised I hadn't dreamed of Rowena for a long time. She hadn't appeared in my dreams in any shape or form and I hadn't heard her voice in my ears. I hadn't been called upon to do battle with her over Christabel for months. Now, she was simply a memory, a friend whom I thought of frequently, but with affection and not dread. And with the disappearance of the raging Rowena had gone that temporary yearning for her child, that one and only urge towards motherhood I have ever had. I felt faint at the thought of how near I had come to being called upon to test that urge – I would have failed. For Rowena, motherhood was necessary, whatever the consequences for the child; for me, it was not. It would have been going against the grain. But I am glad I felt it, that overwhelming urge, I mean. Without the brief experience of such a craving, I might never have understood why women like Rowena defy our society, break moral codes and make their own way. I wanted very much to understand. Now I do. I fought for Christabel and I lost, but in the defeat lay my victory.